Twice dead…A living nightmare

The discovery of a blood-encrusted stiletto knife in journalist Emmeline Kirby's bag at Heathrow Airport sets in motion a chain of events that ensnares everyone she holds dear. The body of Sebastian Jardine is soon found in the boot of Superintendent Oliver Burnell's car, leading to accusations that he and Emmeline conspired to commit murder. Desperate to clear their names, she turns to Philip Acheson of the Foreign Office for help. But when two Special Branch officers arrive to arrest him, he is forced to go on the run.

Gregory Longdon, Emmeline's husband and a jewel thief/insurance investigator with ties to the criminal classes and MI5, is the only man Philip can trust. Gregory is on his own quest to prove her innocence in a game that makes no sense. Jardine was no stranger. His old friend was a former Interpol agent, who soured on the law and succumbed to his baser instincts. The real problem is Jardine died five years earlier. A fancy pink diamond with a murky provenance that men are willing to kill to possess holds the key to the truth. From London to Malta, Emmeline and Gregory are drawn into a web of corruption and revenge. Will they forfeit their lives for justice?

KUDOS for *Viper's Nest of Lies*

"Feuds and treachery and a complex coil of a plot—perfect summer reading." - Tessa Arlen, author of *A Woman of WWII* mystery series *and In Royal Service to the Queen*

"The story races along like a ride in a convertible on the cliffs near Monte Carlo—full of hairpin turns and shocking revelations."
- Tracy Grant, author of *The Westminster Intrigue*

Praise for the Emmeline Kirby-Gregory Longdon Series

"Another exciting foray into the world of international intrigue, dark secrets, and double dealings. Along the way, Daniella Bernett always takes me to new places and teaches me new things. This series just keeps getting better and better!" -Alyssa Maxwell, author of *The Gilded Newport Mysteries*

"I absolutely adore this fabulous crime thriller series. There is always action and adventure, a lot of red herrings, thrills aplenty and all with a touch of humour. Daniella Bernett writes such wonderfully complex and immersive plots [where] the tension and suspense builds…towards a chilling conclusion." -*Bookliterati Book Reviews*

"Murder, mayhem, intrigue, secrets and possible treason…a lot of twists and turns….The characters have a depth to them….I'll definitely be back to read more of [Daniella Bernett's] books and not only in this series, if this is her caliber of writing." -*Novels Alive*

"Scintillating…theft, murder and general mayhem….styled to mirror the writing of classic Golden Age authors. With strong characterization…writer Daniella Bernett has enhanced a series which…has the potential to gain a strong following." -*The Dorset Book Detective*

Acknowledgments

I would like to thank Editor Susan Humphreys, who gave my book the extra polish it needed and created the beautiful cover.

My continued gratitude to the Mystery Writers of America New York Chapter and the International Thriller Writers.

I would like to thank bestselling author Tracy Grant, who has been on this journey with me from the beginning. My deepest thanks also go to authors Alyssa Maxwell, Tessa Arlen, Emma Jameson and Kate Quinn, with whom I became friends via Facebook and exchange lively ideas about writing and life.

Other Books in the Emmeline Kirby/Gregory London Series

Lead Me Into Danger
Deadly Legacy
From Beyond The Grave
A Checkered Past
When Blood Runs Cold
Old Sins Never Die

VIPER'S NEST OF LIES

An Emmeline Kirby/Gregory Longdon Mystery

Daniella Bernett

A Black Opal Books Publication

GENRE: ROMANCE/MURDER MYSTERY, INTERNATIONAL THRILLER, AMATEUR DETECTIVES

VIPER'S NEST OF LIES
Copyright © 2021 by Daniella Bernett
Cover Design by Transformational Concepts
All cover art copyright © 2021
All Rights Reserved
Print ISBN: 9781953434555

First Publication: SEPTEMBER 2021

Published by Black Opal Books **http://www.blackopalbooks.com**

To my mother and my sister Vivian,
I can never adequately express my love for you.

CHAPTER 1

Gregory grabbed their bags off the carousel in Terminal 5 at Heathrow Airport. "Let's go home," he said as he pressed a kiss against Emmeline's dark curls.

She cast a sidelong glance at him, a smile upon her lips. "Mmm," she murmured with a nod.

It had been a lovely few days in Edinburgh. They had done their best to put that harrowing business up in Tobermory with Noel Rallis, Lord and Lady Starrett, and the Russian defector behind them. But it was definitely time for them to go home.

Home. The word had an alluring cachet. A place where they could settle into married life, at last. They were still newlyweds. The wedding had been just shy of three weeks ago. A heady time for any couple. Only fate had a perverse sense of humor and forced them to cut their honeymoon short. Gregory sighed inwardly at the memory that had set their last imbroglio in motion. What other couple on their honeymoon would overhear a man attempting to hire an international assassin? Was it an ominous omen about their marriage? He certainly hoped not. Couldn't the world simply leave them alone to get on with their life in peace?

He tried to shake off these morose thoughts as they passed

the WHSmith bookstore and headed toward the exit to catch a taxi to Holland Park.

A security officer with a shadow of gray stubble spreading across his cheeks and a gleaming bald head stopped them. "Miss, would you mind stepping over there?" he asked politely as he indicated with his chin a table about hundred feet away, where two of his colleagues were standing. "We are conducting random checks."

"Certainly."

Gregory's mobile started to ring. He drew it out of his jacket pocket. "I'll join you in a minute, darling." He gave her a wink.

She nodded and followed the officer.

"Hello," he said as he watched Emmeline place her bag on the table.

"Sorry, I couldn't make your wedding, Longdon, but then I wasn't invited."

Gregory froze. Nerveless fingers pressed the mobile closer to his ear. It was a voice he hoped he would never hear again. "Swanbeck," he hissed.

"I thought I'd send a wedding gift anyway. I hope you enjoy it. Give my love to Emmeline."

The connection was severed.

Gregory's gaze slithered over to Emmeline.

"Did you pack your bag yourself?" the officer asked her, as he searched through it.

"Yes," she replied with a smile.

He stiffened and straightened up. "Then how do you explain this?"

Between his thumb and forefinger, he held a stiletto knife with a brown crust of dried blood.

Emmeline's eyes bulged wide. A cold, suffocating dread clutched at her chest, squeezing the air from her lungs.

She licked her lips with the tip of her tongue. Her mouth

was parched. Even sand-driven winds couldn't make the Sahara this dry, she reasoned illogically.

"I—I…" But her brain refused to string any words together that would be deemed a suitable and coherent response.

There were no words for *this*.

Her gaze flickered nervously between the two officers, before returning to the offending weapon with its sinister, telltale trace of violence. She gaped at it. Errant thoughts, all of them laced with fear, swirled round and round her mind.

She took a step backward, but the officer's bony hand flashed out and clamped down on her upper arm. She could feel his fingers through her jacket biting deep into the fleshy part of her arm. It hurt and was quite unnecessary. What he needed was a good, swift kick in the shin.

A scream was trapped in her throat. This was all a terrible mistake. Despite the way it looked, she hadn't done anything.

"Where do you think you're going?" he snarled.

She straightened her shoulders and drew herself up to her full height. This didn't have quite the effect that she would have liked, as she was only five-foot-two and both officers were over six feet. Still, as Gran would say, a little bluster goes a long way sometimes.

Emmeline finally found her voice and shrugged off his grasp. "I'm not going anywhere. Do I *look* like a murderer? I'm a journalist."

The officer's partner threw his head back and gave a derisive snort. "Miss, that means absolutely nothing. We've seen all sorts. The worst criminals are the ones who look as innocent as lambs. They think that they can pull the wool over our eyes and get away with anything."

Her eyes narrowed and she pursed her lips. *Oh, such an amusing pun. Fancy yourself clever, do you? Think again,* she scolded silently.

She tossed her chin in the air. "The only way that knife"—she pointed at the gruesome weapon with a forefinger—"could have gotten into my bag is if someone planted it there, either in Edinburgh after it was checked or *here* at Heathrow. It's fairly obvious that someone is trying to frame me."

"Is it? We've heard that before too," the one who had searched her bag replied cynically. He snatched her arm again. "Now, come on. You have a lot of questions to answer, miss."

She struggled to free herself. "Let go of me. You're making a mistake."

They were beginning to cause a scene. But as she swiveled her neck around, she noticed that Gregory was no longer standing where she had left him. Her eyes darted desperately around the arrivals area, but he was nowhere in sight. She felt the blood draining from her cheeks and her body went slack.

Where was he? Had he seen what had happened to her? Was he in trouble too? For trouble with a capital T this most certainly was.

The two officers closed ranks, flanking her on both sides and effectively trapping her between them. One of them scooped up her bag in a single motion and waved a hand impatiently to disperse the crowd hovering around them.

As they walked slowly past the baggage carousels, Emmeline ignored the nervous whispers and the anxious glances being cast in her direction. Her only concern was for Gregory.

"Wait a minute." One of the officers drew up short and said over her head, "She was with a chap." He peered down his nose at her. "Where is he?"

"Chap? I have no idea who you mean," she replied nonchalantly. She stared back at him without blinking.

"Hmph. We'll get him."

Ha. You're no match for Gregory, she thought with pride.

He'll run rings around you.

This sense of triumph was transitory. Gregory wasn't here and she had no idea where he was. She bit her lip. Her mind was racing as they dragged her along. If someone—God forbid—had been killed, where was the body? And why put the knife in her bag? Why would anyone want to implicate her? Who hated her that much?

She drew in a ragged breath. All at once, she knew the answer. There was only one person. Alastair Swanbeck.

༒

Gregory had stood there for several seconds with his mobile suspended in mid-air, as he watched Emmy murmuring brief responses to the officer going through her bag. When the chap discovered the knife and held it aloft, the knot in Gregory's stomach gave a wrenching twist. All his fears were confirmed. His first impulse was to rush to his wife's side. But survival instinct took control and he thought better of it. That was exactly what Swanbeck wanted. To have him and Emmy trapped. Swanbeck wouldn't kill them. Oh, no. At least not so soon. First, he wanted to see them squirm.

Gregory took his eyes off Emmy for only a few seconds to scan the faces of the travelers in the arrival's hall. There was no one who looked familiar. Damn. Swanbeck had to be here. He could feel it in the marrow of his bones. However, he couldn't hang about waiting to be snared by his enemy's net. He had to get out of the airport. That was the only way he could save them both.

One last glance strayed toward Emmy. His body tensed when he saw the officers take hold of her. He told himself that she would probably be safer in their custody. He wanted to believe that was truth. It was a risk, but he had to take it.

Time to move.

He kept his head down and sliced his way through the throngs of travelers. He didn't want to attract any undue attention, so he kept his pace swift without breaking into a run. Once out on the pavement, he slipped into the taxi rank behind a rather tired-looking woman with two boys, who were under the age of five and chattering away without a care in the world. He flashed a smile at her, before casually tossing a glance over his shoulder. As far as he could tell, no one was following him.

A taxi rolled up, he hopped in, and they were pulling away from the curb within seconds.

Gregory allowed his tense muscles to uncoil slightly as he murmured his destination to the driver.

He pulled out his mobile and punched in a number he had come to know by heart over the last several months.

Despite the situation with Emmy, a smile touched his lips when he heard the gruff, familiar voice rumble in his ear, "Burnell."

"Oliver, old chap, your phone manner leaves a lot to be desired."

"Longdon? What the devil do you want? I thought you and Emmeline were still in Edinburgh."

"We're back in London. Is that joy I hear in your voice? Does that mean you missed me?"

"Hmph," Burnell grunted. "Sanity and calm return to my life when you are not around, even if I have to deal with the Boy Wonder." The latter was a reference to Assistant Commissioner Keith Cruickshank, the superintendent's much younger boss and the embodiment of a snobbish prat with IDEAS.

"If you've called simply to make a nuisance of yourself, I'm going to ring off because I have work to do."

"I actually rang to consult you in your official capacity. I'm in a taxi on my way to Scotland Yard," Gregory replied seriously.

The superintendent must have sensed the change in his tone. "Why? What's happened?" he asked suspiciously. "And why isn't Emmeline with you?"

"She's in a spot of bother at the airport." He didn't want to go into the details with the driver listening. "I'm afraid it might be our friend Swanbeck's doing. I'll explain when I get to the Yard."

Burnell exhaled a long breath, before he exploded, "Bloody hell." Then he must have put his hand over the phone because his words were muffled. However, Gregory heard him bellow for Sergeant Finch.

"Where are you now?" the superintendent demanded loud and clear once again.

"Surprisingly, the traffic is moving at a fair clip. I should be there in about twenty minutes."

"Finch and I will be waiting for you. I should never have gotten out of bed this morning. Why does trouble trail after you like cheap cologne? If it was you at the airport, I'd leave you there to rot."

"Oliver, you have such a way with language. It's heartwarming to see how much you care."

"Stuff it, Longdon."

CHAPTER 2

etective Superintendent Burnell and Detective Sergeant Jack Finch were waiting on the pavement outside the Dacre Street entrance to New Scotland Yard. Burnell, hands curled into tight balls thrust in the pockets of his navy overcoat, was pacing back and forth. His bulk made him impervious to the November chill. However, he was not immune to the droplets of drizzle that had found their way between the gap of his shirt collar and the back of his neck. He mumbled something unintelligible, as he impatiently pulled up his coat collar around his ears to keep out the damp.

Finch held his tongue. He could see fury and concern vying with one another in the depths of his boss's blue eyes. The same emotions were probably reflected in his own eyes. The sergeant's jaw clenched, when he thought of Emmeline at the airport ensnared in God-knows-what plot concocted by Alastair Swanbeck. Damn and blast. It had been months since anyone had heard a whisper about Swanbeck. They had all allowed themselves to be lulled into a false sense of security. Out of sight, out of mind. *Blind and stupid more like*, he cursed silently. That's what they were and now it had come back to haunt them.

These recriminations came to an abrupt halt as a black cab pulled up across the road in front of the St. James's Park Underground station.

"At last," Burnell grumbled when Gregory's handsome form emerged from the back seat. The two detectives crossed the short distance in a few strides as he paid the driver and the cab departed.

"Well?" the superintendent demanded without preamble.

"Good afternoon to you too, Oliver," Gregory replied smoothly. He inclined his head toward the sergeant. "Finch."

Burnell made a dismissive gesture with one hand. "This is no time to observe the niceties of polite society. And it's *Superintendent Burnell*. How many times do I have to tell you?"

A lazy smile tugged at the corners of Gregory's mouth. "As you just said, *Oliver*, this is no time to observe the niceties of polite society."

Burnell's neatly trimmed beard did little to camouflage the fact that his cheeks were growing redder by the second. He opened his mouth to say something, but snapped it shut again.

Finch stepped into the breach, before his boss reached out to put his hands around Gregory's throat. His gaze flitted between the two adversaries. "You should both be ashamed of yourselves," he reproached. "Can't you stop your ridiculous sniping for one moment? Emmeline is what's important. Or have you forgotten about her?"

The smile vanished from Gregory's lips. He took a step closer to the sergeant. "I never forget about Emmy." There was a dangerous edge to his voice that revealed the extent of his concern for his wife.

Well, they all knew how much he loved her. Emmeline's feelings were just as strong. Hadn't she defended Longdon on numerous occasions when no one else would?

"You're absolutely right," Burnell acknowledged contritely, head bowed slightly. "We're being fools. Now tell us what's happened, Longdon."

Gregory nodded and clapped the superintendent on the shoulder. In a few words, he related everything that had taken place from the moment he and Emmeline landed at Heathrow until he made his hasty exit after Swanbeck's call, leaving her behind.

"And here I am," he concluded. "We all know Emmy's been stitched up. It's no coincidence that Swanbeck rang me at the precise instant that the officers were going through her bag. He had to be in the airport, watching."

"Yes," Burnell murmured. "Finch, get on to the airport. We need to check the CCTV footage."

"Straightaway, sir." Finch pulled out his mobile and dialed a contact of his in security at Heathrow.

"How the bloody hell did the bastard get back into the U.K.?" Burnell said more to himself than anyone else. "There's an international warrant out for his arrest."

"Oliver, Swanbeck probably waved a great deal of money under the nose of some disgruntled airport worker, who was willing to plant the knife in exchange for a chance to retire early to a villa in Ibiza or some such place."

Burnell frowned. "Yes," he mumbled. "It usually boils down to thirty pieces of silver."

Gregory's cinnamon gaze raked his face. "How are we going to get Emmy?"

"*We*? You are not going to do anything, Longdon. This is a police matter. You will get into the next taxi that comes along…"

Gregory cut him off to protest. "You can't expect me to go home and put my feet up with a nice cuppa, when my wife is entangled in God's knows what malicious scheme of Swanbeck's."

Burnell continued as if Gregory hadn't spoken. "You will go straight to Holland Park and *remain* there"—one eyebrow shot up to emphasize this point—"until we ascertain the situation. Is that understood?"

Gregory slipped his arm around the superintendent's shoulders. "Oliver, forgive me for being so abrupt. I'm terribly worried about Emmy."

"As we all are, naturally. Therefore, the best thing you can do is to steer clear of the airport. Let us handle it. I promise we'll ring you the minute we have any news."

Gregory's lips convulsed into a smile. "You don't know how it eases my mind that the case is in your capable hands, Oliver." His smile grew wider. "But it's simply not on. I'm coming with you, like it or not. Shall we go, chaps? We've kept Emmy waiting far too long."

Burnell shrugged off Gregory's arm and glared at him. "I don't like it. Not one little bit. You know I could have you arrested and confined to your house."

Gregory folded one arm across his chest, brought his other arm up, and rested his chin on his hand. His brow furrowed and he made a show of giving this last statement a good deal of thought. Finally, he responded, "As far as I can gather, you are perfectly within your rights to do so. But you won't."

"How can you be so sure?"

"Because Emmy would never forgive you."

Burnell's chest swelled with a weary sigh. He gave a curt nod at the sergeant. "Get the car, Finch. It seems we're all going to the airport."

☙❦❧

Emmeline had been detained in a gray, windowless room for over two hours. It was empty, except for the table in the center where she sat huddled, her arms wrapped around her body. Her fingers were blue because the chill had seeped into her bones. Apparently, hardened criminals didn't merit a modicum of heat or even a cup of coffee. She could kill for a good strong espresso just at this moment.

Since the officers had deposited her in this sterile, airless cupboard, not a single soul had come to see her. Had they forgotten about her? Or perhaps they realized their mistake? If so, why hadn't anyone come to tell her that she was free to go?

However, the overarching question that hissed in her ear was *where was Gregory*?

A frisson that had nothing to do with the chill slithered down her spine. Then she shook her head. *Stop being a fool*, she scolded herself. *Gregory is fine.*

But what if he wasn't? What if Swanbeck had him? What if he was hurt? What if he was locked up in another horrid little room just like this one? *What if…*The questions trailed off in her mind, too appalling to even to put into words.

The chair made a horrible scraping noise against the floor, as she pushed herself to her feet. She began stalking the length of the room, too restless to sit still any longer. With each footstep, her nerves were stretched more tautly. Soon they would reach their breaking point. She pressed a fist to her stomach to quell the fluttering that suddenly erupted deep within her.

She couldn't be held here forever. Someone would come for her soon.

Startled, she sucked in her breath and whirled round when the door rattled on its hinges and opened. There, standing between her and freedom was a hulking, unsmiling security officer with salt-and-pepper hair and gray eyes that burned with hostility behind his spectacles. She hadn't seen him until this point. She swallowed the lump that had lodged in her throat and steeled herself for whatever was in store.

"The police have a few questions for you."

CHAPTER 3

Police?" A tremor in her voice betrayed her effort to appear calm. "But I keep telling you I haven't done anything. Someone is trying to…"

The rest of her sentence died on her lips, when Superintendent Burnell stepped around the airport security officer and came into view.

Her muscles unwound. She wanted to weep with relief. Now, everything would be all right. She opened her mouth to say something, but clamped it shut again when she caught the imperceptible shake of Burnell's head.

Right, they're not supposed to know one another. Better that way for both of them.

The rumbling of Burnell's throat as he cleared it seemed to bounce off the walls. "Naylor," he barked at the security officer. "What the devil is all this nonsense about?"

Although he spoke to the officer, his deep blue gaze never left Emmeline's face. She gave a bewildered shrug of her shoulders.

"A knife is not nonsense, Superintendent Burnell," was Naylor's haughty rejoinder. "And I'd say a bloody one"—with the air of a conjurer, he produced the weapon in question, which was now sealed in a clear plastic bag—"is a very serious matter indeed. To my mind, anyone who has such an item in his or *her* possession"—he jerked his chin in Emmeline's direction—"is intent on criminal mischief and has gone too far by taking a human life."

Burnell made an impatient gesture with his hand. "Let me be the judge if any crime has been committed."

"If?" Naylor bristled. "What more do you want?"

The superintendent took a step closer to him, his gaze dueling with the other man's arrogant one. "A body would help for a start. I'm funny that way. If Mrs. Longdon harmed, or God forbid, killed anyone as you are alleging, where's the *corpus delicti*?"

"Well, the thing is…You see…" The security officer's voice trailed off. It was the first time since they had entered the room that Naylor's swaggering confidence abandoned him.

"I'm listening," Burnell prodded, biting back a smile at the other man's discomfiture. Naylor was puffed up with his own self-importance and didn't deserve any mercy. He probably treated the airport as his own personal fiefdom. The superintendent recognized the type.

"We haven't found a body, dead or otherwise, either on her flight from Edinburgh or anywhere in the airport," Naylor admitted reluctantly.

"*No* body, you say." Burnell's mouth broke into a smile that didn't reach his eyes. "I find that fascinating."

Naylor's nostrils flared at the rebuke. He drew his shoulders back. "Nevertheless, the fact remains that the knife was found in Mrs. Longdon's bag."

"Hmph," Burnell grunted. "She has no criminal record whatsoever. From what I understand, she has led an unblemished life and is a model citizen. In my professional opinion, I very much doubt that she would wake up one day and decide to become a murderer for no good reason."

Naylor tapped his forefinger to his temple. "Maybe she's

not quite right in the head."

"She doesn't look like a lunatic to me."

One of Naylor's shoulders twitched in an indifferent shrug. "Lunatics are clever. They're good at hiding their true natures."

"There speaks the amateur psychologist. How jolly." Then, after a pause, Burnell snapped, "Don't be ridiculous. What's obvious to me is that the knife was planted in Mrs. Longdon's bag."

"Which is what I've been saying all along, but no one would listen to me," Emmeline muttered under her breath.

He pretended he hadn't heard her and went on, "I'll wager you received a tip that spurred you to conduct the impromptu bag search."

"We did in fact, but"—Naylor rubbed the back of his neck, flustered—"We only have Mrs. Longdon's word for it that the knife is not hers," he offered by way of defense.

"I'm a journalist, not a cold-blooded killer." Emmeline spat the words at him, no longer content to stand by while the two men discussed her as if she weren't in the room. Her fear had been replaced by an anger that was kindling into a raging fire in the center of her chest. "My job is to find the truth. It wouldn't hurt you to do the same, instead of jumping to conclusions and harassing law-abiding citizens."

Burnell thought that Naylor was fortunate that Emmeline was only slicing him to pieces with those dark eyes of hers. He almost pitied the man, almost. But really, it was Naylor's own fault. He shouldn't have made her lose her temper. It demonstrated an egregious error in judgment. Ah well, he supposed everyone had to make their own mistakes in life.

"We're about done here, Naylor. It's time you released Mrs. Longdon."

"What?" Naylor asked, clearly outraged at the way things had devolved. "You're not going to arrest her?"

"Until you show me evidence to the contrary, I see no reason to prolong this farce." He relieved Naylor of the plastic bag with the knife. "I'll take this with me back to the station to have Forensics check it for fingerprints." He gave him a sour look. "Though, I think we'll only find those of your staff."

"I can't just let her go."

"I'm afraid you don't have any choice. I'm also taking Mrs. Longdon with me to make a formal statement. At the station."

"I'll…I'll have to inform my boss."

"You do that." Burnell paused. "But make it fast. The law doesn't like to be kept waiting."

Naylor's fingers curled into tight balls. The glance he cast at the superintendent was one of pure indignation at being summarily dismissed on his home turf.

He pivoted on his heel without another word. The door rattled savagely on its hinges in his wake.

"I thought the pompous sod would never leave," Burnell murmured. He shook his head and changed tack. "Well, never mind. This will soon be over. Are you all right, Emmeline?"

She nodded. "Just a bit shaken and bewildered. They marched me straight into this room, after they found the knife in my bag. I've been sitting here alone staring at the four walls. I was going out of my mind. But everything is better now that you're here. What I'm more concerned about is Gregory. I haven't seen him since we separated in the arrivals area. Do they have him too? Is he all right?"

He gave the small hand that grasped at his sleeve an awkward pat. "Don't worry about Longdon. He's fine. That man has nine lives, if not more. He rang me and told me what was happening to you. He hopped in a taxi and came straight to the Yard, before anyone could snatch him too."

Emmeline squeezed her eyes shut. He could see some of

the tension easing from her body. "Thank goodness." She swallowed hard. "I was so worried."

"I left him outside with Finch. I thought it best not to muddle things with a touching reunion. Better to keep this an official matter. For all we know, the entire security team could be comprised or only a few chaps could be on Swanbeck's payroll. Plenty of time to find out once we've gotten you away from the airport."

"Swanbeck." The dreaded name dripped from her lips. All her fears were confirmed.

Burnell fixed his sober stare on her face. "Yes," he replied softly. "There's no doubt about it. The bastard…Sorry. That call Longdon received on his mobile was from Swanbeck." She nodded dumbly, her shoulders sagging forward slightly. "He was playing with Longdon. A tease to let us know that he was back. He rang off almost immediately."

"So, we have no idea where he is or what his next move will be?"

Burnell's mouth twisted into a grim line. The silence that filled the air between them spoke volumes.

"Don't worry, Emmeline. You have my word that the Yard will do everything in its power to protect you and Longdon."

She straightened her spine and lifted her gaze to meet his. She favored him with a crooked smile. "Of course, I trust you and Sergeant Finch without reservations. I know Gregory does too."

The superintendent raised an eyebrow at the latter comment, but let it go.

She wrung her fingers. "It's just…We know that Swanbeck is unpredictable and he's capable of anything. *Anything at all*." Her voice trailed off in a whisper.

He patted her arm again. His mind failed to find the right words to reassure her. Perhaps, it was because Swanbeck's resurfacing disturbed him more than he was willing to admit.

"Where the devil is Naylor?" he growled as he stalked toward the door and pounded on it with his open palm. "I swear I've never seen a more inept chap in my life. He makes the Boy Wonder look like a genius."

Burnell was gratified to see that this outburst brought a smile to Emmeline's lips. He shrugged. "You must admit that I'm right."

"Assistant Commissioner Cruickshank doesn't realize how lucky he is to have such dedicated detectives as you and Sergeant Finch. I can't even begin to thank you for dropping everything to come to my rescue."

Before he realized what was happening, Emmeline reached up and brushed his cheek with a kiss.

Burnell waved a hand in the air. "Nonsense," he replied gruffly to cover his embarrassment at her gesture. "It's all in a day's work. It's obvious to anyone with eyes that someone was trying to frame you."

"Yes, but who was stabbed? And was the person merely injured or is there a dead body hidden somewhere in the airport?"

"Those are questions Finch and I will deal with once you're safely away from here." He pounded on the door again. "Naylor," he bellowed. "Stir your lazy self and open this door. I don't have all afternoon."

It was another five minutes before the door open again and the ever-friendly Naylor reappeared.

He sniffed, but stood aside to allow them to pass. "The boss says you can take her." Apparently, he did not share his boss's opinion but was unwilling to challenge his authority.

The superintendent gave him a curt nod. "About bloody time." He waggled his fingers impatiently at Emmeline. "Come along, Mrs. Longdon. Your ordeal is over."

He took her by the elbow and propelled her out the door ahead of him.

He turned back to Naylor. "I will be putting it in my report about the disgraceful treatment that Mrs. Longdon has received."

He left the security officer standing there with his jaw hanging open.

Once out in the airport, Burnell picked up his pace. Despite his solid bulk, he could move more swiftly than a man half his weight.

They didn't speak as he guided Emmeline up an escalator. They barely registered the Pret A Manger, Mulberry, Kurt Geiger and Reiss as they continued down the long corridor.

He saw the question in her darting eyes as they walked between the duty-free stores that flanked them on either side. "I promise you he's here. He insisted on coming. As a precaution, I didn't want Longdon anywhere near you until I had time to assess how things stood. He's waiting up ahead with Finch."

The next second, the corridor opened up and the British Airways customer services kiosk came into view. She caught a glimpse of Gregory and Finch, their heads bent together in conversation.

"Gregory." She broke free of Burnell's grasp and ran to her husband.

Gregory glanced up at the sound of his name and covered the remaining distance between them in a few strides. His arms closed around her in a protective embrace. He buried a kiss among her dark curls.

"Are you all right, darling?"

She nodded and burrowed her face against his chest, inhaling his scent. "I was worried about you." She tilted her head back to look up into his eyes. "When I glanced around, you were gone. I'm so glad you were able to get away. Superintendent Burnell told me it's Swanbeck."

Her husband grimaced and took both of her hands in his.

"It's my fault that he's in our lives. If you hadn't met me, you'd be safe."

She pressed a hand to his cheek and gave him an impish grin. "And bored to death. A girl needs a bit of danger now and then to keep things interesting."

His lips quirked into a half-smile. "I married a strange woman."

"There's no accounting for taste. That's for certain," Finch murmured out of the side of his mouth as he joined them. "She's the only one who would have you."

Gregory, an arm still around Emmeline's waist, turned to the sergeant. "What was that, Finch?"

"Nothing. Don't mind me." Then to Emmeline, he said, "Delighted to see you. I knew the guv would have you out of there in a tick." He lowered his voice. "Bullying comes naturally to him."

She bit back a smile. "That's not fair and you know it."

Finch spread his hands. "You have to admit, he knows how to get things done."

"Ah, Oliver, the man of the hour," Gregory hailed the superintendent, who shot him a warning look in response.

"*Superintendent Burnell*," he enunciated his title and surname in a clipped tone. "If it had been you, I would have left you to your fate."

"You don't mean it." Gregory cast a quick glance around. "It's simply a question of not wanting to show how much you care in public." He batted his eyelashes coquettishly at the superintendent.

Burnell bristled. "The devil it is. Public or private, it makes no difference, Longdon."

"Stop it both you," Emmeline commanded. "Please don't spoil things with your ridiculous bickering. Sometimes you're worse than Maggie's twins."

"Emmy is right. Shall we call it a truce, Oliver?" Gregory

extended a hand to Burnell, who stared it for a moment before grudgingly shaking it.

"Truce," he agreed.

"For today," Gregory added with a wicked grin.

Burnell groaned and rolled his eyes toward the ceiling. His lips moved in what appeared to be a silent entreaty to the Almighty.

Emmeline cleared her throat, which had the effect of drawing the attention of all three men. "I'm grateful to both of you," she said to the two detectives.

Finch gave a casual shrug. "All in a day's work. It's our job to see that criminals get locked up, *not* the innocent. We know you…"

"Perhaps that's the problem," a male voice suggested gravely. "You know what they say about familiarity and contempt."

They looked round in unison to find Naylor hovering by Burnell's elbow. Malicious glee twisted the airport security officer's mouth into an ugly line. "You should have made your getaway, when you had the chance."

He grabbed Burnell roughly by the arm.

"Eh? What's the meaning of this?" the superintendent asked as he tried to break free of the other's man hold.

Naylor glanced over his shoulder and nodded to two approaching officers. "You'll make things much easier on yourself, if you come quietly."

"If your pride has been wounded, I could care less, Naylor," Burnell snapped. "I'm an officer of the law."

Naylor snorted. "Are you now? I hate people who abuse their position, especially if it's one of trust. You should be ashamed of yourself. But I suppose criminals never are."

"What are you driveling on about?" Burnell's gaze narrowed, perplexed by the direction of this conversation.

"Why don't you answer *my* questions? That is your black

Volvo with the Metropolitan Police parking permit sitting at the curb outside the terminal, isn't it?"

"Obviously, you already know that it is. What does that have to do with this demonstration in stupidity?"

Naylor ignored the question and plunged on with smug satisfaction, "I thought so. I merely wanted confirmation. Then it is my duty to take you into custody, until the proper authorities can take over."

Burnell's ulcer gave a warning flutter. Finch took a step forward, but the superintendent gave a slight shake of his head that stopped him in his tracks.

"What do you mean by proper authorities?"

"Murder is far above my pay grade," Naylor tossed back casually.

Burnell frowned. "Who's been murdered?"

"No idea who the bloke is, but he was discovered in the boot of your car."

CHAPTER 4

H e was stabbed to death." Naylor's lugubrious tone echoed upon the air, as his gaze snaked over to Emmeline. "Rather a nasty-looking wound to his rib cage." He paused for effect, clearly reveling in having a captive audience hanging on his every word. "Remind me again, Mrs. Longdon, about that knife that was found in your bag. You *claim* that you never saw it before. And yet, we now have a dead body on our hands. A man who happens to have been stabbed. I've never believed in coincidences."

"Poor sod. You must have suffered terribly as a child because of your lack of imagination," Gregory suggested facetiously. "Or am I getting muddled and this is an over-active imagination that has conjured up this farce?"

Everyone's attention shifted to his face, whose handsome features bore an insouciant expression. Only Emmeline saw the tension in his shoulders and wondered how they were all going to extricate themselves from this hell of Swanbeck's making.

"A dead body is not a dream, sir," Naylor retorted with asperity.

No, it's a bloody nightmare, Emmeline's brain screamed.

"The way I see it," he went on, "Mrs. Longdon stabbed the victim and Burnell here"—he jerked a thumb at the superintendent and shook his head in disgust—"a man charged with upholding the law—was going to scarper with the body so that he could dispose of it where it would never be found. The only problem was Mrs. Longdon didn't have time to get rid of the knife before my colleagues discovered it. And here we are now." He concluded with a malevolent smile.

Burnell blinked. He was at a loss for words. His glance darted to Finch, then Gregory, before finally settling on Naylor.

"Are you stark raving mad?" he exploded. His nostrils flared and his cheeks were flaming beneath his beard.

Naylor seized Burnell's arm again. "From where I stand, you're the one who's mad for even thinking you'd be able to get away with it. You and Mrs. Longdon have a lot of explaining to do. We're going to hold you, until the police arrive."

His gaze swept over the little group. His pointy, pink tongue flicked out between his thin lips as he thought things over. Then he said to the two other officers, "Chaps, I think we need take all of them in. Who are you two gentlemen by the way?" He directed the question to Finch and Gregory.

"They're nobody," Burnell growled. He silenced the protest rising to Finch's lips with an icy glare. Gregory merely held his gaze. "Never saw them before in my life. Just two concerned citizens who happen to be outraged by your abuse of power."

Naylor sniffed. "We'll see about that." His stony brown stare latched onto Gregory. "You, sir, appear to be very cozy with Mrs. Longdon. You wouldn't by chance happen to be Mr. Longdon."

Gregory favored him with a smile, but something dark and ominous kindled in the depths of his eyes. However, when he spoke his tone was silky. "The name's Toby Crenshaw." This wasn't a lie because it was the name he had been born with, but that was a lifetime ago. A forgotten memory, almost. Gregory Longdon was the man he had been for years.

"As the superintendent here just said, my friend and I"—he shot a pointed look at Finch—"were merely passing through the terminal, when you and your 'chaps'—for want of a better word—decided to harass him and this lady. It's quite outrageous behavior, don't you think, Alfie?" he asked Finch.

The sergeant swallowed hard and played along. "Never seen anything like it, Toby."

Naylor's gaze flickered between the two of them. "Hmph" was his skeptical response.

"Nobody plays me for a fool." His upper lip curled into a sneer. "Take them all in."

Before anyone had a chance to move, a plump middle-aged woman dragging two oversized suitcases jostled her way into the middle of the group, determination to reach her gate etched in every line of her face.

"Madam, have a care," Naylor admonished. "This is official business."

At this, the woman halted, dropped one case squarely onto his foot, and held his face in the crosshairs of her frosty blue stare.

"Official business, is it? Ha," she replied with asperity. "Nobody in this airport seems to know their business. I've got to catch a bloody plane to Madrid in forty minutes, but a rather silly girl has just informed me that the gate has changed. Boarding has started, but I've got to cross to the other end of the terminal. Can you imagine?" She bridled. "I call that bloody inconsiderate. So get out of my way. I'm not going to miss my plane."

While the woman railed at a cowed Naylor wincing in pain, Burnell managed to inch closer to Finch. He hissed out of the corner of his mouth, "Off with the pair of you. Go on." He inclined his head without turning to look at the sergeant and Gregory. "Get the Boy Wonder. He'll know how to deal with these fools."

Burnell couldn't believe he was actually placing his and Emmeline's fate in Assistant Commissioner Cruickshank's hands. *God help us*, he thought morosely. But the situation left him with little choice. He sighed. Needs must.

"But, sir, the car…" Finch ventured.

The superintendent cut him off. "There's nothing we can do about it now. Just *go*."

"Emmy." Gregory's voice was low, barely a whisper, but it caught his wife's eye.

She didn't dare say a word, but she gave him a weak smile.

Gregory nodded. He and Finch started to back away, half a step at a time. Naylor and his colleagues were still focused on the outraged woman, who was lecturing them without mercy.

Naylor put his hands up in surrender. "Right, madam. I'll have a cart drive you directly to your gate. Don't worry. You will not miss your flight."

It was only when he pulled out his radio that he noticed that Gregory and Finch were a hundred yards away.

"Oi, stop," he yelled.

Gregory and Finch turned and broke into a run. Without a backward glance, they rounded a column and were gone.

Naylor whirled on his colleagues. "Pinter, Webb, after them," he barked. "If they leave the airport, you're sacked."

Pinter and Webb needed no other incentive. They peeled off in pursuit of their quarry.

Naylor was seething. He muttered that in his nearly thirty years on the job, nothing like this had ever happened.

A string of curses flowed uninterrupted as he grabbed Burnell's wrist and clamped a handcuff around it. He reached out with the intention of placing its companion around Emmeline's wrist.

But once again he was thwarted. Apparently, today was not his day.

"I wouldn't do that, if I were you," said an extremely attractive fellow with sandy blond hair and bemused chestnut eyes.

Emmeline gasped as the man slipped his arm around her waist and drew her against his body. He towered over her. She struggled against him, but she couldn't break free of his grasp. He was too strong.

"Please don't fuss," he admonished politely.

Naylor and Burnell both took a step forward.

"Ah. Ah." The man gave a curt shake of his head. "At this moment, there's a gun pointed at this lovely woman's back," his plummy voice warned in a conversational tone. "It would distress me tremendously to have to shoot her. So, I'd advise against doing anything rash."

He took a step backward, never loosening his hold on Emmeline. People ogled them, but they scuttled away like skittish rabbits, unwilling to get involved in this drama.

"Now, let me tell you what's going to happen. The lady and I are leaving the airport."

"The devil you are," Burnell snarled. "What do you want with her? She's of no value to you. Let her go."

The man flashed a smile. It would have been disarming, if he weren't threatening Emmeline's life. "Everyone has value, Superintendent Burnell," he replied pleasantly.

Emmeline's mind was racing and her heart was thundering against her chest. She had to get away from this stranger, who was most likely one of Swanbeck's cronies. But how? If she kicked him in the shin, she was certain he would make good on his threat to shoot her. The hard object digging into her kidney made her reassess her options. Perhaps she would have a better chance to escape once they were outside the terminal?

"Let the woman go," Naylor echoed softly. He held his hands up and waved them in calming motion. "Whatever you want, we can discuss it quietly. No need for tempers to flare." At this stage, his primary concern was to defuse the situation. No one wanted more dead bodies scattered about the airport.

The man offered them another smile as he put more distance between them. "You appear to be under the delusion that I'm upset. I assure you I'm not. Now, this is becoming rather tedious. Emmeline and I are leaving."

She craned her neck to look up into his face. "Who are you? If Swanbeck sent you, he can go to the devil." She couldn't keep the anger bubbling in her throat from entering her voice. "You're a fool, if you think you can kidnap me in broad daylight."

The man chuckled. "I see the stories about your temper were not exaggerated. Ah, well. I like a woman with spirit."

His amusement only served to inflame her further. *I'll wipe that smile off your face*, she fumed. *See if I don't, you arrogant bastard.*

By this time, they had stumbled out of the terminal. He took her by the elbow and dragged her to the head of the taxi rank, earning dirty looks and shouts of disapproval from the weary travelers who had been patiently waiting their turn.

He whistled and a taxi rolled up. He opened the back passenger door and shoved Emmeline inside. Before she could open her mouth, he slammed it shut. He leaned his elbow on open window in the front and told the driver. "Holland Park. The lady will give you the address."

Emmeline stared at him in astonishment. She quickly wound down the window.

"Wait. Who are you?" she shouted as he stepped back onto the curb.

A smile played about his lips. "Roger Delahunt. Tell Longdon the slate is wiped clean now."

"You know Gregory? So you're not—" she stammered in confusion at this perplexing turn of events. "What about the gun?"

Delahunt drew out his curled fist from the pocket of his Barbour jacket. "Nasty things guns. Someone could get hurt," he quipped.

He threw his head back and laughed, as her jaw dropped. "Go," he shouted at the driver.

Emmeline slumped back against the seat and clicked the seat belt into place as the taxi merged into traffic.

Her journalist's mind was reeling. *Roger Delahunt, who are you? And* what *is your connection to Gregory?*

Myriad questions followed in rapid succession, but they too would have to wait until she saw her husband again.

❧❦❧

Gregory and Finch split up the instant they were out of sight of Naylor and his officers. Each man stood a better chance, if he were on his own. Gregory would make his way back to the house in Holland Park, while Finch would go directly to Scotland Yard. He would ring Assistant Commissioner Cruickshank *en route* to apprise him of the situation.

The sergeant prayed that airport security hadn't contacted Cruickshank yet. He wanted to be the one to break the news to the Boy Wonder. Surely, Cruickshank would see that Swanbeck was trying to stitch up Burnell and Emmeline as part of a depraved revenge scheme.

The Boy Wonder would stand by Burnell, an officer with a stellar record, wouldn't he? Finch bit his lip as he jumped into a taxi. A niggling doubt tickled the back of his brain. He inhaled a deep lungful of air and punched Cruickshank's number into his mobile. In a few minutes, he would know.

Gregory caught a glimpse of Finch disappearing through a revolving glass door at the other end of the terminal. He sighed with relief. He hoped Emmy was all right. He cursed himself for leaving her behind *again*, but at least Burnell was with her. Oliver would see to it that she didn't come to any harm. This thought assuaged his guilt a bit.

That only left himself. Gregory walked at a sedate pace, his eyes never left the Way Out sign. Only a few more feet stood between him and ground transport.

He was about to plunge through the revolving door, when a hand clamped on his shoulder and twisted his arm behind his back.

"Nice and easy, Longdon. You've caused quite enough problems today," a male voice grunted through clenched teeth. "Now, *move*."

Gregory couldn't resist. But really, what choice did he have? This chap was rather presumptuous. After all, they hadn't even been introduced properly.

"I fear I must decline your offer, delightful as it sounds. I'm afraid I have another appointment."

The man slammed him against the wall. The wind was knocked from his lungs for several seconds. The man pressed his forearm against the back of Gregory's neck, which in turn squashed the side of his face harder against the wall.

It turned out that this chap, who was becoming more disagreeable by the second, was Webb, one of security officers who had come to assist Naylor.

Webb leaned in close, his hot breath brushing Gregory's ear as he dropped his voice. "Swanbeck has message for you, Longdon."

"Does he?" Gregory replied out of the corner of his mouth. "Tell Alastair his manners leave a lot to be desired and that there are more civilized ways of communication."

Webb elbowed him in the kidney, which sent a burst of pain radiating through his body.

"Shut up," Webb snarled. In that instant, Gregory could barely catch his breath, let alone muster the energy to hurl a witty *bon mot*. So he held his tongue and listened.

"Either you return the Blue Angel or you're going to wish you were dead." He increased the pressure of his arm against Gregory's neck. "Today's events are only a preview of the misfortune that awaits you, your wife and your friends, if you're foolish enough to ignore Swanbeck's polite request."

"Request?" Gregory quipped, his voice hoarse. "I could have sworn that was an ugly threat. But perhaps I'm just a suspicious fellow by nature."

This earned him another jab to the kidney.

"Keep up the jokes and you'll be laughing all the way to your pretty little wife's grave."

A primitive roar was ripped from Gregory's throat. He whirled round, the pointy part of his elbow connecting with a satisfying crunch against Webb's jaw.

"Oof." Webb swayed slightly, stunned by the unexpected blow.

A frightened gasp went up around them, which Gregory disregarded as he turned the tables on his newfound foe. He shoved Webb's back against the wall. The other man's hazel eyes darted wildly to the right and left, desperately seeking an escape route, as Gregory's fingers closed around his windpipe.

"Let me make one thing perfectly clear, old chap." His voice dripped acid. "If you or Alastair, or anyone else, comes anywhere near Emmy, you will regret it for whatever is left of your *very* short life."

Webb, feeling emboldened once again, shot back in a rasping tone, "Don't—make—me—laugh. You don't have it in you, Longdon. Everyone knows it. You're just a petty thief.

All talk and charm."

Gregory increased the pressure of his fingers. "Alastair made a mistake coming back."

"No, *you* made the mistake, when you decided to steal his property," Webb sneered. "If you don't return the Blue Angel, Swanbeck is going to see to it that your wife and that fat superintendent are locked away for murder. And it will be all your fault." He managed to chortle.

A knot formed in the pit of Gregory's stomach. He called on every ounce of willpower to remain calm and in control. He drew in a breath through his nostrils. He couldn't allow his anger and fear for Emmy's safety to cloud his judgment.

He loosened his grip a fraction. "Blue Angel? If Alastair has found religion, I'm certain a man of the cloth is far better equipped to answer any questions he may have about God. After all, that's the clergy's stock in trade," he concluded with a roguish smile that teased and only served to irritate Webb further.

"We both know that the Blue Angel is a twelve-carat blue diamond," Webb hissed. "And you stole it after the Sotheby's auction."

"Oh, *that* Blue Angel. Why didn't you say, old chap? I thought we had embarked on a philosophical discussion about the divine. Silly me." The other man emitted a low growl, but Gregory went on, "Now then, I'm a law-abiding citizen. I was on hand at the auction as Symington's representative to ensure the safe transfer of the diamond into the buyer's hand. There my involvement ended. The buyer was a Russian gentleman by the name of Igor Bronowski. If Alastair has an issue, I suggest he takes up with Mr. Bronowski."

"Bronowski is dead, as you are well aware."

Gregory snapped his fingers. "So he is. My memory is not what it once was."

He had the pleasure of seeing two pink stains color Webb's cheeks. They eyed each other warily for several seconds.

"What's going on here?" another security officer called from several hundred feet away. "Clear a path," he ordered the crowd of gawkers.

Gregory quickly let go of Webb and straightened the other man's now crushed and wrinkled collar. "Must dash, old chap. I'd like to say it's been riveting, but that would make me a liar."

With a sidelong glance at the approaching officer, Gregory took a half-step toward the revolving door and freedom.

Webb gripped his sleeve. "This isn't over, Longdon," he mumbled. "Swanbeck always wins. One way or the other."

Gregory shook off his hand and plunged through the door seconds before the other officer closed in.

Webb's words echoed in his ear, as he raised a hand to hail a taxi.

Swanbeck always wins. One way or the other.

CHAPTER 5

Superintendent Burnell drummed his fingers in an angry tattoo on the table in the same claustrophobic closet of a room, where Emmeline had been detained a few hours earlier. Every time Naylor's weasel face, with its spiteful grin of amusement danced before his eyes, the drumming picked up in intensity.

His ulcer rumbled in sympathy. He wasn't afraid. Everything would get sorted in the end. He placed all his trust in the law. He had to. His entire adult life had been dedicated to upholding it. The law would not let him down. Justice would prevail. The law did not punish the innocent. Anyone with eyes and an ounce of brains could see from a mile away that he and Emmeline had been framed.

Anyone with an ounce of brains, he ruminated. On the other hand, there was the Boy Wonder, who had surely been informed of the situation by now.

Hmm, the Boy Wonder.

Burnell pursed his lips. "Perhaps I *should* start worrying," he said aloud.

The door handle rattled, jarring him from these thoughts. He looked up to find the unctuous Naylor, a smirk on his lips, ushering his fearless leader into the room.

Burnell sighed wearily as he placed his palms on the table and pushed himself to his feet. "Sir," he murmured.

"I'll leave him to you, Assistant Commissioner Cruickshank," Naylor ventured, giving him a deferential nod.

Cruickshank inclined his head, but he didn't speak until the door had closed behind him.

He gestured at the chair. "Sit down," he ordered Burnell, as he took the seat opposite.

The Boy Wonder folded his hands in front of him. He fixed his stare on Burnell.

The superintendent supposed the look was intended to be stern, but if it was, it failed miserably. Cruickshank appeared more like a petulant child, who had been denied his favorite toy.

Cruickshank's brow furrowed. *Is that what passes for thinking or does he merely have indigestion?* Burnell wondered.

At last, the assistant commissioner cleared his throat. "Burnell, why is it that of all the men under my command…"

Burnell wagged a forefinger in admonishment. "Don't forget the women, sir. They are an integral part of the team," he offered unhelpfully with a smile.

Then he frowned. *Dear Lord,* he realized, *I'm beginning to sound like Longdon.*

Cruickshank scowled at him, but went on, "—you are the only one who causes strife. You are a senior officer." He gave a disappointed shake of his head. "You should be setting an example."

The superintendent's fingers bit into his knees under the table, as he sought to retain his composure. "Surely, sir, you don't believe that I'm capable of murder?" he asked, disbelief echoing in his voice. "Do you think that Finch and I drove across London to the airport with a body in the boot?"

"Don't be ridiculous, Burnell. What do you take me for?

An idiot?"

The superintendent pressed his tongue against his cheek. *I'm assuming that's a rhetorical question and you don't really want my opinion.*

"Of course, I don't think you murdered that fellow. But once again, you've given the Met a black eye."

Burnell's fist curled into a tight ball. "Sir, this is Alastair Swanbeck's doing. It's his way to get revenge against me and the Longdons for disrupting his unsavory dealings with Bronowski."

Cruickshank waved his hand impatiently in the air. "Yes, yes. But you see how it looks. The word has already leaked out to the press. Goodness knows how. My mobile was ringing nonstop in the car on the way over to the airport. I finally had to turn it off."

"Respectfully, sir, *stuff* appearances." Cruickshank stiffened at this rebuke. "The Met should be more interested in finding out who the victim is and catching Swanbeck."

"Naturally. I don't need you to tell me how to conduct an investigation, Burnell. I am in charge after all."

Indeed, you are. More's the pity, Burnell lamented to himself.

"Forensics is already scouring your car and two other teams are making inquiries."

"What about Finch, sir?"

"He's at the station. After the scene earlier with airport security, I thought it best that he remains out of the way for the moment."

That's the only intelligent thought that has ever crossed your mind, Burnell mused.

"That only leaves you, Burnell. I'm afraid I can't play favorites. I have no choice but to suspend you, until we can get this sorted." He paused. "And we're going to have to take you out in hand cuffs."

The superintendent slammed the table with his open palm. "Bloody hell, sir. This is exactly what Swanbeck wants. You're playing straight into his hands."

Cruickshank's jaw tightened into a hard line. "Sit down, Burnell," he commanded. "You are in no position to dictate orders. You're lucky that I don't dismiss you from the force outright. I have cause. Your file is bulging with complaints from former Assistant Commissioner Fenton."

Burnell glared down his nose at him. *Fenton? How dare the Boy Wonder throw Fenton in my face.*

"Hmph." He grunted in disgust. "So, the Met will take the word of an incompetent and corrupt official over a detective who has dedicated his life to the law? That's more than reprehensible. It's unconscionable."

"It is not a question of taking sides," the Boy Wonder replied tersely as he fiddled with his cuffs. "There are procedures to be followed. Everyone is treated equally under the law."

"Not from my vantage point. We were stitched up. You just acknowledged it a moment ago. The knife in Mrs. Longdon's bag and the dead man were carefully staged. And yet, you're treating me as if I'm the criminal. Swanbeck is playing you for a fool."

"That's quite enough, Superintendent Burnell," Cruickshank roared as he surged to his feet. He gave his suit jacket an impatient tug to straighten it. "It's time to go."

He pounded on the door with his closed fist and called for Naylor.

"May I ask a question, sir?"

"What is it?" Cruickshank couldn't keep the irritation from creeping into in his voice.

"Since you are now in charge of the investigation, can you tell me what happened to Mrs. Longdon? Is she all right? Did you catch the fellow?"

Cruickshank shot a quizzical glance at him. "What do you mean? I thought Miss Kirby…I mean Mrs. Longdon—I'll never understand why the devil such a woman married Longdon," he muttered under his breath." Burnell bit back a smile. Obviously, the Boy Wonder was still smarting from Emmeline's snub the first time they met. "But that's neither here nor there. I thought she was being held here by security. That's what Finch told me."

"Ah," Burnell responded gravely. "Finch and Longdon had already made their escape, before things got a bit tricky."

"Tricky? I don't like the sound of this."

"Well, it's not good news, sir. While Naylor and his colleagues were attempting to detain Mrs. Longdon and me, a man with a gun abducted her." The Boy Wonder's puppy-dog brown eyes stared back at him without blinking.

Burnell frowned in what he hoped appeared to be concern. "I'm surprised Naylor didn't inform you." *Not really, the arrogant bastard didn't want to advertise his incompetence.*

Cruickshank was prevented from saying anything because the door was flung open. Naylor's frame filled the threshold. The same surly expression was plastered across his features. "Right, are you ready to take the prisoner?" he demanded.

"Not quite yet," Cruickshank replied crisply. "I have a few questions for you. I'd also like to have a word with your superior."

Burnell flashed a broad smile at Naylor. *What goes around, comes around. I believe the Boy Wonder has a pair of handcuffs that will fit you like a glove.*

❧❦❧

The taxi drew to a halt before the house in Holland Park. Gregory hurriedly paid the driver and bounded up the steps. He had the key poised in mid-air, ready to slip into the lock, when the door was wrenched open.

Without a word, Emmeline threw her arms around his waist.

He caressed her dark curls and pressed a kiss to the top of her head. "Did you really think that you could get rid of me that easily? You're stuck with me for life. I needn't have to remind you that you promised to love, honor, and obey."

Her head snapped back, and she impaled him with her gaze. "I never said obey, so you can remove that word from your vocabulary this instant." She exhaled a low sigh as her fingers interlaced with his. "None of this is a laughing matter. It's a nightmare."

"Yes, well, we'll get through it," he said philosophically as he nudged her inside and closed the door behind him. "We always do. How about a nice cuppa?"

As if on cue, they heard the kettle screaming in the kitchen. She gave him a wan smile and scurried down the hall. He ducked his head into the living room as he followed her. He was fully expecting to see Burnell ensconced on the sofa, but the room was empty.

"Where's Oliver?" he asked as he lowered himself onto a chair at the blond wood table in the center of the airy kitchen. Two cups and saucers with tiny pink rosebuds were already set out. "I'm surprised he left you here all alone. I call that ungallant. I'll have words with him the next time I see him."

Emmeline whirled round the teapot still in her hands. "You most certainly will not. Superintendent Burnell is still at the airport. That idiot Naylor is still holding him."

He frowned. "And he let you go?"

She turned away to the stove and sloshed some hot water into the pot to warm it. "Not exactly," she replied as she calmly dumped the water into the sink, tossed in a heaping spoonful of tea leaves in the pot, and poured a boiling cascade over them.

He waited as she put the pot on the table between them and took the chair opposite. "I was kidnapped," she said matter-of-factly.

Gregory arched one eyebrow upward. "You were *what*, my darling?"

"It's perfectly true, I assure you. Naylor clamped handcuffs on poor Superintendent Burnell and was about to do the same to me, when this chap materialized out of nowhere and put a gun to my back..."

"A gun?" he spluttered.

"—and dragged me off. It was either a dead body at their feet or let me go. So, Naylor, paragon of courage, and his men opted for a tactical retreat." She reached out for the pot. "I think it's steeped enough." She poured him a cup and then one for herself.

She took a tentative sip of the steaming liquid and peered at him over the rim of her cup. Her eyes gleamed with amusement.

He smoothed down the corners of his mustache and his gaze held hers. "Emmy, my love, there's something you haven't told me."

"Now, there's a turn of events. Usually, the shoe is on the other foot."

He waved a hand in the air. "Never mind that. How is it that you've managed to escape a 'kidnapper?'"

"He sent his compliments, by the way." She lifted the cup to her lips again.

He leaned back and casually hooked one arm around the chair. "The kidnapper?" She nodded. "That was very civil of him."

She set down the cup again. "I thought so. He also said that the slate was wiped clean."

A brief silence ensued. A faint smile played about Emmeline's mouth.

At last, she relented and put him out of his misery. "His name was Roger Delahunt."

CHAPTER 6

Delahunt?" Gregory murmured. "What the devil"—he shook his head—"I can't believe it. The last time I saw Roger…" He shrugged. "Well, it doesn't matter. Where is he now?"

Emmeline shook her head. "I have no idea. He bundled me off in a taxi as soon we got outside on the pavement. He could be anywhere. Perhaps he was catching a flight?"

Gregory lifted his cup to his lips and took a distracted swallow of his tea. "Mmm. I don't think so."

"How did he know who I was?" she demanded.

He flashed one of those smiles that melted her heart—and was intended to distract her. "Darling, your reputation precedes you. You are one of the preeminent journalists of your generation."

She refused to be swayed by his charm. She wanted answers. "Rubbish. Who is he and what's his connection to you?"

He lifted her hand to his lips and grazed her knuckles with a kiss. "Emmy, I'm your husband. You can't grill me like one of your sources."

"Oh, no? Think again."

Her jaw tightened and her chin jutted in the air. That

stubborn expression that he was thoroughly acquainted with etched itself onto her features.

Inwardly, he sighed. *Was the honeymoon over already?*

"Why so suspicious? You act as if he's a criminal. He came to your rescue."

"And I'm grateful—not that I believe for one moment we're out of the woods because we don't know who the victim is and Swanbeck is back—but how do I know Delahunt isn't a criminal? He knows you."

Gregory put a hand to his chest in mock disbelief. "You think that *I* associate with criminals?"

"I don't think. I know. It takes one to know one. You were a jewel thief." She held up a hand to halt the protest rising to his lips. "*Were* being the operative word. As in the past. Don't forget I know about the ruby necklace. Just because I love you, doesn't mean I have my head buried in the sand."

He took another sip of tea to cover his smile. "Well, it's a relief to know you love me."

She made a moue at him. "Charm will get you nowhere. I'm your wife. I'm immune. Start talking."

"Helen and Maggie would have something to say about your harsh treatment of an innocent man."

"Let's leave Gran and Maggie out of this discussion. They're biased when it comes to you."

"For a journalist, your choice of words leaves a lot to be desired. I prefer discerning. You do them a grave injustice. Helen and Maggie have refined tastes and recognize quality when they see it."

In spite of herself, Emmeline laughed. "I married a man with delusions of grandeur."

His mouth broke into a wide grin. "Darling, you know what they say? So often one can't appreciate what's right in front of one's nose."

"Hmph. I have eyes. I know the man I married. How do

you always manage to deflect the conversation away from the subject at hand when it doesn't suit you?"

He glanced down at his nails. "It's rather vulgar to boast, but it takes a certain amount of talent and skill."

She rolled her eyes at the ceiling and then she lowered her gaze to meet his again. "What am I going to do with you?"

"I have a few ideas. Would you like to go upstairs to our room so that I can share them with you?"

She reached out and traced a finger along his jaw. Her mouth curved into a smile. "Seduction is not going to work either. Who is Roger Delahunt? And why is the slate wiped clean now?"

"Has anyone ever told you that you have a one-track mind?"

"It's called perseverance. It's the only way to get to the truth."

"You said yourself he was gracious. A Good Samaritan who wasn't afraid to step into the fray. I find that rather admirable these days. Why not leave it at that?"

She shook her head.

He threw his hands in the air. There was nothing for it. He would have to tell her.

"Roger is a former…colleague. We had similar…business interests." She lifted an eyebrow. "For a time we were rivals, but then we became friends. I haven't seen Roger in a few years. The last I heard, he had retired to a villa somewhere near Villefranche along the Côte D'Azur."

"Retired? He looked like he's around your age."

"He's three years younger. Lucky him, I say. He made wise investments."

"You mean he stole his way into a fortune."

Gregory cleared his throat. "That's a rather cynical observation, Emmy. Sometimes I think the things you've seen as a journalist has made you jaded."

She crossed her arms over her chest. "Tell me the rest of it. All of it. What happened?"

He folded his hands on the table. "After a string of successful…deals, Roger thought no one could touch him and he became a bit careless. You must understand that the business world we worked in was small. Everyone knows each other, if not personally then by reputation. Petty rivalries and jealousy are common. Sometimes they are taken too far."

"As it did in Roger's case?" she prompted softly.

He nodded. "It's not my place to go into details, but one night I found Roger in my flat. He was barely conscious and bleeding like a sieve. He'd been shot." She gasped and put a hand to her mouth.

His hand curled into a fist. "I brought him to hospital. It was touch-and-go that first night, but Roger survived. Once he was strong enough, I helped him to get out of England. He had to disappear for a while. There was no guarantee that the blokes who attacked him wouldn't come after him again. I had a fairly good idea who had been responsible. I'm happy to report that they are now guests of Her Majesty's prison system."

"It sounds a bit like Swanbeck."

Gregory gave a grim shake of his head. "No, Alastair is even more ruthless."

"And he's intent on destroying our lives, as he proved today at the airport." Her voice cracked slightly. "Will we ever be free of him?"

He took her small hands in his larger ones. "Emmy, he's bound to make a mistake. Oliver will catch him. It's just a matter of time."

"Let's hope it's before he kills us."

⁓⁓⁓

It was another hour before Assistant Commissioner Cruickshank and Superintendent Burnell left Heathrow. To Burnell's delight, Naylor and his supervisor, a rather insipid fellow named Grey who was as colorless as his name, found themselves subject to a proper dressing down by Cruickshank on the topic of proper procedures and full cooperation with the Met.

As the assistant commissioner's car pulled away from the curb, Burnell slid a sideways glance at his boss's profile.

Perhaps, the Boy Wonder is not that bad after all, Burnell reflected. Just as this thought crossed his mind, he gripped his thighs hard. *What* am *I saying?* he reproached himself. *I think I was locked in that room for too long and the lack of oxygen has addled my brain.*

"Burnell," the Boy Wonder broke the silence and turned his earnest gaze on him, which made the superintendent grit his teeth. He knew it was going to be a pearl of wisdom.

"Yes, sir?"

"Just because of the lax manner Naylor and his men conducted themselves, doesn't mean I have forgotten your part in this distasteful affair."

Burnell leaned back and stroked his beard. *Oh, yes, definitely a pearl of wisdom.*

"And what part would that be, sir?" he asked sweetly. "If you'll recall, I didn't murder our victim and I certainly didn't stuff his body in the boot of my car as a memento of the dirty deed."

Cruickshank's ginger eyebrows knit together and he gave an exasperated sigh. "Why do you always make things so difficult? This is what I was getting at earlier. You are one of my most senior men and you're always putting your foot in it. Just be thankful I didn't drag you out of the airport in handcuffs."

"Respectfully, sir, Mrs. Longdon was being detained under false pretenses. It was my duty to ensure that she was freed as quickly as possible."

The Boy Wonder threw his hands up in the air. "How do we know Mrs. Longdon is not guilty? She is married to a criminal. Longdon probably put her up to it. Or they did it together. All I know is that when those two are around, we have nothing but trouble."

"Sir, you know as well as I do that Mrs. Longdon doesn't have a corrupt bone in her body. She has dedicated her career to finding the truth. She's a damn good journalist."

"Hmph," Cruickshank sneered. "She can't be that upstanding, if she married Longdon. There is something definitely wrong with her. And now the tiresome woman has gotten herself kidnapped."

Oh, there is a litany of things wrong with Longdon, but not Emmeline—except perhaps her temper and her stubborn streak. But then, none of us are perfect.

"I think that's a bit unfair. I don't think Mrs. Longdon woke up with the intention of getting kidnapped. Aside from that, she and—although it goes against the grain to admit it—Longdon have helped us to solve several cases."

The Boy Wonder merely grunted, as he tapped a tattoo on his knee. In the end, he said, "I have no choice, but to suspend you, Burnell."

The superintendent's fist curled into a tight ball. "But, sir..."

The Boy Wonder held up a hand. "I can't place you in charge of the case, when the victim was found in your car. The press is already circling like buzzards. It's only going to get worse. A few days leave will do you good."

"Sir, I don't need any leave. I would be more useful working to discover who the victim was and how he's connected to Swanbeck. We both know that Swanbeck poses the biggest threat at the moment," Burnell replied, struggling to keep his tone level.

"I'm sorry, Burnell. My hands are tied. I'm going to put Inspector Halliday in charge of the case. Finch will assist him."

His gaze drifted to the window. Now that his decree had been issued, his flow of words appeared to have dried up. Burnell, on the other hand, silently let loose a string of curses.

After several moments, Cruickshank murmured without looking at Burnell, "Of course, far be it from me to tell you what to do during your leave. If it were me, I'd take a holiday. But everyone is different. On the other hand, I realize that man is a social creature and needs to keep in touch with his friends and colleagues, like Finch for example, even if one is not in the office. As Sally would tell you, I'm far too busy to keep track of such friendships."

One of Burnell's eyebrows rose and his ears perked up suddenly. What was the Boy Wonder saying?

Cruickshank swiveled his head around to fix his brown stare on the superintendent's face. "It's really a matter of out of sight, out of mind. If you're not at the office getting under foot, it's not my place to tell you how to spend your leisure time. That would be an intrusion of privacy. I make it a policy never to get involved in the private lives of my subordinates."

The superintendent's mouth broke into a grin. He extended a hand to his boss. "Of course not, sir. Thank you."

Cruickshank hesitated a moment before clasping the proffered hand. "I have no idea what you're on about. But I'd like to remind you that discretion is always the better part of valor."

CHAPTER 7

Burnell's mobile began vibrating in his inside jacket pocket. He drew it out and sat on the edge of the seat. "It's Finch, sir," he told Cruickshank, who nodded, his body tense with anticipation.

The superintendent turned his attention back to the call, steeling himself for the worst. "What is it, Finch?"

"Sir, Emmeline is all right." Burnell slumped back. "Thank God for that. Where is she?"

Cruickshank's brow puckered in a question, but he held his tongue.

"She's at home. Longdon has just returned as well. He said that one of Swanbeck's lackeys, the security officer called Webb, attempted to detain him."

"Webb? Well, we knew Swanbeck had at least one man on the inside at the airport. Send a team to bring Webb in for questioning. I'll be at the station shortly."

The Boy Wonder cleared his throat noisily. "I mean tell Inspector Halliday, since he's in charge of the case now. As you know, I have been suspended."

Out of the corner of his eye, he saw the Boy Wonder give an approving nod.

"Sir, Cruickshank is a nutter and a prat to boot," Finch

complained in his ear.

Burnell bit back a smile as he shot a speculative glance at the Boy Wonder. "That is common knowledge. But perhaps we can have a nice chat over coffee, now that I have all this free time on my hands. I'd be delighted to catch up with a colleague."

There was a brief pause. "Sir, are you quite all right? Is your ulcer bothering you again?"

"As well as can be expected under the circumstances. I'm here in the car with Assistant Commissioner Cruickshank. I could pass on any information you may have for him, such as whether there has been any sign of Swanbeck."

"Ah. Nothing on Swanbeck. May I ask what you are going to be doing now that you're suspended?"

"Since I find myself with all this free time, I thought I'd visit some old friends."

"I see. These friends wouldn't happen to live in Holland Park, would they?"

"Clever chap."

"Right. I'll try to get away from the station as soon as possible. I'll meet you at Emmeline and Longdon's house. Then you can explain everything."

"Yes, that would be best. I hope to speak to you again soon, Finch."

He severed the connection and turned back to Cruickshank.

Before he opened his mouth, the Boy Wonder said, "I take it Mrs. Longdon is alive and well." Burnell gave a curt nod. "That's all that matters for the moment. I'll expect a report from Finch. Otherwise, I don't want to hear even a whisper about you. Unless, of course, as a concerned citizen you hear word about Swanbeck and find out our victim's connection to him. Any other interference with the case while you are on suspension would be most improper."

Burnell schooled his features into a solemn expression. "Sir, I assure you that I'm the soul of propriety."

⌘

Finch had barely settled down on the sofa in the living room in Holland Park, his teacup halfway to his lips, when the doorbell rang. Emmeline hurried out into the hall. There was a murmur of voices and within seconds Burnell was following her into the room.

"All hail the conquering hero," Gregory greeted him with his usual flippancy. "Or is that the prodigal son?" He took a sip of tea and peered at Burnell over the rim of his cup, his eyes gleaming with mischief. "I always get it muddled."

Emmeline gave him a disapproving shake of her head and then asked the superintendent, "Would you like a cup of tea and some biscuits? It's been a harrowing afternoon."

Burnell lowered himself heavily onto the sofa beside Finch with a grateful sigh. "I wouldn't say no to tea. Thank you, Emmeline."

A hush fell over the room as she poured him a cup and then settled herself. They waited until he took a few swallows and devoured two shortbread fingers.

His gaze scoured Emmeline's face. "Thank God you're unharmed. I was relieved when Finch told me that you were home. How the devil did you manage to get away from that chap?"

Her gaze strayed to Gregory before offering Burnell a sheepish smile. "I was never actually in any danger." The superintendent raised an eyebrow. "It appears the chap who abducted me was…a friend of Gregory's. His name is Roger Delahunt."

Burnell shot a glance at Gregory. "Longdon," he growled.

Gregory set his cup down gingerly on the coffee table and

raised his hands in the air. "It's no good giving me the evil eye, Oliver. I was just as surprised as you when Emmy told me. I haven't seen Roger in several years."

"Do you really expect me to believe this Delahunt just happened to be wandering around Heathrow and decided to spirit your wife away?" he demanded.

Gregory leaned back in the wing chair and casually crossed one leg over the other, propped his elbows on the arms, and steepled his fingers over his stomach. "Oliver, it's your choice whether you believe it or not. It happens to be the truth."

"Truth," Burnell scoffed, "You wouldn't know the truth, if it fell from the sky and hit you on the head. And it's *Super-intendent Burnell*, as you well know."

A lazy smile tugged at the corners of Gregory's mouth. He clucked his tongue. "Really, *Oliver*. You're among friends. Relax. Let your hair down." He flicked an impish glance at the thinning wisps of hair on Burnell's crown. "Oh, dear. Perhaps that's a bit difficult."

"Keep it up, Longdon. One day soon, you'll be rotting in a jail cell and I'll be the one laughing on the other side of the door."

Gregory's grin only grew wider. "Promises, promises."

Emmeline leaped to her feet, the teapot held aloft, in a bid to change the subject and ease the tension in the air. "More tea, Superintendent Burnell?" she asked as she scowled at her husband. To her annoyance, he winked at her.

"Anyway," she said after the superintendent had accepted a second cup and she resumed her place. "I'd never met Roger Delahunt. I had no idea he knew Gregory until he bundled me into the first taxi that came along."

"Where is Delahunt now?"

She gave a helpless shrug of her shoulders. "I don't know. I left him standing on the curb. He could be anywhere."

"That's no surprise, if he's one of your friends," Burnell griped to Gregory. "The name doesn't ring a bell, but I have no doubt that Delahunt is another thief."

Gregory's eyes raked over the superintendent's features, which were creased with irritation. "I don't know what you're on about, Oliver. But I'm a law-abiding citizen and so is Roger. You shouldn't go around casting aspersions. You could do irreparable damage to a chap's reputation. I needn't have to remind you about the strict slander laws we have in this country."

Burnell huffed a laugh. "Your reputation is like a piece of Swiss cheese. Full of holes."

"You are in a tetchy mood today, Oliver. Is it your ulcer again?"

The superintendent perched himself on the edge of the sofa and wagged a thick finger at Gregory. "My ulcer would be a damn sight better, if you weren't constantly aggravating me."

"Admit it. This is all merely bluster to cover how worried you were about my welfare." Gregory fluttered his eyelashes for emphasis. "You're a teddy bear at heart."

Burnell made a gurgling sound in the back of his throat. "The only one I was worried about was your wife."

Gregory took a long swallow of tea. "If you say so."

Burnell gripped his cup and saucer so tightly, his knuckles showed white. "Enough," he commanded through clenched teeth. "We don't have time for your usual rubbish. We have bigger problems on our hands."

The bemused expression evaporated from Gregory's features. He inclined his head in deference. "You're quite right, Oliver. My apologies."

This mollified the superintendent somewhat. "That's more like it." Then to Finch, he asked, "Have you been able to find out anything about the victim?"

The sergeant gave a bleak shake of his head. "There was no identification on him. He's in his mid- to late thirties. Well-built, health-looking, if one doesn't count the stab wound between his ribs. I spoke to Dr. Meadows. He promised to do the postmortem as soon as possible. He said that the Boy Wonder is a fool and sends his sympathies on your predicament. He expects to see you on Friday for your usual pint at the pub."

Burnell's curled into a crooked smile. "Good old John. What about witnesses?"

"We couldn't find anyone who had seen the attack." Finch reported ominously. "If there was a witness, no one has been willing to step forward."

The superintendent slumped back against the sofa and heaved a weary sigh. One eyebrow quirked upward. "CCTV footage?"

Finch permitted himself a small smile. "After Naylor's and his men's shameful performance, airport security was falling over backward to cooperate. They made copies of the tapes from the last twenty-four hours." He bent down and drew out several CDs. "I told Inspector Halliday I would review them, but then you rang and I came directly here." He waved them in the air. "I don't suppose you'd like to take a peek, would you, sir?"

Burnell straightened up. "Certainly not," he answered sententiously. "That would be most inappropriate, as I've been suspended."

"Of course, it would," the sergeant murmured, as he cast an expectant look at his superior officer.

"I'm surprised at you, Finch. Removing evidence from the station." He shook his head. However, he couldn't keep eagerness from his tone.

He licked his lips and flicked a glance at Emmeline and Gregory. "We also have two civilians in the room. One of them is a journalist, who should not be privy to the evidence that has been discovered thus far." He gave Emmeline a pointed look.

"Oh, we don't mind at all, Superintendent Burnell. Besides, if you'll remember, Gregory and I signed the Official Secrets Act, so there's no problem," Emmeline chimed in with a sweet smile as she scooted closer to him. "You forge ahead. Feel free to use my laptop." She waved vaguely in the direction of the secretary desk in the corner of the room that overlooked the garden. "We have just as much of a vested interest in finding out the truth as the police. You know that we could be of some help." Her smile grew wider.

"Besides we're on the same side, Oliver," Gregory interjected.

"You're on no one's side except your own, Longdon," the superintendent tossed back. He held up a hand. "However, in extraordinary circumstances beggars can't be choosers." He jerked his head toward Emmeline's laptop. "Pop them in, Finch."

They hurried across the room as a group. As Emmeline typed in her password to log on, Burnell intoned, "Whatever is discussed in this room is off the record. Is that understood, Emmeline?"

She stiffened slightly. Silence hung upon the air for several seconds. Then, she nodded. "Understood. But for the record"—she swiveled around slowly and hooked one arm around the back of the chair—"I intend to get to the bottom of this mystery and clear my name and yours."

Burnell inclined his head. "Noble as always. But we have to do this by the book, otherwise Swanbeck will have won. And we can't have that."

Her chin jutted in the air. "Over my dead body will he win," she replied as she extended a hand to Finch for the first CD.

"Emmy." Gregory's voice held a note of warning.

"Don't Emmy me. I *will* find out the truth."

"A story is not worth your life," Burnell offered gently. "Let the law take its course."

She turned to the monitor as the first images of the terminals and concourses popped up. "The law is too bloody slow because justice is blind," she complained. "Sometimes it needs a bit of nudging in the right direction."

The three men exchanged exasperated looks. In the defiant mood she was in, it was useless to argue. Instead, they huddled around her, all their attention focused on the people moving to and fro through the airport. No one spoke.

After the first CD with six hours' worth of images, Emmeline rubbed her eyes with the heels of her palms. They had fast-forwarded through a good portion of it, as they reasoned the murder must have occurred fairly close to the time that Emmeline and Gregory's flight from Edinburgh had landed. But she still felt drained. Her vision was slightly blurred as she tilted her head back to ease a cramp in her neck. Her gaze fell upon Gregory. His face was set in taut lines. He gave her shoulders a distracted squeeze. His frustration was transmitted through his fingers.

She opened her eyes wide and with renewed purpose inserted the next CD. "One of the cameras must have caught something." She wondered if she was trying to convince herself or the others.

Fifteen minutes went by and it was more of the same. And then, Finch yelled, "Stop. There." He pointed at the frozen image. "That's the victim."

"You're sure?" Burnell asked.

Finch nodded. "Yes, sir. I'm positive."

"Right. Emmeline, play it."

They watched the victim weaving his way along the concourse in Terminal 5, a carry-on gripped tightly in one hand.

He craned his neck around to toss a nervous glance over his shoulder. At one point, he darted into WHSmith and disappeared from the screen for a few minutes.

"He's being followed," Burnell murmured, as he stroked his beard. "But who is it?"

They held their collective breath as the victim came into view again. He hovered on threshold for a few seconds, twisting a magazine between his hands. It appeared as if he were waiting for someone. He glanced at his watch and shook his head. A startled expression trespassed his strained features, when he looked up again. Clearly, he had been unsuccessful in shaking off whoever had been shadowing him. He clutched his bag and flung the magazine into the nearest rubbish bin. He plunged into the throng of humanity, brusquely elbowing people aside, manners forgotten, no longer caring. He was running for his life.

If he had kept moving, he might have made it out of the airport safely. But then, everything becomes crystal clear with hindsight. That last glance over his left shoulder was his fatal mistake. The blow came from in front of him and to the right. To all outward appearances, it could have been two men in a hurry bumping into one another. However, the little group glued to the computer knew better. It was over within seconds. At first, the victim didn't realize anything. Then his hand grabbed at his side. They could read the horror on his face when he pulled his hand away. His killer never stopped. He just kept walking. His face was obscured by a flat cap that was pulled low over his brow. Child's play for a professional. That is, if murder can be considered a game.

"Play the rest of it," Burnell directed, as he stroked his beard. "Maybe we'll see which way he went."

Emmeline nodded wordlessly and did as she was bid.

Once again, they watched with rapt attention. Before the victim collapsed to the floor and passersby realized that a murder had taken place, Webb and another security officer swept into view. They bundled the man into a wheelchair and in the blink of eye were out of camera shot.

"My guess is that they took the victim to a maintenance room or storage area and kept him out of sight, until they could dispose of the body," Finch suggested. His brow creased as he shook his head. "But there's something wrong."

Burnell met his uneasy gaze and nodded. "Murder is always wrong, but I agree with you. There's something haphazard about the way it was carried out. So many things could have gone awry."

"And Alastair is nothing if not meticulous," Gregory ventured.

"Precisely," Burnell said. "I think it was a crime of opportunity. A chance encounter between Swanbeck and our victim. Were they strangers? Or was it simply a matter of settling old scores?"

"The victim could very well have seen or overheard something he shouldn't have and he had to be silenced," Finch offered.

Burnell scowled at the monitor. "Yes, what better place than an airport to get lost."

"But sir, how did Swanbeck know that Emmeline and Longdon were returning today or for that matter that they weren't in London?"

Burnell heaved a weary sigh as his gaze reluctantly settled on Emmeline and Gregory. "I hate to say it, but Swanbeck could be tracking your movements."

Emmeline drew in a sharp breath and reached up to clutch her husband's hand.

A heavy silence closed in around them. They had all been afraid that this could be the case. It was just that no one had dared to utter it aloud.

Gregory was the first to speak. His tone was calm and

matter-of-fact. "That explains how the knife could have gotten into Emmy's bag, but Alastair couldn't have been sure that you and Finch would be the officers sent to the airport to investigate."

"Unless he's tapped your mobiles," Burnell replied, as his practiced eye scanned the living room. He waggled his fingers at the husband and wife. "Get your mobiles. We'll check them now." Then to Finch, he said, "Tell Halliday what we suspect, without mentioning my name of course. Suggest that a team be sent to sweep the house. You can't be too careful where Swanbeck is concerned."

Emmeline and Gregory scurried off to get their mobiles, while Finch drew out his to ring Inspector Halliday.

Within seconds, husband and wife had returned. "Oliver, our mobiles are clean. I've checked," Gregory said, but he turned them over to the superintendent anyway.

Burnell popped them open performed his own examination just to satisfy himself. "Damn and blast," he muttered. "That means Swanbeck's spies have bugged my phone at the station."

Finch heard and nodded grimly. He passed on their suppositions to Halliday, listened for another minute and then concluded his conversation.

"Sir, Inspector Halliday is going to have your office swept from top to bottom. By the way, he wanted you to know that he doesn't believe the accusation against you and he's going to do everything in his power to see that you're cleared of this ridiculous charge as soon as possible."

Burnell permitted himself a half-smile. "Halliday's a good man and an honest detective."

"Oh my God. It can't be," Emmeline exclaimed. She had settled herself in front of the laptop, while this exchange was taking place. She was staring at the screen, eyes wide.

"What is it?" Burnell snapped.

Emmeline shook her head, as she hit the pause button. She lifted her dark gaze to his face. "I just saw Roger Delahunt."

"Where?" the superintendent demanded, eyes narrowing, brows knit together.

Reluctantly, she allowed the tape to roll again and touched the screen with her forefinger. "There." She took a deep breath. "Picking up the victim's carry-on and hurrying away in the opposite direction."

Burnell's head shot up. His deep blue stare found its target. "Longdon," he growled.

Gregory put his hands up. "It's no good using that tone, Oliver. I have no idea what Roger was doing at the airport. I told you before I haven't seen him in several years."

"Why should I believe you a word that comes out of your mouth?"

"It happens to be the truth. And we all know how much you prize the truth," Gregory quipped. "You have that in common with Emmy." He gave his wife a loving smile.

Burnell snorted. "You and the truth don't even have a nodding acquaintance."

Gregory contrived to appear hurt by this remark. "All I want to do is my civic duty to help the police solve the crime and keep society safe."

"Bollocks," the superintendent retorted and immediately regretted his outburst. He turned to Emmeline, slightly shamefaced. "Sorry for the language, but your husband..." His sentence trailed off as he threw his hands up in the air in exasperation.

Gregory sniffed. "And here I was about to impart another nugget of information. I assure you, it's something you're dying to know."

Burnell folded his arms over his broad chest. Through gritted teeth, he replied, "I very much doubt it."

"Why are you always so cynical? You should have more

faith in your fellow man."

Burnell groaned and rolled his eyes toward the ceiling. "I'm not in the mood for a philosophical discussion. If you have something to say, spit it out."

Gregory sighed. "I suppose I've kept you in suspense long enough." He paused, his gaze sweeping over each of them in turn before coming to rest once more on the superintendent's face. "The victim's name was Sebastian Jardine."

"What?" Burnell exploded, his cheeks flaming beneath his beard.

"I did say it was something you wanted to know. Oh, and more thing," Gregory added casually, "It's quite disconcerting to see Jardine, in the flesh so to speak, because he died five years ago."

CHAPTER 8

ll this time we've been sitting here and you didn't breathe a bloody word," Burnell challenged, his voice rising.

"Be fair, Oliver. You didn't ask me about Jardine. If you'll recall, you were more interested in poor Roger, who I must point out once again came to Emmy's rescue." Gregory concluded this speech with an ingenuous smile that did nothing to dampen the mischievous gleam in his eyes.

"What are you and Delahunt up to?" the superintendent snarled. "And what do you mean Jardine died five years ago?"

"Which question would you like me to answer first? Or am I meant to choose the one I like best?"

"Gregory," Emmeline hissed out of the corner of her mouth. "Don't make things worse."

He rested his hand on her shoulder. "Darling, how much worse can they get?"

"I could have you thrown in jail for perverting the course of justice for a start," Burnell countered acidly.

"Oh, Oliver, sometimes you can be too melodramatic for your own good."

"*Superintendent Burnell.*" The two words flew across the

air as if honing in on a target.

The only problem was they merely bounced off Gregory. He sighed and patted Burnell on the arm indulgently. "All right, Superintendent Burnell. There, do you feel better now?"

Burnell shook off his grasp. "Whenever I'm near you, I feel ill because I know disaster is not far behind." He took a step closer toward Gregory, his fists clenched tightly at his sides. "You're always bloody hiding something."

Gregory gave a sad shake of his head. "You know I'm certain that your pessimism is the root cause of your ulcer." He nodded sagely, rubbing his chin in imitation of the superintendent. "Yes, the more I think about it I'm certain it is. If you had a sunny disposition like mine"—he beamed at the detective—"you'd be as fit as a fiddle."

"Sunny disposition? It's more like the dark cloud of the plague looming over everything. Now, enough of this rubbish. Start talking."

"We're all a bit on edge today. Perhaps another cup of tea would do us all good. I'll make a fresh pot, shall I?" Emmeline suggested as she stepped between the two men. She threw a pleading look at Finch.

"What a good idea," Finch replied as he came to her aid and tugged the superintendent toward the sofa. "Sir, why don't we sit down?"

Meanwhile, Emmeline hurried toward the doorway and called over her shoulder, "Gregory, I need your help with the tea."

He raised an eyebrow. "Do you, darling? Complicated recipe is it? I'd be glad to share my expertise." Then, to Burnell and Finch, who had settled themselves on the sofa, he said, "Ah, well, a dutiful husband is always in demand."

She pursed her lips and her dark eyes narrowed as she waited for him to cross the living room. When he reached her side, she gave him a shove into the hall. But she flashed a smile at the two detectives, before her head disappeared round the door.

"Longdon's for it now," Finch quipped, a grin playing upon his lips.

Burnell gripped his knees. "Yes, well. He had better start unburdening his soul when he comes back, if he knows what's good for him."

"Don't worry, sir. I'm certain Emmeline is laying down the law at this very moment."

The superintendent pounded a fist against his thigh. "Hmph. The law," he groused. "Longdon goes out of his way to flout the law at every opportunity. Why does the man insist on hiding things?"

Finch spread his hands wide. "I suppose because everything's a game to him."

"This is deadly serious," the superintendent retorted through gritted teeth. "It's not a game."

"Surely, sir, you don't suspect Longdon had anything to do with the murder?"

Burnell slumped back and squeezed his eyes shut. Several seconds elapsed before he opened them again. "No, he's bloody infuriating and I'd like to throttle him most of the time, but Longdon's no murderer. We both know that." He exhaled a weary breath. "Swanbeck is the obvious suspect. However, we wouldn't be doing our job if we ignored the possibility that it could be someone else."

Finch nodded. "The question is who?"

"The only way we'll find out is if Longdon tells us. Because"—his fist curled into a tight ball again—"as always, he's the only one with all the answers. God how I hate being out of the loop. It's ironic if you think about it. Almost laughable." But there was no mirth in his voice. "I've been suspended and maybe the only person who can get me reinstated is a thief. Don't you find that amusing, Finch?"

The sergeant's lips parted to respond, but he was prevented from doing so. Perhaps it was just as well. What could he have said?

"Are my ears burning, Oliver?" Gregory asked as he entered the room, Emmeline close on his heels. "I'm touched that you missed me so much," he went on as he placed the tea tray on the coffee table. "But really, we've only been gone a few minutes."

Emmeline gently bumped him out of the way with her hip and gestured with her chin toward the wing chair he usually occupied. "Remember what we discussed" she mouthed.

He winked and gave her a cheeky salute, as he lowered himself into the chair.

"Now then, Superintendent Burnell," she said as she handed him a steaming cup of tea. "Gregory has promised to answer *all*"—she cast a pointed glance at her husband—"your questions."

Gregory propped his elbows on the arms. "Indeed, I have. You don't know how eager I am to help the law"—he waved an elegant hand at the detectives and beamed at them—"as represented by you fine gentlemen."

Burnell and Finch exchanged an exasperated look and shook their heads.

"Longdon, why do you take a perverse pleasure in making everything so difficult?" Finch asked.

Gregory pressed a hand to his chest and assumed an innocent expression. "Me? I wouldn't dream of it. On the other hand, everyone needs a bit of excitement."

Burnell took a long swallow of tea seemingly to steady his rattled nerves and then carefully set his cup and saucer on the coffee table. His eyes locked on Gregory. "Who is Sebastian Jardine?" His voice was pitched low, but there was a hard edge to it.

"Seb is—was—a man of many tongues."

"*Longdon*," the superintendent thundered in warning.

Gregory put up a hand in defense. "Truly, Oliver. I'm not joking. Jardine was a linguist. He was fluent in eight languages that I knew of. He had a natural ear. He could pick up a language like that." He snapped his fingers to emphasize his point. "He had a brilliant mind. He received a double first from Cambridge and became a fellow. He taught history for a time."

"So how did a man like that wind up dead at the end of a knife?"

Gregory frowned. "Seb was restless. He was always looking for a challenge and he had wanderlust in his soul. He thought his gift for languages could help him fulfill his desire to see the world. He also had a penchant for puzzles. What better way to indulge both his talents? He submitted his CV to Interpol hoping to do good in the world. Interpol was more than happy to accept a man of Seb's intelligence into the fold."

"A mate of yours working at Interpol?" Finch asked incredulously. "Now, I've heard it all. It's no wonder you were never caught. Jardine was feeding you inside information, so that you could stay one step ahead of the police."

Gregory sniffed. "I really don't know what you're implying. I am, and always have been, a model citizen with a deep reverence for the law."

The two detectives exchanged a skeptical look and shook their heads.

"Go on," Burnell prodded. "I can't wait to hear the rest of it. Jardine obviously took a wrong turn somewhere along the line, if he's lying dead at the morgue. But according to you, he rose from the dead like Lazarus only to be killed—permanently."

A shadow fell across Gregory's face. "Yes," he whispered.

Then in a stronger voice, he went on, "Seb was with Interpol for three years, but unfortunately he couldn't seem to find his niche. He decided to look for greener pastures. He offered his services as a translator to anyone with money. The richer, the better since those with money are always jet setting about and want things at their fingertips." A sad sigh escaped his lips. "I'm afraid his noble intentions abandoned him. He wasn't particularly choosy about the company he kept."

"So, what you're saying is that it's quite possible that Swanbeck could have hired Jardine as a translator?"

Gregory nodded. "Alastair or one of his cronies. My guess is that Seb overheard something that he shouldn't have." He leaned forward in his chair. "And the fool tried his hand at blackmail."

"And paid for it with his life," Burnell concluded with a grimace. "What the devil did he learn?"

One of Gregory's shoulders twitched upward. "When it comes to Alastair, his hands are so dirty it could be anything."

Only the clink of china could be heard as each sipped his or her tea, their minds mulling over the unsavory possibilities.

"It all boils down to Delahunt," Finch observed. "Clearly, the only reason he was at the airport today was to meet Jardine."

Emmeline shuddered, thinking of Delahunt's attractive face and laughing brown eyes as he put her into the taxi. "That makes him a target now too." She put a hand to her mouth and drew in a ragged breath. "What's even more un-settling is that he's roaming around out there alone and we have no idea where to find him."

"Delahunt's not alone," Burnell pointed out matter-of-factly. "He has Jardine's carry-on bag." He pounded his fist against his open palm. "I want to know what's in it."

"Something Swanbeck desperately wants back and he's willing to kill to get it," Finch murmured.

Burnell's glacial stare impaled Gregory. "I hope your friend hopped on the first plane out of the country. Otherwise, he's playing with fire." He wagged a finger at Gregory and issued a stern warning. "If I so much as hear a whisper that the two of you are hatching some scheme, Emmeline or no Emmeline, I'm going to throw you in jail."

Gregory didn't flinch. "Oliver, I assure you I've told you everything that I know."

"Which is precious little," the superintendent countered. "As usual."

"What can I say? I'm a man of few words."

Emmeline had only been half-listening to this habitual war of words between her husband and Burnell. She cleared her throat. "What if Delahunt decides to pick up where Jardine left off?"

"Then God help us all," Burnell intoned lugubriously.

CHAPTER 9

T he next day, Fate decided to give them all a bit of a reprieve. Prince William and his longtime girlfriend, Kate Middleton, announced their engagement, at last. The prospect of a royal wedding in the near future bumped everything else to the back pages of the all the newspapers. Even the item about an unidentified dead man being discovered at Heathrow in the boot of a car belonging to Superintendent Oliver Burnell, who until that moment had been a well-respected detective in the Metropolitan Police. The brief account of this still-evolving story indicated that Burnell had been suspended pending the outcome of the investigation. A single paper brashly posited whether this could be another sad case of a copper gone bad. The paper, naturally, was not *The Clarion.*

Also missing from the front pages was the startling news that during a routine search yesterday at the airport, a bloody knife had been found in the baggage of *The Clarion*'s editorial director of investigative features. The same scurrilous paper that had cast aspersions upon Burnell's integrity was the only one astute enough to question whether the two incidents could be connected. Emmeline flung that particular rag across her office and damned it to the darkest corners of hell.

Granted it was not a mature thing to do, but it was better than screaming at the top of her lungs or alternately strangling someone. She hoped it would be a few more days before she and Burnell were thrown to the wolves. She knew how ruthless her colleagues could be with such a juicy double story. She couldn't blame them really. After all, she understood only too well. But it just didn't feel especially comfortable when one was on the receiving end of all the media attention.

Right. She placed both hands on her desk and pushed herself to her feet. As Gran always said, worrying never helped anyone. It simply drained one of the energy to fight. And fight she must. For herself and Gregory, and poor Superintendent Burnell, who had been dragged into this mess because he was a dedicated servant of the law. The fight for the truth was never easy, but it was always worth it.

What could she do at the moment? Of course, she couldn't cover the story about herself and the fact that she had been detained at the airport for several hours. That would be a conflict of interest. She had agreed to go down to Scotland Yard that afternoon to give her statement to Inspector Halliday and Sergeant Finch. Thankfully, she wasn't under arrest. That meant she was free to do what she did best. Ask questions.

She smiled and gathered up her handbag. She could follow up on the lead about the now twice-deceased Sebastian Jardine. She was more than a little curious about his interlude at Interpol. Instinct told her that his death—the most recent one—almost certainly had to do with his time at the agency. Her few contacts at Interpol were either unwilling to help her with this story or ordered not to.

She needed to speak with someone outside Interpol, perhaps from another agency. Someone well-versed in the vagaries of government—and its intrigues. Someone she could trust. Hugh Carstairs immediately came to mind. She and Gregory had just worked with him on that foul business involving Noel Rallis and Lord Starrett. The only problem was she had no idea where Carstairs was at the moment. That only left Philip, her best friend Maggie's husband. Philip wouldn't refuse to speak with her—well, he could, but she hoped he wouldn't. Therefore, the best plan of attack was to get him off balance. She was going to hop on the Tube and simply appear at his office. She had a secret an ally in Philip's secretary Pamela, which didn't hurt. Philip was just as dear a friend as Maggie, but sometimes he was much too cautious and tried to put her off a story for any number of reasons. She supposed it was the diplomat in him. But Pamela would help to wear Philip down, in the event he chose to be a bit unco-operative.

ↁↂↁ

As Emmeline had anticipated, Pamela was more than willing to squeeze her into Philip's diary. He was out at a meeting, but he was expected back shortly. Pamela ushered Emmeline directly into his office, rather than having her wait in the antechamber, which was Pamela's domain and where she ruthlessly controlled access to her boss.

"Better to spring you on him," the secretary whispered conspiratorially. "More difficult to boot you out, if you're already in his office. Not that Mr. Acheson has ever done so, but men can be distinctly odd at times, don't you find?"

They both giggled and Pamela glided out of the office to get a tray with tea.

Emmeline settled herself on the claret-colored leather Chesterfield sofa in the corner to the right of the door and allowed her eyes to wander over the handsome room she knew so well. It was more like a gentleman's study than an office. The plush red wall-to-wall carpeting covering the floor muffled one's footsteps, while an elegant mahogany desk dominated the center of the office. Two arm-chairs in the same claret leather faced the sofa and were clustered around a highly polished oval coffee table made of cherry. This cozy area nestled next to a large window that overlooked King Charles Street. On the opposite side of the room near the desk were two mahogany bookcases with glass doors, through which she spied leather-bound tomes.

As she formulated a list of questions in her head, Emmeline's eyes alighted on a photo of Philip and Maggie and their twin sons. Not for the first time, Emmeline felt a stab of guilt. Maggie, like most people, thought her husband worked for the Foreign Office's Directorate of Defence and Intelligence. However, a small group, which included Emmeline, Gregory, Burnell and Finch, knew he really worked for MI5, Britain's counterintelligence agency.

This revelation came to light earlier in the year, when she was trying to find out who had killed her colleague Charles Latimer. Her investigation subsequently turned into a hunt for a Russian spy in the Foreign Office. Philip had sworn her and the others to secrecy about his employment at MI5, going so far as to have them sign the Official Secrets Act. He didn't want Maggie worrying unnecessarily. Emmeline understood his concern. And yet, sometimes it made it difficult to look Maggie in the eye.

The sound of the door opening tore her from these thoughts. Philip's tall, lean frame emerged on the threshold. She sat up straighter preparing to launch into her opening gambit, but he hadn't noticed her yet.

With his hand still on the doorknob, his blond head swiveled round to respond to something Pamela was saying. "What was that?" he asked.

"You have a visitor, Mr. Acheson. I'm just coming with the tea."

Emmeline watched Philip's profile. His lips were pursed

and his brows knit together, as though he was scrolling through his mental diary. He held the door open wider to allow his secretary to enter.

"What visitor? I know for a fact that I didn't have another meeting scheduled until this afternoon with the French ambassador."

These words were barely out of his mouth, when his gaze fell on Emmeline. His blue eyes widened for a second and then narrowed.

Pamela scuttled past him and set the tea tray on the coffee table. "As you can see, Miss Kirby"—she shot an apologetic glance at Emmeline—"I'm sorry. I mean Mrs. Longdon is here to see you. She didn't have an appointment, but of course she doesn't need one. I knew you would be more than happy to see her." She straightened up and spun round. She beamed up at her boss. "I can tell by the expression on your face that you are. I'll leave you to it and get back to my work." She inclined her head to Emmeline. "Mrs. Longdon, always a pleasure to see you."

Emmeline smiled. "And you, too, Pamela. Thank you."

Philip pressed his tongue against his cheek and slipped one hand into his pocket, as Pamela breezed out the door.

Just before she disappeared, she tossed over her shoulder, "It's no use giving me that Gorgon stare, Mr. Acheson. It doesn't frighten me one bit because I have nerves of steel."

"Well, some kind of nerve anyway," he retorted as the door closed with a soft click behind her.

Philip sighed and crossed over to the coffee table and lowered himself into one of the armchairs opposite Emmeline.

She perched on the edge of the sofa and reached for the tea pot. Holding it aloft, she asked with a sweet smile, "Shall I be Mother?"

They were both silent as she handed him a cup and poured one for herself.

Philip took a sip and over the rim of his cup said, "It's only been a few days. I didn't expect to see you again so soon."

Emmeline settled back against the sofa and flapped a hand at him. "It couldn't have slipped your mind that you and Maggie have invited us to lunch at your house on Sunday. I would be hurt if it did." She concluded with a pout.

He took another swallow of tea. "No, I haven't forgotten about Sunday. But today's Tuesday. There can be only one reason why you have ambushed me in my office *again*. You want information." He leaned back and propped his elbows on the armrests and took a swallow of tea. "Whatever it is, the answer is no."

Emmeline set her cup and saucer down on the table. She sniffed. "Ambushed? That's rather harsh for a friend, wouldn't you say?"

He crossed one leg over the other and shook his head. "In your case? No. I think it's completely apropos."

Emmeline cleared her throat and held his gaze. "The thing is…something happened yesterday at the airport. Well, two things actually, which we're quite certain are linked. It's rather complicated."

"We? As in you and Longdon. Where the two of you are involved things are always complicated, especially if it concerns your husband."

"That's utterly unfair. I should be offended. Besides if it makes you feel any better, Superintendent Burnell and Sergeant Finch are quite in the thick of it."

Philip groaned. "Terrific. That means it's much worse than I thought."

"I never realized until this instant that you have a rather negative outlook on life. How does Maggie put up with you?"

"Never mind about the state of my marriage. You had better tell me what the trouble is all about."

"The word trouble never crossed my lips."

Philip snorted. "You know, sometimes you can be quite amusing." He went quiet for a moment. "This is *not* one of those times. I'm not promising anything, but I'm willing to listen."

Emmeline gave a conciliatory nod and confided every detail about what occurred at the airport from the moment the knife was found in her bag to what they had seen on the CCTV tapes.

"Jardine hasn't been officially identified yet, but it's probably only a matter of days before the police do. I must find out about his time at Interpol. What precisely did his work involve? Why did he leave and decide to offer his linguistic skills to those of dubious morals and flexible ideas about the law?"

"You mean like your husband."

She threw him a withering glance. "That remark does not deserve a response. I have to find the truth to clear Superintendent Burnell's name. We both know that he's one of the finest police officers on the force. I can't allow Swanbeck to use him as tool to exact his revenge on us."

"As always, your intentions are extremely noble. Swanbeck is guilty as sin, but we're going to have a devil of a time trying to prove it. Don't forget you're not out of the woods yet."

Emmeline's heart lifted at these observations. "So you'll help?"

Philip tilted his head to one side and met her gaze. "Was there ever any doubt that I would?"

She shrugged. "One never knows. You could have gotten too big for your britches."

He guffawed. "Not a chance with you, Maggie and that one out there"—he jerked his thumb toward the door on the other side of which they knew Pamela was hard at work— "ready to beat me into submission." He pressed a hand over his heart and bowed his head. "I am but a humble servant."

Emmeline laughed for the first time since this nightmare began. "The martyr role doesn't suit you."

Philip shrugged. "Yes, well. There are a couple of things that intrigue me. Why is Swanbeck so convinced that Longdon has the Blue Angel?" He gave her a pointed look. She met it without flinching. "And how is Delahunt mixed up in this mess?"

Emmeline spread her hands wide. "I have no idea what drives Swanbeck. Gregory has left his old life behind. He most definitely does *not* have the diamond. We all know Bronowski is the one who must have made the switch."

"Hmph," Philip snorted. She could tell by his expression that he was not as convinced about Gregory's innocence as she was.

"Gregory does not have the Blue Angel," she repeated more forcefully.

Are you sure? a voice whispered inside her head. *Remember Tarasova's ruby necklace.*

She tossed back a gulp of tea. *Gregory* has *reformed. He has a legitimate job now,* she argued with herself. *He made a promise.*

The cold tea tasted bitter on her tongue. *Keep telling yourself that. Maybe it will become true. And by the way, promises can be broken.*

Oh, shut up. What do you know? she silently spat back.

"Emmeline, are you listening? You've gone a funny shade of puce. Look, I didn't mean to upset you any more than you are already. Let's just say that I view Longdon as a work in progress and we'll leave it at that, shall we?"

Her head snapped up. "What? No. I'm mean yes. You're wrong about Gregory, but I don't want to argue about it now." She took a deep breath. "I have to meet with Inspector Halliday and Sergeant Finch this afternoon to give my formal statement. I'll try to see if I can winkle out any information from them about the investigation in the process. In the interim, perhaps you could reach out to some of your contacts to find out something about Jardine?"

He nodded and rose to his feet. "Yes, I'll have a quiet word with one or two chaps. I can trust them to keep it under their hats. You just worry about yourself and Longdon. Burnell can take care of himself. I'll ring him later."

She accepted the hand he extended and stood as well. "Would you? I'm sure he'll appreciate that. There's no need to see me out. I know you're busy and I've already taken up too much of your time." She reached up and brushed his cheek with a kiss. "Thank you, Philip."

He put his hands on her shoulders. "What are friends for? I'll let you know the instant I find out anything. I only ask one thing."

"Ask away," she said with a smile.

His grip tightened on her shoulders. "Be careful. Don't put yourself in harm's way. Journalism is a noble calling, but a story is not worth your life."

She patted him on the arm. "You're like a mother hen. You worry too much. Have I ever deliberately placed myself in a dangerous situation?"

"Too many times for me to count."

CHAPTER 10

Gregory had spent a rather dull morning at the office completing some paperwork on his last case. Once again, he had prevented Symington's from making a generous payout on a claim that had turned out to be false. A wealthy hedge fund manager, who was going through a nasty divorce, had devised an elaborate ruse to make it appear that his priceless coin collection had been stolen. Therefore, his lawyer had argued in court filings, the collection could not be sold with half the proceeds going to his wife. Gregory had smelled a rat from the outset. It had taken very little effort for him to prove that the hedge fund chap had stolen the coins himself. He never stopped marveling at amateurs and their sloppy planning, as he made a final note in the file.

His persistence in the case had earned him Symington's undying gratitude. In the company's eyes, he could do no wrong. He couldn't help but chuckle.

Gregory checked his watch. Ten-thirty. He sighed. The meeting for his next case was not until this afternoon. However, he couldn't muster any enthusiasm for it. He was merely going through the motions of reading up on the client. He was too preoccupied. First and foremost, he was worried about Emmy with Swanbeck lurking in the background. She had forbidden him to accompany her to Scotland Yard for her interview with Inspector Halliday. He silently cursed his wife's stubborn streak. At the same time, his mind was awhirl with speculation about poor Seb Jardine and the deception that had cost him his life. And, what the devil did any of this have to do with Roger Delahunt?

He gave a frustrated shake of his head. He had no answers, only more questions. That left him to his own devices for the rest of morning. Well, there was no rest for the wicked.

He smoothed down the corners of his mustache and pushed himself to his feet. He shot his cuffs and straightened his immaculately cut Savile Row suit jacket. Since the dead man at the airport had yet to be officially identified as Seb, Gregory thought a little visit to his old friend's flat was in order. *Before* the police got in there and mucked things about. He could have a good look around at his leisure without any interference. After all, he reasoned, coppers were so overworked, wasn't it his civic duty to help them out if he could? Of course, it was.

With a smile on his lips, he popped his head round his boss's door and told him that he would be out the rest of the day on a case. His boss waved him away with a distracted "Off you go then" and nary a question about what case precisely he was working on.

He took the lift straight down to the garage. After his contretemps at the airport yesterday with Webb, all his nerves tingled with wariness as the doors slid open. He stepped out into the garage and casually drew out his mobile from his inside pocket, seemingly checking if he had any messages. But in that one brief instant his eyes roamed about the garage to make sure that he didn't have any unexpected visitors waiting for him.

The garage was empty, as it should be in the middle of the morning on a weekday. The knots in his muscles eased a fraction. He saw his blue-gray Jaguar quietly gleaming in its spot. His ears strained for echoing footsteps as he crossed to his car, but there weren't any. He was quite alone. But that didn't stop him from making a complete circuit of his car to check for anything odd, before he slipped in behind the wheel. Since his friend Rupert had died in a car bomb explosion over the summer, Gregory always went through this ritual thanks to Swanbeck.

Gregory started the ignition and exhaled a long breath. He put the car in gear and guided it toward the exit onto Leadenhall Street. He merged into traffic and headed west toward Seb's flat in St. John's Wood. Leadenhall soon became Cornhill. As he slid past the Royal Exchange and the Bank of England, Webb's voice popped into his head.

Either you return the Blue Angel or you're going to wish you were dead.

Gregory's fingers tightened on the wheel. "You're never getting your hands on the Blue Angel, Alastair," he said through clenched teeth. "Haven't you learned that a lady never responds to threats?"

He would simply have to find a way to protect Emmy *and* keep the Blue Angel. He was a clever fellow after all. It shouldn't be too difficult a task.

⌘

Gregory skirted Regent's Park along Park Road. At the roundabout, he turned onto Prince Albert Road. Within minutes, he was pulling the car into a spot halfway down the block from the graceful Art Deco building in St. John's Wood where Seb's flat was located. He had done a bit of checking in the morning and Seb was still listed as the owner.

Once again, Gregory marveled that his friend had been living in plain sight all these years only a stone's throw from his old flat in Primrose Hill. Even if Seb wasn't in London often, how was that possible? And how was it that he hadn't known that his friend was still alive? He shook his head in disbelief as he locked his car and started to amble up the block. More importantly, what dangerous game had Seb been playing since he left Interpol?

Gregory's silver tongue and innate charm made it child's play to wangle his way past the uniformed porter and onto the lift, which carried him up to Seb's flat. As he stepped off the car on the third floor, Gregory inclined his head and murmured "Good morning" to an elderly woman who had been waiting for the lift. He lingered there until the doors slid closed.

The corridor was empty. Therefore, he didn't have an audience when he entered Seb's flat without the assistance of a key. He was a master of ingress by other means. A key was merely superfluous.

He pressed the door closed behind him and shot the bolt. He scooped up the mail that was scattered across the creamy wall-to-wall carpeting beneath his feet. He flicked through it. There was nothing of interest. Nothing that gave him any sort of clue as to what his friend had been involved in. He dumped the pile on a console table and drifted into the spacious living room to his right.

Although sparsely furnished, it was a cheerful room. The sun's golden lashes pierced the row of windows along one wall and tumbled forth, spilling late morning light into the room. Gregory's footsteps were lost in the plush carpeting as he crossed to the pair of striped moss green-and-beige sofas facing one another across a Queen Anne coffee table in the center of the room. The table's surface was coated in a fine layer of dust, but not as much as he would have expected if the flat had been shuttered for several years. Clearly, Seb had been living here all the time that the world had assumed that he was dead. Or at least someone had been staying here recently. This last thought was far from comforting.

Gregory proceeded to rummage among the cushions looking for…he had absolutely no idea. He moved on to the elegantly carved glass-fronted cabinet. Seb's inlaid wood and mother of pearl chess set took pride of place. He remembered his friend was a master chess player. Seb could have competed among the world's best, if he had had any ambition. But he had no desire for accolades. Seb simply liked the challenge of the game. A glance at the handful of *objets d'art* surrounding the chess set told Gregory there was nothing to be found in the cabinet.

He spun on his heel and turned his attention to the bookshelf along the opposite wall. He riffled through the pages of several books, but he hadn't really expected to find a secret note tucked among their pages. Alas, that only happened to the hero in films. The search of the small desk next to the shelf proved to be equally as disappointing.

A frustrated sigh escaped his lips as he wandered out of the room into the kitchen across the corridor. He knew Seb would have left something behind as insurance, especially if he was tangling with Swanbeck. But *what* was it? And *where* had he hidden it? He groaned inwardly. If only Seb had come to him to ask for help, instead of going after Alastair alone.

The kitchen was spotless. Nothing was out of place. Damn and blast. He slammed his open palm against the marble countertop of the island in the center. He had the sudden urge to throw a few pots and dishes about to create a bit of disorder on the outside to complement the turmoil and worry roiling his mind. He lifted his hand to open a cabinet above the stove, when he heard a muted noise coming from the direction of one of the bedrooms. He rather doubted that this pristine building was overrun by mice and the police would have made their presence known the instant he set foot in the flat.

So that only left one other possibility. An uninvited visitor.

A smile spread over his face. How terribly thrilling. And here he was thinking today would be a dull day. Of course, Emmy wouldn't approve of him confronting an intruder, especially as he had no idea whether the chap was armed. But happily, his dear wife wasn't here and if he was careful, she would never find out.

Gregory seized the nearest pan at hand and eased his way out into the corridor on the balls of his feet. Lithe as a cat, he made his way along the wall toward the master bedroom. Even a ghost would have had to strain its ears to hear his approach.

When he was only a few steps from the door, he saw the knob turning. He held his breath and raised the pan above his head ready to lash out.

The door swung open and his hand came down in an arc. At the last second, he managed to deflect the blow.

"Bloody hell, Roger," he cursed, as the knot in his stomach unwound.

Delahunt grinned back at him, an amused gleam in his brown eyes. "Hello, Greg." He relieved him of the pan, judging its weight. "Had I known you were cooking lunch I wouldn't have had a full English breakfast." He patted his flat stomach. "As it is, I don't think I could eat a bite."

"Thank you for coming to Emmy's aid at the airport yesterday," Gregory said ten minutes later as he eyed his old friend over a cup of tea in the kitchen. "But I should have coshed you over the head when I had the chance. What the devil are you up to?"

Delahunt ignored the question. "Your wife is rather lovely."

"I won't argue with you there. Emmy's one in a million."

Roger took a sip of tea. "I was quite surprised when I read in the paper that you had married again." He paused. "I only spent a few minutes with Emmeline, but she's…quite different from Ronnie." His gaze held Gregory's and a heavy silence filled the space between them.

"Yes," Gregory murmured at last and swallowed the rest of his tea in one gulp.

"What happened to Ronnie?"

Gregory set his cup and saucer down on the countertop. "We divorced obviously."

"That goes without saying. Emmeline doesn't strike me as the type of woman who would share you."

Gregory huffed a laugh. "No, she's not. She's a bit on the jealous side. But then, I gave her no cause to doubt me. She also has a temper."

Roger shook his head and gave a low whistle. "Dear, oh dear. If I were you, I wouldn't stray."

Gregory's voice held a gruff note. "Never. Emmy's more to me than life itself. I lost her once. I don't intend to again." He busied himself pouring another cup of tea. "Ronnie's dead by the way," he tossed out nonchalantly.

One of Roger's brows arched upward. "Is she? I know one shouldn't speak ill of the dead, but I'm rather glad. You were too good for her. I don't know why you ever…" He bit off his last words.

"No, no. You're quite right. I was a complete and utter fool. I allowed Ronnie to turn my head. You knew her. She was sexy and exciting. Like that blasted apple in the Garden of Eden." He took a sip of tea, scalding his tongue in the process. "She was murdered in April in Torquay."

This elicited another whistle from Delahunt. "Well, I can't say that I'm surprised. She was always like the bubonic plague."

"We were there. Emmy and I."

"So that means…"

"Emmy met her? Oh, yes, they met."

Roger leaned across the island. "How…awkward." This was uttered with all the understatement that only an Englishman could muster. "Emmeline didn't kill her, did she?" He put up his hands in the air. "Not that I would blame her, you understand."

Gregory snorted. "Don't be daft. My wife doesn't have a corrupt bone in her body. She's a defender of truth and justice."

"Greg, you always did like living on the edge. Does she know about your past?"

Gregory permitted himself a wry smile. "Yes and no."

Roger nodded knowingly. "Ah. So she only knows what she's been able to find out. And the rest?" He left the question hanging in the air.

Gregory's shoulders twitched in a shrug. "Emmy's job keeps her quite busy enough. I'm a considerate husband. Why burden her?"

"I see. That means you're still on the game, despite outward appearances to the contrary."

"I'm a law-abiding citizen these days."

Roger folded his arms across his chest and smirked. "Of course, you are. You're also playing with fire. There will be hell to pay, if your wife discovers the truth."

"She already knows the truth. I love her."

"But will that be enough? Especially considering that hot temper of hers. A woman like Emmeline doesn't like to be lied to. You can't have it both ways."

Gregory made a dismissive gesture with his hand. "Since when have you become an expert on women?" Then changing the subject, he asked pointedly, "Speaking of playing with fire *and* lies, what the devil were you and Seb mixed up in?"

Roger's gaze slid away. "Seb?" His tone was all innocence.

"Yes, Seb Jardine. Our mutual friend. The chap who

owned this flat. The chap who was murdered at the airport yesterday. The chap whose bag you snatched before anyone realized what had happened."

Roger lifted his eyes to meet Gregory's gaze, but he held his tongue.

"Why was Seb blackmailing Alastair Swanbeck?" Gregory pressed, adamant that he would have an answer one way or the other.

"You never used to ask so many questions. It must be a nasty habit you picked up from your wife."

"Leave Emmy out of this."

"I'm afraid I can't, old chap. Don't you know that when you save someone's life, you're responsible for her?"

Gregory favored him with a smile. "Emmy's *my* wife and I can take care of her quite well. Thank you very much."

"It didn't look like that from my vantage point at the airport."

Gregory felt the muscle in his jaw pulsing just below the skin. "Roger, I consider you a friend, but we both know that you're no knight in shining armor. So stop pretending otherwise. Where is Seb's bag?"

CHAPTER 11

Burnell caught a glimpse of Philip's blond head reflected in one the mirrors, as he entered Café Richoux on Piccadilly. Philip was seated in one of the forest green leather banquettes a short distance from the door. He lifted a hand in greeting. The superintendent murmured to the hostess that he was meeting a friend and pointed in Philip's direction. She gave him smile and nodded.

Burnell ambled over and reached across the marble table to shake Philip's outstretched hand. The superintendent cast a glance round the restaurant, as he lowered his bulk in the chair facing Philip. Although he had passed by often, he had never actually set foot inside. With its red floral wallpaper, mirrors and marble tables, the ambiance was warm and inviting. It was the perfect spot to share conversation with a good friend over a nice cuppa or a quiet meal. Under other circumstances, he would have allowed himself to relax and abandon his cares for a brief interlude. Only this wasn't one of those cozy occasions. His cares were so weighty that his ulcer was doing somersaults. Not a good sign at all.

As if reading his mind, Philip asked, "How are you holding up?"

"Oh, you know." He waved a hand airily and assumed a

nonchalant expression. "The British way. Stiff upper lip and all that. Thanks for the call and the lunch."

Philip flicked his napkin open and spread it across his lap, as he opened his menu. "Lunch is my pleasure. This is one of my favorite haunts, when I can get away. However, you have Emmeline to thank. She's quite worried about you. Not to say that I'm not. I'm damn concerned by this sticky mess. But she's ready to charge the ramparts of the Tower of London if need be to clear your name."

At the mention of Emmeline, one corner of Burnell's mouth quirked into a smile. "Well, we both know that sometimes she gets carried away. I hope you persuaded her that I can take care of myself."

Philip cocked his head to one side. "*Can* anyone change Emmeline's mind? We both know she's stubborn as a bulldog."

They both chuckled.

"But seriously now, how are you?"

The smile vanished from the superintendent's lips. He pounded a meaty fist against the marble tabletop, making their cutlery jump. "Bloody angry," he growled.

This outburst attracted several startled glances.

Philip pursed his lips. In soothing tones, he murmured, "Naturally. Why don't we order? A little food will help settle your nerves. We'll soon have this sorted out."

"Sorry," Burnell mumbled, as he picked up his menu. "I'm angry because I allowed myself to be lulled into a false sense of security since there hadn't been a peep about Swanbeck in months. We all *know* he's as slippery as an eel. I should have been more vigilant." His fingers tightened on the menu. "My gut told me that we hadn't seen the last of him. I should have—"

"You can't blame yourself."

"No?" Burnell hissed through clenched teeth as he leaned

across the table. "Who else is there?"

"Don't be maudlin. You know that you're a damn fine policeman. Your dedication to the law is unparalleled."

The superintendent grunted. "And we all see where that has gotten me."

Although the words held a bitter edge, Philip could see that some of the tension had melted away in his companion. "I don't know about you, but I'm ravenous."

Burnell nodded in agreement as his gaze fell on his menu. By the time the waitress appeared at his elbow a few minutes later, they had made their choices. They both had opted for the French onion soup as a starter, but the superintendent blatantly ignored the scolding tones of his doctor swirling around in his head and ordered the fish pie. To hell with his diet. He would begin watching his weight *after* this Swanbeck nightmare was resolved. Until then, he needed sustenance. From the dawn of time, men were hunters and gatherers. They could not possibly survive on bread and water alone. He was definitely on a hunt. The hunt of his life.

Burnell glanced down at his protruding stomach, but felt no stab of embarrassment at the fact that Philip had selected the lighter Welsh rarebit for his lunch. After all, he reasoned, the younger man was married to an extremely attractive wife. It went without saying that Philip would want to remain in trim form. *Chacun à son goût*, as the French say. To each his own. Every man had his priorities. At this moment, Burnell's was filling the gaping crater that had opened up in his stomach.

Although the food was more than satisfying, Philip and Burnell's conversation in hushed tones was grim. They were realists and abundantly aware of the gravity of the superintendent's predicament. It would have been an insult to Burnell's intelligence, if Philip had offered him platitudes that gave him false hope.

And so, they parted outside the restaurant on a hand-shake and Philip's promise to do everything in his power to help the superintendent. "I've already made a few calls. There are a few more things I'd like to check. I'll ring you in a couple of days, if I've discovered anything useful."

"That's more than anyone could ask," Burnell replied gratefully.

ღჄღჄ

On the short walk back to the Foreign Office, Philip mulled who else he could discreetly approach about Swanbeck and the murder accusation hanging over Burnell's head.

By rote, he ambled down Whitehall and through the Corinthian columns of the Foreign Office's main entrance. The guards recognized him and bid him good afternoon. His footsteps echoed loudly as he crossed the elegant hall with its high, vaulted ceiling, gilded walls and red-veined marble columns. His frowning countenance as he climbed the red-carpeted Grand Staircase dissuaded one or two of his colleagues from approaching. At the top of the landing, he turned left and followed the corridor until he came to his office at the far end.

A sigh escaped his lips as he entered the antechamber, causing Pamela to break off from her typing. "Problem, Mr. Acheson?" Her pleasant voice was infused with concern as she looked up at him expectantly.

He nodded. "You could say that."

"Does this have anything to do with what Mrs. Longdon came to see you about this morning?"

Philip gave her a slightly lopsided smile. "How did you guess?"

"You had that look."

He raised an eyebrow. "'That look?' I didn't know that I had particular expression when Emmeline drops by for a chat."

"Oh, yes," Pamela replied matter-of-factly. "It's a mix of earnestness and exasperation, and concern."

Philip sighed again. "Yes, I'm worried about Emmeline *and* Superintendent Burnell. Things couldn't be blacker for them at the moment and it's all because of Alastair bloody Swanbeck."

Pamela wrinkled her nose with distaste. "Swanbeck? Is that villain back in the picture? I thought he'd run away to lick his wounds after that dreadful business over the summer."

"He did, but apparently only to regroup. He's back with even more malice in his heart, if that's possible. He doesn't simply want to hurt Emmeline, Longdon and Burnell. He wants to *destroy* them."

"You mean if he has a heart. In my experience, men like Swanbeck crawled out from under a rock and never shed the dark mentality with which they were born."

Philip nodded wearily. "Thank you, Dr. Freud, for your analysis. Any messages while I was at lunch?"

Pamela dutifully handed over a stack of pink slips of paper. He flicked through them. Nothing that couldn't wait. He waved them in the air. "I'll return these later. I don't want to be disturbed for the remainder of the afternoon, unless it's the Prime Minister."

"Of course, Mr. Acheson."

His hand was on the doorknob to his office, when Pamela cleared her throat. He shot a glance over his shoulder. "Yes, Pamela, what is it?"

"I'm assuming that if Mrs. Acheson rings, the do not disturb does not apply to her and I'm to put her straight through?"

A smile tugged at Philip's mouth. "Do I look like a man who has lost his mind?"

Pamela was smiling too. "No, sir. You appear to be quite rational, but I just thought I'd check."

"Well now that you've proven beyond a shadow of a doubt that you're the model of an efficient secretary, get back to work." His words may have been stern, but his tone was light-hearted.

He pushed the door shut behind him and marveled once again at how fortunate he had been to have hired Pamela three years ago. He couldn't have asked for a more loyal, hard-working and conscientious secretary. He could trust her with the most sensitive issues that crossed his desk, and her lips would remain forever sealed.

After two hours of quietly badgering some of his contacts for any information about the late Sebastian Jardine and Swanbeck, he felt drained. He pressed the intercom on his phone.

"Yes, Mr. Acheson?" Pamela's crisp tones echoed in his office.

"I find myself in need of reviving. Could you please bring me some tea?"

"Certainly. Would you also like a plate of biscuits?"

"No, just the tea. Thanks."

"I'll have a pot ready for you shortly."

He was about to thank her, when he was interrupted by the intrusion of male voices. Then Pamela asked politely, "Yes, gentlemen, how may I help you?"

Apparently, she had deliberately left the speaker on so that he could hear. Why? Who were these chaps?

"Hammond and this is Wakefield. Special Branch" was the terse response to his silent question.

"I see," Pamela murmured. "How can I help you?" she repeated.

"You can't. We're here to see your boss."

"I'm afraid Mr. Acheson is not in. He had a luncheon appointment and then he was going directly to a meeting with Prime Minister."

"You're lying."

A cold tendril of dread clutched at Philip's chest. He rose warily and rocked on the balls of his feet.

Pamela's calm, professional voice hovered upon the air. "I beg your pardon, sir? If you don't believe me, I can ring Number Ten and you can speak to Mr. Acheson in person. However, I don't think the Prime Minister would be pleased at the interruption. Can't you tell me what this is all about? I assure you I have all the top security clearances and am privy to all of the matters Mr. Acheson is dealing with at the moment."

Good girl, Philip thought. *Find out what they want.*

The one named Hammond scoffed, "Not this business, unless you want to join Acheson in jail."

Philip didn't wait to hear more. First, Emmeline and Burnell. And now this. Whatever cooked up charge had brought Special Branch here, he knew for a certainty it was another of Swanbeck's calculated lies.

Philip was already moving as he heard Pamela's sharp intake of breath. "Jail? What do you mean?"

"We're not at liberty to say."

He eased open the top drawer of his desk. His fingers fumbled around for a few seconds, until they curled around the cold steel of his Beretta nine-millimeter gun taped to the back. He yanked it out and jammed in the magazine with a satisfying click. Then, he snatched up his mobile and punched in a number. The phone rang only once.

"Hello, darling." Maggie's voice caressed his ear. In his mind's eye, he could see his wife's beautiful smile.

"Maggie, just listen carefully," he whispered briskly before she could say more.

Philip could feel her tense at the other end of the line. "Darling, go home and pack some clothes for several days. Then, go and collect Henry and Andrew from school and take them to my parents' house. No——" His brain was racing furiously. Special Branch would be sure to check. "No, I have a better idea. Hop on the train and take the boys down to Helen's in Swaley."

"Philip, are you mad?" Maggie bristled. "Simply show up on the poor woman's doorstep with the boys in tow? I couldn't possibly impose."

"Nonsense. You know Helen would be tickled to death. She adores our little monsters."

"That's as it may be. Why are you whispering? What's going on? You're frightening me."

He tried to inject a calmness he did not feel into his tone. "Maggie, trust me. I love you and everything will be right as rain in a few days. Don't ask me any questions. Just please, *please* do as I ask. Get the twins and go to Helen. Ring her once you're on the train, not before. I'll be out of touch. I'll ring you in a few days."

Once I know it's safe. But he didn't dare utter these words out loud.

CHAPTER 12

Emmeline slammed the receiver down. That had been the third call she had fielded about the discovery of the bloody knife in her bag.

Damn, damn, damn, she fumed silently. How had her colleagues heard about the incident so quickly? Neither Inspector Halliday nor Sergeant Finch had made a public statement. As far as Scotland Yard was concerned, the circumstances seemed to be highly suspect. Halliday and Finch, unofficially, had concluded that the knife had been planted. They simply had to go through the motions for appearances sake. She even had to admit that Assistant Commissioner Cruickshank, annoying officious prat that he generally was, in this instance was being extremely decent and had shown some common sense. Could it be she had been wrong about him? Hmm, she would reserve judgment on Cruickshank for another day.

Right now, she had to find answers to so many questions. Who was Sebastian Jardine? Obviously, there was more to the man than anyone realized. Did Gregory know the truth and he wasn't saying?

No, she scolded herself. She would no longer doubt Gregory. She had done too much of that in the past and look where it had gotten them. He was her husband now. She had to trust him. Otherwise, the alternative was too unsettling to contemplate.

She took a deep breath and channeled her racing thoughts. Why was Jardine murdered? How had he gotten mixed up with Alastair Swanbeck?

Swanbeck. She shivered involuntarily. Would she and Gregory ever be free of the fiend?

She shook her head. No use being maudlin. Worrying never helped anyone, as Gran was wont to remind her. She had to find irrefutable, concrete proof of his crimes to finally bring Swanbeck to justice. But where to start? The man had been in hiding for months, until he rang Gregory at the airport.

No one could vanish without a trace. Swanbeck must have left a trail. She simply had to find the right thread to pull to unravel the entire ball of yarn. What was the man's weakness? She tapped a tattoo on the desk with her pen.

It came to her in a flash. Money. Swanbeck was never satisfied with his thriving illegal empire. He always wanted more. Her Majesty's government had frozen all of Swanbeck's assets in the U.K. But a savvy and cunning entrepreneur always has money stashed away in bank accounts all over the world, some secret and some in countries that were more than willing to turn a blind eye for a price. To find Swanbeck, she would have to follow the money until she struck gold.

A renewed sense of purpose sent a jolt of adrenaline coursing through her veins. At last, a lead. Well, the first step on the road to a lead. She reached for her phone and rang a reliable source she had cultivated at the Financial Reporting Council, who might be able to point her in the right direction. In this day and age of global commerce, the business world was a small one. In the end, no one could escape scrutiny, good or otherwise. Her source would most certainly be aware of the rumors swirling about Swanbeck's illicit dealings.

Yes, money was the devil's trap. She just hoped Swanbeck's greed would be his undoing.

⌘

Philip tossed his mobile on the desk, after he severed his call to Maggie. He didn't dare use it again until this whole nightmare was over. He couldn't afford to have Special Branch tracing his movements. Pamela couldn't stall the two agents in the antechamber much longer. At most, he only had another couple of minutes. Precious seconds ticked by as he swiveled his chair round and reached underneath.

His nimble fingers immediately found the mobile he had taped to the underside of the chair. Next to it was an envelope with one thousand pounds that he kept in case of emergencies. His current predicament most definitely constituted an emergency.

He ripped the tape away and crumpled the torn envelope. He stuffed the money in his wallet. In one fluid motion, he grabbed his suit jacket off the back of his chair and tucked the mobile in the inside pocket. He shrugged on the jacket as he crossed to a door that led out into the corridor.

He had barely pulled the door closed behind him, when Pamela and the two agents burst into his office.

"Satisfied now?" he heard Pamela ask. "If you'll recall, I *did* say that Mr. Acheson was out." Her tone held a mixture of asperity and outrage.

"Acheson's mobile is on the desk," Hammond pointed out, an air of triumph in his tone.

Pamela gave an exasperated—and exaggerated, Philip thought—sigh. "Again you mean. Mr. Acheson is always leaving his mobile behind. And they say women are forgetful." She clucked her tongue. He could only imagine the long-suffering expression on her face. "I'll have to ring the Prime Minister's office to let him know. If you gentlemen are quite finished, I'll see you out."

Philip bit back a smile, but he didn't linger to hear Hammond's response. There was no rest for the wicked.

The challenge now was to get out of the building without stumbling into the hostile arms of the two Special Branch agents.

He kept his head down, chin tucked into his chest, and avoided making eye contact with anyone as he made his way along the gallery at a brisk clip. He couldn't afford to be waylaid by one of his colleagues or to attract undue attention to himself. The red-carpeted Grand Staircase was only a few feet ahead of him.

The blood was pounding against his temples as he trotted down the stairs and sliced his way across the hall. Someone called his name, but he kept moving without acknowledging whoever it was.

In another minute, he pushed through the doors and passed between the Corinthian columns of the main entrance and out onto King Charles Street. He hesitated for only a fraction of a second to a cast glance over his shoulder. No one appeared to be following him. But then, he had no idea what Hammond and Wakefield looked like. He had only heard their voices.

He turned left, his feet taking him toward the arcade that led onto bustling Whitehall. Then what?

჌ჄჄ

"Roger, I asked you what was in Seb's bag?" Gregory demanded a second time, his tone was laced with irritation.

He could see that behind the warm brown eyes, Delahunt's brain was rapidly calculating the odds of offering a lie.

Gregory placed his hands on the island that separated them

and leaned toward his erstwhile friend. "I would hate to think that you're contemplating fobbing me off with a lie."

The lines of Roger's face crumpled into a wounded expression. He put a hand to his chest. "That hurts, Greg. There's such a thing as loyalty. Would I do that to you?"

Gregory snorted. "In a heartbeat."

Roger opened his mouth, but whatever lie he settled upon would have to wait because Gregory's mobile screamed to life.

He drew it out of his pocket and frowned at the unfamiliar number.

"Look, you're busy, Greg. I wouldn't dream of keeping you a minute longer," Roger said as he took half a step backward. "I'll just go."

Gregory grasped Roger's sleeve, before he could make a dash. "We're not finished. You're not leaving this flat, until I have the answers I want."

Roger sniffed. "That's a bit high-handed, I must say."

"Lump it" Gregory mouthed as he pressed the button on his mobile. "Longdon," he declared.

"Good. I've caught you."

Gregory's eyes widened. "Acheson?" He fell into his usual flippant manner. "Were you lonely and needed to chat?"

"I can't believe I'm saying this. But I think you're the only one who can help me."

Gregory's nerves tingled and he was immediately on the alert. "What's happened?"

"Swanbeck. Two Special Branch agents came to arrest me at the office. Pamela stalled them to give me time to escape."

Gregory's jaw tightened. "Bloody hell. Are you sure?"

"First, Emmeline and Burnell. Come on. It's too much of a coincidence," Philip scoffed. "This has Swanbeck's fingerprints all over it."

Gregory nodded in grim acknowledgement of the truth. "Where are you?"

"I just jumped into a cab on Whitehall. We're stuck in some traffic. Look, I need you to get in touch with Villiers. I daren't trust anyone else."

Gregory grimaced at the sound of Villiers's name. The man was an acquired taste. He pinched the bridge of his nose between his fingers. However, if it hadn't been for Villiers, he wouldn't be here today. For all his machinations, Villiers hadn't hesitated to step in front of him and take a bullet. The last time he saw Villiers was in the hospital just after his surgery.

He exhaled a weary sigh. "Yes, of course I'll go see Villiers," he replied finally. "But look here, Acheson, we can't have you wandering about on your own. I'm in Sebastian Jardine's flat in St. John's Wood. Have the cab drop you near Regent's Park. If anyone's following you, it may throw them off track. We'll meet you in Queen Mary's Rose Garden and come up with a strategy on what to do next."

"We? Is Emmeline with you? I don't want her dragged deeper into this thing than she already is."

Gregory flicked a glance at Roger, who shot him a questioning look but didn't utter a word. "No, Emmy's not here. To my surprise, I found my old mate Roger Delahunt in Seb's flat."

"Delahunt? Isn't that the chap who helped Emmeline at Heathrow?"

"That's one." His gaze narrowed. "Roger seems to be on the spot these days when trouble is brewing. You can help me wangle the whole story out of him." Then another thought struck him. "Speaking of wives, what about Maggie?"

"I told her to pack some things for a few days and take the boys down to Helen's in Swaley. Swanbeck would never bother to chase them down there. Maggie was more than a bit outraged that I had suggested she hop on the train without ringing ahead. She'll get over it."

"Helen won't mind at all. At least Maggie and the twins will be out of Swanbeck's line of fire. Now, we just have to worry about Emmy."

He didn't like the fact that his wife was roaming about London firing off questions that were certain to provoke Swanbeck's ire.

"Mmm" was Philip's response. Apparently, he shared the same concerns about Emmy.

Gregory shook his head, as if to physically prevent his mind from dwelling on sinister scenarios. Emmy would be fine. As long as he kept an eye on her. Which was never easy. He sighed. Why did he have to fall in love with a stubborn, independent woman?

"Roger and I are leaving now." He gave Delahunt a gentle shove out of the kitchen. "We'll be in the park."

"I know we've rubbed each other the wrong way at times, Longdon," Philip appeared to be searching for his words, "but for what it's worth, I'm grateful for your help."

One corner of Gregory's mouth twitched into a smile. "Water under the bridge, Acheson. I'll ring Oliver and Finch to let them know what's happened."

"Good idea. See you soon." With that, Philip rang off.

"Greg, you don't really need me to meet with your friend. I'd be a third wheel," Roger offered with a sheepish grin, as Gregory propelled him out of the flat and into the corridor.

Gregory kept a firm hold on Roger's upper arm as he jabbed the button on the lift. "I'm not letting you out of my sight."

"It's nice to know one is wanted," Roger mumbled with the air of a martyr.

CHAPTER 13

Emmeline glanced up from her monitor at the sound of light tapping on her door. Her mouth broke into a broad grin, when she saw Nigel Sanborn's pleasant face.

He returned her smile. "Are you in the middle of something or do you have a few minutes to spare?"

"I wouldn't be doing my job, if I wasn't in the middle of a story. However, I always have time for you, Nigel."

The corners of his eyes crinkled and she saw a flash of teeth. "I'm flattered."

She motioned to the chair opposite and waited until he lowered himself into it. The two of them had hit it off from the moment they had first met. Nigel was the corporate counsel for Sanborn Enterprises, which owned the *Clarion*. He was more than that, though. He had become a good friend and now, he was family since he was Gregory's cousin. Nigel's older brother Brian was the chairman and managing director of the company. Gregory had been estranged from the Sanborns for twenty-five years. Ever since he ran away when he was seventeen. Their rapprochement only occurred over the summer. After Nigel and Brian's father, Max, was murdered. She shuddered as the image of Max Sanborn's face floated before her eyes. Such a corrupt brute of a man. It was hard to believe that he had sired two such wonderful sons. Nigel and Brian were a credit to their mother, Mireille. But enough of family history.

"You don't usually pop by during the day," she said as she propped her forearms on her desk and rested her chin on her hand, "unless I've asked you to vet a story to make certain everything is above board from a legal standpoint before we go to print." She shot him a concerned glance. "So, I can only assume you're here because of what happened at the airport." She pursed her lips. "Sanborn is worried that it might damage the company's and the *Clarion*'s reputations."

Nigel leaned back in his chair and crossed one leg over the other. He scoffed, "The one who single-handedly sabotaged Sanborn's reputation was Dad, and Dad alone. Poor Brian had to shoulder the Herculean burden of restoring the company's good name. It's taken him months and a lot of closed-door meetings, but he's done it. Therefore, you're wrong. I'm here at Brian's behest to reiterate that Sanborn and the *Clarion* will stand by you no matter what else Swanbeck tries. We are prepared for a lengthy and ugly court battle, if that's what it takes. You are family in every sense of the word."

Emmeline swallowed the lump in her throat. His words touched her more than she could say. "Thank you," she replied hoarsely.

Nigel slapped his thigh. "Good. Now that we've settled that, where do things stand?"

She cleared her throat and became all business. "Inspector Halliday and Sergeant Finch have unofficially concluded that the knife was planted in my bag. They just have to go through the motions of an investigation."

Nigel gave a nod. "I would expect no less. What about Superintendent Burnell?"

She slumped back in her chair. "That's more complicated.

I'm sure you've heard that he's been suspended."

A sigh escaped Nigel's lips. "I suppose Assistant Commissioner Cruickshank had no choice under the circumstances."

"No, he didn't. One point in Cruickshank's favor is that he doesn't believe Burnell's guilty."

"He'd be a fool if he did."

"Cruickshank also has given Superintendent Burnell tacit authorization to investigate the case, as long as he does it behind the scenes. He's keeping in touch with Sergeant Finch. Out of sight, out of mind. Cruickshank can't be seen to be giving preferential treatment to the superintendent, even if he is the best man on the force."

Nigel's mouth quivered into a ghost of a smile. "Glad to see your journalistic scruples are not allowing you to show any bias."

She made a moue at him. "This conversation is strictly between us. But you know I'm right about Superintendent Burnell. Anyway, I had a word with Philip. He promised to talk to the superintendent. To buck up his spirits. Philip also said that he would try to discover what he could about Sebastian Jardine, the dead man." She held Nigel's gaze. "Jardine was a friend of Gregory's." She concluded softly.

Two vertical lines appeared between Nigel's brows. "Hmm. Was he?"

She nodded. It was obvious he was not pleased by this revelation. It was bad enough that Swanbeck was back in their lives, even if they had no idea where he was lurking.

After an interval, he asked, "Did Toby..." From time to time, he and Brian still slipped and reverted to the name Gregory was given at birth: Toby. He had been Toby Crenshaw before he had run away and embarked on a career as a jewel thief. "Did Gregory know Jardine was in London?"

She shook her head and hesitated. "Gregory...Everyone really...thought Jardine was already dead."

Nigel sat forward, hazel eyes widening in disbelief. "What? This gets worse by the second."

"I'm afraid everything is extremely dire where Swanbeck is concerned." She pursed her lips and frowned.

"From the little Gregory has said, Jardine was a brilliant scholar who spoke several languages. He was a fellow at Cambridge for a few years. He taught history, but he got bored. Jardine was seized by wanderlust and yearned for adventure. He ended up working for Interpol and then he decided that he could earn more money by offering his linguistic services to those whose ventures are highly lucrative and flagrantly illegal."

"Lovely." Nigel's voice held an edge of annoyance mingled with frustration. "How did Gregory manage to surround himself with such people before he met you?"

Emmeline spread her hands wide and shrugged, but she said nothing.

He pounded his fist against his open palm. "It's Dad's fault. Gregory would never have run away, if hadn't been for Dad."

Yes, Max had a lot to answer for, she thought. But he was dead and couldn't hurt anyone ever again. They couldn't allow themselves to be distracted by the past. *And yet, wasn't it because of the past that they were all in this predicament now?* instinct told her.

Nigel shook his head and pushed himself to his feet. "Right, I don't like any of this. If it were up to me, I'd take you off the Jardine story. In my opinion, it's far too dangerous." He put up a hand to silence the protest that had leaped to her tongue. "But I'm not here to censor you." His gaze locked on hers. "And you know it. It doesn't mean I have to like it, though."

"Life is full of things we don't like," she mumbled. "I'm a journalist. I have to ask questions to find the truth.

Sometimes the truth is ugly, but the public has a right to know. Sebastian Jardine deserves justice. He can no longer fight for himself."

"Why does it always have to be you?" he asked pointedly, his voice tinged with exasperation.

"Because I wouldn't be able to look myself in the mirror otherwise."

His lips pressed together in a tight line and he ambled toward the door. With his hand on the knob, he tossed over his shoulder in parting, "Keep me informed of your progress. And make certain you and that reckless husband of yours *stay* alive."

She gave a curt nod. "Of course." Then she relented slightly. "Don't worry, Nigel. We have the truth on our side."

"The truth is what got Sebastian Jardine killed." With that, he flung the door open and sailed out into the newsroom.

"Thank you for that cheery bit of wisdom," she groused aloud to her office.

She thrust her chin in the air and turned back to her computer. She had no intention of dying anytime soon.

However, a niggling little voice in the back of her mind whispered, *"L'homme propose, mais Dieu dispose."*

ↄ◌ↄ

Gregory paced back and forth as Roger lounged on the bench, legs stretched out in front of him and crossed at the ankles. They had agreed to linger in Queen Mary's Rose Garden for another ten minutes to give Philip time to slip away to a MI5 safe flat to wait for word from Villiers. Gregory had suggested that Philip contact Hugh Carstairs. At this point, Carstairs was the only one aside from Villiers at MI5 that they could trust. The problem was no one knew where Carstairs was at the moment. Except, of course, Villiers. Because

Villiers knew everything and told no one anything.

Their unwelcome conversation kept replaying itself in Gregory's head. It was all such a bloody mess.

Roger broke into his thoughts. "You know you've got a face like thunder. Sit down or you'll wear out your shoes."

Gregory whirled round and glared at him. "You were absolutely no help with Acheson."

"Why should I tell him anything? You have to admit his story sounded rather dodgy to me. For all I know, it's a trap to lure us out and you dropped us right into it."

Gregory groaned as he plopped down on the bench. If it had been five years ago, he would have agreed with Delahunt. But not now.

He stared straight ahead at some point in the middle distance without really seeing the stray faded bloom here or there or the curving path. "Acheson is not a friend. But we respect one another. He's the husband of Emmy's best friend." He turned to face Roger. "I trust him and so should you."

Roger sniffed and folded his arms across his chest. "If you say so. I trust you and by extension Emmeline, so I'll give Acheson the benefit of the doubt."

Gregory gave a resigned nod. He couldn't really blame Roger. In their business, they were conditioned to live by their wits. Trust was a luxury.

"I suppose that's progress. Since you trust me, answer my question about Seb." Delahunt's features became a blank mask. Not a muscle moved. "For God's sake, Roger," Gregory snapped in exasperation, "He wasn't like us. Seb was always on the straight and narrow. He followed the letter of the law. What pushed him to mix with thugs and criminals?" When Roger still remained silent, he endeavored to appeal to his sense of humanity. "Seb was our friend."

Delahunt cleared his throat and rose. "Greg, you're a good

friend. One of the best. But Seb is not who you or any of us thought he was. Everything about him was a lie."

Gregory frowned up at him as the first droplets of drizzle moistened his face. "How very cryptic. What the devil is that supposed to mean?"

"I'm simply telling you the truth. That's what you wanted."

Gregory surged to his feet. "You haven't told me a bloody thing. You keep talking in riddles." He caught Delahunt's sleeve. "I can see you're in dire straits because of whatever Seb dragged you into. Let me help you. What was in Seb's bag and where is it?"

Roger gently shook off Gregory's grasp. "Just walk away. This is not your problem. Seb doesn't deserve your loyalty. You're a married man. Your pretty wife should be your priority."

Through clenched teeth, Gregory hissed, "What do you think I'm trying to do? I have Swanbeck out for blood again and he was somehow connected to Seb." He took a step closer to Delahunt. "If anything happens to Emmy because you refused to tell me the scheme you and Seb were plotting, I *will* kill you."

Roger huffed a laugh. "Oh, Greg, come off it. We both know you don't have it in you. Violence is beneath you."

"None of us knows what we're capable of until we're pushed too far."

"Go and see this Villiers chap about your friend Acheson. As for this other business"—Roger's shoulders twitched in a shrug—"Take my advice and walk away." And that's precisely what he did, hands thrust in his pockets and without a backward glance.

Gregory knew one thing for certain. There was no way he was dropping the matter.

CHAPTER 14

Burnell had been incensed when Gregory had rung him the day before to tell him about Philip. The superintendent's anger was fueled in no small part by self-disgust. Despite his better judgment, he had gotten his hopes up that Philip, with his high-level government contacts, would swiftly extricate him from the cloud that hung over his career. With Philip under suspicion, that prospect appeared bleak at best.

Burnell's chest heaved a sigh infused with frustration. Then, he drew his shoulders back. Only the weak wallowed in self-pity. And yet, he had to admit he felt like he was floundering. It was an alien and disconcerting sensation because he had always been in control of every case. But now, he was on the outside and Swanbeck was the puppet master pulling all the strings.

Damn Swanbeck to hell, Burnell swore silently, not for the first time—nor the last. Although it served as a release valve for some of his tension, cursing ultimately was a waste of breath. It was because of criminals like Swanbeck that his ulcer was rumbling like Mt. Etna these days.

His mind was awhirl, he stalked down Millbank, past Parliament and into Victoria Tower Gardens. Loitering in front of *The Burghers of Calais*, the bronze replica of Rodin's famous statue, was Finch as agreed. The sergeant looked like a restless tiger. Obviously, he wanted to be elsewhere. Burnell knew how he felt. He was itching to be in the thick of the investigation. It was ironic. His career was at stake and he had to rely on others for information and evidence to clear him.

He called out to Finch, who swung around and waved a hand. The sergeant waited until Burnell had reached his side and then they found a bench overlooking the Thames.

"How are you holding up, sir?" Finch asked once they had sat down.

"How do you think?" Burnell snapped. He regretted the harshness of his words as soon as they slipped out of his mouth. Never a demonstrative person, he squeezed Finch's shoulder. "Sorry. I'm not myself."

The sergeant flashed a broad grin. "Don't worry, sir. I usually ignore your bluster. I'm immune to your moods by now."

Burnell grunted a laugh and wagged a plump finger at him. "I'd have a care, Sergeant. I'm still your boss and don't you forget it." There was no rancor in his tone, though.

"I wouldn't dream of it. It's more than my life is worth." Then Finch's smile evaporated, and he became serious. "Sir, you'll be back at the Yard in no time. I assure you that Inspector Halliday and I are working hard to see to it."

Burnell nodded wearily. "I know you're a damned fine detective. Halliday's smart. I'm glad the Boy Wonder put him on the case."

Finch cleared his throat. "I hate to admit it, but Assistant Commissioner Cruickshank has been remarkably decent. He's not his usual…"

"Pompous prat self," the superintendent finished for him.

The corners of Finch's mouth twitched. "I'm just a humble sergeant. It would be inappropriate for me to speak ill of a senior officer. However, as you've nailed the peg on the head, yes."

"Ever the diplomat. You'll go far, Finch. Now then, enough chitchat. What's going on with the case? Any leads?"

"Halliday and I have officially concluded that the knife was planted in Emmeline's bag. Halliday will make a statement to the press today."

Burnell slumped back against the bench and tipped his head back to watch the clouds scudding across the cerulean sky. "Well, that's something. We all knew it, but at least it's official. It takes the pressure off Emmeline."

Finch exhaled an exasperated breath. "As much as the pressure can be eased, when Swanbeck is in the picture."

Burnell's lowered his gaze and searched Finch's earnest, concerned face. He was certain that the worry reflected in the sergeant's eyes mirrored his own. "Yes," he murmured. "Longdon told you about Philip."

Finch nodded morosely. "It appears Swanbeck is coming after whoever has crossed him. I wonder who's next." He pounded one fist against his thigh. "Damn Longdon. He brought Swanbeck into our lives."

Burnell sighed. "You know my feelings about Longdon." He pressed his tongue against his cheek as he gathered his thoughts. "But if we're honest, we can't really lay the blame for Swanbeck's crimes at Longdon's feet."

"No, I suppose not," Finch replied grudgingly.

"No matter what Longdon is—and he's great many things, I grant you—he's not a vicious murderer and we both know he'd give up his life to protect Emmeline."

"That's true. That's his only redeeming quality. Maybe married life will reform him—if he can be reformed at all."

"If anyone can do it, I'll lay my money on Emmeline. However, she's the one who is the most vulnerable in Swanbeck's machinations. Her questions tend to make people very nervous. And yet the more resistance she faces, the more she presses forward until she has her answers."

"I admire her tenacity. Really, I do," Finch asserted. "But at the same time, I cringe every time she puts her own safety at risk for a story."

"Yes, it's a problem. That's why it's our job to protect society. You and Halliday have a surveillance team watching Emmeline and Longdon, don't you?"

The sergeant gave a curt nod. "It was one of the first things Halliday did. Two plainclothes teams round the clock."

This reassured Burnell somewhat.

"Any luck finding what rock Swanbeck has been hiding under or what he's been up to these past few months?"

"Nothing yet. I've been on to Interpol. They're checking from their end. His assets here in the U.K. are frozen."

Burnell pursed his lips. "Swanbeck isn't stupid." He leaned forward, his hands hanging between his knees. "A man like Swanbeck must have secret accounts and shell companies all over the world. We need a financial expert to do some digging. No one vanishes off the face of the earth, unless he's dead. And we know for a fact that Swanbeck is alive."

"I spoke to Emmeline yesterday. She had the same idea. Find the money, find the man." Finch shot a sideways glance at the superintendent. "She's doing her own investigation."

Burnell groaned. He was not surprised, but he didn't like the sound of it. "Of course, she is. She's a smart young lady. That's what makes her a threat. Did she find out anything through her sources?"

"No." Then Finch corrected himself. "At least, she hasn't *told* us anything."

"That, too, sounds very much like Emmeline. Watch her like a hawk. What about this friend of Longdon's, Delahunt?"

"Longdon caught up with him yesterday."

"Good. What did Delahunt say about Jardine and Swanbeck when you questioned him?"

"Not a lot." Finch cleared his throat. "Nothing, in fact. I haven't questioned him nor has Inspector Halliday. Apparently, Delahunt drifted off after he and Longdon met with Mr. Acheson in Regent's Park. Longdon has no idea where he is. He's looking for him."

Burnell jumped—well, as much as his portly frame allowed him to jump—to his feet. "Damn and blast. What was Longdon thinking? Delahunt is our only link to Jardine."

Finch spread his hands wide and shrugged.

Burnell paced back and forth in front of the bench muttering under his breath for a couple of minutes, before dropping back down and sending a tremor through the wooden slats of the bench. "You have to find out what flight Jardine arrived on. Maybe it will give us a clue as to where Swanbeck has been hiding these past few months."

"I already have D.C. Cooper checking all the flight manifests."

Burnell nodded his approval. He leaned back and folded his arm over his broad chest and stroked his beard meditatively with the other hand. "Delahunt," he mumbled, as he puzzled it out loud. "Did he arrive in London with Jardine? On another flight? Or was he already at Heathrow and were they simply going to make an exchange?"

"Sir, I've gone through the CCTV footage again. I'm fairly certain that the only reason Delahunt was at the airport was to collect Jardine's bag. I think the exchange was supposed to be quick. Done in plain sight without anyone realizing what was going on."

"That bloody bag. We still don't know what was in it or where it is?"

Finch shook his head. "Presumably Delahunt has it."

"If Swanbeck is involved, we can't assume anything. In

any case, Delahunt didn't have the bag with him when he spirited Emmeline away to the taxi." Burnell frowned. "How did he know she was in a bind? Longdon said that he hadn't seen Delahunt in years, let alone at the airport."

"Perhaps Longdon is lying. I don't know where he went after we separated. He could have looped back to meet Delahunt. We know that he's not above bending the truth to suit his purposes."

"Yes, that silver tongue of his has a way of twisting things around. But, I don't think so this time, though."

"I'll defer to your judgment as my superior officer," Finch replied, skepticism echoing in his tone.

Burnell threw him a pointed glance. "None of your cheek."

Finch bit back a smile. "No, sir. To get back to the CCTV footage, I've watched the critical moments before and during the attack on Jardine several times. I think that Swanbeck's men, Webb and that other security official, were taken by surprise. You only have to look at their expressions to see that."

The superintendent sat up alert. "Are you suggesting that someone other than Swanbeck wanted Jardine dead?"

"Yes. Initially, we all agreed that the attack appeared to be a crime of opportunity. Not Swanbeck's style at all. I think Jardine had something Swanbeck wanted badly. Swanbeck wouldn't have had him killed until he had recovered whatever it was. I think Swanbeck's plan was to have Webb and his colleague take Jardine to a maintenance or storage area to interrogate him. That's why we see them prepared with the wheelchair in the tapes. However, someone in the crowd had another agenda and that involved assassinating Jardine—before he could reveal the secrets he knew."

Burnell nodded. "Your theory makes sense. You've also made our lives more complicated because now we have Swanbeck *and* a hired killer roaming around London."

"Swanbeck is a work in progress, but I think I know who Jardine's murderer is."

The superintendent gaped at Finch in admiration. Then he snapped his jaw shut. "Don't keep me in suspense. Do tell?"

"The murderer's face was obscured by a flat cap and I'm still working on the identity. But I believe it's a woman."

Burnell trusted Finch's instincts. "What makes you so certain?"

"It's the way the killer's body moves. Men's hips are straight and their gait tends to be too. One would have to be blind not to notice that a woman's hips are curved, even those who are very slim. Women's hips sway back and forth as they walk. There's a natural, fluid rhythm to the motion. That was what struck me about Jardine's murderer. Once the idea planted itself in my head, I scoured the tapes again but kept my attention glued on the murderer. She didn't break stride after she stabbed Jardine. She kept walking until she reached the women's toilet at the other end of the terminal. In strolls an assassin, ten minutes later a woman in a long skirt, boots and a tartan shawl comes out. She was wearing a hat and kept her chin tucked into her chest, so we never see her face on camera. She was carrying a rather large shopping bag, which she promptly dumped in the nearest rubbish bin. That was the last glimpse I had of her. I couldn't find her on any of the tapes. I'd wager anything that woman is the murderer. Her sex made her perfect for the job because, rightly or wrongly, we tend to think of men as contract killers."

"Sharp eye. Well done, Finch. Get onto Interpol and MI6 See what information they have about known female assassins. We have to stop this woman from exercising her lethal skills again."

CHAPTER 15

Emmeline was sifting through the material that her source at the Financial Reporting Council was able to pass on with a clear conscience. Although it wasn't much, it was a start nonetheless. She made notes as she did some digging into the list of shell companies. The first two had yielded nothing. All of the ships in Swanbeck's line were registered in Valletta, Malta. Was that significant? Or was it merely an accounting ploy to ensure that the company paid as little taxes as possible? Swanbeck had long used his ships to trade arms. Was he now running his empire from Malta? Was he branching out into some other illicit business such as smuggling? She tapped her pen against her desk. The country did have a history of welcoming those with dodgy morals and bank accounts overflowing with cash.

Hmm, it was something to be getting on with at any rate. She did a quick Internet search and found the website for the Malta High Commission. She reached for the phone and punched in the general number. A pleasant female voice answered after the second ring. Emmeline identified herself as the editorial director of investigative features at *The Clarion* and explained that she would like to speak to someone about a story she was working on about corruption. She was put through to press inquiries, where a gen-tleman politely brushed her off. Likely, he did not want to be bothered. He recommended that she contact the Ministry of Foreign Affairs in Valletta directly.

She groaned as she severed the connection, but she was not going to be put off. She clicked on the Ministry tab at the top of the commission's home page. She scanned the list of the various directorates to determine which one could possibly know anything about Swanbeck. She decided she would start with the Directorate of Global Issues, International Development and Economic Affairs. The brief description on the website indicated that it dealt with issues associated with human rights, disarmament, terrorism, maritime matters, sanctions and export control, among others. Swanbeck had certainly dipped his toes in those areas at one point or another.

She took a deep breath and waited, as the line for the director of Global Issues rang. The director's secretary picked up. In a congenial tone, Emmeline repeated her entire speech. However, the secretary's response was terse and clipped. The director did not speak to the press over the phone. She would have to submit her list of questions in writing and he would get back to her. The secretary provided the director's e-mail address and promptly terminated the conversation.

Emmeline slammed down the receiver. She was getting the distinct impression that no one wanted to talk to her. Why was that? She dug her hands through her curls and shook her head in frustration. She knew that this wasn't going to be easy. Swanbeck was a shrewd, if unscrupulous, businessman and he would take whatever steps were necessary to keep the law from getting its hands on his ill-gotten gains.

She pinched the bridge of her nose and squeezed her eyes shut. She would send a bloody list of questions, but would the director of Global Issues deign to respond? And how long would it take? She had to find the answers. Fast. So many lives depended on her uncovering the truth.

She should feel relieved that the police had cleared her of any wrongdoing. Instead, she was consumed by guilt—and anger. Things remained black as pitch for Superintendent Burnell and became blacker as each day passed. She pounded her fist on her desk. And now Philip was forced into hiding all because she had sought his help. Poor Maggie must be climbing the walls.

Her eyes popped open. "Ooh," she growled. She could kick herself. However, she snatched up her phone and viciously punched in her grandmother's number.

She drummed her fingers on the desk. On the second ring, Helen's slightly out-of-breath voice murmured "Hello" in her ear and then became muffled as if she had covered the mouthpiece and was carrying on another conversation.

Emmeline couldn't help but smile. Her grandmother was the one constant in her life and could instantly make any situation better. "Hi, Gran. It's me. I just wanted to check if everything was all right with your guests."

"Emmy? Hello, love. Oh, we're having a grand old time aren't we, boys?" In the background, Emmeline could hear the excited voices of two highly active five-year-olds concurring enthusiastically. MacTavish, her grandmother's mischievous Scottish terrier, made his presence known as well by unleashing a stream of barks. He always seemed to sense when she was ringing Helen.

"The boys and I were playing hide-and-seek." Another bark. "Sorry. And MacTavish too. There do you feel better, you little devil?" Helen chided playfully.

Emmeline giggled, when this elicited an affirmative bark. "I'm glad to hear that the house is still standing. How's Maggie holding up?"

"Andrew, Henry, why don't you take MacTavish and go

into the kitchen," Helen said. "I'll be there in a minute to make some cocoa for all of us. I have a few things I must discuss with Emmy first."

By the cheers and barks in response, Emmeline surmised this suggestion met with everyone's approval. As the boys were running out of the room, a couple of "Hi, Auntie Emmelines" drifted to her ears. Then all was quiet.

"Emmy, I don't mind telling you that whatever it is all of you are mixed up in this time, I don't like it." Helen's tone was stern.

Emmeline's throat constricted. "Why has something happened?" she asked anxiously. "Have you seen strangers hanging about?"

"No, I have not and no one had better try anything."

Emmeline exhaled a sigh of relief. "You had me worried."

"You should be worried. This whole situation is worrying. What was this nonsense I read in the papers about a knife being found in your bag at the airport? And *why* did I have to discover it from the papers? Hmm."

Emmeline swallowed hard. "Oh, you found out."

"Of course, I found out," Helen retorted indignantly. "I thought you learned when you were five years old that you couldn't hide things from me. I *always* find out."

Emmeline groaned inwardly. More's the pity. Aloud she said, "Yes, Gran. It's Scotland Yard's loss that you never joined the force."

"I'm not amused, Emmy. I know this is something dangerous. And I don't believe a word of what they're saying about Superintendent Burnell either."

"You shouldn't. It's a tissue of lies. Gregory and I are trying to find out the truth."

"Good. Now, what are you doing about Philip? *Where* is he?" Helen demanded. "That boy has a lot to answer for. Maggie is beside herself, the poor dear. I don't blame her."

"I can only imagine. Where is she now?"

"I sent her off on a long walk, while I kept an eye on the boys. She's tried ringing Philip a dozen times. His mobile is off. It's unforgiveable. I'll throttle him the next time I see him."

"Gran…"

Helen cut her off. "Don't Gran me. I know you and that handsome husband of yours are in trouble *again* and Philip is somehow involved. I know better than to ask any questions."

So you'll settle for lecturing instead, Emmeline speculated.

"You've stopped listening, young lady. I can feel it."

Emmeline sat up straighter in her chair, as if her grandmother were standing in front of her wagging an accusatory finger. "I'd never do that. I know there is wisdom in your every word."

"Hmph. I see you've been taking lessons in flattery from that charmer you married. Well, it won't work."

Emmeline bit back a smile. "You seem to gush like a schoolgirl, when the purple prose flows from Gregory's lips."

"Don't try to change the subject, Emmy. You take far too many unnecessary risks. But all of you are not going to listen to an old woman—"

"Oh, come on. You're more spry than women fifteen years younger and you know it."

Helen ignored this and plowed ahead. "—so I won't waste my breath. Maggie and the boys are welcome to stay here as long as they like. As for the rest of you"—she took a deep breath—"Be careful. Make sure Philip rings his wife as soon as possible. And you will tell me everything. And I do mean *everything*, once this is all over."

"Yes, Gran." She sketched a little salute in the air, even though Helen couldn't see it. "We have our marching orders. One last thing."

"What's that?"

"I love you."

She could feel Helen's smile and heard her tone soften. "Oh, my precious girl, you had my love from the first day you curled your tiny fist around my finger. That's why I worry about you so much. And Gregory too. Sometimes I think the pair of you don't have any sense. Instead of concentrating on more important matters, you're off chasing murderers and all sorts of other unsavory criminals."

"Gran, what could be more important than seeing that the guilty are punished?" Emmeline asked, incensed.

"My great grandchild. That's what. He or she could have been coming along nicely by now. But no, you two had to cut your honeymoon short," Helen groused. "You call two nights a honeymoon? It's disgraceful, if you ask me."

I don't recall asking, Gran, Emmeline reflected. Aloud she said, "We've only been married for *three* weeks."

"What are you waiting for? Goodness knows that you and that dashing devil have wasted enough time. If Maggie and I hadn't taken matters in hand, you would still be dithering about aimlessly."

Emmeline couldn't believe her ears. Helen's words were the epitome of British understatement.

"You know things were extremely complicated…"

Helen interrupted, "And *who* made it that way? Quite unnecessarily, I might add."

Right, Emmeline had to nip this in the bud before it spiraled out of control. "Must dash. I have a story to write. I'll ring again in a couple of days."

She exhaled a long breath, as she replaced the receiver. She shook her head and clucked her tongue. *Oh, Gran. A baby already? Really?*

She bit her lip. It's not that she didn't want a baby. She had always wanted children. But…in her heart of hearts…she was afraid. She knew she would be utterly shattered, if she lost another baby. The aching emptiness. Her eyelids stung and tears constricted her throat. She couldn't go through that again. Not a second time.

She drew in a shuddering breath and pushed these fears from her mind, as she impatiently swiped at an errant tear that had escaped down her cheek. Work. She needed to focus on work. But at the moment, everything was upside down for everyone. Burnell. Philip. She had to find something to help them.

Her mind lingered on Philip. "Damn, damn, damn," she muttered. She was hoping that he had gotten in touch with Maggie, at least to let her know that he was all right.

What did it mean? Where was he? Did Special Branch track him down? Did Swanbeck's lackeys catch up with him? Was he hurt? This last question made her shiver involuntarily.

She placed her palms on her desk and pushed herself to her feet. She couldn't stay here allowing her imagination to conjure up all sorts of terrifying scenarios. She'd go mad. She needed answers and the only way to get them was to ask questions.

She gathered up her notebook and handbag and shrugged herself into her coat. First, she was going to pop by the Foreign Office to see whether Pamela had any word from Philip. She didn't want to risk a call, in case Special Branch had tapped Pamela's phone. Then she was going to Scotland Yard to make a nuisance of herself, until someone gave her a morsel of information she could use.

She was reviewing her list of questions in her head, as she exited Sanborn Enterprises. The wind blowing off the churning gray-green waters of the Thames huffed with chilly dampness. The charcoal clouds above wept, moistening her cheeks with a misty drizzle. With her luck, it would start bucketing down because she had rushed out of the office without taking her umbrella.

As she squinted up at the sky trying to decide whether she should risk it or run back upstairs, she felt a tap on her shoulder.

"If it isn't Shylock herself, out and about wreaking havoc."

She stiffened, gritting her teeth and cringing at the sound of that oh-so-despised male voice.

Emmeline tore her gaze from the sky and turned slowly on her heel, steeling herself for what was certain to be a thoroughly unpleasant encounter.

She squared her shoulders and tilted her head back slightly to look up into the face of Ian Newland. He was the last person she wanted to see. Ever.

"What do you want, Ian?" Her tone was brusque and unforgiving.

His lips twisted into a malevolent sneer. "Still as prickly as ever I see. I guess they don't teach you bloody Jews any manners."

Emmeline's nails bit into her palms, as she balled her fists at her sides. "I have better things to do with my time than listen to you spewing your usual taunts and insults. I'm extremely busy, so if you'll excuse me."

She tried to step around him, but he blocked her path. "Yeah, busy ruining people's lives. That's what you're good at, you little Jewish bitch."

She eyed him coldly. "Get out of my way before a I call a constable."

"Why? So you can spread your lies about someone else like you did about me? You had me sacked from *The Times*. And not only that—" He took a step closer. She felt his warm breath brush her cheek. "You've seen to it that no one will hire me. I've been forced to freelance for grubby rags."

White-hot embers of fury kindled in the pit of her stomach and her tongue lashed back at him. "You sabotaged your own career, Ian. You're your own worst enemy. You went against all the tenets of good journalism." She enumerated on her fingers. "You made up stories; failed to corroborate your facts; and stole your colleagues' work. You're nothing but a cheat and a liar. I had nothing to do with you being dismissed."

Newland snorted. "Cheat and liar? Me? That's rich coming from you. You greedy Jews are always trying twist things to your advantage. You were born trying to cheat the world. I see that once again you've managed to pull the wool over Scotland Yard's eyes with your sweet and innocent act." He took another step forward, doing his best to intimidate her by looming. There was barely any space between them. "First, you wormed your way out of a charge for the Victor Royce murder over the summer and now that chap at Heathrow." He shook his head. "How do you do it? Or should I say who did you sleep with?"

Emmeline's hand whipped out and landed a stinging blow to his cheek. "You vile pig of a man. Get out of my face," she hissed savagely.

Newland touched his cheek, but merely laughed. "The truth hurts, doesn't it?" His voice dripped with venom. "I'm just getting started. It's going to hurt very, *very* much. I promise, you will pay. You're not getting away with a second murder. I'm going to make it my mission to see that every paper in London considers you *persona non grata*. Your name will become notorious. You'll *never* work again." He paused, his upper lip curling back to reveal his cigarette-stained teeth. "Alastair Swanbeck pays good money for any information about you and your thief of a husband." He leaned in and whispered in her ear, "He hates you even more than I do."

Emmeline sucked in her breath, cold tendrils of fear coiling themselves around her lungs. "*Swanbeck*? Is he here in

London?" Bile rose in her throat. "You're working for him?"

Newland threw his head back and a malicious chuckle rumbled from his throat. "Sorry, love." Out of his mouth, this word was anything but a term of endearment. "I don't have to answer any of your questions. I'm just going to sit back watch you squirm."

"Emmeline, is this chap bothering you?"

She whirled around, blood thundering in her ears, heart pounding in her chest, to find Roger Delahunt peering down at her, his brow puckering in concern.

His unexpected appearance had momentarily thrown her off balance. She blinked up at him in confusion. "What? I…"

"Who the devil are you?" Newland barked.

The smile that touched Roger's lips did not reach his eyes. He took Emmeline gently by the elbow and nudged her aside. "Excuse me. This will only take a moment," he murmured, as he planted himself in front of Newland.

They were virtually the same height and therefore could glare at one another at eye level. Roger cleared his throat. "Would you care to repeat all that poisonous rubbish?"

Newland's icy blue eyes narrowed, and his mouth tightened into a thin line. "Move along and mind your own bloody business." He turned to Emmeline and spat, "Why don't you keep your lovers on a leash?"

She opened her mouth to hurl a barbed retort at him, but Roger held up a hand and forestalled her.

He shook his head and clucked his tongue. "Not only is that the wrong answer, mate, it's frightfully rude."

Newland's lips twisted into a smirk. "We're not mates."

Roger's frosty smile widened. "Thank God for that. To be honest, I would rather shoot myself, if that were true." He cast a quick glance over his shoulder and saw that they were beginning to attract an audience. His gaze locked once again on Newland's arrogant face. "In fact, I feel quite embarrassed standing here in your presence. Because clearly you crawled out from under a rock."

Newland's nostrils flared and his eyes ignited in a flash of anger mingled with irritation.

He pitched his voice low. "You've got a big mouth." He jerked his thumb in Emmeline's direction. "Just like her. And one day quite soon, I'm going to see to it that you choke on your words."

The ugly threat hung upon the air, sending a frisson down Emmeline's spine. She slid a sideways glance at Roger, but his sangfroid was firmly in place. She, however, fervently wished they could melt away and pretend that they had never run into Ian Newland. The only thing was she knew that was going to be impossible.

She tugged on Roger's sleeve. "Let's go. He's not worth it," she implored.

Some of the tension eased from his face as he smiled down at her. "In a moment." He patted her hand, as he pried her fingers from his arm. "I promise. Someone has to make sure the gutter press is put in its place."

The words were said to Emmeline, but they found their intended target.

A crimson flush quickly spread from the base of Newland's jaw to the tips of his ears. Emmeline bit back a smile. Although his conscience was never bothered about lying to grab a headline, she knew Newland craved to be thought of as one of journalism's brightest stars rather than merely a third-rate hack.

Through gritted teeth, he snarled, "You'll regret your interference." His tone thrummed with fury, as his gaze flicked between them. "Both of you."

Roger's eyes widened in innocence. "I seem to have struck a nerve. Or are you simply prone to hysterics? If that's the case, I suggest checking into the nearest psychiatric clinic. I hear they work miracles these days with the criminally insane."

A primitive sound gurgled in Newland's throat and his chest heaved. He shoved past Roger, but he had only taken a few steps when he spun round on his heel. "You've just dug your own grave."

Roger inclined his head and gave him a cheeky salute. "Right, duly noted." He shot his cuff and casually glanced at his watch. "I think we're done here. Ready to go, Emmeline?" She nodded mutely.

He tucked her arm through the crook of his elbow and guided them away from the still fuming Newland. They didn't break stride until they had turned a corner down a side street.

He drew her aside and took her by the shoulders. "Are you all right?" She saw the concern in his eyes.

She swallowed hard. "I'm all right."

Roger hadn't released her. "You're sure? That brute didn't hurt you, did he?"

She shook her head. "Ian was born a bully. I should be used to his repugnant insults by now."

"No one should have to put up with such disgusting behavior."

She laughed, but it was devoid of mirth. "Oh, Roger, wake up and look at the world around us. Nothing has changed in centuries. Jews have always been the target of hateful insults—and much worse. Sometimes these ideas are couched behind platitudes and polite smiles. Others are more brash and spew their venom to your face. But the bottom line is that anti-Semitism is always there."

Roger remained silent. After all, he couldn't deny what she had said was true. He didn't know what it was like to endure these demeaning encounters. But she had felt it on her own skin. And each time, it made her tremble with rage. She had not—and would *never*—allow herself to be cowed by such viciousness.

She stared off at some point over his left ear. This was not the moment to explore this ongoing struggle with prejudice.

She drew a shuddering breath and lifted her eyes to meet his gaze. "Until now, I thought Ian was harmless. I did my best to ignore his bigotry. But not anymore." She caught Roger by the arm. "He's working for Swanbeck. Or Ian at least knows where he is. He boasted about it. It's obvious Swanbeck is playing on Ian's weaknesses to further his own battle against us. Swanbeck and Ian are two peas in an unholy pod."

CHAPTER 16

"Don't worry, Emmeline," Roger murmured soothingly, as he gave her shoulders a reassuring squeeze. "Greg won't allow Swanbeck to touch a hair on your head. For that matter, I won't let anything happen to you either." This was uttered more softly. "You know the old saying, 'If you save a person's life, you're responsible for them.'"

She smiled and gave him a gentle shove. "I can take care of myself just fine. There is no need for you to feel responsible for me."

"Why not agree to disagree on that score, shall we? For the time being, you and Greg are stuck with me."

She suddenly impaled him with her gaze. "Oh, yes? And where have you been the past twenty-four hours? Where did you go after you parted ways with Gregory in Regent's Park? You do know that the police need to question you? I'm on my way to Scotland Yard now." She touched his arm. "Why not come with me and speak to Sergeant Finch and Inspector Halliday?"

She started dragging him in the direction of the London Bridge Tube station.

Roger shook himself free of her grasp and put up his hands

in surrender. "My head is spinning. Do you ever take a breath? Or is the secret to your success your ability to breach people's defenses with your questions?"

"Stop stalling." She gave him another prod with her elbow. "I have a strong suspicion you have all the answers to the untimely demise of Sebastian Jardine."

He gave her a broad grin and pressed a hand to his chest. "I'm flattered, but I'm afraid you'll be disappointed. What I know is paltry at best."

She raised one finger in the air and flashed a triumphant smile at him. "Ah so, you admit it. You know *something*."

Roger groaned. "Do you make it a habit of cornering Greg like this?"

"Never mind my husband for the moment. We were talking about you and what you know."

"Were we? I seem to recall keeping mum, while you did all the talking and speculating."

Her eyes narrowed. "Hmph. In my experience, people who deflect and try to change the subject have something to hide."

He licked his lips, as his eyes raked her face. She could see that his mind was furiously calculating whether to risk a lie.

At last, he cleared his throat. "You give me far too much credit. I'm merely a ship passing in the night."

"Or the airport, as the case may be," she countered.

"Exactly." He patted her arm. "Got it in one." He glanced at his watch. "Is that the time? I'm terribly late for an appointment, so I must leave you. I'm sure you understand." Then he became more serious. "I don't think you need to worry about that Newland fellow. At least not today."

"Why won't you help us? After what Ian said, Swanbeck is here in London. I don't need to tell you how dangerous Swanbeck is, especially if you've crossed him. He most certainly is after you too, since you took Jardine's bag. What were you and Jardine involved in? And what was in the bag?"

Roger gripped her by shoulders and drew her close so that his lips were near her ear. "I am helping," he whispered. "Not for Seb's sake, but for yours. And Greg's," he added belatedly. "I already told Greg that Seb was not the man everyone thought. Seb was full of hatred and consumed with revenge. Leave it at that and trust me. Let me handle things in my own way. And take my advice, drop the story about Seb. It will only make things worse for you, if you don't."

She pushed him away. "I can't do that. I refuse to cower in a corner. I have to find the truth. A man was murdered. He deserves justice."

Roger sighed. "Actually, Seb probably got exactly what was coming to him. With the games he was playing his entire life, it's surprising that he lasted this long."

Emmeline stiffened. "How can you talk about your friend like that? Don't you want the truth to come out?"

"The truth is ugly."

"So is murder," she shot back.

"Emmeline, it's not your job to save the world. Let it go."

"No, it's my job to fight for the truth. My friends are in trouble. I will do everything I can to save them. You met Philip yesterday. His wife is my best friend and they have beautiful five-year-old twin boys. Philip is in hiding now because I asked him to find out about Jardine. And poor Superintendent Burnell is accused of Jardine's murder. So you see, I can't let it go."

"Acheson appeared to be pretty resourceful. I'm sure he'll be all right, as will the copper. Besides, Acheson asked Greg to talk to someone called Villiers. They both seemed to think that this Villiers—whoever he is—would be able to help. Although I must admit that Greg didn't look too happy about it."

"Mmm, Villiers," Emmeline murmured, remembering her

past encounters with the secretive deputy director of MI5. "One never knows where one stands with that man."

ⅇᴔⅇᴔ

Laurence Villiers, tall, lean, distinguished with his head of thick wavy silver hair, closed his umbrella and gave it a good shake on the pavement in front of the curved bay windows, before opening the door and stepping inside Hatchards, London's oldest bookshop which was nestled next to Fortnum & Mason on Piccadilly.

He hooked his umbrella over his forearm as he cast a cursory glance at the bestsellers on display on the table at foot of the staircase. He picked up a book and made a show of flicking through the pages. As he set it back down and reached for another book, he allowed his keen eyes to casually roam around his surroundings, assessing his fellow customers without seeming to do so. His antennae were on the alert, his fingers tense around the book's spine.

Satisfied that no one was other than what he or she appeared to be, he carefully returned the book to the pile, and slowly ascended the winding staircase. His steps were slow and measured. His hand skimmed the smooth wooden banister, not quite holding on for support.

He was more than a bit annoyed to find himself slightly winded by the time he reached the landing on the first floor. Any other sixty-eight-year-old man, who had been shot and gravely wounded four months earlier, would have recognized that the body needed rest and time to heal. Villiers viewed it as a sign of weakness. He had returned to work a few weeks ago, against his doctor's order. After all, what did doctors know?

Every other floorboard creaked beneath the mint green and royal blue fleur-de-lis patterned carpet as Villiers strolled toward the crime fiction section. He pretended to peruse the shelves with eager interest.

Only a couple of minutes had elapsed, when a man cleared his throat noisily behind him. His heart started to race, but he forced it to slow down.

Damn the man, Villiers cursed silently. *How did the fellow manage to creep about like a cat? Not even the air moved.*

Villiers didn't turn around. Instead, he reached for a Ruth Rendell novel on an upper shelf. Out of the corner of his mouth he hissed, "What was so urgent that we needed to meet?"

"Believe me, I don't consider these interludes festive social occasions," Gregory replied as he came to stand at Villiers's side. "It's rather a case of *noblesse oblige*."

Villiers snorted as he flicked a few pages in his book and slid a sideways glance toward Gregory. "Since when have you developed delusions of grandeur? We both know you are anything but noble. *What* do you want?"

"Pardon me, sir," Gregory said as he reached for an Ian Rankin mystery and took the opportunity to eye Villiers coldly. He pitched his voice low. "The only reason I'm here is because of Acheson. Two Special Branch agents appeared at his office yesterday to arrest him. He's packed off his wife and children to the country and gone into hiding. He needs help and feels that you're the only one he can trust. God help him. We both know you're as slippery as they come." Villiers made an impatient gesture with his hand at this last remark. "Acheson didn't dare contact you himself because he doesn't know whether your phone is bugged or who may be watching."

Villiers face remained impassive, but he snapped shut the book. "Bloody hell. Why is it the first time I'm hearing about this?"

"Bureaucratic red tape?" Gregory quipped facetiously.

"Everyone knows civil servants work at a snail's pace."

Villiers grunted. "This is far from amusing."

Without a second glance, Gregory replied through clenched teeth, "Do I look as if I'm joking? Emmy and I have Swanbeck breathing down our necks again."

Villiers drew in a sharp breath. "Swanbeck has reared his head at last? He'd be a fool to return to London."

"Be that as it may, everything points to it. My only concern is Emmy."

"Of course. Let me guess. She's waving the red flag in front of the bull as usual, isn't she?"

"If anyone is noble, it's Emmy. Her dedication to finding the truth is admirable." Gregory held his body still. Only a muscle in his jaw twitched. "It's also damnably infuriating."

"Hmph. On that point we agree." Villiers added grudgingly, "Congratulations on your marriage, by the way. I hear the wedding took place the twenty-ninth of October. Three weeks ago."

Gregory's eyes widened in surprise. "Thank you for your good wishes," he murmured uncertainly. Did he detect a hint of injured pride in the older man's tone? His gaze scanned Villiers's face. Surely his *éminence grise* did not expect to be invited to the wedding?

An uncomfortable silence filled the space between them.

Villiers sighed and was the first to break it. "I suppose you had better tell me the whole sordid story."

They drifted toward the olive-green Chesterfield leather sofa tucked in a corner in front of a window that overlooked Piccadilly. They retired to opposite ends of the sofa. Villiers's countenance was pinched and watchful. He sat with his legs splayed and his Burberry trench coat still tightly belted, as if he would pounce on anyone who dared approach. By contrast, Gregory exuded an air of calm that belied the tension knotting his nerves. He casually crossed one leg over the other and balanced the Rankin mystery novel on his knee.

They were quite alone. The only one who was privy to their conversation was an elegant bust of a Grecian young woman, who loomed over the sofa. But she had held her tongue for hundreds of years, so there was no danger that she would begin spilling her secrets now.

Without mincing words, Gregory launched into a narrative about what had taken place in the last forty-eight hours from the instant the airport security officers had asked to check Emmy's bag to her detention at Heathrow; to Burnell's intervention and subsequently being framed for murder; and finally, his meeting with Acheson and Roger in Regent's Park the previous afternoon.

He had debated whether to tell Villiers about Roger's role in these grave matters. In the end, he had decided to do so because Villiers being Villiers had an uncanny knack of finding things out that one hoped would never see the light of day. Roger was a big boy. He would simply have to fend for himself. On the other hand, Emmy was the one who was exposed and, therefore, the one at greatest risk.

When Gregory had finished, he quietly closed his book and continued to stare straight ahead. He didn't have long to wait for Villiers's reaction.

"The situation is worse than I thought," the older man declared phlegmatically. "I have never known a woman to whip up such a tempest in her wake. How does your wife manage to do it?"

Gregory didn't look at him. Although a faint smile touched his lips, his fingers were tapping an angry tattoo on the book, which rested precariously on the armrest. "I know you're the master of deception, but don't you dare twist things around. You know damn well that the only reason that Emmy has come to Swanbeck's attention is because all those years ago I agreed to 'help' you and MI5 from time to time. For the good of 'Queen and Country.'" He huffed a bitter laugh. "Patriotism has a lot to answer for."

Villiers flicked an imaginary speck of dirt from his coat and groaned. "You never used to be so hysterical."

"I can get up and leave," Gregory threatened. "I'd like nothing more than to wash my hands of you once and for all."

Villiers raised the back of his hand to his mouth to cover an exaggerated yawn. "But you won't." He inclined his head slightly and studied Gregory's stony profile. "Because no matter how much you protest, you love the adrenaline rush of the game. You'll never give it up. That's why you also steal jewels."

Gregory slowly rose to his feet. He came to stand before Villiers. His handsome features were relaxed, with a hint of their usual mischievousness. He turned up the collar of his raincoat. "I'm afraid you're under a misconception. As I often have to remind dear old Oliver, I'm a law-abiding citizen. You forget I am the chief investigator at Symington's."

"You're not fooling anyone. How do you think a man of your reputation was hired for that job?" Villiers sneered. "Once a spade, always a spade."

Gregory offered him one of his most engaging smiles. "One man's spade is another man's diamond."

Villiers cracked a rare smile. "And of course, you're an expert in diamonds…and rubies, and sapphires, and emeralds. Anything that sparkles really."

Gregory ignored this remark. "Are you going to do something about Acheson?"

Villiers stood, and with an irritating deliberateness tightened his belt before replying, "It seems I'm left with little choice. Now am I?" He held Gregory's hostile stare. "I always have to clean up the messes others leave behind."

"How terribly ungallant," Gregory scoffed. "You manipulate people into doing what you want to achieve your secretive goals and yet, you despise them." Gregory took a step toward him and poked his chest. "I always knew you were a cold-hearted bastard. I suppose that's a prerequisite for the job."

Villiers seized his finger and gave Gregory a small shove backward. "Are you quite finished with your tiresome insults? I must tell you that I'm not impressed. I've been called worse over the years."

Gregory tossed his head back and chuckled. "Oh, I don't doubt it. And yet, I seem to have touched a nerve." His gaze held a challenge. "Why is that?"

Villiers flapped a hand at him. "Don't be ridiculous. You're the one who has changed. That wife of yours has made you soft. She's a distraction that you can ill afford. She's going to get you killed one day. You were much sharper when you were on your own."

Gregory balled his fists at his sides. His voice held a dangerous edge when he spoke. "I never asked for your advice. My personal life is off limits. Emmy is my wife and she's going to remain that way. Just because you're made of stone and don't know what it is to love someone else, doesn't give you the right to ruin other people's lives."

He turned to walk away, but he halted to toss over his shoulder, "Use that tremendous influence you wield to help Acheson."

Villiers swallowed the lump in his throat and snatched Gregory's sleeve. "Stay out of mischief," he growled. "I don't want to be forced to come to your rescue. *Again.*"

Gregory gave a jerk of his chin and shook off Villiers's hand. There was nothing left say.

Villiers remained rooted to the spot. He would wait five minutes before he left Hatchards. He watched as Gregory skirted a table, his back ramrod straight and his shoulders held rigid.

Once Gregory had disappeared between the opening between two shelves, Villiers drew in a ragged breath. "You're wrong," he said aloud. "I *do* know what it is to love so much it hurts. That's why I left you and Clarissa. There's no room in an agent's life for a wife and son."

This last thought lingered in his mind as he reached for his umbrella. Images of Gregory as a toddler and now as a man flashed before his eyes.

Villiers suddenly felt old and bone-tired. *Did I make a mistake, Toby?* he asked himself.

For once, the deputy director of MI5 didn't have an answer.

CHAPTER 17

Emmeline hovered outside Assistant Commissioner Cruickshank's office, pen and notebook in hand, ready to pounce the instant he opened the door.

"Miss Kirby, I told you," Sally, his highly efficient, slightly pompous secretary, entreated. "The assistant commissioner is extremely busy. He cannot give you an interview."

Although Superintendent Burnell and Sally had a frosty— and that was being diplomatic—relationship, Emmeline had always gotten on with the rather fusty secretary, who guarded her boss like a tigress does her cubs. Therefore, she tried charm. It always worked for Gregory.

She offered Sally a broad smile. "Oh, come on, Sally. I recognize that you have an important job…"

Sally tucked a long strand of chestnut hair that had dared to slip out of place and preened. Emmeline was pleased to see the ghost of a smile quiver upon the other woman's lips. "At least someone does," the secretary murmured. "If you only knew what I have to deal with on a daily basis"—she gave a disapproving shake of her head—"to shield the poor assistant commissioner."

Emmeline nodded and schooled her features into what she

hoped was a sympathetic expression. *Cruickshank "poor?"* She had to choke back a laugh. Sally had a blind spot when it came to Cruickshank, as she had with his predecessor Fenton. There is always a danger placing someone on a pedestal, as they all found when Fenton tumbled down into a mire of ignominy.

"—It would make your head spin." Sally's voiced jarred Emmeline back to the present. She realized she hadn't been listening. "Superintendent Burnell has a particular talent for making a nuisance of himself."

Emmeline's back stiffened at the secretary's disparaging remarks about Burnell. However, it would not do to get on Sally's bad side at the moment. "Yes, of course. I suppose it comes down to clash of personalities."

"You're too kindhearted," Sally scoffed. "But then, you don't have the misfortune to know the superintendent like I do." She exhaled a long-suffering sigh. If she were the heroine in a Victorian play, Emmeline was certain Sally would have touched her wrist to her forehead in melodramatic fashion to emphasize her point. "Frankly, I was not surprised to hear that he is accused of murder. That man has an ugly temper that matches his lack of respect for authority."

Emmeline pressed her lips into a thin line. It took all of her self-control not to give vent to the acerbic rejoinder dancing on her tongue. She needed an interview. Throttling Sally would not help her find the answers to clear Burnell. Therefore, she suppressed her murderous instincts and cajoled, "Please, Sally. You know me. I don't do hatchet jobs on the police. I do my best to present both sides of the story. To do that properly I need information." She waited a moment before continuing. "The public has right to know what the police are doing to protect them. I promise I'll only be five minutes." She surreptitiously took a step toward the office.

"Surely, Assistant Commissioner Cruickshank can squeeze me in."

The door flew open unexpectedly throwing both women off balance for a moment. Cruickshank stalked out, his ginger head bent over a file. "Sally, I need you to…"

He stopped short when he lifted his gaze and came face-to-face with Emmeline. His eyes narrowed as they locked on her. "Ah, Miss Kirby…I mean Mrs. Longdon."

"Kirby is all right," she mumbled. "I use my maiden name professionally." She offered him a smile.

He made an impatient gesture. "That's as may be. What are you doing here? No, wait." He put up a hand before she could utter a word. "Let me guess. You want an update on the Jardine case." She nodded eagerly. "I'm afraid you've wasted a trip. I'm not at liberty to divulge anything to the press at this time. This is an ongoing investigation."

"Assistant Commissioner Cruickshank, you must be able to give me *something*. I can't believe that the Metropolitan Police has not made any progress. The least you can do is to tell me whether you're going to charge Superintendent Burnell with murder."

Cruickshank made a gurgling sound at the back of his throat. There was a spark of annoyance in his eyes. "Miss Kirby, I don't have to tell you anything. In fact, nothing that has transpired in the past few minutes is on the record. My official response to *any* of your questions is 'No comment.'"

Emmeline pressed her point. "If you're not prepared to charge Superintendent Burnell, does that mean that you have doubts about whether he is guilty?"

"Good afternoon, Miss Kirby." His tone was clipped, as if he would somehow betray himself by using too many words. Then to Sally, he said, "Would you please come into my office?"

Sally inclined her head toward Emmeline, gathered up her

pad and was close on her boss's heels. She firmly closed the door to the inner sanctum behind her.

"Right," Emmeline said aloud. "You've had your chance to make a statement. Now, you've left me no choice but to hunt down the answers myself."

She smiled when she caught a glimpse of Sergeant Finch at the far end of the corridor. "Just the person, I wanted to see," she mumbled. At least she could rely on him to give her a little morsel. Even if it was off the record.

Finch seemed to sense that he was the subject of intense scrutiny because his reddish-brown head swiveled round, his gaze immediately finding her. He gave an infinitesimal nod and gestured with his chin toward the lift.

A lead at last, her brain cheered, as she slowly crossed the floor.

Finch was already standing before the lift by the time she reached it. He pressed the button without glancing at her. "The guv's office," he whispered out of the corner of his mouth.

She nodded as the doors slid open. There were two PCs in the car when they got on, so they refrained from engaging in any conversation. Finch kept his gaze on the doors. When they opened on the seventh floor, the PCs stood aside to allow Emmeline to get off first. Finch stepped out last and waited until the constables had disappeared down the corridor. Then he took Emmeline by the elbow and guided her toward Burnell's office.

Only after he had locked the door and they were quite alone, did Emmeline start asking questions. "Have you spoken to Superintendent Burnell? Is he all right?"

The sergeant smiled and waved her to a chair. "The guv is a tough old bird."

"I very much doubt he'd appreciate being described as a 'tough old bird,'" she chided, giving a disapproving shake of her head.

Finch's grin widened. He hitched a hip on a corner of Burnell's desk and left one leg dangling off the edge. "He's not here, is he?" Then in a more serious tone, he said, "He's restless and frustrated at being kept on the side lines, but he's fine. I promise you he is," he added reassuringly, as if reading the concern that must be etched on her face. "We met yesterday. He's going to make some discreet calls to some retired Interpol agents with whom he's worked over the years.

"The guv's actually more worried about you. And Longdon to a lesser extent." These last words were offered grudgingly.

She put a hand to her chest. "Me? You and Inspector Halliday have cleared me of any involvement in Jardine's murder." Her eyes searched the sergeant's face for confirmation and relaxed when he gave a curt nod. "So Superintendent Burnell need not be worried. I'm hard at work on the story."

"That's why the guv is concerned. He's afraid that as usual your aggressive"—Finch put up a hand to forestall the protest rising to her lips—"albeit thorough reporting is placing you in harm's way." His voice softened. "Swanbeck is out there. You know he's out for blood and won't stop until he destroys you and Longdon."

She slumped back and shivered involuntarily. "If I didn't know it before, it was made patently clear to me just a short while ago."

Emmeline proceeded to tell him about how she had been waylaid by Ian Newland outside Sanborn Enterprises' offices. She drew in a shuddering breath when she had concluded her tale. The incident had disturbed her more than she had realized.

Two vertical lines appeared between Finch's brows and his forehead was puckered in concern. He started to reach for the phone. "I'll have Newland picked up and brought into the station."

She sat forward and placed a restraining hand on his arm. "Please don't. I think it will only make things worse. He hasn't done anything."

"Yet," he snarled. "Newland threatened you. Bold as brass, he told you that he holds you personally responsible for his career taking a downward spiral. It's harassment at the very least."

Emmeline sat up straighter in her chair. "Listen to me, Sergeant. Ian is a bully and a coward at heart. Yes, he's full of hot air and puffed up with a sense of his own self-importance. But I think when push came to shove, he would bolt if he had to commit murder. He just doesn't have it in him."

"All the more reason to bring him in. There's nothing like the prospect of being banged up in the nick to put the fear of God into a weasel."

In spite of herself, Emmeline smiled. "You have such a charming way with words."

She saw some of the tension ease from his body. He replaced the receiver and inclined his head. "Something was bound to rub off, since I find myself in your company so often lately." He pursed his lips. "What disturbs me the most about your revolting encounter is that Newland admitted his smear campaign is being financed by Swanbeck."

Emmeline swallowed the lump that lodged itself in her throat. Her voice was hoarse when she spoke. "He didn't dare put it into words, but Ian virtually admitted that Swanbeck is back in London."

Finch slapped his thigh. "The sheer audacity of the man is astounding. He enjoys nothing more than rubbing our noses in it." His jaw clenched in a rigid line. He pounded a fist against his open palm. "What does Swanbeck want?" He flicked a glance at her. "Aside from revenge. What was his involvement with Jardine?" He went quiet, allowing his gaze to linger on her face. "Delahunt knows. It's obvious he was working with Jardine."

She looked down at her hands in her lap. "Yes," she replied. She lifted her eyes to meet his. "I did everything in my power to persuade Roger to talk to the police. He refused. He begged me and Gregory to drop matters. He said it was safer for us that way. But it's madness. Roger is just as much a target of Swanbeck's ire as Gregory and I are. More than likely he can identify the lackey who killed Jardine. Roger scooped up Jardine's bag only minutes after he was murdered."

"Yes, that damn bag," the sergeant muttered under his breath. He threw up his hands in the air. "We'll leave that point for the moment. I think I may have something on Jardine's killer."

"Oh, yes?" Emmeline dug out her pad and pen from her handbag and leaned forward in anticipation. All her senses were alert and tingling with anticipation.

He gave her a pointed look. "Off the record."

She gave an exaggerated sigh. "If it means giving me something"—she closed her notebook and folded her hands in her lap—"then I have no choice but to agree. Proceed, Sergeant."

"Right. I've watched the tapes from the airport several times."

"And?" she prompted.

"And I think the killer is a woman."

She lifted an eyebrow. "A woman? Are you sure?"

He nodded. He repeated the theories he shared with Burnell.

"Well, that adds a new wrinkle to the case," she observed. "This woman could still be working for Swanbeck. I suppose she could be his lover. But Swanbeck doesn't strike me as the type of chap to inspire blind loyalty in anyone, much less love. The secret to his power is that he rules by fear."

"Yes," Finch concurred. "Swanbeck's lackeys are normally men, but he could have hired her for this one job because no one would suspect a woman of carrying it out. On the other hand, Jardine's murder could have no connection to Swanbeck."

She cocked her head to one side and asked skeptically, "Is that likely? It's too much of a coincidence."

"We agree. But it's the policeman's lot to follow up all the possibilities."

"Yes, of course. As do I."

"Emmeline." There was a note of warning in his tone. "Don't make me regret telling you what we suspect. You can't print a word of it. We don't want to alert the woman—whoever she is—or Swanbeck."

She flapped a hand at him. "You should know me better than that by now, Sergeant Finch."

His lips pressed into a thin line. "Mmm, yes. Quite well, in fact. That's why I don't like the gleam in your eye."

"Gleam? I'm certain that's merely a trick of the light."

"Now you sound like your bloody husband."

"Don't be silly. Although Gregory and I are married, we are two distinctly different people."

"The only difference is that he's a criminal and you're not. Other than that, you're both reckless. Though I must admit that Longdon tends to be to a lesser extent than you."

She sucked in her breath. "I should be deeply offended by that remark."

"But you're not because it's the truth. And we all know how much you prize the truth."

She sniffed. "It is completely unfair to use my own words against me."

A laugh bubbled up from his throat. "We wouldn't have you any other way. The guv and I just wish you'd exercise a bit more caution. We'd much prefer to have you alive and pestering us than lying on the cold altar of the truth in a corner of the morgue."

She remained silent for several seconds. "I won't give up on the story."

"Do you ever?" he shot back.

She smiled up at him and scooted to the edge of her chair. "You know we can help each other."

He folded his arms over his chest and one eyebrow arched upward.

She ignored his pointed look and rushed on, "After all, we're after the same things. Truth and justice." She favored him with another smile, as she casually opened her notebook again. "What can you give me to tell my readers?"

"Talk to the Boy Wonder."

She shook her head. "I already asked Cruickshank. Apparently, his lips are sealed as tight as a clam. The official line he's spouting is 'No comment.'"

"Then I can't oblige you."

"Oh, come on. I wouldn't have to quote you directly. You could be *a source close to the investigation*. I'm certain if Superintendent Burnell were here he'd be more than happy to give me something."

Finch snorted. "We both know that's not true. Emmeline, I can't jeopardize the investigation."

"I'm not asking you to do so. I simply want a lead that I can pursue on my own."

"Didn't we just go through this not five minutes ago? It's much too dangerous."

She rose to her feet and hitched her handbag over her shoulder. "There's something called freedom of the press. The public has right to know that the police are doing everything in their power to keep them safe."

"An admirable goal, but that's not why you're chasing

after this story." He paused, holding her gaze. "Well, not the only reason. It's because there's nothing you enjoy more than working out a complicated puzzle."

She opened her mouth to say something but changed her mind.

He wagged a finger at her. "You see, you can't deny it."

Emmeline tossed her chin in the air in defiance. *Ooh, why did he have to hit the nail squarely on the head?*

She sighed. Discretion was the better part of valor, wasn't it?

"Truce," she offered at last. "I'll use the official statement Scotland Yard put out. However, you can't prevent me from following up on the matters we discussed off the record today."

"That's fair enough."

"But do I have your word that you'll give me an exclusive the instant you have a crack in the case?"

"You mean the same way you'll promise to come to us, if you find out anything about Jardine or Swanbeck *before* it's splashed over the front page?"

Emmeline adopted an innocent expression. "That goes without saying. I'm all for cooperation," she replied demurely.

She extended a hand to him. He stared at it for a second before clasping it. Then she sauntered toward the door, only stopping to give him a cheery wave over her shoulder.

As he watched her go, Finch was left with a growing sense of unease in the pit of his stomach. He was too young to have an ulcer. But after his frank discussion with Emmeline, he could well understand how Burnell's ulcer had been born.

CHAPTER 18

Superintendent Burnell hunched his shoulders, shrugging deeper into his trench coat. Despite his umbrella, he was being pelted by fat droplets of rain that were being blown at an angle into his face.

As he waited for the light to change, he wondered for the millionth time why he hadn't accepted that early retirement package he had been offered a few years back. He let his mind imagine it. This instant he could have been roasting in the sun in a villa in Torremolinos like so many of his former colleagues who had cashed in their lot and moved to Spain. He savored the dream for a few moments, a faint smile touching his lips. He never would have heard of Alastair Swanbeck or Sebastian Jardine. He would have been a happy and contented man far from the madding crowd at Scotland Yard.

The light changed and the golden images of the Costa del Sol dissolved into the damp, dreariness of London and reality. It was merely a dream he indulged in from time to time, like a chocolate bonbon one devoured when craving a treat. In his heart of hearts, Burnell knew he would never leave London nor retire.

Unless I'm pushed out, the little voice inside his head intoned lugubriously. Which at the moment appeared to be a strong possibility.

All he had ever wanted since he was a boy was to be a policeman. His parents had wanted him to become a barrister, but he couldn't have spent his days in a stuffy courtroom kowtowing to supercilious judges. He had wanted to defend the law, not recite it from memory. Thus, he had stood his ground against his parents' entreaties and entered the force. Had it been thirty years? He couldn't believe it. He was proud of his steady rise through the ranks, despite the obstacles put in his way by former Assistant Commissioner Fenton and now the Boy Wonder.

But would his career be remembered for how it ended? With all his accomplishments torpedoed by a thug like Swanbeck.

"No," Burnell growled as he dashed across the Strand. "Over my dead body." His outburst had earned him curious glances from those hurrying past him. He hadn't realized he had spoken aloud. Well, they could all go to the devil. He had a right to grouse, if he wanted.

Burnell ducked into The George, the lovely little pub in a black-and-white Tudor-style house that faced directly onto the Royal Courts of Justice—the home of the Court of Appeal and the High Court of England and Wales since the late nineteenth century. He shook off the rain clinging to him, welcoming the warmth that beckoned him to linger inside for a while. The pub had character. The color scheme probably had a lot to do with it. Everything was awash in red—the walls, the leather banquettes, and the chairs. A number of ornate portraits, light fittings, and stained-glass decorated the walls and wooden partitions. Oak beams ran across the ceiling giving The George a historic air. The pub opened out towards the back, where there was a cozy seating area and a fireplace—a perfect place to escape to on a rainy autumn afternoon like today. It also was ideal, when one wanted to have a quiet word with someone away from prying eyes and ears.

It was one o'clock and the lunch crowd was in full force. However, Burnell was in luck. The man he was there to meet was already ensconced on a banquette at a small table along the window. His head was bent over the *Times* crossword, a pint at his elbow from which he was taking occasional sips between scribbling down his answers. He glanced up, his brow furrowed in concentration. No doubt he was mulling over the next clue.

His mouth broke into a broad grin when he caught a glimpse of Burnell hovering inside the doorway. He raised his hand and waved at the superintendent. Burnell nodded, but he had to squeeze past two barristers and a group of clerks from a nearby chambers to reach the table.

He thrust a hand out, when he had finally reached the man's side. "Terence. Terry, it's good of you to meet me at such short notice."

To the outsider, Terence Dunbar could have been mistaken for an accountant or a professor. But that guess would be incorrect. Terry had one of the sharpest police minds in the U.K. and Europe. He had used his inherent talents at Scotland Yard for twenty years and then during a five-year stint as a criminal intelligence officer at Interpol. Two years ago, he decided he'd had enough and retired.

Now, Dunbar pressed the superintendent's hand between both of his and pumped it up and down for several seconds. "It's been a long time, Oliver."

Indeed, it had, Burnell agreed. However, the years had been kind to his friend. Terry was a bit thinner, but in no way did he appear frail. Only a few lines marred his face. His cheekbones seemed to be more pronounced than the superintendent remembered, and his friend's steel-gray hair was creeping farther back from the dome of his forehead. Aside from those changes, Terry exuded the same fierce intelligence mingled with a sense of humor.

Dunbar waited until Burnell had shed his coat and slipped into the chair opposite. "I'm sorry to hear about your spot of bother at the moment," he murmured. His shrewd slate-green eyes clouded with sympathy, which made the superintendent flinch. He didn't need anyone's pity.

Dunbar shook his head. "It's bloody outrageous, if you ask me."

Burnell was prevented from answering because a waitress materialized at his elbow. The next few minutes were taken up with decisions about lunch. Burnell ordered a beer and ri-beye steak sandwich, while Dunbar opted for one of their homemade sausage rolls.

As the waitress drifted away, the dull murmur of conversation thrummed around them. Burnell hooked one arm around the back of his chair, his gaze traveling around the room, assessing the other patrons with his practiced eye.

"I need to pick your brain, Terry, about Sebastian Jardine. From what we've been able to gather, he worked at Interpol for a time. Did the two of you ever cross paths? Everyone else who I've approached about Jardine has shut me down. Why is that?"

He saw Terry stiffen. His features were suddenly pinched with tightly controlled anger. He took a deep gulp of his beer and slammed the pint down. He cast a sideways glance to his left and right. "Jardine was bad news." His tone was clipped. "Interpol is still trying to rid itself of his stench."

Interesting. Burnell took a swallow of his own drink and waited. But Dunbar fell into a brooding silence.

Burnell cleared his throat. "Are you going to leave me hanging or are you going to tell me the rest of it?"

Dunbar met his gaze. "Look, why do you want to know about Jardine? He's dead anyway and good riddance. Surely, you have bigger problems to concentrate on at the moment."

The superintendent leaned across the table. "But you see, Jardine *is* my problem. He's the man I'm accused of murdering at the airport."

His friend sat bolt upright, his eyes bulging in surprise. "What? That's impossible. Jardine died in 2005."

Burnell slumped back. Terry had confirmed Longdon's little bombshell, which didn't help matters. "Yes, that's what someone told me. But it seems Jardine's death—the first one—was some sort of a ruse. So, I put it to you again. What did Jardine do at Interpol and why won't anyone talk about it?"

The waitress, a bright smile lighting up her face, appeared with their lunch. After wishing them a hearty appetite, she left them alone.

Terry shoved away his plate, glaring at his sausage roll in disgust.

"It looks perfectly edible to me," Burnell ventured, as he tucked into his sandwich.

"I've lost my appetite," Terry mumbled. "The subject of Jardine leaves a bitter taste in one's mouth."

The superintendent chewed thoughtfully for several seconds and then remarked, "They say confession is good for the soul. Why not unburden yourself? It will make you feel better and could very well help me out of this mess." He took another bite of his sandwich. "Come on, Terry, it's me you're talking to. I've seen the worst of humanity over the years. Nothing can shock me."

Dunbar tapped his finger on the table and gave a curt nod, as if coming to a conclusion after an internal debate. He took a swig of his beer. "Right. Where to begin?"

He rested back against the banquette and rolled his pint between his hands. "I was a criminal intelligence officer in the Fugitive Investigative Support division in the General Secretariat. I was based at the headquarters in Lyon. It was supposed to be a three-year secondment from the Met, but my term was extended another two years.

"Jardine was hired as an analyst near the end of my first year. As you can imagine, Interpol's vetting process is comprehensive and thorough. It has to be. But Jardine slipped through the cracks. Don't get me wrong. His credentials and background appeared—and were—stellar. A double first at Cambridge. Then he became a fellow and taught history, and he was a linguist. He was a gift that fell into the agency's lap. But Jardine came to Interpol with his own sordid agenda of revenge.

"He was hired as an analyst in the Project Portfolio Management Office, which is part of the Executive Directorate for Partnerships and Planning." Terry put up both hands in the air. "I know it's a mouthful. Suffice it to say that Jardine did research and drafted policy reports. For the first few months, he was producing great work. Then he started accessing the databases for things that were not part of his remit at all."

"Like what?" Burnell asked.

"It was subtle at first and no one really noticed. However, a pattern began to emerge. Jardine was interested in only one thing, Malta. Playground of the superrich and international money-laundering haven. Criminals with money to burn can buy a Maltese passport. It's known as 'a Golden Visa.' It's legal, but it's one of the dirtiest schemes in this century. If I tell you that revenue from the sale of passports is estimated to reach fifty million euros next year, a fourteen million euro increase over this year, you can understand why the scheme remains popular and lucrative for the government. Corruption is rife in Valletta. Officials are getting their palms well-greased, I can assure you. As for criminals, the scheme allows them to evade law enforcement, and more importantly, prosecution back home. Suddenly they are absolved of their past sins and have a clean slate. And now, they can move freely and make investments in EU countries. You won't be surprised to hear that the Russians and Chinese are big fans.

"Then we have the Mafia. Malta's strategic location in the middle of the Mediterranean makes it quite attractive for organized crime groups involved in all sorts of trafficking, ranging from drugs and firearms to oil smuggling, among other illicit endeavors." Terry took another sip of his beer. "There was a report I read earlier this year, which found that the country's favorable tax system and other business opportunities provide an array of incentives for organized crime to establish companies there."

Burnell had stopped eating long ago. He leaned back in his chair and folded one arm over his chest, while he stroked his beard with the other hand. "Naturally I was aware of Malta's reputation, but not all of these details. What does Malta have to do with Jardine's murder?"

"Everything," Terry explained. "He lived in Valletta between the ages of four and ten. His mother, Rosalie, escaped with him—and I do mean bolted—in the dead of night from Catania in Sicily. You see, Jardine was her maiden name. She had been born on Malta. Her father was in the British army and he had been stationed on the island. He was a bit strict and young Rosalie rebelled. She fell in love with a young Italian who she crossed paths with on the island one summer. His name was Matteo Pappalardo."

Burnell's ears perked up at this nugget. He hissed, "Pappalardo? Not the Cosa Nostra boss who terrorized Sicily and all of Italy throughout the 1960s and early 1970s. Wasn't he killed by one of his lieutenants?"

Terry tapped the side of his nose. "Got it one. Rosalie and Matteo were married only a month after they met. Her parents were livid. They banished her from the family home and cut her off. Rosalie, like all young people at that age, shrugged off their disapproval and settled into life by her husband's side in Catania. Nine months later, they welcomed a healthy baby boy, Sebastiano. For the first years of his life, the boy had the world at his feet. Matteo kept accumulating power and the money followed. However, this inspired jealousy not only from rival families, but from some within his own organization. Until one day, it reached a boiling point and his second-in-command, Luca Cannizzaro, shot him at point blank range without batting an eye and took over the business. What is not widely known is that Cannizzaro murdered Pappalardo in front of Sebastiano, who was four at the time."

"Hence his mother's nocturnal flight to Malta," Burnell muttered.

"Yes. Rosalie quickly reverted to her maiden name and thus Sebastiano Pappalardo overnight became your dead man, Sebastian Jardine."

"How did they end up in England?"

"One day, she caught a glimpse of Cannizzaro—with two of his thugs hovering in tow—shaking hands with some high-profile government official outside a restaurant on Republic Square in Valletta. Rosalie had dreaded for years that Cannizzaro would find her. She knew he would stop at nothing until he eliminated her son—Matteo's heir and the only witness. Sebastian was a loose end. As long as he was alive, he posed a threat to Cannizzaro's organization.

"Rosalie didn't wait to find out whether Cannizzaro knew she was on Malta. She fled again leaving behind a man with whom she had been living for all intents and purposes as his wife. They had a child together, but Rosalie didn't think twice. Her erstwhile husband killed himself about six months after she left."

Burnell gave a low whistle. "Poor sod. So much for love in paradise."

Dunbar nodded grimly. "Sebastian was Rosalie's entire

world. She would do anything to protect him. Therefore, the only place she felt she would be safe now was England. Like the prodigal returning to the fold, she begged her parents for forgiveness and promised never to go against their wishes again. Her father had been transferred back home by that time. After thirty-four years in the service, he had decided to retire. He and his wife had sold their London flat and bought a house in Surrey. This is where Sebastian grew up. No one, except his grandparents, knew of his ignominious beginnings. Rosalie had died a few months after their return."

The expression on Terry's face told Burnell that this last remark was significant. "Oh, yes? She was still quite young. Had she been ill?"

"No, there was nothing natural about Rosalie's death. She had come up to London to do some shopping and to see a play with a friend. She was hit by a car as she stepped off the curb at Waterloo Station. Witnesses said that the car came out of nowhere. She had no time to react. She died at the scene. The driver was never found."

"Hmph," Burnell grunted. "Cannizzaro settling old scores."

"I have no doubt about it, but there was no way to tie it to him. Young Sebastian became an orphan. His grandparents raised him, but he never forgot his mother and what she had drilled into his head about his ill-fated, ruthless father Matteo. She poisoned her son's mind and made him vow to avenge his father one day. If she was consumed with hatred for Cannizzaro, Rosalie loathed his wife, Stefania, who was her sister-in-law, Matteo's younger half-sister. If she had been born male, Stefania should have been the one to run the family business. As it was, Matteo, who was far less intelligent, was anointed king when their father died. Stefania was furious. Their father must have foreseen what would happen. In his will, he left her the Pink Courtesan as a consolation prize.

Ever heard of her?"

Burnell frowned. "Somehow I don't think she's the Scarlet Pimpernel's mistress," he quipped facetiously.

Dunbar permitted himself a wry smile. "You're right about that, Oliver. But the Pink Courtesan knows how seduce men with her charms. It's a fifteen-carat, oval-shaped fancy vivid pink diamond ring surrounded by white diamonds and set in platinum."

Burnell dropped his head and stared into the depths of his pint, wishing he could drown in it.

A diamond? No, no, no. Not again, his brain groaned as his ulcer sent up a distress signal. He shook his head and tossed back a swig of his beer, as Longdon's roguish face flashed before his eyes. *Why does it always have to be diamonds? And a* fancy *one at that.*

He cleared his throat. "Fancy vivid pink?" he croaked, his mouth suddenly parched. "It sounds…expensive."

Dunbar snorted. "It's worth more than we'll ever see in two lifetimes. The Fancy Vivid category is the highest possible for pink diamonds."

"Naturally," Burnell muttered under his breath.

"The ring had belonged to Matteo's mother," Dunbar explained. "Rosalie had coveted it from the day she set foot in Sicily, especially because Stefania treated her with utter contempt. After Matteo died, Rosalie felt she was owed something for marrying into the Pappalardo family. This is what she had told Sebastian. He grew up with the notion that he had been swindled out of his birthright. He vowed to get it all back and make those who stole his life from him pay a steep price."

Burnell eyed Terry over the rim of his pint. He clucked his tongue. "It's the same old story. Revenge twists the mind and gnaws away at you bit by bit, until it's the only thing that makes you get up in the morning."

Terry exhaled a weary sigh. "That was Jardine in a nut-shell. Everything he did in his life had one goal: get back the diamond and make Cannizzaro, and by extension Stefania, pay for cheating Rosalie. Ultimately, it's what got him killed."

"At the rate Jardine was going, it was only a matter of time. So, someone at Interpol finally stumbled onto the truth and he was dismissed because of his connections to a notorious Mafia family."

"Not exactly. The family bit came out months after he'd left the agency. By the way, he left of his own accord. But he would have been sacked, if he hadn't. He saw the writing on the wall. However, what started to make people nervous was the discovery of his friendship with a chap he met at the Cambridge Union, the university's debating society. His friend was just as brilliant by all accounts. I'm certain his name rings a bell."

Burnell raised an eyebrow in askance. "Don't tell me you're going to make me guess."

Terry gave a curt shake of his head. "Jardine's bosom mate was *Alastair Swanbeck*."

The superintendent felt as if he had been pitched into a black hole. "Bloody hell."

CHAPTER 19

After her meeting with Sergeant Finch, Emmeline had hopped on the Tube and gone directly back to *The Clarion*. The information that Finch had passed on had sent a jolt of adrenaline coursing through her veins and helped to give focus to her story on Jardine's murder and his connection to Swanbeck. Although the latter remained an elusive thread at the moment. But no matter.

Now, she had to try to find the mystery woman who was the prime suspect. Who was she? Where was she? She couldn't simply have vanished. The woman must have left a trail, Emmeline reasoned.

She exhaled a frustrated sigh. Finch had told her about the woman in confidence. How could she write the story without breaking her promise to him? In good conscience, she could not. Although others—she gritted her teeth—like the despicable Ian Newland, wouldn't think twice about betraying such a confidence, it went against every rule of journalistic integrity by which she lived.

She couldn't jeopardize Scotland Yard's case. And yet, it was a legitimate story. She drummed her fingers on her desk. Was there a way she could get the information from someone else?

She sat up straighter in her chair as an idea flashed into her mind. Perhaps, her angle could be what was being done to keep the public safe in an era of heightened concern about terrorism? The average citizen or traveler wanted to know that he or she could go to the airport and not have to worry about being stabbed or physically harmed in any other way. Yes. Her mouth broke into a smile. Naturally, she would have to interview Heathrow security officials to give the story authoritative substance. She already knew one official who was eager to redeem himself in the eyes of his bosses, the public, and Scotland Yard. The pompous, self-important Naylor. He was the sort who would preen at seeing his name in the paper and, therefore, would be more than willing to talk. Naylor would want to stress to the public that Jardine's murder was an isolated incident and solely a police matter. She would wager anything that if she framed her questions in just the right way, she could get Naylor to discuss the woman seen on the CCTV tapes. He would want to point out that she targeted Jardine and no one else.

Emmeline reached for her phone. Yes, she had her story without compromising Sergeant Finch. It would cast doubt about Superintendent Burnell's involvement in the murder. Assistant Commissioner Cruickshank would have no choice but to restore him to duty, allowing Scotland Yard to get on with the job of finding the real culprit.

And, hopefully, a small voice whispered in her head, *it will lead to Swanbeck, so that we can all rest easy and not have to look over our shoulders anymore.*

Emmeline got her story from Naylor. He had been even more loquacious than she could have hoped. It would be the leader on tomorrow's front page. All in all, a good day's work. She prayed that it helped Burnell's cause.

Now, if she could only do something for Philip. She bit her lip as she left the building. Yes, he was a trained MI5 agent and a diplomat to boot, but she was worried. Why hadn't they heard from him? She knew Gregory was going to meet Villiers today. As much as she disliked the man, Villiers was the only one in this situation who had the power to look into Special Branch's charges—whatever they were. It was utterly ridiculous.

She was still fuming on this point, when Gregory slipped his arm around her waist and suggested that they have dinner at their favorite Italian restaurant near Covent Garden. Her mood brightened considerably, and she readily agreed. She looped her arm through his and they hailed a cab.

Only after they had ordered, and the wine arrived was Emmeline finally able to tell him what she had discovered from Finch about the woman who the police suspected had murdered Jardine.

He reached across the table and took her hand, rubbing his thumb along the soft web of skin between her thumb and fore-finger. "Emmy, was that wise?"

Her fingers stiffened within his grasp and she tried to tug her hand back. She didn't want to argue. And yet, she had nothing for which to reproach herself. "I was simply doing what any good journalist would do: following a lead. Besides, Nigel reviewed the article and gave his blessing to run with it."

He inclined his head to one side, his gaze skimming her face. "That's as may be. From a legal standpoint, it may pass muster. But you're being deliberately coy, darling, and it doesn't suit you. There was more to it than simply following a lead and you know it."

She did manage to wriggle her hand free. It was absolutely unfair for him to be so devastatingly handsome—and so right.

She tore her eyes from his intense scrutiny to peer into the rich ruby depths of her Montepulciano d'Abruzzo, as she twirled the stem of her wineglass between her fingers.

She took a long swallow, savoring the delicious wine before it slid down her throat. Finally, she sighed and lifted her gaze to meet his again. "I was doing my job," she repeated. He gave her a pointed look but remained silent. "But I was hoping it would help to clear Superintendent Burnell."

"And?" he pressed.

She glared at him. "And what?"

He flashed one of those smiles that melted her heart and at the same time vexed her. "While it's admirable you're using the power of the press to see that a miscarriage of justice is not carried out against our cuddly Oliver, there is an underlying reason you wrote that damn story."

She tossed her chin in the air defiantly. "Oh, yes? Enlighten me," she challenged.

He leaned across the table and lowered his voice. The smile was still on his lips, but a muscle in his jaw tightened. "Yes, you infuriating woman. You want to draw out Swanbeck by making yourself a target yet again."

His words hung in the air between them, angry, bitter and tinged with concern.

She didn't respond immediately, instead taking another lingering sip of her wine. She lifted the glass in the air, admiring its color in the light. "This wine is absolutely delicious." She shot him a sideways glance out of the corner of her eye. Gregory's lips were pressed together, and his shoulders were hunched and tense. "I'm a journalist, not a detective…"

He interrupted, "You seem to forget that fact quite often, my darling."

"—All I do is to make sure that the public knows the truth," she went on, ignoring him. "I would never interfere with a police investigation. On the other hand, if I come across a vital piece of information, I can't ignore it."

Gregory took a gulp of his wine and glared at her. She was

certain he hadn't tasted it at all. Such a pity, she thought.

He set the glass on the table and smoothed down the corners of his mustache. "Emmy, Swanbeck already tried to kill you once. Why give him a second chance?"

"Because he's still out there," she hissed through clenched teeth, no longer able to contain the anger that had been simmering below the surface. "Until he's behind bars, we can't get on with our lives. That's why."

She slumped back in her chair and folded her arms over her chest, daring him to reproach her actions further.

"I married a mad woman," he mumbled at last. "You're playing with fire. Oliver, Finch, and even that fool Cruickshank would tell you to stay out of it. And I'm sure they have."

"You know I can't do that. No journalist worth her salt would give up this story."

"I seem to remember something about it being better to be safe than sorry."

She snorted. "Safe? That's rich coming from you with the life you've led. I've only scratched the surface about your wicked past. I'm certain that there are hundreds of other things that I still don't know." She wagged a finger at him. "But stand warned, husband dear, I intend to find out every last, dark secret."

His usual playful, charming smile touched his lips. "Wicked?" He clucked his tongue. "Really, Emmy. You make me sound like a villain in a Victorian novel. As for secrets, I'll admit to a…misspent youth." His smile grew wider. "You can't condemn me for anything more sinister than that."

"Hmph," she grunted, but some of the anger of a moment ago had dissipated. The knots in the pit of her stomach unwound. She reached across the table for his hand. "What are we doing?"

He laced his fingers through hers and gave a slight shake

of his head.

"I just want"—she exhaled a weary sigh—"everyone to leave us alone. It's not unreasonable. I don't want to be afraid anymore."

"Lest I point out the obvious, darling"—he lifted her hand to his lips and brushed her knuckles with a soft kiss—"putting yourself in Swanbeck's crosshairs will not bring tranquility to our lives."

She rolled her eyes at him. "If only we knew where he's been hiding, it would be half the battle. Then maybe we could find out his connection to your late, lamented friend Jardine. And we could clear Superintendent Burnell and restore his reputation."

"Emmy, you can't right all the world's wrongs."

"No, just the little corner that affects us." She held his gaze. "Gregory, the truth matters."

"You matter more to me than any truth, which, I must say, can be overrated at times."

"This is not a laughing matter."

"No, that's precisely the point. We're dealing with a ruthless criminal, whose natural milieu is the dark underbelly of society. Swanbeck rubs shoulders with all sorts of nasty chaps. For them, killing is an amusing pastime."

"All the more reason to discover evidence to put him away for life. That means we must find him. Don't you want your friend's murderer to be caught?"

"The police have to find Swanbeck," he corrected.

"All right, the police. But there's no rule saying that we can't do some digging on our own, is there? It's our civic duty to help."

His right eyebrow arched upward. "I suspect that the police will not share your sanguine opinion."

She dismissed this observation with an impatient wave of her hand. "Why are you being so argumentative tonight?"

"Call it the voice of sanity."

"Ha. Ha. No, let's think about it. There must be someone who's in contact with Swanbeck. Someone who may—" She bit back the rest of her sentence as Ian Newland's sneering face flashed before her eyes and their conversation replayed itself in her mind.

Gregory's brow creased into a frown. "Darling, someone who *what*?"

His eyes searched her face for an answer. She knew he was going to be upset when she recounted her encounter with Ian. She drew in a ragged breath. Best to get it over with. She plunged in and told him about the incident with as minimum fuss as possible.

His eyes narrowed and his lips pursed as each word tumbled out of her mouth. When she was finished, the only thing he said was "I see."

She didn't like the cloud that darkened his features. She smiled and rushed on, trying to inject a positive note into her voice. "Nothing happened. That's what counts. And Roger was wonderful. Ian backed down almost immediately. It shows that he's a coward at heart."

"Yes," Gregory murmured as he took a thoughtful sip of his wine. "Good old Roger. He seems to be everywhere and nowhere these days. Naturally, he didn't tell you what he's been up to." She shook her head and he took another long swallow of wine. "No, of course not. But he's up to his bloody neck in this business." He leaned back in his chair and his eyes came to rest on Emmeline's face. "I wonder what game he's playing."

She could not answer his question because the same thoughts had been racing through her own mind. She didn't like Gregory worrying, though. "Whatever it is, I'm glad Roger happened to be on the spot. Yes, I would have been able to extricate myself from two tricky situations, but it was nice to have someone there for support."

"Yes, of course. And I'm grateful Roger was there, but…"

She squeezed his hand. "No buts. We'll simply have to trust Roger. Ian is the real problem. From what he let slip, he's in contact with Swanbeck. I spoke to Sergeant Finch and he can bring Ian in for questioning."

"Ye-es." Gregory drew out this word. He wasn't listening. She was certain that his thoughts were still concentrated on Roger.

It was a welcome interruption, when the waiter arrived with their dinner. As he set their plates in front of them, she said, "Oh, lovely. I'm famished." She took up her fork and knife and sliced into her veal, but her gaze lingered on Gregory.

A change of subject was needed. "You never told me how your meeting went with Villiers. What did he say about Philip?"

The pained expression etched in every line of Gregory's face spoke volumes.

"Ah, that well," she mumbled as she popped a forkful of veal into her mouth.

This at least coaxed a ghost of a smile to his lips. "You know the old devil. Everything is always a damn secret. I feel as though we're always going round in circles. He seemed completely unaware about Acheson, but then again that could be an act."

Reluctantly, he related his wearisome conversation. The only bit Emmeline remained ignorant of was Villiers's observation about her being a distraction that was going to get Gregory killed one day.

Only a man with a death wish would have told his wife something certain to provoke a violent reaction.

CHAPTER 20

The next day was a Wednesday. Laurence Villiers always lunched at his club on Pall Mall on Wednesdays. Like clockwork, his sleek black Mercedes drew up in front of the gleaming white building with its sturdy Doric columns at noon. The driver walked around the car and held the rear door open. Villiers stepped out, immaculate as ever in a charcoal Savile Row suit. He buttoned his jacket, as he casually cast a quick glance up and down the road. His trained eye didn't detect any unwanted friends. Good.

He nodded at his driver. "Thank you, Ralph. Be back at the usual time."

He waited until the car had pulled away from the curb, before proceeding up the marble steps at a sedate pace. Once he was in the shadow of a column, he took a moment to go over the scene one last time. But there was nothing out of the ordinary, so he stepped into the bastion of male exclusivity.

His footsteps echoed as he glided across the black-and-white tiled marble floor of the foyer. He plastered a smile on his lips and inclined his head as Smithers, the concierge, bustled toward him and made his usual fuss.

"Your usual table has been reserved in the dining room, Mr. Villiers, and here are the latest editions of all the papers, as you requested," Smithers informed him with his usual efficiency. "Will you be needing anything else?"

"Thank you, not just now, Smithers," he replied smoothly and started to head in the direction of the dining room. Then he stopped and spun around on his heel and commented, seemingly as an afterthought, "Sir Cyril Spencer mentioned he might be at the club today."

"Indeed, he is. Sir Cyril arrived about a quarter of an hour ago. I believe he's in the library. I can have a message sent to him, if you'd like to see him."

Villiers waved a hand in the air. "No, no. That's not necessary. I was merely curious. It's nothing urgent. I'm sure I'll bump into him later," he replied nonchalantly.

"Very good, Mr. Villiers. If that's all, I'll be getting back to my duties."

"Yes, by all means. Don't let me keep you."

After he enjoyed a leisurely and rather pleasant lunch with a fellow member he hadn't seen in several months, Villiers made his way to the billiard room. He found the game a mindless bore, but he knew that Spencer, the head of Special Branch, fancied himself an amateur expert.

Spencer was hunched over the green baize, elbow pointed upward, as he surveyed the table. He flicked a glance toward the door as the air moved and Villiers slipped into the room, pressing his back against the door. Spencer's clear blue eyes narrowed, and his lips twisted into a grimace. His gaze returned to the table and he drew his arm back, letting loose his shot. The ball went wide, rolling to a halt at the opposite end of the table. Villiers bit back a smile. So much for the club's resident champion.

Villers pushed himself away from the door as Spencer straightened up. "Bad luck, old chap," he mumbled. The words lacked sincerity.

Spencer rested his hands atop the cue and waited until

Villiers reached his side. His eyes never left the face of the deputy director of MI5. His gaze held a mixture of shrewd intelligence and haughty arrogance, a combination which tended to rub those who had the misfortune of coming into contact with him the wrong way. Villiers suspected that the pomposity masked a man plagued by insecurities. Perhaps that was why Spencer had two ex-wives? And didn't he recently marry a woman twenty years younger? Villiers clucked his tongue in silence and wondered how long it would last. Ten years Villiers's junior, one couldn't deny that Spencer's lean physique and arresting features would catch the eye of the ladies. But it was his abrasive personality that was his downfall in the end.

"Villiers," Spencer said in a tone bordering on a snarl. "What do you want? As if I didn't know."

Villiers's fingers itched to wipe the smirk off the other man's lips, but he quashed down his distaste. "I see that you still have the manners of a mongrel, Cyril."

"It's Sir Cyril these days," Spencer corrected, stressing the title. "Do show some respect to your betters, Laurence."

Villiers sniffed and made a show of casting a glance around the room. His shoulders twitched in a shrug. "Betters? It's only you and me here. I wasn't aware that any respect was due. You're still the same bastard who clawed his way up the ladder, not caring whose career you ruined to get to the top. I wouldn't be surprised if you blackmailed someone to get your title."

He felt a stab of pleasure at seeing Spencer's face turn an angry shade of puce. With jaw clenched, the head of Special Branch chalked up his cue and turned his attention to his game once again. He let loose an angry shot—missing again, Villiers noted spitefully—before he spoke. "Laurence, I'm busy, if…"

Villiers shot a pointed look round the table. "Yes, I can see. Extremely busy," he quipped.

Spencer stood up, back ramrod straight and dropped his cue with a clatter. "Right. Let's not mince words. Say what you came here to say and get out."

Villiers inclined his head and smiled. "How refreshing. One knows where one stands with naked antagonism, as opposed to feigned politeness." He hitched a hip on the edge of the table. "What possible reason could you have to arrest Philip Acheson? And why wasn't I informed before your chaps stormed into his office like two bulls in a China shop?"

Spencer's mouth broke into a malevolent grin. "Because he's one of your golden boys and you would have warned him." He paused for a beat. "As you did. I don't know how you managed it."

"Don't be ridiculous," Villiers snapped. "I wouldn't be here, if I had spirited Acheson away."

"Wouldn't you?" Spencer sneered. "From my point of view, you doth protest too much, Laurence." He put up a hand to forestall Villiers's protest. "You know *exactly* where your boy is. This is merely an attempt at plausible deniability. It won't work, though. We'll find him."

"Believe what you like," Villiers retorted, his tone holding thinly disguised outrage. "What's the bloody charge?"

Spencer clapped him on the shoulder. "Sorry, old chap. It's on a need-to-know basis."

Villiers surged to his feet. "I'm the deputy director of MI5, I *need* to bloody know."

Spencer gave an infuriating shrug. "Apparently someone very high up felt you couldn't be trusted with the sensitive details." He clucked his tongue. "I wonder why that was? In any case, it's above my pay grade. I was just following orders."

"I seem to remember the Nazis spouting the same kind of rubbish," Villiers shot back.

"You've overstayed your welcome." Spencer jerked his chin at the door. "Time for you to leave."

Villiers adjusted his suit jacket and shook his head in disapproval. "It's appalling the hoi-polloi they allow into the club these days." With that, he turned his back on Spencer and crossed to the door.

His hand clasped the handle, when Spencer's voice stilled him. "I'd have a care who was calling the kettle black. I can bring you down, old man, if I set my mind to it."

Villiers chuckled and tossed back over his shoulder. "That would be rather reckless, even for you, Cyril. I know where all the bodies are buried."

∽∾∽

"Insufferable *parvenu*," Villiers muttered under his breath as he stalked across the foyer, heedless of the greetings of several members he passed. The bitterness of his conversation with Spencer lingered on his tongue. He cursed the need to demean himself by broaching the subject of Acheson with a weasel like Spencer.

He burst out of the club in such a huff that he was momentarily blinded by the sun and had to shield his eyes from the glare. But the crisp, biting breeze helped to alleviate the pressure of the blood hammering against his temples. Within seconds of his descending the steps, his Mercedes appeared and rolled to a stop at the curb. Ralph bustled around the car to open the door for him.

"Ralph, you're a welcome sight. I—" He broke off when the muzzle of a gun was jabbed into his rib cage.

"Nice and easy, Villiers," the man, who he now saw was not his driver, whispered in his ear. "We wouldn't want to splatter your brains all over the pavement, would we?"

Villiers resisted as the man tried to shove him into the back seat. "Who the devil are you? And where is Ralph?" he growled.

The man managed to dump him unceremoniously onto the leather banquette, knocking the air from his lungs and jarring the parts of his body that still hadn't recovered fully from the gunshot wound over the summer.

His captor's face loomed above him. "No questions. You're not in charge at the moment, Mr. Deputy Director." He pressed Villiers against the seat with the splayed palm of one hand as the other pointed the gun at his heart. "Sit back and enjoy the ride."

He slammed the door and sprinted to the front. He was behind the wheel and merging into traffic in the blink of an eye.

Villiers cleared his throat. "You can tell Spencer that I'm not impressed with this rather infantile display. I'll have his guts for garters."

His captor chuckled. "I'm certain Sir Cyril would be quite amused at how easy it was to drive off with the great deputy director of MI5. No mess. No fuss. Nice and quiet. That's what I'm paid to do. Unless"—he craned his neck around to lock eyes with Villiers—"someone takes it into his head to be uncooperative. In that case, I'm afraid the gloves are off. You're an intelligent man. Don't make the wrong decision."

Villiers gripped his knees so hard the thin skin across his knuckles blanched and stretched taut. He was not afraid because fear was not a word that was part of his vocabulary. However, he hated not being in control of the situation.

"If you're not one of Spencer's chaps, who are you working for?"

The man swiveled to face forward again. "Don't be so impatient, Mr. Villiers. Anticipation is half of the fun. All will be revealed in good time."

CHAPTER 21

When Emmeline had arrived at the paper that morning, the little red light on her phone was flashing. There were three voicemails awaiting her. All of them were from Sally, requesting that she ring Assistant Commissioner Cruickshank at her earliest possible convenience. With each message, Sally's tone became more insistent and clipped.

Emmeline didn't have to guess what was so urgent. Cruickshank had seen the article. She knew she would have to face the music. She had rung him to try to smooth the matter over as best she could. After he had harangued her for ten minutes, she had done her best to diffuse the tension. As diplomatically as possible, she reminded the assistant commissioner that the public had a right to know the progress being made in the case, especially if the police were investigating one of their own. She pointed out that the press and the police were essentially on the same side. Cruickshank hadn't shared this opinion, but she had persevered. She told him that there was no need for them to be enemies because they both were after the same things: truth and justice. Therefore, it was in Scotland Yard's best interest to cooperate with the press to see that its side of the story was conveyed, without jeopardizing the case or public safety of course.

When their conversation had come to a conclusion, she had managed to reach a truce, if somewhat strained, with Cruickshank. The rest of her morning had been spent making calls to sources. She remained frustrated because her efforts thus far to trace Swanbeck through his tangle of illegitimate businesses had been time-consuming and had yielded nothing. At one stage, she had gotten excited about a nugget she had discovered about an offshore account. Ultimately, like everything else that had appeared promising, it turned out to be a waste of time.

A man could not vanish off the face of the earth, she reasoned, unless he was dead. And Swanbeck had made it a point of letting them know that he was *not* dead.

"Think," she said aloud to her empty office. "What do we know about Swanbeck?"

She tapped her pen impatiently against her notebook.

He was arrogant. She swallowed hard. He was consumed with revenge. He enjoyed nothing more than to taunt them and play games. Look at how he had rung up Gregory on his mobile at the precise moment the security officers had discovered the knife in her bag.

Her thoughts lingered on this last point. Swanbeck liked to dangle clues before their eyes, and then he sat back and laughed as they scrambled to make sense of them.

Clues, she repeated. Had he left them a clue to his whereabouts, and they hadn't put the pieces together yet? She frowned in concentration. Her mind sifted through the memories of the tumultuous events of the summer. The Royces, Swanbeck, the murders of Pavel Melnikov and Yevgeny Sabitov.

What was it that she was missing? Because a niggling voice in the back of her mind kept whispering that she was close. It was just out of reach. Then her eyes grew wide, and it struck her.

The locket.

The bloody silver filigree locket that Swanbeck had left in her hotel room in Edinburgh. At the time, she had dismissed it as a cruel joke. But what if it also was part of his cat-and-mouse game? To keep them off guard and jumping at shadows?

Yes, that was precisely Swanbeck's objective.

She gathered up her handbag and her coat, and hurried out of her office. She was waylaid by a reporter as she pushed the button on the lift. He had wanted to discuss his idea for a new investigative series. She listened with only half an ear, nodded at all the right points and gave her assent to go with it. He was a brilliant reporter, and she knew he would do a thorough job. As the doors slid open, Christine from Research hustled over to ask a question. Emmeline waved her off and stepped into the car. "Sorry. I can't stop now. I must dash home. I promise we'll speak as soon as I return from lunch."

The doors closed and she was alone. She leaned back against the car, as she racked her brain. *Where* was the locket? She should have thrown it and the accompanying note. But she hadn't. She didn't know why she had kept it. Perhaps instinct had told her it was important? Something else she hadn't done at the time was to tell Gregory about Swanbeck's "gift." It only would have upset him. Goodness knew they had had enough to worry about. Now, she was left with no choice. She had to tell him.

And she would. Once she found the locket.

∽∾∽

Gregory had found a file with a new case waiting for him, when he entered Symington's gleaming offices on Lime Street. He flicked through the police report. A robbery of a financier's penthouse in a relatively new residential development on Horseferry Road in Westminster. The man was known to be a collector of Old Masters and Impressionist paintings. Several paintings worth millions and a number of pieces of his wife's jewelry had been stolen.

Gregory sighed. The police had given Symington's access to the penthouse and agreed to share all their information. Both the police and the insurance company were eager to get the matter resolved as quickly as possible, preferably by recovering the stolen items. However, he knew it was going to pose a challenge. It was a virtual certainty that the paintings had already made their way into private collections and would never see the light of day again. His only hope was to track down the jewelry. At least on that score, there was a glimmer of a chance that the pieces would be returned to their owner.

Damn and blast, he swore silently. He had hoped to be able to sneak off to Jardine's flat in St. John's Wood again. Roger's unexpected appearance the last time had interrupted his search. Now, all of that would have to wait. Unless. His eye fell upon Kathleen, one of the junior investigators who was keen to make her mark. She'd be thrilled if asked her to accompany him to the scene of the crime. After making an initial assessment, he could leave her at the penthouse to follow up with the police and take notes. He had watched her in the field and read her reports. She was professional, supremely able, and meticulous with details. It was a pity more of the investigators didn't share her work ethic.

Kathleen must have sensed his scrutiny because she looked up. He flashed a smile and signaled to her. When she reached his desk, he said, "I have a new case and I'd like you to assist me. Fetch your coat. I'll brief you in the car."

Gregory's opinion of Kathleen's skills was reinforced when they arrived at the penthouse. He allowed her to question the owner and his wife, as he spoke to the inspector in charge of the case. He didn't leave until he had surveyed every room with his expert eye. He asked Kathleen to look into a couple of discrepancies and draft the preliminary report. She barely noticed when he departed.

Half an hour later, the lift deposited him on Seb's floor in the building on Prince Albert Road. Once again, the corridor was quiet. He was inside the flat in mere seconds. He pressed the door closed behind him and bolted it. He leaned his shoulder blades against it and stood still, listening. No sounds of someone moving about. No Roger.

What did that mean? Had Roger found what he had been looking for the last time he was here? And what the devil was *it* in the first place?

Right. He pushed himself away from the door with determination. No use driving himself mad trying to fathom Roger's motivations. He made his way into the living room. He stood in the middle of room and turned in a slow circle, taking in everything with a fresh eye.

He decided to start with the pair of striped moss green-and-beige sofas. He took out the cushions, slid his fingers along every seam and crevice, got on his hands and knees and fumbled underneath. He came up empty-handed.

The bookshelf and Seb's desk received the same painstaking inspection. Again, Gregory had nothing to show for his troubles. The last place to check in here was the glass-fronted cabinet. As on his previous visit, the inlaid wood and mother of pearl chess set captivated him with its craftsmanship and beauty.

He cocked his head to one side. "Could Seb have hidden his secret in plain sight?" Gregory asked himself.

He unlatched the cabinet's doors and with steady hands gently lifted out the chess set. He set it down on the coffee table and lowered himself onto one of the sofas. His fingers caressed its smoothly polished surface, turning it this way and that. He opened it up and examined each intricately carved mother of pearl piece, giving each one a twist to see whether any were hollow. One and all were frustratingly solid.

He slumped back against the sofa, glaring at the chess set. For he was now certain that the answer was sitting in front of him. "I know you're here," he said. But how could he coax it to give up its secret?

He rested his elbows on his knees. His eyes narrowed and he sat up bolt upright, when he realized that the base of the set was thicker than it should be. He drew it toward him and flipped it upside down. His mouth broke into a smile, when a hollow echo came in response to the tap of his knuckle.

His eyes narrowed. There must be a lever or catch. Where was it? His fingers poked and prodded. The bottom suddenly sprung open revealing a drawer, which was home to a single black velvet box.

Gregory placed the chess set down on the table and reached for the box. He flicked open the lid with his thumb. His breath caught in his throat, when the diamond's facets trapped the sun's rays and winked back at him.

"You brazen vixen. It's been far too long," he cooed as he freed the Pink Courtesan from its velvet prison.

He was still admiring the diamond's blushing complexion and graceful curves, when a whisper of movement made him half-turn. But it was too late. Something—he assumed it was a ten-ton brick—came crashing down against back of his neck, sending a white-hot jolt to rattle the top of his skull. Stars floated before his eyes. He was falling. Falling. Faster and faster. All the while, the Pink Courtesan's mocking laugh chased him as he hurtled deeper into the abyss.

"Nothing…but a…common whore," he groaned.

The second blow landed against his kidney, stealing the air from his lungs and sending searing daggers of pain across every sinew of his body. He tried to claw his way back from the blackness enveloping him.

"Forgive me…Emmy," he mumbled.

Oblivion's seductive embrace was too tempting to resist.

CHAPTER 22

Emmeline was grinning broadly and filled with a sense of triumph. She had found it. The box containing the cursed locket that Swanbeck had sent her and his note. She raced down the stairs, almost twisting her ankle on the last step in her haste.

She righted herself and burst into the living room and picked up the phone to call Gregory. His mobile rang and rang, and finally was answered by his voicemail. Damn. She left a message for him to ring her as soon as possible.

Disappointment surged through her. She opened the box in the palm of her hand and stared at the locket. Instinct told her that it would lead them to Swanbeck.

"Damn," she muttered aloud. She hoped Gregory would get her message soon.

She bit her lip. She should tell Sergeant Finch. A *mea culpa* for the article about the mystery woman at the airport. But she had wanted to share the news with Gregory first.

Her shoulders twitched in a reluctant shrug. Oh, well. She started dialing Finch's number at Scotland Yard, when the doorbell rang.

That was odd. Who would be popping by in the middle of the day? Normally, she and Gregory would be at work. She waited. The bell buzzed again. Several insistent times, in fact. Then the person started banging on the knocker.

"Emmeline, it's Roger. Open the door," his muffled voice implored.

She hurried out of the living room and quickly unbolted the door.

She looked up into his face, which was pinched with strain. "Roger, what are you doing here? What's the matter?"

He jerked his chin over his shoulder. "I've brought something that belongs to you."

She frowned at him in confusion. "What?"

"Your husband." He stepped aside and her gaze shot to Gregory's blue-gray Jaguar parked at the curb. "He said you'd be home."

She could see him struggling to get out of the passenger seat. The door was half-open. He appeared drunk or...*hurt*. She shoved Roger aside and bounded down the steps. She threw the door open and took Gregory's face gently between her hands.

"Darling, are you all right?" She noted that his gaze was slightly unfocused. "Gregory?"

She pressed her mouth near his ear and whispered, "Can you hear me?" She caressed his hair, which elicited a moan. Her gaze locked on his again.

"The old head's been through the wars a bit this afternoon," he replied hoarsely.

"Right. Let's get you inside and I'll ring the doctor." She was about to call to Roger, but he was already by her side.

"Allow me," he said, as he slipped an arm around Gregory's waist and helped him to stand.

He swayed on the balls of feet. However, the ghost of a smile touched his lips. "I'm fine, Emmy. Don't worry," he said reassuringly. He must have read the concern in her eyes.

"Of course, you are. I have no doubt about it," she

asserted. She was surprised at how calm her voice sounded. She nearly convinced herself. Nearly. "Come on."

She put her arm around him and they had him on the sofa in the living room within a couple of minutes. They propped his feet up and placed some cushions under his head.

Emmeline tenderly probed the back of his head and was alarmed when her fingers encountered the lump the size of a goose egg. Gregory flinched, his lips pressing into a thin line.

His eyes found hers. "Perhaps you could leave off the detective work at the moment."

She nodded mutely and fumbled for the phone, which she had dropped on the coffee table when she when to the door.

He cleared his throat and tried to sit up, but he slumped back down. "No doctor."

"Gregory, you're hurt and..."

"No doctor," he repeated more forcefully.

"At least, let me get you some ice," she countered.

"No. I'll be right as rain in a few minutes." This time he did manage to sit up and placed both feet on the floor. He flashed her a smile. "You see, I'm perfectly fine."

"Emmeline, he's a little worse for wear that's all," Roger interjected. This earned him a withering look from her.

"Men," she huffed. "And you have the nerve to call me stubborn."

Gregory clasped his hand around the back of her neck and with an effort drew her toward him to place a kiss on the tip of her nose. "That's because you are."

She loosened his grip and stood up. "I don't know why I bother with you."

He chuckled but regretted it almost immediately.

"Serves you right," she remarked. "You ought to—" She broke off when the doorbell sounded for the second time that afternoon. "Not again. Who can that be now?"

Roger put up his hands. "Stay with your husband. I'll get

rid of whoever it is."

She came to sit beside Gregory and twined her fingers through his. With her eyes glued on him, her ears strained to learn who was the new visitor.

After a brief conversation in the hall, Roger returned with Superintendent Burnell and Sergeant Finch on his heels. "Coppers," he mumbled, as he jerked his thumb over his shoulder.

"I apologize for intruding, Emmeline, but the paper said you could be reached at home." Then, he turned to Gregory. "Up to your old tricks, I hear, Longdon," he intoned with a hint of smugness.

Even though he was injured, Emmeline saw a mischievous glint in Gregory's eye.

"Oliver, you old teddy bear. I know underneath that gruff exterior, you're beside yourself with worry. I'm touched."

"Yes, touched in the head"—the superintendent tapped his temple with his forefinger—"if you think I care what happens to you."

He caught Emmeline's eye and must have seen the effort she was making to remain calm. "Sorry, Emmeline," he mumbled contritely. "I know you're upset." She inclined her head.

Burnell's gaze narrowed, and he raised an eyebrow. "Are you all right?" he asked Gregory grudgingly, as he lowered himself into the wing chair.

Gregory squeezed Emmeline's hand and gave Burnell a crooked smile. "I'll live."

Burnell grunted and settled back in the chair.

Finch sat down beside Emmeline on the sofa and Roger took the chair next to Gregory.

Emmeline gave Finch a sheepish smile. "I know you must be upset with me. I had Cruickshank on the phone and he read me the riot act. I had no intention of jeopardizing the case. I simply wanted to…"

Burnell cut across her. "We know what you wanted. And I'm grateful." He gave her a rare, but sincere, smile. "I'll weather this storm. I put my trust in the law," he said solemnly. "If I can't trust the law, then my whole life would have been a waste and I can't bring myself to believe that."

"Bully for you," Gregory chimed in. "We all have to believe in something."

To prevent this conversation from escalating, Finch told Emmeline, "I admit that I was furious initially." She opened her mouth to say something, but he raised a hand to prevent her apology. "However, your article was perfectly objective and corroborated by sources, as always." He sighed. "Look, we couldn't have kept quiet about the woman for much longer anyway. No matter what the Boy Wonder says. Your article proved that too many people are aware of it."

She smiled at him. "Thank you for being so generous. I don't think I would have been. My temper tends to get the better of me sometimes."

Finch grinned at her. "Really? I hadn't noticed."

She felt her cheeks burning at this good-natured dig.

"Good." Burnell slapped his armrest. "Now that we've gotten all that out of the way"—he directed the full force of his forbidding stare on Roger—"We meet again, Mr. Delahunt."

Far from being discomfited, Roger inclined his head. He rose and extended a hand to him. "No hard feelings, I hope, Superintendent Burnell. As I saw it, the situation at the airport called for a drastic intervention."

"Mmm," Burnell replied noncommittally, ignoring the proffered hand.

"My concern was entirely for Emmeline. I assure you," Roger went on smoothly.

Burnell stroked his beard. "Very chivalrous."

Roger beamed as he sat down once again. "Thank you. One does one's best."

The superintendent rolled his eyes. "Two peas in a pod," he grumbled. "It comes as no surprise that you and Longdon are mates."

"Do I detect a hint of jealousy in your tone, Oliver?" Gregory queried in mock concern. "There's absolutely no need. A special place in my heart will always belong to you. But it's gratifying to see that one is held in such high regard." The corners of his eyes crinkled with laughter.

"Stuff it, Longdon. Obviously, that conk on the head didn't knock any sense into you. Or respect for that matter."

"Oh, but I have the utmost respect for *you*, Oliver. You must know that."

Emmeline gave him a quelling look. "Enough" she mouthed.

Gregory patted her hand. "You're quite right, Emmy." He attempted to school his features into a serious expression.

"Sorry," she offered Burnell with a small shrug of resignation.

He made a dismissive gesture with his hand. "It's all right. You're not his keeper." He shifted his gaze to Gregory again. "Why did someone decide to bash your head in? What have you done?"

Gregory put a hand to his chest. "*I* haven't done anything, Oliver. I resent the tone of the question. There are desperate scoundrels in the world, if you haven't noticed."

The superintendent snorted. "Yes, I count you and Delahunt among them."

Roger sniffed. "I don't know about you, Greg, but I'm deeply offended."

"I'll get to your story shortly," Burnell told him. "First, Longdon will regale us with his dubious exploits of the day. Why don't you start by telling us about the Pink Courtesan?"

Gregory eyes widened in surprise and his mouth twitched into an impish grin. He sketched a little salute at the superintendent. "Top marks for your detective skills. Don't tell me that she's been sharing her favors, Oliver?"

"*Superintendent Burnell*," the older man growled through gritted teeth.

Gregory gave him a cheeky wink. "Certainly, *Superintendent* Burnell, if you insist. But it's quite silly to stand on ceremony, when you're among friends."

"Longdon." Burnell's voice trembled with a note of warning.

Gregory raised his hands in surrender. "All right. Don't get your knickers in a twist."

"Who is this woman?" Emmeline asked, trying to tamp down the jealousy swelling in her chest.

"The Pink Courtesan is not a woman," Gregory explained. "She's a flawless fifteen-carat, oval-shaped fancy vivid pink diamond ring. She's surrounded by white diamonds."

"Oh, I see." This news was unsettling. She had hoped his escapade with Tarasova's ruby necklace was a minor relapse. She would hold him to his promise to walk the straight and narrow. Wasn't their marriage worth more than any jewel?

To preempt another outburst from the superintendent, Gregory prudently launched into an account of his decision to search Jardine's flat again and his discovery—and loss— of the Pink Courtesan. Roger became very still, keeping his counsel throughout Gregory's narrative. With each word, though, the blood drained from Roger's cheeks.

"Naturally, you had no idea that you'd find the diamond in Jardine's flat?"

Gregory crossed his heart with two fingers and held them aloft. "Upon my word of honor…"

"Honor?" Burnell snapped. "That's a contradiction in terms where you're concerned."

"You wound me, *Oliver*. I don't know how I'll get over your heartless cruelty."

"Lump it. If you've quite finished, shut your mouth and listen to what I found out about your friend Jardine and that bloody diamond with the ridiculous name."

Emmeline rested her elbows on her knees and leaned toward the superintendent, eagerly devouring everything he had learned from Terence Dunbar about Sebastian Jardine's true identity as the scion of a notorious Mafia family in Sicily; to his "rebirth" in Malta; how he and his mother had returned to England; and, finally, to the circumstances surrounding his hiring by Interpol and his resignation. The only point at which Burnell hesitated was when it came to Jardine's friendship with Swanbeck. His gaze lingered on Emmeline's face.

She drew in a sharp breath and sat up straighter. Gregory draped his arm around her shoulders and murmured, "Don't worry, darling." By the inflection in his tone, she could tell that he was just as shocked as she was by this revelation.

Her eye fell on the coffee table and the box containing the locket from Swanbeck. With a hand that was not quite steady, she reached out and scooped it up.

She cleared her throat. "There will never be a good time to tell all of you about this." She removed the lid and lifted the locket out of the box. It swung back and forth between her fingers like a pendulum.

She felt Gregory stiffen beside her. "Where did you get that, Emmy?" Two vertical lines had etched themselves between his brows.

Her mouth went dry. She had dreaded this moment. Wordlessly, she passed Swanbeck's note to him and waited. It didn't take long.

He winced, when his head shot up. The paper crackled, as he flapped it in the air. "Why didn't you tell me about this?"

She found her voice at last and gestured at him with her

hand. "This is why. I knew you would react this way."

"Can you blame me?" he countered.

"Longdon, what does it say?" Burnell interrupted.

Gregory tossed the note across the coffee table in disgust. "Read it for yourself."

"*My dearest Emmeline,*" the superintendent murmured aloud. "*A small token to remember me by. I have to go away for a while. Think of this as adieu, rather than goodbye. I will never forget you. Or Longdon. All my love, Alastair.*"

When Burnell had finished, he handed it to Finch. "When did you receive it?" he interrogated Emmeline.

She swallowed hard. "I found it in my hotel room in Edinburgh over the summer, after everything that happened with…with the Royces."

"You mean you've had it all this time?" The superintendent's hands curled into tight balls on his knees. She could see that he was making a supreme effort to keep his temper in check.

She nodded. "I'd forgotten about the locket. It was stuffed at the back of a drawer." She slid a sideways glance at Gregory. "I don't know why I kept it. But today," she persevered, "it struck me that it might give us a clue to where Swanbeck is hiding or at least where he has been. Gregory, please." She touched his hand lightly. "Take a look at the locket. It's not something you would find here in the U.K. Of all of us, you're the one who is an expert when it comes to jewelry."

His eyes still simmered with cinnamon fire. However, he took the locket from her. He rolled it in the palm of his hand, running his finger over the filigree details. It was delicate and light, gossamer strands of finely spun silver creating a floral design. With his thumb nail, he flicked open the latch and peered at the empty interior. He snapped it shut with a soft *click.*

"Well?" Burnell prompted impatiently.

Gregory eased his body back against the sofa. He smoothed down the corners of his mustache. "In my opinion, it's an antique piece from Malta or Gozo. The Maltese have a long tradition dating back to the Phoenicians. They spread the technique throughout the Mediterranean and beyond of weaving fine threads of gold or silver together in intricate motifs."

Burnell pounded one fist against his open palm. "Malta again."

The adrenaline began to sluice through Emmeline's veins. "I was right." She couldn't keep the triumph from ringing in her voice. "I think we're on to something." Then she told them about Swanbeck's ships being registered in Valletta and the run around she had gotten when she called the High Commission and Ministry of Foreign Affairs. Swanbeck had to be in Malta. At last, a solid lead.

She gave Gregory a gentle peck on the cheek, which he accepted a bit stiffly. Apparently, he was still smarting over her belated disclosure about the locket. He had no right to be standoffish, after all the secrets he had kept—and continued to keep—about his past.

"Finch, I suggest you inform Halliday and the Boy Wonder about our suspicions that Swanbeck is in Malta or at least was at some point in the last five months," Burnell recommended. "Also, check whether any flights from Malta landed at Heathrow around the time Jardine was killed."

Finch nodded. "Jardine's name wasn't on any of the passenger lists we reviewed thus far, but he could have been traveling under an alias. Now that we've narrowed it down to one destination of origin, perhaps we'll get lucky. We'll start with Air Malta and check some of the private charter services as well. Excuse me." He took out his mobile as he rose and stepped into the hall to make the call.

The superintendent propped his elbows on the armrests

and steepled his fingers over his protruding stomach. His gaze locked on Roger. "You've been very quiet, Delahunt."

Roger gave him a watery smile. "I was just following your instructions, Superintendent. I'm merely a bystander. But I'm quite appalled by everything that I've heard today. Shocked, really."

Burnell returned his smile, but there was something dangerous about it. "Why don't I believe you?"

"An inherent lack of faith in your fellow man?" Roger ventured.

"Very droll. I don't like coincidences." He jerked his chin at Gregory. "Ask your mate Longdon, he'll tell you. Coincidences set my mind to thinking. And you're a walking coincidence. A magnet for mayhem, in fact. Like this afternoon. Did you attack Longdon?"

These words hung upon the air.

"I didn't hit Greg," Roger replied, his tone soft. His eyes drifted to Emmeline. "You must believe me. I didn't take the diamond either."

"You know a lot more about Jardine and Swanbeck than you've shared to this point," Burnell pressed. "Out with it, before we have another body on our hands and on your conscience."

Roger's smile slipped slightly. His glance fluttered between Burnell and Gregory.

"There's no blood on my hands, so don't try to stitch me up for Seb's murder."

"No one's trying to frame you, Delahunt. All we want is the truth."

He ignored the superintendent and directed his comments to Gregory. "You should have listened to me and walked away. The *truth* is Seb was nobody's friend, especially not yours. Just leave it that."

Gregory's brow creased in annoyance. "We can't. A

man's been murdered and unless the culprit is caught, he or she may kill again. Aside from that disturbing prospect, I can't rest easy until Swanbeck is no longer a threat to my wife." His tone was even, but it held a steely edge.

Roger raked a hand through his sandy-blond hair and surged to his feet. "Fine. How do you think Swanbeck found you again?" he spat back.

CHAPTER 23

Villiers was surprised when the car drew to a stop in front of St. Martin-in-the-Fields, the neoclassical Anglican church built in Portland stone at the northeast corner of Trafalgar Square.

His captor put the blinkers on and flicked his gaze to the rearview mirror. "This is where you get out, Mr. Deputy Director."

"Church? You must be joking," Villiers scoffed. "I'm an atheist. I avoid church like the plague." He folded his arms over his chest and glared mulishly at his captor.

The younger man swiveled around slowly. He rested the muzzle of his gun atop the corner of his seat. Villiers heard a muted *click* as the fellow drew back the safety catch.

"Today is the day you find religion." He made a brusque gesture with the gun. "Out."

Without warning, the door was flung open. A large hand reached in and seized Villiers by the lapels, dragging him out onto the pavement.

His captor chuckled and called to him, "This is my associate Mr.—Jones. He's going to escort you into the church. Just to make sure you don't stray."

Mr. Jones, one paw clamped in a vice-like grip around

Villiers's arm, slammed the door with his free hand. They watched as the car eased into the traffic and then disappeared around a corner.

Jones, a slim man in his thirties with chestnut hair and icy blue eyes, roughly drew Villiers toward him so that there was no space between their bodies. The muzzle of a gun dug uncomfortably into Villiers's rib, but he was damned if he'd give the chap the satisfaction of seeing him flinch.

Jones's warm breath tickled his ear as he whispered, "I'd advise against any heroics." He flashed a malicious grin and leaned his weight against the gun, pressing it harder. "You're too old for a start and I can't answer for the consequences. If you try to run, I *will* shoot you. I don't have any qualms about it. In fact, I'll quite enjoy it."

Villiers had no doubt that this was an utterly sincere statement. He shot a glance to his left and right, calculating his options. There were too many people in the vicinity. He couldn't risk an innocent bystander getting hurt or worse, killed.

He sniffed. "It seems I'm left with very little choice," he retorted, each word infused with disdain.

"Good. Now that we understand each other," Jones went on cheerfully, "We're going to walk up the steps and into the church. I will turn you over to another associate and we will never see each other again."

Villiers snapped his fingers in mock disappointment. "I'm going to miss your sparkling wit."

"Remember what I said," Jones growled as he tugged Villiers up the flight of stone steps.

"You mean your charming threat? How could I forget? It was so affectionate and sentimental."

Jones gave him a shove that nearly caused Villiers to tumble forward. "Move, old man, before I rip out your tongue."

As he recovered his footing, Villiers murmured out of the

side of his mouth, "Temper, temper. I suggest cutting back on the caffeine. It would do wonders for your nerves."

Jones grunted and wrenched Villiers's arm, dragging him across the imposing Corinthian portico comprised of eight columns and over the threshold into the church.

Although Villiers was not a religious man, he did have an appreciation for art. His breath caught in his throat and his eyes marveled at the elegant details on the barrel-vaulted ceiling. The creamy plaster panels were decorated with cherubim, clouds, shells, and scroll work. The church was airy and filled with light.

Their footsteps echoed off the polished parquet floor as they sauntered up the main aisle. As it was a Wednesday, there was no lunchtime concert taking place. Only a few people were scattered about the church, their voices a low buzz mingling with the reverent, almost serene, hush enveloping them. Some wandered around admiring the architecture. Others sat in the pews, their heads bent, hands folded, seeking solace in prayer.

They halted about halfway up the aisle. "Sit," Jones commanded, placing a hand on Villiers's shoulder and pressing him down onto the pew. He plastered a disingenuous smile on his lips and hissed, "My colleague will join you in a minute. Stand up and I will put a bullet in your knee."

Villiers matched his smile. "I would say that parting is such sweet sorrow, but then I'd be lying and stealing from Shakespeare. And I would never dare to sully the Bard's genius by wasting his words on a common thug like you."

He was pleased to see that this slight hit home. Jones started to raise his hand as if to strike him.

Villiers wagged a finger at him. "Ah, ah. I wouldn't if I were you. We are in the Lord's house after all. He would take great offense and hurl a lightning bolt at you through the beautiful ceiling. That would be a pity."

Jones curled his fingers into a tight ball, spun on his heel, and stalked off.

Villiers permitted himself a chuckle.

"Like father, like son, I see," a male voice whispered over his right shoulder. "Obviously, Longdon gets his glib tongue from you. Or should I call him by the name he was born with? Toby Crenshaw."

Villiers drew in a ragged breath. His skin prickled with apprehension.

Longdon. Toby Crenshaw. How did it come out? his brain screamed. A swirl of questions hurtled around his mind in rapid succession. Acheson was the only one who knew. But he swore he'd never reveal the truth. Did he trade the information to get Special Branch off his back? None of us ever knew what we would do, until we were pushed too far. And yet, Acheson was scrupulously honest. He was not the type to betray such an explosive secret.

All these thoughts assailed Villiers in a matter of seconds, leaving him dazed and more than a little off kilter. But when he spun around to confront his accuser, he had schooled his features into an impassive expression and slowed his breathing. Only an icy unease settled upon his chest, making his heart pound against his ribcage.

"You have a rather vivid imagination. I'm guessing you must be an author of cheap, sensational novels. Mr.—what, by the way?"

The man, who Villiers judged was of medium build and must be in his late forties, had deep-set eyes the color of jet. He didn't think anyone's eyes could be darker or more watchful than Emmeline Kirby.

Damn the woman, Villiers cursed. *Why did Toby have to fall in love with* her? He dug his fingers into his knees. *All of this is her fault. She never stops asking questions.*

The man's voice jarred him back to the present. "You

nearly convinced me with your patrician, stiff-upper-lip scorn. It had just the right amount of holier-than-thou contempt. However"—he rested his elbow on the back of the pew and leaned toward Villiers—"I *know* the truth. And soon the world will find out that the deputy director of MI5 has a son, who is a notorious international jewel thief." He waited to let these words sink in. "Unless you do exactly as I say."

Villiers sniffed. "Blackmail, really? How cliché," he replied phlegmatically. "I'm amazed that you think that anyone will believe your fanciful tale."

"I wouldn't take this so lightly. Imagine the whispers that will hurtle around Whitehall, when it gets about that you and your son may have betrayed the country's secrets." He clucked his tongue. "Naughty, naughty. Remember, I have nothing to lose and everything to gain. On the other hand, it's your forty-year career that will go up in smoke. *Poof.*" He snapped his fingers. "Gone in the blink of an eye."

Villiers clapped his hands. "Oh, bravo. I must say that was good. The snapping fingers added the perfect dramatic touch." He sighed. "But it has failed to frighten me."

"Shut up and listen, Villiers," the man retorted, his patience at an end. "You have seventy-two hours to see that Alastair Swanbeck's assets are unfrozen and to wipe his record clean…"

"*Swanbeck,*" Villiers cut across him, his voice trembling with fury. "You're mad. Swanbeck deserves to rot in a cell for the rest of his miserable life. It's too bad we don't have hanging anymore."

"I'd have a care what you say about Mr. Swanbeck. He holds your career and the lives of your son and his nosy wife in his hands. I assure you he'd like nothing more than to destroy all of you. But he's mellowed in the past few months. Therefore, he's willing to give you a reprieve, *if* he gets his money back."

Villiers snorted. "Pull the other leg. You really expect me to believe that Swanbeck will slink off into anonymity?" He waved his hand dismissively. "Please. It beggars the imagination. I'd have to be as mad as old King George to absolve Swanbeck of his crimes. There are so many that I've lost count. Besides, I could care less what happens to Longdon or Emmeline Kirby."

The man's mouth curved into a lupine leer. "I must compliment you on your bravado, Villiers. You're being a fool if you think Mr. Swanbeck wouldn't hesitate to…"

"To kill, maim, extort, steal, smuggle?" Villiers suggested. "Mind you, Swanbeck is desperate and on the run. I suppose he's willing to give anything a try." He paused. "Tell him I'm not interested in his offer." He stood up and peered down his nose at the man. "I'm not for sale." His tone dripped with venom.

"I wouldn't put Mr. Swanbeck to the test." The man stood up as well. "He's a man of his word."

Villiers tossed his head back and laughed. "A man of his word? How terribly amusing. Honor is an alien concept to Swanbeck. He's as slithery and spineless as a snake."

"You'll regret it to your grave, if you underestimate him." He buttoned his suit jacket and leaned in toward Villiers. "You have seventy-two hours to think over Mr. Swanbeck's generous offer." He slipped out of the pew and started to walk away. Then, he turned around. "I nearly forgot. Silly of me, really. Mr. Swanbeck has one other condition."

"Oh, do tell. I'm fascinated."

"He wants the Blue Angel. It's a deal breaker, I'm afraid. No diamond, then you all go down in flames. So don't be hasty about your decision. Why don't you toddle off home and have cozy chat with your son and daughter-in-law? All of you are intelligent. Mr. Swanbeck is confident you'll see it his way in the end. Check the papers tomorrow and you'll see a sample of what's in store, if you don't agree to his terms."

The man spread his arms wide in a gesture that encompassed the entire church. "You're in the right place to seek divine guidance. Maybe He will endow you with the wisdom of Solomon and you'll see the light."

Villiers was rooted to the spot. He gnashed his teeth as he watched the man amble down the aisle and pass beneath the magnificent Walker organ. With its 3,000 pipes, it was considered the finest organ in London.

The organ came to life and music filled the church. But all Villiers could hear was a funeral march.

It was his own.

CHAPTER 24

Gregory's gaze never left Roger's face. After an interval, he cleared his throat. The sound was terribly jarring in the tense silence that had closed in around them.

"What are you talking about—Jardine and Swanbeck?" His tone was even and neutral, but Emmeline could see the muscle pulsating along his jaw.

"Oh, for God's sake," Roger exploded. "Don't tell me you didn't suspect. How do you think Swanbeck tracked you down?"

"I…I thought Ronnie whispered her sweet poison in Swanbeck's ear out of spite because Emmy and I were together again." Emmeline reached for his hand and gave it a squeeze.

Roger huffed a bitter laugh. "You're half right. Seb and Ronnie played you for a fool from the beginning."

Gregory stiffened, his brow puckering in confusion. "Seb *and* Ronnie?"

Emmeline exchanged a look with Burnell. The stunned expression on his face likely mirrored her own.

Ronnie? her brain railed. *The infamous Veronica Cabot. When would they ever be free of her ghost?*

"Yes," Roger hissed, "they hatched up the scheme between them."

"But why? We'd never crossed paths until—" Gregory broke off as he sifted through his memories.

"Until Monte. It all started that night in Monte."

Emmeline frowned. "Monte?"

"Monte Carlo," Gregory elaborated.

"This has always been about the Pink Courtesan," Roger continued.

"That cursed diamond again," Burnell muttered.

Roger turned to him. "You're right about that. The Pink Courtesan has certainly proven to be a curse for old Greg."

The superintendent rounded on Gregory. "You stole it, didn't you? This bloody mess is nothing but a long-running feud among thieves, isn't it?"

For the first time since Roger made his shocking declaration about Jardine and Veronica Cabot, formerly Longdon, Gregory's mouth curved into a bemused smile.

"No, Oliver. I hate to shatter your illusions, but I didn't steal the alluring pink minx. I won her. Fair and square."

Burnell's brows shot up and his eyes widened in disbelief. Clearly, he had not—nor had anyone else for that matter— anticipated this answer.

"What do you mean you 'won' it?"

Gregory crossed one leg over the other. "Exactly that. Lady Fortune was on my side that chilly New Year's Day in 2000 at the casino in Monte. I started off playing roulette but watching the wheel spin round and round soon became tedious."

"I wouldn't know," the superintendent murmured irritably. "I've never been a gambling man nor set foot in *Monte*. I don't see the fascination."

"Monte is always larger than life. One is quickly seduced by the ambiance," Gregory observed, "particularly when the champagne continues to flow, the stakes are high, and the pot keeps growing before your eyes. One thinks that with the next roll of the dice or draw of a card, 'I can have it all.'" He wagged a finger in warning. "That's where the danger lies. That's the instant when people throw caution to the wind and end up losing it all."

"But not you, of course," Burnell remarked, his voice laced with irony.

Gregory flashed a smile at him. "Oliver, I'm disciplined. I never lose control, and know when to stop. Therefore, I always win."

"Hmph" Burnell grunted. He flapped a hand at him. "Just get on with it. We're not interested in your philosophy of gambling."

"As you wish. A gentleman had just left the table where a brisk game of Vingt-et-Un was taking place. I drifted over and took his seat. There were seven other punters. Two women and five men. A young fellow—an Italian, I think, or he could have been Spanish—had only a small stack of chips in front of him. It was evident he had been losing badly. He was knocking back martinis like a man in the desert gulping water. I don't know how many he'd already had by the time I joined the game. His eyes were a bit glazed, and his brow was damp with perspiration, but he stubbornly played on.

"As usual, the cards were on my side that night. I won three rounds and, in the process, wiped out the poor chap's paltry winnings. He didn't have a single euro to his name. I felt rather sorry for him. I thought he'd finally give up and walk away. He opted to stay. He wanted to win back his money. He begged me to play one more round. To entice me, he drew out of his pocket the Pink Courtesan and placed it on the table." Gregory smiled at the memory. "The offer was too tempting. So we played. And he lost."

"No surprise with the diamond as the prize," Finch

mumbled. "Did you cheat?"

Emmeline sucked in her breath, outraged on her husband's behalf. But he merely chuckled and patted her hand. "A gentleman never cheats, Finch."

"I hadn't realized we were talking about a gentleman," the sergeant countered.

"Your humor must be an acquired taste. Isn't that so, Oliver?"

"Both of you put a cork in it," Burnell reprimanded. Then he asked Gregory, "So this fool handed over the diamond and sulked off to lick his wounds in private?"

"Far from it. He cornered me in the bar. He told me the Pink Courtesan was an heirloom of sorts and he couldn't allow it out of the family. He was virtually in tears thanks to all the alcohol he had guzzled. He was babbling on about family honor. Frankly, he wasn't making a great deal of sense. He pleaded with me to return the diamond. He said he would pay anything. All I had to do was to name my price.

"I asked him how he intended to pay me, when he had lost all his money. He gave some vague answer that's not even worth repeating. In the end, I took pity on the poor chap and gave him back the Pink Courtesan."

"*You what?*" Burnell bristled and leaped to his feet. "You don't seriously expect us to believe you turned over a diamond worth..."

"It sold for nearly thirty-three million pounds earlier this year at Christie's in Geneva," Gregory informed him matter-of-factly. He gave a nonchalant shrug of his shoulders. "What can I say? I keep up with the latest news."

The gathered company gaped at him, as each tried to digest the nugget of information he had just tossed out for consumption.

"Everything is quite true, I assure you. I'm a man of principle, after all."

Emmeline was the first to recover. "I always knew you were. I believe you, darling," she said loyally and chided herself for doubting him earlier. She gave him a kiss and then fixed her eye on the other men in turn, daring any of them to say another word against him.

Burnell plopped back down in the wing chair and shook his head, flabbergasted.

Roger broke the silence. "Seb didn't know any of this."

"No one did," Gregory replied.

Roger grimaced. "If only he had, Greg. Your misguided sense of decency hammered the nail in your coffin. You were doomed the minute the Pink Courtesan crossed your palm. And now, by extension, Emmeline has been drawn into this cauldron of vendetta. Seb ultimately turned against Swanbeck too. And all because of that bloody diamond. The vicious cycle won't end until you and your wife are dead."

❧❧❧

Villiers, his blood like ice water, staggered out of St. Martin's-in-the-Fields church in a daze. He blinked as his eyes became accustomed to the sunshine. He was disturbed to see that his hands were trembling. He thrust them deep into his coat pockets. His mind was a jumbled morass of errant thoughts.

He couldn't see a way out. Everything he had worked for all his life. *Gone.* And Toby would be dragged down with him. A voice in the back of his mind—his conscience? did he even have one?—questioned whether Toby hadn't been condemned from the day he was born, simply because he was the son of a man whose career at MI5 meant more to him than a family. Villiers shook his head. This was not the time for regrets and self-recrimination. The past couldn't be undone. It was the *past.* And yet, it made the present a living nightmare for all concerned.

In the midst of this churning mental turmoil, Villiers was cognizant of the fact that he was not overly upset about Emmeline, although she faced the same threats. He told himself dispassionately that he was not totally devoid of feeling. It's not like he wanted to see the woman dead. He simply wished she was out of the picture—forever. Her intrusive inquisitiveness had only served to fan the flames and bring things out into the open. She, and the rest of the Fourth Estate for that matter, failed to grasp that it was far better to keep the public in the dark. The truth was best left to the professionals like himself, who understood all the nuances and could handle the consequences. Where did her expertise lie? She lobbed hand grenades without giving a damn about where they landed or the collateral damage they inflicted.

"Sir," a familiar male voice tore him from his vexing reverie.

Villiers whirled round when he felt a hand on his arm. He curled one hand into a fist, prepared to strike a blow if necessary.

His eyes widened in surprise and his body relaxed, when he saw Philip standing before him, a flat cap pulled low over his brow to hide his face.

"Acheson," he whispered, as he clutched his sleeve in relief. "Where the devil have you been the past two days?"

Philip cast a furtive glance around him. "Sir, we're rather exposed here on the stairs." He took Villiers by the elbow. "I suggest we go back inside the church or start moving."

Villiers stared at him transfixed. He tried to shake off Philip's hand. "Swanbeck knows."

Philip's blond brows knit together. "Knows what?"

Villiers ignored the question. "You're the *only* one who knew the truth. The only one." He gathered fistfuls of Philip's jacket. "You promised to keep your mouth shut. You scheming liar. I never should have believed you." He shook Philip so violently that his teeth rattled. "You're nothing but an opportunist. All you cared about was saving your own skin."

Philip clamped his fingers around Villiers's wrists and finally managed to loosen his grip. "Steady on, sir. You're upset. You're not making sense."

Villiers took a step toward him, his face inches from Philip. "You'll pay for this." His voice dripped ice. "That's a promise."

CHAPTER 25

Roger paced in front of the fireplace liked a caged lion. At last, he collapsed in the chair across from Gregory. "I was hoping you'd never found out. I wanted to clean things up. To make up for…" His sentence trailed off and he shrugged. "You helped me out of my spot of bother. I wanted to return the favor."

"You know the saying about a friend in need," Gregory murmured. After a pause, he said, "You owe me—us—nothing but the truth. Tell us the rest of it. Every detail about Seb, Ronnie, and Swanbeck. We're wandering about blind. What are we up against?"

Roger gave a resigned nod of his head. "Right. Seb was at the casino the night you won the Pink Courtesan. He had been following the other chap, who happened to be his cousin, Marco Cannizzaro."

Emmeline and Gregory exchanged a weary look.

"Cannizzaro's father, Luca, was the one who had murdered his father. As the superintendent told us. Since Seb was at university, he'd been gathering information on Cannizzaro and the family. He was very patient. It took him years to plot his plan of revenge. Seb found out that the Cannizzaros had moved to Malta a few years after he and his mother had fled to England. Luca attempted to sanitize the family's image, but it was only on the surface. Suffice it to say the Mafia decided to expand its influence beyond Sicily and Luca found Malta to be a tax haven ripe for the picking. Today, it operates an online gambling network that launders its proceeds through a series of companies based in Malta.

"Luca bought politicians, body and soul, ensuring that the authorities never interfered in the family's business. He pushed his middle son, Antonio, to become a politician, further cementing the Cannizzaros' hold on the government. The oldest son, Bruno, entered the family business. He was Luca's most trusted adviser. Your friend Marco, the youngest son, was the wild one. He was a playboy. His only interests were women and gambling."

"How is this connected with Seb and the diamond?" Gregory prompted.

"Marco, fool that he was, took the diamond to Monte Carlo hoping to make a fortune for himself by selling it to a high-roller. The only problem was the lure of the tables proved too strong and he started gambling in the afternoon before he even had a chance to make a pitch to anyone. His money ran out very quickly and he was forced to use the Pink Courtesan as collateral. He flashed the diamond about to make everyone think he could pay his tab. He continued to lose. You came across him at that stage, Greg.

"What you didn't know is that Seb had followed Marco to Monte Carlo. He somehow found out that Marco had the diamond with him and was planning to it get back, by force if necessary. Seb was in the casino. He was outraged when Marco so casually turned over the diamond to you. From that moment, his cousin was forgotten and you became a target of his hatred. In his view, he had been cheated out of what was rightfully his yet again and you were just as despicable as the Cannizzaros.

"The bit I'm not clear on is how Seb became entangled with Ronnie, but they were together at that point." Roger broke off and held Gregory's gaze. "I'm sorry."

Gregory's jaw tightened. "Not your fault." His tone was clipped. "Go on. Don't hold back on the gory details."

Emmeline rested her hand on his knee without uttering a word. He slipped his arm around her shoulders and drew her to him. The last thing she wanted to hear about was that scheming witch Veronica Cabot, but the woman was dead and couldn't hurt them anymore. She leaned into Gregory and listened to the rest of Roger's story.

"Anyway," Roger went on, "Seb and Ronnie hatched a two-pronged attack to get close to you all with the goal of getting the Pink Courtesan. They found out your name and then it began. Seb seemingly bumped into you in the bar by chance and struck up a conversation. He could be charming when he wanted to be. You agreed to meet up back in England. You'll recall that although he lived in Cambridge, he often came up to London. And that's how your"—he hesitated—"your friendship began."

Gregory nodded his assent. "I can't believe I was taken in by all of it. I never suspected a thing."

"Yes, well." Roger coughed as his gaze slithered over to Emmeline. "Now, we come to Ronnie."

"You don't have to tiptoe around the subject," she said briskly, as she tossed her chin in the air. "I met the viper back in the spring. I experienced first-hand her vicious games."

Burnell and Finch squirmed and studiously avoided glancing at her, as they remembered the events that had taken place at the Royal Devon hotel in Torquay. Gregory's eyes clouded with pain and guilt. Emmeline knew he would never be able to forgive himself for what happened with Veronica Cabot. It had taken Emmeline a long time to trust him again, but she had made peace with it all. She knew Gregory loved her. She trusted him. She had to. A marriage without trust is worthless.

Roger smiled at her. "She didn't hold a candle to you, Emmeline. That's the truth." She inclined her head at the compliment.

"Tell me," he lowered his voice conspiratorially, "with that temper of yours, did you scratch her eyes out?"

A burst of laughter erupted from Emmeline lightening the mood in the living room. "I nearly did," she admitted sheepishly, as heat suffused her cheeks.

Roger winked at her. "My money would have been on you. Ronnie certainly gave you just cause."

"All right, Delahunt," Burnell growled impatiently. "Get on with it. We all know what the oversexed Lady Cabot was like. Why did Jardine take you into his confidence?"

"Seb and I were old friends. I would run into him from time to time. He wanted someone to listen to him without making judgments. He needed an outlet for his anger. That made him eager to tell me the details of his evil plot. Meanwhile, he was completely unaware that Greg was a mate. I flattered Seb by marveling at his ingenuity and made him promise to keep me posted. He thought I was a kindred spirit, so he did."

Burnell shook his head. He was obviously disgusted by the layers of deception. "Is there much more to this saga?"

"I'll give you the abridged version in deference to Emmeline. A month after Seb crossed paths with Greg in Monte, Ronnie made her move on him in London." He coughed. "Things heated up quickly and by that June Greg and Ronnie were married. It was far from a conventional marriage. Ronnie took to disappearing for months at a time and then she would return, as if they had never been apart. During those absences, she and Seb used to meet to discuss strategy. They were frustrated that they still hadn't been able to find the diamond. This put a strain on their romantic relationship and eventually they parted ways."

"That's probably when Ronnie started looking for bigger fish to fry and sunk her claws into Sir Frederick Cabot," Gregory interjected.

"I'm not certain about the timing, but it fits," Roger replied. "Seb regretted ever getting involved with Ronnie..."

Gregory huffed a bitter laugh. "Ronnie was a typhoon. She left a trail of regret and misery in her wake."

"What Seb regretted the most," Roger continued, "is that he ever told her about the Pink Courtesan. It was too much of a prize. She was willing to do anything to get her greedy paws on it. She thought if you were banged up in the nick, as your wife she would gain control of all the marital assets and have all the time in the world to search for it. That's why she set the coppers on you in Rome. The only problem was you scarpered and here we are today."

"What I don't understand," Emmeline ventured, when he had finished, "is how Jardine managed to get the diamond back and what Swanbeck has to do with any of this."

Gregory rubbed his head tenderly. "My head would like to know who snatched the Pink Courtesan from me for the second time in my life."

"Once really, Greg, since you willingly returned it to Cannizzaro in Monte," Roger corrected. Then to the group, he said, "As the superintendent told us, Seb had been chums with Swanbeck since university. They had lost touch for a while, though. Swanbeck suddenly renewed the friendship, when Seb went to Lyon to work for Interpol. His time at the agency was mutually beneficial for both of them. Seb dug up information on the Cannizzaros' illicit businesses. He wanted to hit them where it hurt. Swanbeck played on his obsession for revenge and, when it suited him, threw Seb an occasional bone about the Cannizzaros. In exchange, Seb felt it was only fair to warn him about investigations that Interpol intended to launch against him. Swanbeck convinced him that these probes had no merit. That's how he has been able to stay one step ahead of the authorities all these years.

"Swanbeck finally persuaded Seb to come and work for him. After a year, things started to sour between them. Seb was shocked to discover that Swanbeck had been doing business with Luca Cannizzaro for years. He was livid, when he realized that Swanbeck had been using him to safeguard his and the Cannizzaros' business interests. Overnight, Seb became a loose cannon that had to be dealt with quickly. Seb anticipated that Swanbeck would try to kill him, so he preempted him by faking his own death.

"Being a dead man had certain advantages. He never had to look over his shoulder and he could focus on his vendetta without distractions. When he heard about the sale of the Pink Courtesan earlier this year, he thought the day had finally arrived to punish Greg for selling the diamond to which Seb considered he had no right in the first place. Imagine his horror when he found out that Swanbeck was the one who had bought the diamond. Consumed with rage he decided to kill two birds with one stone. He prostrated himself at Swanbeck's altar, seemingly seeking forgiveness. Swanbeck is no fool. He was skeptical about his desire for a rapprochement, particularly when he thought Seb was dead. But Swanbeck adhered to the philosophy of keeping your friends close and your enemies even closer. In his view, Seb was both.

"However, Seb had an ace up his sleeve. As a gesture of goodwill, he served up Greg on a platter for Swanbeck to feast on. He told him that Greg was the anonymous seller of the Pink Courtesan and had set out to bilk him out of as much money as possible. This proved to be a master stroke. Seb was welcomed back into the fold. While Swanbeck was distracted with Greg, Seb bided his time and meticulously gathered evidence to bring down his former friend. He also told me that he had recovered the Pink Courtesan. He didn't say how he had managed it, though. Seb was on his way back from his last trip to Malta, when he was murdered at Heathrow. And that's the whole sordid tale."

Roger plopped down in the chair again, apparently exhausted after regaling them with the torturous machinations of Jardine's revenge plot.

Burnell stroked his beard meditatively. "Hmm. Eye-opening and disturbing. But you haven't told us quite everything, have you?"

Roger raised a sandy brow in askance. "I shared all the relevant facts. I would have thought it's more than enough to be getting on with. I hope you chaps at Scotland Yard don't expect me to do your jobs for you." He offered the superintendent an ingratiating smile.

Burnell stared back at him stone-faced. "Where is Jardine's bag? And what did you intend to do with its contents?"

೧౬౧

Philip didn't recognize the man standing before him. Never had he seen Villiers in such an agitated state. The man had always been cool, aloof, and self-assured. Now, his nostrils flared with barely controlled rage and his eyes held a deadly glint.

"Sir," Philip tried again, his tone soothing. "I assure you I haven't breathed a word to anyone about your…connection to Longdon."

"Then how did Swanbeck find out?" Villiers snarled.

"I have absolutely no idea." Out of the corner of his eye, Philip was aware of the constant bustle around them. "We can't stay here. You must realize that." He gestured with his chin. "Why don't we go across the road to the Caffè Nero?"

It was his favorite haunt. The coffeehouse was opposite Trafalgar Square and a stone's throw from the Foreign Office. He would often nip round in the afternoon for an espresso or cappuccino. It would be a risk since Special Branch was after him, but he had to get Villiers out of the way.

Villiers didn't budge.

"Sir, please. I realize you're upset, but you'll only make matters worse if you carry on like this. I am not the enemy. We're on the same side."

"Not from where I'm standing," Villiers shot back.

Philip tugged his cap lower over his forehead. "Whether you like or not, at this stage we're the only ones who can help each other. You're going to have to trust me."

Villiers's probing gaze raked Philip's face, but there was a subtle change in his demeanor. *Please let me have broken through*, Philip urged silently.

Villiers finally relented. "I'm left with no choice," he grumbled.

He thrust his hands deep into his pockets and stalked off down the steps. Without turning around, he called, "Get a move on, Acheson."

CHAPTER 26

oger's flicked the tip of his tongue over his lips. All eyes in the room were riveted on him. He didn't flinch, meeting each probing gaze in turn. By the expression on his face, he was furiously trying to come up with a plausible answer.

"We're waiting, Delahunt," Burnell prompted.

Roger favored Emmeline with a smile. "Any chance of a cup of tea?" He rubbed his throat. "I'm parched after all that talking."

The superintendent turned to her and gave a curt shake of his head. Then to Roger, he said, "There are glaring omissions in your story. Fill in those gaps."

"I would have thought that you're sick of the sound of my voice by now."

"To be brutally honest, I wish our paths had never crossed." Burnell rested his elbows on his knees and leaned forward, allowing his hands to dangle loosely between them. The fierce intensity of his gaze imprisoned Roger. "But in the interest of the law and justice, I'm obliged to deal with you. I advise you to tell us the truth. It would go far better for you in the long run."

Roger slumped back. "Well, that's gratitude for you, I must say. *I* haven't done anything wrong. Swanbeck is the villain in all this." He appealed to Gregory. "You believe me, don't you?"

"To a point" was Gregory's cautious reply, an edge of wariness in his tone. "What are you hiding?"

Roger threw up his hands in surrender and sighed. "All right. It's the papers." The words were dragged out of him with great reluctance. "The bag is a treasure trove of evidence against Swanbeck."

Burnell's mouth curved into a smile. In that instant, he bore a striking resemblance to the Cheshire cat. "Ah. I'll wager it came as grave disappointment that the diamond wasn't in it. Where is the bag now?"

Roger folded his arms over his chest and replied mulishly, "In a safe place."

"I would hope so, if the material is as explosive as you say. Of course, you had every intention of turning it over to the police?"

Roger hesitated for a fraction of a second before responding. "Naturally."

"And why haven't you?" Burnell asked with a sweetness that rang false.

"Oh, you know," Roger remarked vaguely. "What with this and that, I simply didn't get around to it."

"Hmm. I see. I hope you weren't planning to blackmail Swanbeck."

Roger's features contorted into an expression of mock outrage. "It never crossed my mind."

The superintendent exchanged a skeptical look with Finch.

"That's good to hear. Because as you are aware blackmail is illegal."

Roger nodded. "And very nasty too."

Burnell smiled again. "I'm glad we agree on that point. Therefore, I assume the minute you leave from here, you'll rush out to retrieve the bag from its hiding place and then go directly to Scotland Yard. Or better yet, Finch can accompany you. Just to make sure it gets into the proper hands." He clapped the sergeant on the shoulder.

Finch grinned at Roger. "Of course, sir. Anything to protect the public."

"That's not necessary, really," Roger countered. "I'm perfectly capable of finding my own way to Scotland Yard."

"But I insist," Burnell asserted. "We wouldn't want you to get lost."

"That's hardly likely."

"We're not well-acquainted. For all I know, you could have a poor sense of direction."

"Give in gracefully, Roger," Gregory counseled. "Oliver isn't a bad sort once you get to know him."

Burnell scowled at Gregory. "*Superintendent Burnell*, for the millionth time."

⁂

Philip's eyes darted everywhere as he pushed open the door of Caffè Nero. The aroma of ground espresso beans assailed his nostrils. The floorboards creaked slightly as he and Villiers climbed the three wide, flat wooden steps and made their way past the counter to the back of the café. Philip gestured with his chin toward a table with cracked leather armchairs which had seen better days but were surprisingly comfortable. He always chose this table, when it was free because it afforded him an uninterrupted view of the door and the entire café. No one could take him unawares. It wasn't too crowded today and none of the other patrons had raised a head when they had entered, nor did anyone cast a glance in their direction. Still, it was best to be prepared for any eventualities.

"I'll get us some coffee. What would you like, sir?"

Villiers removed his trench coat and dropped heavily into one of the chairs. "A double espresso," he grunted. Then, his tone softened as he appeared to remember his manners. "Thank you, Acheson."

Philip nodded as Villiers, his jaw clenched and a scowl etched on his face, turned away to glance out the window that overlooked Admiralty Arch. Cars, taxis and other vehicles ducked in and out of the monument's shadows as they made their way along the Mall.

When Philip returned a few minutes later with their coffees, Villiers hadn't moved. Either he hadn't noticed when Philip lowered himself into the chair opposite and placed the espresso in front of him, or he was deliberately ignoring him. The man's stillness was unnerving.

Philip noisily cleared his throat.

Villiers sighed. "I'm quite aware of your presence." He tore his gaze from the window. His face was haggard. The lines bracketing his nose appeared deeper and his eyes were clouded with a mixture of worry and irritation.

"Right then." Philip settled back in his chair and lifted his cup to his lips. He took a grateful sip of his espresso and allowed it to stimulate his brain. He needed the jolt after the strain of constantly looking over his shoulder the past few days. Judging by the little Villiers had revealed thus far, there was an even bigger storm looming. He tossed back the rest of his coffee and steeled himself for what was yet to come.

The minutes stretched out as Villiers stared at him without blinking. At last, he gave a nod, as if coming to a decision reluctantly.

"Trust has never come easily to me. It's not part of my nature. And it's a luxury we can ill-afford in our business."

The words spilled out slowly. "To trust, one has to let one's guard down. It's a loss of control." He reached out for his coffee and took a long swallow before continuing. "I have always been in control." His voice petered out to a whisper.

Philip took advantage of this lull and ventured, "As John Donne wrote, 'No man is an island.' There's always an element of risk involved, but then nothing is guaranteed in life. We're in a similar position, sir, and all because of Swanbeck. We can't allow him to win. We have to fight back. Not just for us, but for the others. No matter how we stumbled into this cloak-and-dagger world, we do what we do because we believe in the law and justice and protecting society."

Villiers's mouth quirked into a crooked smile that reminded Philip of Longdon for a brief second. Then the moment was gone.

"You should have been a philosopher, Acheson."

Philip returned his smile. He was relieved that things had finally thawed. As if tiptoeing through broken glass, he broached the delicate subject of Longdon. "Sir, I didn't breathe a word to a soul about"—he pitched his voice even lower—"your relationship to Longdon. My lips have been sealed. If Swanbeck found out, it wasn't from me."

Villiers set his cup on the table. His fingers bit into his knees, clamping them so hard that his knuckles were distended. Philip could see that he was making a supreme effort to rein in his ire.

"Yes, I know that you're an honorable man," he replied gruffly. "I apologize for suggesting otherwise even for a second. I wasn't thinking clearly."

"It's not surprising. A man had just threatened not only you but your…your son and daughter-in-law."

Villiers groaned. "That woman." He rubbed a hand over his face. "That bloody woman. If it hadn't been for her and all her poking and probing where she had no right to stick her nose…" His sentence trailed off.

Philip's back stiffened at this disparaging observation about Emmeline. "Sir, none of this is Emmeline's fault." His words held a sharp tang of bitterness.

"Isn't it?" Villiers shot back, once again on edge. "If Toby hadn't entangled himself with her, he would have been safe now."

Philip leaned across the table and hissed, "Don't you dare make this about Emmeline. She's an innocent bystander in…"

"Ha." Villiers laughed, but the sound was harsh and grated on the ears. "Innocent? There's nothing innocent about Emmeline Kirby. She's cunning and calculating. She would do anything to have her byline splashed across the front page." Villiers's gaze simmered with anger. "She's a loose cannon. She fires off questions without giving a second thought about the consequences. She doesn't know the meaning of the word discretion."

Philip's blood thundered through his veins. He was outraged on Emmeline's behalf. "I wonder at your temerity. Emmeline believes in honesty and the truth. Something we tend to ignore in our business."

Villiers wagged a finger at him. "Oh no, don't play that card. You know as well as I do that sometimes we have to lie to get to the truth, which often is vile."

"I'm not denying any of that. But it's no justification for your comments about Emmeline. She's a good journalist with a strong sense of moral integrity. You brought up the *vile* truth. Well, here it is, sir. You're a master at manipulation. You threw Longdon into Walter Swanbeck's lair. Your own son. You had no qualms about it because your mission was vital and the end justified the means. But Longdon got in over his head. You seem to forget that if it hadn't been for a twist of fate, your son and *not* Swanbeck could have ended up dead."

"Walter Swanbeck was a criminal. Toby killed him in self-defense. The world is a better place without the likes of him. I assure you no one was crying over his death," Villiers said derisively.

"No one except his son Alastair, who has made it his life's ambition to see that Longdon pays," Philip snapped. "So you see, sir, this chain of events can all be traced back to you."

"If you're trying to shame me, forget it. I make no excuses for what I did. It was all in the line of duty. I would do it all over again," Villiers retorted defiantly. "My career has been dedicated to Queen and Country. I will not allow that thug or anyone else to take everything from me."

Philip dropped his head and groaned. It was astounding how blind and self-involved this man was. He threw up his hands in resignation.

"You're utterly wrong about Emmeline." He raised a hand to prevent another scathing tirade. "But there's nothing I can say to change your mind on that subject. At the moment, we have more important things that require our attention.

"I followed you all the way from your club to St. Martin's-in-the-Fields. I saw that chap drive off with you. For once, I thanked God for London traffic. I hopped into a cab and had you in sight the entire time. You were never in any real danger. I was prepared to step in at the first sign things were getting too hot. I was in the church, hanging about in the shadows when you were talking with Swanbeck's lackey in the pew. I didn't dare get closer, though." He held Villiers's gaze. "What does Swanbeck want?"

"Only the world. That's all," Villiers scoffed. "The bloody bastard wants to have all charges against him dropped and all his assets unfrozen. Oh, and the deal breaker, apparently, is the Blue Angel."

Philip raised an eyebrow. "The Blue Angel? Igor Bronowski bought it at the Sotheby's auction over the summer. Why would Swanbeck think…" He broke off in confusion.

"Swanbeck is convinced Toby has the diamond."

"But that's ridiculous. Isn't it?"

Villiers spread his hands wide and shrugged. "Your guess is as good as mine."

Philip frowned, searching through memories of that heated auction. He had been there with Burnell and Finch. There was no way Longdon could have stolen the diamond. And yet, they were talking about Longdon. Anything *was* possible, when it came to jewels.

Villiers's sigh drew Philip back to their vexing conversation and all its ramifications.

"Swanbeck has given me seventy-two hours to meet his demands. I'm amazed at his generosity," Villiers spat facetiously. "Should I fail to comply, he promises to unleash his vengeance by announcing to the world that Toby is my son and has done little jobs for MI5 over the years. His emissary 'Mr. Jones' also said that if I wanted a preview of what is in store, I should read the papers tomorrow."

"Sounds ominous." Philip shook his head. "It's pure blackmail."

Villiers snorted. "When has blackmail ever been pure? It's all about power."

They fell into a sulky silence.

Philip was the first to break it. "Sir, you know as well as I do that you have only one choice." His voice was barely above a whisper.

Villiers pounded his open palm on the table making their demitasse cups rattle on their saucers. "No," he growled.

This outburst drew several curious looks. Philip smiled and shrugged his shoulders in apology, before addressing

Villiers again. "Sir, you must tell them."

Villiers's brows knitted together. "Them? Oh, you mean Emmeline Kirby too."

"She's his wife. This affects both of them," Philip went on reasonably.

A range of emotions chased themselves across Villiers's features. Philip waited, allowing him to gather his thoughts and make a decision.

"I can't have my reputation destroyed. I've worked too hard all these years."

His career, Philip noted sourly, *not what it would do to Longdon.*

Villiers slumped back in his chair, suddenly appearing older than his years. He swiveled his head to peer out the window. Without looking at Philip, he said, "This was a secret I thought I would take to the grave. Toby was better off without me. I was never meant to be a father."

"Nevertheless, it doesn't change the fact that he's your son," Philip pointed out. *And you watched over him from afar all these years*, he added silently.

"Hmph. That means we were both cursed."

CHAPTER 27

Finch stood up and waggled a hand at Roger. "Mr. Delahunt, I think it would be best if we were off now. The sooner we get Jardine's bag to the station, the better it will be for all concerned."

"There's no rush surely." Roger lounged back in his chair. "We can spend a few more minutes here with my dear friends Emmeline and Greg. Greg is injured, after all. I have to make certain he's all right."

Burnell rose as well. He jerked his head at the door. "Move. Longdon has a hard head. He'll be fine."

"But…"

The superintendent stopped Roger with a quelling look. "If you don't want to be charged for withholding evidence, I suggest you leave *immediately*."

Roger sighed and got to his feet. "When you put it that way, I can't refuse, can I?" Burnell shook his head. "Did anyone ever tell you, you have a charming way with words? Really you do, Superintendent. Perhaps you should consider becoming a writer."

"Let's go," Finch called from the doorway.

Roger turned to Emmeline and Gregory. "As you can see, my audience is awaiting impatiently." He bent down to brush

Emmeline's cheek with a kiss and then extended a hand to Gregory. "Take care of yourself."

"The old head's a bit sore, but I'm all right," Gregory replied. He squeezed Emmeline's hand. "Besides, I've the best nurse in the world."

Roger smiled down at her. "I don't doubt it. Lucky man."

"Stop dawdling, Delahunt," Burnell ordered.

Roger inclined his head and shuffled toward Finch, who was lingering in the hall.

Emmeline waved toward the wing chair. "Superintendent Burnell, why don't you stay a little longer? I could make some sandwiches."

Burnell opened his mouth to respond, when the doorbell rang.

Emmeline frowned. "Who could that be?"

"I'll get it." Finch's voice drifted on the air.

The superintendent resumed his seat and the three of them strained their ears to discover who was the unexpected visitor.

The low murmur of male voices mingled together and the next second Finch appeared in the doorway with Philip and Villiers in tow.

Emmeline leaped to her feet and rushed over to Philip. She threw her arms around him. "Oh, thank goodness you're all right."

"Steady on, Emmeline," he replied, gently holding her away.

Her dark eyes searched his face. "We were all so worried about you."

"As you can see, I'm fine."

"Good. I'm relieved to hear it." Then she swatted his arm, hard.

"Ouch," he said rubbing it. "What was that for?"

"For making poor Maggie worry." She pointed at the

phone and commanded, "Ring your wife this instant and tell her that you're safe."

Philip smiled. "I will in a minute. I promise. We need to discuss something first." Over the top of her head, he said to Gregory, "If I had known your wife was in a violent mood this afternoon, I would have reconsidered popping by." Then his gaze narrowed as he took in Gregory. "What happened to you?"

A ghost of a smile quivered upon Gregory's lips. "It's a long story."

Philip nodded as his gaze snaked over to Villiers. "We have a rather complicated matter to discuss with you both."

Emmeline glanced over her shoulder at Gregory, but he was peering intently at Villiers, his jaw clenched. "Where the distinguished deputy director is involved, things are always complicated *and* unpleasant."

Villiers made a rumbling sound at the back of his throat. "Believe me, I wouldn't have intruded on your domestic bliss if I had a choice."

"How jolly," Gregory quipped. He gestured toward the chair Roger had vacated. "I suppose you had better have a seat."

"We'll be going," Finch called from the doorway, his hand on Roger's arm for good measure. "I'll ring you later with an update, sir," he told Burnell.

Burnell waved them off and mouthed "Thanks."

"Superintendent Burnell," Philip said, as he proffered a hand, "do forgive me. I hadn't noticed you until just now."

"It's all right. It was quite evident you had more pressing matters on your mind." He shot a pointed look at Villiers, who inclined his head.

Villiers crossed to the chair Gregory had indicated, while Philip and Emmeline perched on the edge of the sofa.

The suffocating silence made Emmeline's skin prickle

with foreboding. She had never felt comfortable in Villiers's presence. The man was too secretive and arrogant. She felt the tension oozing from Gregory's body. He was eying Villiers warily.

Villiers exhaled a heavy sigh, as his gaze swept over Burnell. "This is a private matter. Your presence is not required, nor wanted." This last word was muttered under his breath.

Burnell's back stiffened at this stinging dismissal. But before he could utter a word, Philip broke in, "Sir, I really think the superintendent should stay. He's a man of the law and has a vested interest in this case."

A shadow fell across Villiers's face and his brow puckered. "But he has no interest in *my* business." His voice trembled with anger.

"Oliver stays," Gregory interjected. The two words flew across the air like two bullets.

Villiers waved a hand in the air and slumped back in his chair. "Oh, very well. Have it your own way."

"As you are a guest in our house, that's precisely what we intend to do" was Gregory's acerbic rejoinder.

"Shall I make some tea?" Emmeline asked in a bid to soothe the ruffled feathers. After all, tea cured all ills. At least, Gran had always assured her that it did. And who was she to go against the wise and all-knowing Gran?

Villiers wrinkled his nose. "I don't intend to stay that long."

Well, that's put me in my place, Emmeline thought sourly. *So much for being polite.* She gritted her teeth and gripped her hands tightly in her lap, as her temper started to kindle in her chest. She knew that if she opened her mouth to give vent—as she longed to do—to the tongue-lashing he richly deserved, it would quickly escalate into something rather unseemly.

Burnell shot her a sympathetic look that said, "Never

mind." She inclined her head and offered him a smile.

Philip cleared his throat. "Sir, don't you think it would be better to get it over with?"

A weaker man would have been intimidated by Villiers's glacial stare, but not Philip. He met the older man's gaze without flinching.

"I must admit I was quite put out, when you appeared on the doorstep," Gregory commented. "True to form, and your natural state of gloom, you have seen fit to insult my wife and our guests." He smiled at Emmeline. "I admire Emmy's sense of self-restraint." Then to Villiers, he said, "She does have quite a temper. Therefore, in the spirit of goodwill, I suggest you tell us whatever you came to say, or leave. Otherwise, I can't answer for the consequences."

Villiers flicked a bitter glance at Emmeline, before his eyes settled on Gregory.

"I never intended for this to come out," he began haltingly, as if searching for the right words. "In fact, it would have been better if it hadn't. But my hand was forced. I make no excuses. I want you to understand that I did what I thought was best..." He broke off. "It was all...a long time ago."

Confusion and curiosity vied in equal measure in the depths of Gregory's eyes. His lips were compressed in a tight line, but he simply waited in silence.

Emmeline had never seen Villiers flustered. He was rubbing his perfectly creased trousers with the palms of his hands. Deep in the pit of her stomach, she felt a flutter of unease and shivered involuntarily. Whatever was coming, she knew it was going to be bad.

The words floated out on the end of a long sigh. "I...I'm your father."

The world seemed to come to a halt. Only the ticking of the carriage clock on the mantelpiece bore witness to the fact that time indeed was marching inexorably forward.

Emmeline drew in a ragged breath, choking on the words which still echoed upon the air. *This is a cruel joke, isn't it?* her brain screamed. *It has to be.*

But no one was smiling.

After sharing a startled glance with Burnell, Emmeline swung her head to study Gregory. He hadn't moved a muscle. She reached out and touched his hand, wishing she could erase the last few minutes.

She was the only one in the room who could understand what must be racing through his mind. Coming so soon after the revelation that Victor Royce, and not Aaron Kirby, was her father, her heart ached for her husband. And yet, their situations were quite different. Aaron Kirby had been a father to her in every sense that counted. He was a kind, loving man, whose face was always wreathed in smiles and made her laugh until her stomach hurt. He and her mother had been her world. Victor Royce, who she had only known for a couple of weeks before he was murdered over summer, was aimable and gentle. She had liked him tremendously. They had shared a lot of things in common, but it wasn't the same as what she had had with Aaron Kirby.

Gregory, on the other hand, grew up with the know-ledge that his father had abandoned him and his mother when he was only three years old. This twist of fate had forced his mother to beg her brother, Max Sanborn, to take them in. She had nowhere else to turn. Max never let them forget that they were under his roof on sufferance and without his charity they would have to fend for themselves. After his mother died, poor Gregory ran away at the age of seventeen. A mere boy still. He had to get away. He couldn't endure Max's vile behavior a moment longer.

Now, after all these years, Villiers dropped this bomb. Her eyes narrowed as she shot a withering glance in his direction. What a heartless man. She wished the earth would open up and swallow him whole.

"The master manipulator playing mind games as usual," Gregory murmured. "I must say it's in extremely poor taste, even for you."

Villiers held his gaze. "Toby, it's the truth."

Gregory's grip tightened, crushing Emmeline's fingers. A vein was throbbing against his temple. "The name is Gregory," he stressed through gritted teeth.

"Now, it is. But you were born Tobias Crenshaw. Toby. Clarissa wanted…"

Emmeline jumped, when Gregory dropped her hand as if he had been singed by hot coals.

"Don't." The single word seared the air. It held a lifetime's worth of venom and rage.

Villiers would not be put off, though. "Toby Crenshaw was my code name. Clarissa wanted to name you after me. I never told her I was an agent. She thought I was a salesman, which explained why I had to travel often."

Gregory shook his head. Clearly, he didn't believe a single thing the older man was saying. "Don't talk about Mum."

"We had five years together," Villiers went on, a ghost of a smile playing about his lips at the memories. "We were happy. I loved Clarissa more than life itself." His voice was thick with emotion.

"You loved her so much that you turned your back on us. Your own wife and son," Gregory snarled.

Villiers cleared his throat. "Clarissa and I were never married, not that it's any excuse. It never bothered her. But for all intents and purposes, we *were* married. And then…then you came along, Toby." Gregory's hand curled into a fist.

"I tried. I really tried to make it all work. But in the end, it simply wasn't possible. I was a field agent. I was being sent on more and more dangerous assignments. There's no room for a wife and child in a spy's life. I couldn't put Clarissa's and your life at risk. I did what I thought was best. I left you."

Tears pricked Emmeline's eyelids. Gregory had said virtually the same words to her several months back. *I loved you, so I left you.* She still felt their sting.

Gregory's nostrils flared, as he took shallow breaths.

"If it's any consolation, I've been watching over you for years. You just didn't know it."

Gregory threw his head back and laughed. The sound was harsh and unsettling. "Is that supposed to make me feel better? Do you want me get down on my knees and thank you?"

Villiers looked away, ashamed for the first time in his life. "I don't want anything," he replied hoarsely.

"That's good. Because the only thing I have for you is contempt," Gregory shot back.

"Steady on," Philip, ever the diplomat, interrupted. "Villiers did jump in front of a bullet meant for you in that tunnel not so long ago, in case you had forgotten."

Gregory flapped a hand impatiently at him. "I'm not likely to forget, am I?" Then he whirled back to Villiers. "While I'm grateful for my life, it doesn't make up for you abandoning us. Nothing will. You weren't there when Mum got sick. You didn't watch her waste away a bit more each day as the cancer waged a war inside her body." A tremor shook his voice. "Until the day she gave up the fight and finally had peace."

"No," Villiers whispered. "I'm sorry." He gave a helpless shrug. "I know the words are inadequate, but I don't know what else to say."

They both fell silent, exhausted by anger and bitter recriminations.

"Why?" Gregory asked, after he had regained some of his composure. "After all these years, why tell me now?"

A muscle in Villiers's jaw pulsated. "Swanbeck."

"What the devil does Swanbeck have to do with this happy

family reunion?" Gregory asked contemptuously.

"The bastard has threatened to tell the world about our relationship and the fact that you've done the odd job for MI5 over the years, *unless* I expunge his record and see to it that all of his assets are unfrozen." He went on to recount the events of how he was kidnapped at gunpoint outside his club until the moment he ran into Philip at St. Martin-in-the-Fields.

"What?" Burnell exploded, outrage ringing in his tone. "That's blackmail."

Villiers inclined his head. "Nevertheless, there it is. I suspect that it's because your wife"—he scowled at Emmeline—"has seen fit to stir the pot *yet again* with her story about that fellow Jardine who had managed to get himself topped off at Heathrow. You're never content to let sleeping dogs lie, are you? You're always poking and prodding with your intrusive questions."

Emmeline drew her shoulders back and sat up straighter. "That's my job. If someone has nothing to hide, then there's no reason he or she should be afraid to talk to me. The public has a right to know the truth."

Villiers smirked, waving a hand at her as if he were a magician performing a trick. "And there you have it out of her own mouth. The most dangerous woman in Britain. She's willing to do anything for a byline, regardless of the damage she leaves in her wake."

"How dare you?" she fired back. "How dare you come into my house and spew your poison?"

Out of the corner of her eye, she caught a glimpse of Gregory's smile. "If you'll recall, I did warn you she had a temper," he murmured. "She will crush you."

She ignored his remark and continued her attack on Villiers. "I'm proud of the job I do. It's important. The truth matters. But of course, someone like you can't see that. You're so used to being in the shadows that lies and deception are your only friends."

Bravo, Burnell cheered silently as he repressed a smile. *Game, set, and match to Emmeline.* He saw Villiers open his mouth again. *I'd quit while I was ahead, old chap.*

"Are you quite finished?" Villiers inquired, a bored expression settling into the creases of his face. He had reverted to his usual aloof and standoffish demeanor.

The smile on her lips didn't reach her eyes. "I'm just getting started," she snapped.

He gave a weary shake of his head. "You are the most tiresome woman I know. Save your histrionics for another day." She sucked in her breath, but he put up a had to forestall another barrage. "The bottom line is Swanbeck has given me seventy-two hours to meet his demands. He's vindictive enough to mean every word of what he says."

Burnell's sat back in his chair and stroked his beard. "What do you think will be the preview he has planned for tomorrow?"

One of Villiers's shoulders twitched in a shrug. "Lord knows. Only you can bet it will be nasty."

"What are you going to do, sir?" Philip asked.

Villiers shook his head. "I wish all of this would go away..."

Gregory cut across him. "You're an expert at making complications disappear. Like you swept Mum and me under the rug, when things got too tricky. Out of sight, out of mind is your motto."

"Oh, do put a cork in it, Toby. You can nurse your wounded pride some other time. I'm certainly not going to give in to common blackmail. On the other hand, I've worked too hard over the past forty years to allow Swanbeck to destroy my reputation all because of you and your interfering wife."

Gregory surged to his feet. "You cold-hearted bastard. Everything is about you."

He lunged at Villiers, bracing his hands on the armrests of his chair.

Emmeline jumped up and was by his side in an instant. She placed a restraining hand on his arm. "Gregory, don't. He's not worth it."

He shook off her grasp without glancing at her. "Sit down, Emmy."

She took a half-step backward but hovered nearby. Gregory's face was only inches from Villiers, his breath ruffling the older man's hair.

"You forget, dear—what shall I call you? *Papa, Father, Dad?*—Anyway, you forget that the only reason I ever crossed paths with Alastair Swanbeck and his father was because you threw me to the wolves with that 'little job' of yours for Queen and Country. This is your mess."

Far from being cowed by Gregory's uncharacteristic display of pique, Villiers shot back, "You were the only one— with the requisite skills, shall we say?—for the job. I sent you in because I needed someone I could trust. We had a leak at MI5. I had to find out who it was and plug it—permanently."

Gregory snorted as he pushed away from Villiers's chair. "Charming. My own *papa* thought nothing of using me as bait." His voice dripped acid. "In the end, you failed miserably because Swanbeck knew exactly what I was about from the outset. The whole thing was a bloody shambles."

Villiers made a dismissive gesture with his hand. "Take it however you like. My job is to ensure the safety of the realm by any means I deem necessary. That was precisely what I was doing. Protecting the U.K. from Walter and Alastair Swanbeck."

Gregory gave a disapproving shake of his head, despite the throbbing radiating up his skull. "And here we are today.

We've come full circle. Alastair is free and inflicting mayhem. So tell me, what did we accomplish?"

"We've reached this point today, *dear boy*," Villiers sneered, a pink flush creeping up his jawline, "because you couldn't resist thumbing your nose at Swanbeck by stealing that damned diamond."

Gregory smoothed down the corners of his mustache. "What diamond?"

"You know perfectly well. The Blue Angel."

A faint smile played about Gregory's mouth. "Everyone knows that Igor Bronowski—a Russian gangster, I might point out—purchased it, likely with ill-gotten gains, at a Sotheby's auction for a ridiculous sum." He gave a casual shrug. "I suppose he was desperate to get his hands on it. That's what obsession does to a man."

"Swanbeck ended up with a fake. He thinks you switched it," Villiers countered.

Gregory chuckled. "I can't help what Alastair thinks. Clearly, this is a falling out among thieves."

"Hmph," Villiers grunted. "I wouldn't be so glib. Swanbeck's lackey made it a point of stressing that the diamond is a deal breaker. No diamond, Swanbeck destroys all of us."

"Then we have a dilemma on our hands. I can't conjure up a diamond out of thin air."

CHAPTER 28

Diamonds," Burnell muttered under his breath. "How I hate diamonds and their fanciful names. The Blue Angel. The Pink Courtesan." He rolled his eyes at the ceiling. "They must all be cursed, like a Black Widow. Lovely at first glance, deadly as sin once you scratch the surface."

"What are you chuntering on about, Oliver? Is your ulcer rumbling again?" Gregory inquired pleasantly, but there was a bemused gleam in his eye. He was sounding more like himself, despite the afternoon's revelations.

The superintendent wagged a finger at Gregory. "Longdon, you're a never-ending source of aggravation for my ulcer." He rubbed his stomach, as if to soothe its inner stirrings. "Today is a case in point. You're lucky you staggered home with only a goose egg on your head because of the Pink Courtesan. And now we wind up in a conversation about the Blue Angel. Your passion for diamonds is going to kill me one day."

"I don't know what you mean. I'm a law-abiding citizen, as I'm continually reminding you. The only contact I have with diamonds is if they are possessions that Symington's clients want insured."

"Pull the other one. No one in this room believes you. You're the only one who could have switched the Blue Angel. And as we are on this theme, I'm quite certain you stole Tarasova's ruby-and-diamond necklace."

Gregory resumed his seat on the sofa and crossed one elegant leg over the other. "Oh, not that again. If you'll recall, as someone with nothing to hide, I submitted to a search on the spot at the Starretts' disastrous party. Your chaps came up empty-handed."

He flicked a glance at Emmeline and patted the place next to him. She pursed her lips, as she lowered herself beside him. She *knew* he had stolen the necklace. She had found it in her clutch and made him promise to turn it over to the police. She assumed he had, since it was no longer where she had put it for safekeeping. Now, she realized he must have hidden it somewhere else. The thing was her lips were effectively sealed. Although she wanted to unburden herself to Burnell, she couldn't without wading through the rough shoals of why she had taken this long to say anything.

Damn and blast, she cursed as Gregory slid his arm around her shoulders and flashed one of his engaging smiles, making her his unwitting accomplice. She offered him a tight smile. *Ooh, how I want to throttle you.*

She could not bring herself to meet Burnell's intense gaze. She was certain he would be able to read the truth in her eyes. As for the Blue Angel, it was absolutely impossible that Gregory had stolen it. She slid a sideways glance at her husband. Wasn't it?

She cleared her throat. "Mr. Villiers, we all know lying is second nature to Swanbeck. Of course, Gregory doesn't have the Blue Angel."

Gregory raised one of her hands to his lips and brushed her knuckles with a kiss. "Thank you, Emmy."

Villiers grunted, Burnell glared, and Philip raised a

skeptical blond brow. Her husband merely beamed at each man in turn.

"At this stage, it makes very little difference," Villiers observed. "This is yet another game to set us chasing our tails. We all know that Swanbeck is going to carry out his plan, whether I meet his demands or not." He leaned forward in his chair, his expression somber. "And I want it to be clear that I have *no* intention whatsoever of doing so."

While they all applauded this stance, it still left them without a plan of attack.

Philip broke the brooding silence into which they had sunk by asking how Gregory came to be attacked that afternoon. This led to explanations about the murky pasts of both the Pink Courtesan and Sebastian Jardine.

At Emmeline's insistence, Philip told them where he had been hiding and what he had been doing for the last two days.

"You've been *where*?" Emmeline demanded incredulously, when he said that her half-sister, Sabrina Royce, had "generously" offered the use of the spare bedroom in her Mayfair flat.

Philip couldn't help but smile at her reaction. "I must say she's been quite nice about the whole thing. She's not a bad sort."

Emmeline shook her head. "How…how did this come about?"

"Actually, Hugh Carstairs arranged everything. It was a stroke of brilliance. No one would think of looking for me at Sabrina's flat."

"I see," she murmured. It made sense. Hugh was MI5 and a friend of Philip's. He also happened to be one of Sabrina's ex-husbands.

An image of a tall, svelte Sabrina, with her mane of lustrous dark hair and emerald eyes danced before Emmeline. Tensions between her and Sabrina had thawed slightly since they had discovered that they were related. But not entirely. Emmeline gritted her teeth. It was primarily because Sabrina was a shameless barracuda. She threw herself in Gregory's path every chance she that presented itself. Naturally, Gregory ignored her. He had taste after all, but it still irked Emmeline.

She pursed her lips. "You should go down to Swaley to be with your wife and sons."

"I would like nothing more. But until all of this is sorted out, Maggie and the boys are much better where they are. Without me."

Emmeline folded her arms over chest and gave him a withering look. "How can you say that?"

"They are safe with Helen. Besides, it's easier for me to try to find out why Special Branch wants to arrest me if I'm here in London."

"There's also a greater chance that Special Branch will catch you." She was fuming. Honestly, men could be so pigheaded. "You can't possibly remain at Sabrina's. Come stay here with Gregory and me. I'll run up now and make the bed in the spare room for you."

She started to rise, but Philip stopped her. "No, Emmeline. Thank you, but no. Swanbeck is after all of us. It would be better if we didn't put all the eggs in one basket and make it easier for him. That's why I didn't come to you in the first place."

Gregory tugged her arm, pulling her back down onto the sofa. "Darling, Acheson is right."

She exhaled a frustrated breath. "Yes, of course. But I don't like the fact that Philip is out there all alone."

"It's not as if I'm an amateur. I know how to take care of myself." He gave her a reassuring smile. "You really mustn't worry. I'm perfectly fine at Sabrina's."

That last remark was definitely the wrong thing to say.

"And I certainly don't like that," she retorted, her tone clipped.

"You can't think that anything will happen. Sabrina doesn't interest me in the least. Maggie is the only woman for me."

"*You* are above reproach, Philip. But Sabrina is another story entirely. A wife won't stop my dear sister from trying something."

"How about if I promise to fight off your sister if she comes near me? I could also bolt my door at night," he added in mock seriousness.

This made Emmeline laugh. "She'd probably break down the door. I'm sorry. I'm being silly. Although I admit that I would have felt better about the situation, if you were staying with Adam rather than Sabrina."

As twins go, Adam couldn't have been more different from Sabrina. Emmeline and Adam had become close in the past few months. She sighed. Oh, well, there was nothing she could do about these arrangements.

Philip nodded. "Good. I'm glad we've settled that point. If nothing else."

Emmeline was suddenly seized by a restless frustration. She got to her feet. She needed to move. To think. She started pacing back and forth in front of the fireplace as the men conferred among themselves. She could feel their eyes on her.

Tick tock. The clock seemed unusually loud. Or was it her nerves being stretched taut as a bow? The minutes were slipping away. *Tempus fugit.*

They couldn't allow Swanbeck to control the situation and dictate terms. There was absolutely no way that she and the others would aid and abet him to escape justice. He had done that for far too long. And yet, without concrete proof of his crimes, they were powerless. The truth remained just out of reach. The bits and pieces that they had painstakingly gathered were sadly only conjecture. They couldn't tie any of it directly to Swanbeck. Assistant Commissioner Cruickshank would laugh in their faces.

She stopped in her tracks. Why didn't she think of it before? "I know where to find all the answers," she blurted out.

Burnell eyed her warily, one brow quirking upward. "Oh, yes?"

"I'll go to Malta." She clapped her hands and beamed.

"No" was the swift, unified, and unequivocal response, as four pairs of male eyes glared at her.

Their tongues tripped over each other as they took turns admonishing her.

"It's out of the question," Villiers intoned with gravitas.

"A complete nonstarter," Philip concurred, his lips twisted with displeasure.

"Have you gone stark raving mad?" Burnell demanded, his cheeks flushing crimson beneath his beard.

The *coup de grâce* came from her darling husband. "Oliver, couldn't you and Finch find a nice, cozy corner in a jail cell for Emmy? Preferably in solitary confinement."

To her chagrin, the superintendent agreed with him. "That's not a bad idea."

She made a moue of distaste at them. "Ha. Ha. I was being serious."

"We know," Philip said. "That's what is so terrifying."

"Emmeline, you can't go Malta alone." Burnell tried to reason with her. "You'd be a sitting duck. You do see that, don't you?" He offered her a rare smile in a bid to persuade her.

It didn't work. "No, I don't," she countered. "It's always better to attack. Swanbeck would be caught off guard, if I went to Malta. He believes if he creates enough confusion to have us running around London like chickens without our heads, we'll give up the hunt for the answers. He's counting on it. Only I *won't* stop until I find the truth about Sebastian Jardine's murder and the Pink Courtesan. Gregory can't go because he has concussion…"

"Do I indeed?" Gregory interrupted her. "I don't recall a qualified doctor diagnosing one."

"You see it proves my point exactly," she continued breezily. "The blow to your head has affected your memory. Besides there's your job at Symington's. You can't disappear for a few days. You'd be sacked." She rushed on before he or the others could stop her. "We must face reality. We've hit a dead end here—pardon the unintended pun. If we want justice, the truth is in Malta."

Gregory's gaze skimmed her face and a faint smile touched his lips. "My hat is off to you, darling." He inclined his head. "You make a forceful and thoughtful argument."

She returned his smile. How she loved this man. "Thank you. I knew you would understand."

"But there is no way any of us will allow you to set foot on Malta."

She flashed a ferocious scowl at him. *Ooh, you traitor. Just you wait until the others leave*, she fumed silently.

He must have sensed what she was thinking because his smile broadened. *Why did I marry you?*

"*Allow*?" She hurled the word back at him, her voice rising an octave. "Since when do I need permission from any of you to pursue a lead?" Her scornful gaze sliced each man to pieces. "I am doing my job. Just like the rest of you."

"Emmeline, be reasonable." Philip put up his hands before an avalanche of vehement protest came tumbling down upon his ears. "No, listen please. Why are you treating us like we're the enemy? All of us only have your best interests and safety at heart." Villiers grunted at this comment, but Philip ignored him. "If the corruption is as widespread in Malta as the superintendent's friend Dunbar has indicated, then you won't know what you're walking into or who to trust. Intrepid journalists like you, lawyers, and others have been killed for attempting to expose the dirty secrets of politicians, businessmen, and the Mafia. You can't turn a blind eye to that. It's a fact."

A strangled sigh escaped from her lips. She couldn't deny the risks posed by the situation. She plopped down on the sofa again and rested her head on Gregory's shoulder. "I can't see any other way to find the truth."

"I have a few contacts at the Maltese High Commission," Philip offered. "I'll pop over to Piccadilly as soon as we're done here and see if I can catch them for a quiet word."

Emmeline sat up and touched his arm lightly. "Is that wise? Special Branch is still looking for you."

He grinned and patted her hand. "Don't worry. I won't make it easy for them. They haven't found me yet."

Before she could express further misgivings, Villiers cleared his throat. "I know Reggie Millbank. He's a career diplomat who was named the British high commissioner to Malta three months ago. We've crossed paths over the years. I'll give him a ring. Perhaps he can give us some insight into the situation on the ground in Valletta. He's sound. He always has his antennae tuned for the latest gossip. Nothing escapes him."

Emmeline inclined her head at him. She was surprised by Villiers's grudging offer of assistance. Or was it selfishness and a desire to protect his reputation? She stared at him, but his face was a mask of inscrutability. At this stage, did it really matter what his motives were as long as they found the answers they needed and Burnell's name was cleared? She supposed not.

In the meantime, to prevent her from doing anything rash, Philip told her that the Foreign Office kept a list of local service providers, including lawyers, that could assist British nationals overseas. He knew for a fact that there was such a list for Malta. Philip emphasized that the providers were neither endorsed nor recommended by the Foreign Office, and the list might not be up to date. However, he suggested she check the list and try contacting the law firms. Perhaps someone might be able to provide them with some information about the political landscape. He cautioned her to be circumspect in her questions.

It was merely a bone that he had tossed out, but Emmeline was willing to pursue any avenue to get answers. She reached up and gave Philip a peck on the cheek. "Thank you." His mouth quivered into a half-smile. "Believe me, it's entirely for my peace of mind. I'd much rather have you making phone calls, than running off to Malta and causing an international incident."

She swatted his arm. "As if I would." She jerked her head at the door. "Go on. Back to my dear sister Sabrina's flat." She wagged a finger at him. "But you had better give Maggie a ring or there will be hell to pay from me *and* Gran."

Philip clicked his heels together, as if she were a general commanding an army. "Message received and understood." Then, he turned to Villiers. "We had better go, sir."

Burnell rose as well. "I must be off too."

Villiers cast a glance at Gregory. For a second, it appeared he wanted to say something. To explain further. In the end, he shook his head, seemingly changing his mind. Or losing his courage when confronted with Gregory's unforgiving expression.

"Yes, right," he murmured. He gave Emmeline a curt nod. "I'll let you know what Millbank has to say."

"That would be helpful," she mumbled as she saw the three men out.

When she returned to the living room, she found Gregory standing by the window looking out on the garden. She crossed the room and slid her arms around his waist, resting her cheek against his back. "Are you all right?" she asked quietly.

He turned around to face her, drawing her close. A ghost of a smile played about his lips. "How could I not be when I have you?" He pressed a kiss against her forehead and rested his chin on the top of her head. "Nothing can hurt me, if I have you."

Except for Swanbeck, she thought as she leaned into him and tightened her grip.

They stood there for a few moments not speaking, just holding onto one another. Then she remembered about Tarasova's necklace. "I meant to ask you. Did you ever return Tarasova's ruby necklace to the police? I don't recall Superintendent Burnell mentioning that it had been recovered."

Gregory broke their embrace and grimaced. "Much as I'd like to linger here with you, darling. I've got to get back to Symington's. You wouldn't want your husband sacked for shirking his responsibilities."

She smiled up at him. "Certainly not." She stood on tiptoe and brushed his lips with a soft kiss. "But you're going to answer my question. One way or another." He made no comment.

"In the meantime," she went on, "I have to check that list of lawyers Philip mentioned. I'll work from home the rest of the afternoon." She gave him a gentle shove. "I'll see you this evening. Be careful."

He let himself out and then she was alone.

She sat down at the antique secretary desk that had been her grandfather's. Her laptop sat open patiently waiting to assist her in her investigations. First, she jotted down notes on everything they had learned that afternoon from Roger, Superintendent Burnell and Villiers to get it clear in her mind and determine what gaps needed to be filled. Once satisfied, she searched the Foreign Office's website for the list of lawyers. There were only eight firms, so it wasn't going to be too tedious a task. She eliminated one firm from the outset because their practice areas would not intersect in any way with either Swanbeck or Jardine. The other seven all did extensive work in the areas of international, corporate, bankruptcy, criminal and maritime law.

No one was able to help her at the first two firms. At the third, she was told in a haughty manner that its policy was never to speak to the press. She made a face at the phone after the man rang off. If she encountered the same attitude at the other firms, she would have to chalk this up to a fruitless exercise. However, nothing ventured, nothing gained. She punched in the number for the fourth one on the list.

This time she asked to speak one of the senior partners, rather than trying the general number.

A rather breathless female voice said, "Hello, Saliba, Mifsud and Zammit Advocates. Giuseppina Zammit's office."

"Hello, Ms. Zammit," Emmeline replied in an affable tone. "My name is Emmeline Kirby. I'm the editorial director of investigative features at *The Clarion* in London and I was wondering if I could ask you a few questions."

"I'm sorry Giuseppina is away at a conference in Paris. I'm Alessia Summergill, one of the associates. I assist Giuseppina. Perhaps, I can help you," she offered.

Emmeline wanted to leap into the air. Finally, someone who was willing to at least listen to her. "I hope so. I'm doing a story about an Englishman, Sebastian Jardine, who was murdered here in London a few days ago. He had made a number of trips to Malta over the past few months. I believe his death may have something to do with his time in Malta and his connection to an international criminal named Alastair Swanbeck."

"I see," Ms. Summergill's husky voice murmured in Emmeline's ear. "Why are you so interested in Jardine?" she asked suspiciously.

Why are you being cagy? Is it a lawyer's natural instinct or do you know something? Emmeline's silently queried, as she tried to tamp down her excitement at this prospect.

"First of all, it's a matter of justice. Surely, you see that. His killer must be captured. But on a personal note, Jardine was a friend of my husband's." She took a deep breath. "And…and unfortunately we've crossed paths with Swanbeck. Over the summer, our inquiries about a completely separate matter exposed some of Swanbeck's illegal business dealings. This forced him to bolt. There is strong reason to believe that Swanbeck has been in Malta all this time. The authorities think he may have obtained a Golden Visa in a bid to evade British law." She broke off to assess the other woman's reaction thus far.

"Please go on," Ms. Summergill encouraged.

"Swanbeck has vowed revenge against me and my husband. He attempted to make it appear that I had murdered Jardine, but Scotland Yard determined that I had been framed. This is another reason we need to find Swanbeck. I was wondering whether Ms. Zammit or anyone else at your firm had heard of Swanbeck or Jardine and might be able to give me an idea whether they had any business interests there. I understand that there is a good deal of corruption in Malta."

The other woman gave a throaty chuckle. "That is putting it mildly. Our lawmakers have corruption in their blood. It doesn't matter who is in office. The names change, but it's always the same in the end. Some are not as bad as others." She sighed wearily. "However, that is not the information you were seeking. You'll have to forgive me. Giuseppina is away at a conference in Paris. I'm trying to catch up on a number of cases. I've been away in England for the last week meeting my in-laws for the first time." She groaned. "It was…quite tense. I was walking on eggshells the entire time. You see, Derek works here in Valletta at the British High Commission. We were married over the summer. It was a whirlwind courtship and his parents were not pleased. They had been hoping Derek would marry the daughter of some friends of theirs."

Emmeline mumbled something suitably sympathetic and wished the woman would get to the point. Patience was not one of her virtues.

"I'm sorry," Mrs. Summergill said, as if sensing Emmeline's frustration, "I know I'm rambling. I'll look through Giuseppina's files to find out whether this Jardine approached the firm for legal advice. But I must caution you, Saliba, Mifsud and Zammit takes client confidentiality seriously. I wouldn't be able to divulge anything Jardine may have told her or one of the other lawyers. Particularly if he was involved with this criminal Swanbeck. It would be privileged information."

"I quite understand, Mrs. Summergill. I certainly don't want you to betray any of your firm's secrets."

Well, I wouldn't really mind, she mused, *but I understand. It's a bit like a journalist's sources. I always jealously guard my sources' identities.*

Aloud, she said, "I would appreciate any help that you are able to provide. Or at least if you can point me in the right direction, since you know the political landscape."

"Don't mention it. Just give me a few days. What is the best number to contact you?"

Emmeline gave her mobile number, thank her again, and rang off.

Most likely it was a dead end. But it was worth a try.

CHAPTER 29

As Emmeline came downstairs to make the coffee the next morning, she was assailed by second thoughts. She shouldn't have allowed Gregory and the others to dissuade her from going to Malta. It was always best to follow one's instincts. And her instincts told her that Malta held the key to everything.

She frowned as she reached the bottom step. Someone had pushed a tabloid through the letter slot. It lay face up on the parquet floor of the hall.

"That's odd," she murmured. The only paper they had a subscription to was *The Times*. A stack of papers was awaiting her on her desk at the office. She always began the day by perusing *The Clarion*'s competitors to see what they were covering.

She was bending down to scoop up the tabloid, when Gregory trotted down the stairs.

She froze and her eyes widened in disbelief. The headline screamed at her in bold letters.

GETTING AWAY WITH MURDER, TWICE.

Her hands trembled as she scanned the story, bile rising to her throat. She was being choked by unadulterated fury.

"Emmy, what is it?" Gregory asked as he reached her side.

She merely stared back at him without uttering a word. He had to pry the paper from her numb fingers, so tightly was she clutching it.

"Ian bloody Newland," she barked, a tremor in her voice.

A range of emotions chased themselves across Gregory's features as he read aloud, "Emmeline Kirby, editorial director of investigative features at *The Clarion*, leads a charmed life. We should all be so lucky. She has escaped the long arm of the law not once, but twice this year.

"Over the summer, she was the prime suspect in the murder of industrialist and philanthropist Victor Royce. Why? It seems Royce changed his will only a week before his death, leaving the bulk of his vast estate to Kirby. It turns out she was his long-lost love child. Or so she claims. By all accounts, she wormed her way into Royce's life. She flattered his ego under the pretense of interviewing him for a series she was writing. But cold and calculating Kirby had a sinister, ulterior motive. She was driven by greed. All she wanted was to get her hands on his money."

Emmeline made a gurgling sound in the back of her throat and put a hand to her mouth. She shook her head. Gregory gave her shoulder a squeeze and read on, "The Metropolitan Police questioned her several times, but she was never charged. The sordid business was swept under the rug, despite the overwhelming evidence against Kirby.

"Now, we come to the shocking murder of Sebastian Jardine, whose body was discovered at Heathrow only a few days ago. He was brutally stabbed. The odd thing is that Kirby was on the scene again. Airport security officers discovered the knife in her bag during a random search.

"Kirby was held for several hours by airport security and then Scotland Yard's Superintendent Oliver Burnell arrived to question her. The story becomes even more intriguing because Jardine's body was ultimately found in the boot of

Burnell's car. Burnell also happened to be the detective who investigated Royce's murder. He was the one who allowed Kirby to go free. Burnell stands accused of Jardine's murder. But did he and Kirby conspire on the dirty deed? Or was it Kirby and someone else is paying the price for her crime once again? The growing pile of coincidences can't be ignored. CCTV footage suggests that a woman was the killer. How does Kirby continue getting away with it?

"Most would say that Kirby is a fairly attractive young woman. Is she using her feminine wiles to seduce those in high places to escape justice? The public has a right to know." Gregory snapped the paper shut.

"You call that an objective story?" Emmeline demanded, no longer able to hold her tongue. "It's typical Ian. All salacious inuendo, no facts or corroboration."

Gregory folded her into his embrace, holding her close. He pressed a kiss to her forehead. "Shh, darling. Everything will be all right. The police know the truth." He waved the paper in the air. "No one will believe this rubbish."

She tilted her head back to look up into his face. Despite his soothing words, his eyes were clouded with anxiety.

"I am not naïve. *The Clarion*'s competitors will jump on the story. Seeing me skewered makes good copy and will help to sell their papers. Those with integrity will take a more tempered approach, but they will still follow up with their own articles and editorials because this is news. The unscrupulous papers, well"—she gave a sad shake of her head—"They're already rubbing their hands together in glee trying to determine how long they can drag this out."

"Bloody Swanbeck," he snarled, as he pressed her against him and rested his chin on top of her head. "This is his little surprise."

"We only have two days to stop him." Her words were muffled against his chest. "We have to find the evidence to connect him to Jardine's murder."

"We will," he reassured her.

She stood back and pinned him with her gaze. "How? We've hit a brick wall. Everything points to Malta…"

"No, you infuriating woman. It's far too dangerous."

She grabbed him by the elbows. "And it's not here in London? Jardine was murdered. You had your head bashed in yesterday. We can't sit back and wait for Swanbeck to launch his next volley. I don't want to be afraid when you set foot out the door that it may be the last time I see you." Tears caught in her throat. "We have to stop him."

"There are better, *safer* ways to go about it than dashing off to Malta."

She regained control of her emotions and hissed, "How? Time is not on our side."

They glared at each other in silence, each not willing to give in.

Emmeline opened her mouth to try to make him see sense, but the phone in the living room started screaming. A weary sigh escaped her lips. "The vultures have started circling," she murmured.

He patted her shoulder. "I'll get rid of whoever it is."

She followed him into the living room and plopped down on the sofa as he picked up the phone. "Hello," he said, his tone clipped.

She saw him stiffen and his brows knit together as he listened. She shot him a puzzled look.

"Not since yesterday," he mumbled down the line. Then, he covered the mouthpiece and whispered, "It's Finch. Roger has disappeared and the police have no idea where the bloody fool is. What?" He turned his attention back to the call. "I was just telling Emmy."

He was silent for a few seconds. "What about the papers?" She saw his jaw clench. "Have you told Oliver? Right, I see.

Yes, I'll let Villiers know. He can get word to Acheson. We'll ring you, if Roger gets in touch with us." He nodded. "Yes, I'll tell her."

Gregory severed the connection and put the phone back on its stand. He shook his head.

"What else did Sergeant Finch say?" she asked warily, girding herself for more bad news. Although how much worse could it get?

"He's seen the paper. Everyone has naturally." Gregory grimaced. "He wanted to assure you that the police have no intention of arresting you now or in the future. Cruickshank is holding a press conference at this very moment to dispute the scurrilous allegations made in Newland's story."

This brought a smile to her lips. "What about Superintendent Burnell? Surely Cruickshank can reinstate him. The holes in the case against him are growing by the second."

His mouth twisted into a crooked smile. "To his credit, Cruickshank has already done so. But it's being kept quiet. No need to stir the pot any more at the moment."

A wave of relief swept through her. "Oh, I am glad. The mere thought that a dedicated detective like Superintendent Burnell could be a killer was outrageous." She paused and held his gaze. "That doesn't change things…about Malta." She tossed her chin in the air defiantly. "You know I'm right."

He shook his head and lowered himself onto the sofa. He took her hand, his thumb rubbing the web of skin between her thumb and forefinger. "Emmy…"

She cut across him. "Everything points to Malta. All the answers are there. I have to go."

"No, Emmy. You're not going to Malta alone." He put up a hand. "Just listen." His gaze held her prisoner. "Think what Helen would do to me if anything happened to you. You can't possibly be that cruel, darling. Do have some pity for your poor husband."

Emmeline couldn't help it. She laughed and pushed him away. "You do talk a lot of piffle." Then more seriously, she said, "Nothing will happen. I'll be careful. I'll go directly to the embassy and speak to Villiers's friend Reggie Millbank." She held his hand between both of hers. "I promise. I'll also drop by the offices of the *Times of Malta*. Perhaps the editor can extend some professional courtesy and share some information with me."

"Are you quite finished?"

"We're wasting time. You do realize that?"

Gregory groaned. "Stubborn woman. Listen. You're not going alone to Malta because *we're* going together. All right? Am I out of your black books now?"

She threw her arms around his neck and gave him a kiss. "Sorry. I thought you were trying to talk me out of it again."

"Perhaps you should trust me more, wife," he murmured against her ear.

She drew back and gave him a wry smile. "I'll take it under consideration. But what about Symington's? You can't simply disappear for a few days."

"Didn't you know? My Auntie Agnes is quite ill." He sighed melodramatically. "The poor dear has no other family in the world. I must go take care of her. I would never be able to forgive myself, if something happened."

She raised a brow and eyed him skeptically. "They won't believe that."

He shrugged. "How will they be able to check? Besides, I've saved Symington's from making several hefty payouts in the past month. I think they can give me a bit of leeway."

She nodded and leaped to her feet. "Right. I'll call the paper and let the editor know what I'm planning. He's extremely supportive, so it won't be a problem. No doubt he's already fielding questions from *The Clarion*'s rivals and would like to laugh in their faces when I come back with a scoop. I'll also speak to Nigel. We owe him at least that much. He won't like it, but he can't stop us. Then, I'll see what's the first available Air Malta flight." She bit her lip. "I hope there's one this morning. Otherwise, I don't know what we're going to do."

He caught her hand and kissed the palm. "We'll figure out something. Make the coffee. I'll be in the kitchen in a minute. I want to ring Villiers and Symington's." He pursed his lips, as he drew out his mobile from the inner pocket of his suit jacket. "And I'll try Roger as well. I wish I knew what he was up to."

Husband and wife each efficiently dealt with these tasks within half an hour. As Gregory surmised, his boss at Symington's accepted his explanation and wished poor Auntie Agnes a speedy recovery. Gregory promised to ring back in a few days. Then followed the call to Villiers. He had no desire to speak to the man. His throat constricted with anger when he thought about Villiers. *His father*. He still felt a bit dazed by the truth. However, Gregory pushed down the churning in the pit of his stomach and rang him.

Villiers had been his usual brusque and professional self, not even a trace of sentimentality could be detected in his voice. He absorbed what Gregory had to say with equanimity. Villiers was wise enough to know it would have been a waste of breath to try to dissuade them from going to Malta. What surprised Gregory was that Villiers said that he would have a charter plane waiting for them at Heathrow. He promised to send his driver round in an hour to take them to the airport. He would see to it that the security officials didn't give Gregory and Emmeline any problems. They would be whisked directly to the plane. The only stipulation Villiers made was that Acheson would go with them. It would get Philip out of Special Branch's crosshairs, while Villiers tried to get to the heart of the matter and smooth interagency relations. It also was a way to ensure that Emmeline and Gregory didn't get into too much hot water in Malta. Gregory acquiesced gracefully. In fact, he welcomed having someone else to watch over Emmy. Sometimes—too often lately—she had deliberately placed herself in harm's way to root out the truth. The day would come when she asked one probing question too many. He shook his head, which made him wince. She would make him old before his time. But then, he couldn't live without her.

He checked his watch and pushed himself to his feet. He had to change and help Emmy finish packing. Then a strong cup of coffee before they left for the airport.

As he slowly climbed the stairs, he wondered what was awaiting them in Malta. Nothing good. Of that, he was certain.

CHAPTER 30

The flight crew shut the door as soon as Emmeline and Gregory stepped aboard. Philip was already on the plane. He had been watching for their arrival and dipped his head in greeting. Husband and wife had barely settled into their seats and were still fastening their belts, when the low rumbling of the engines whirred through the cabin. Within a minute, they were pulling back and had started taxiing down the runway. They were cleared for takeoff relatively quickly. As they rose higher and higher into the clouds, Emmeline tried to ignore the flutter in the pit of her stomach. Her gaze slithered over to Gregory, who winked and gave her a lopsided smile. But before he turned his face to look out the window, she caught a glimpse of apprehension in the depths of his eyes.

In three hours and ten minutes—barring any headwinds—they would be in Malta. The die was cast. They would not leave until they had the truth. She closed her eyes, her fingers gripping the armrests. She hoped they wouldn't be taking whatever they discovered to the grave.

Emmeline felt a moment's trepidation, when she descended from the plane and entered the terminal. Her gaze darted everywhere. The last time she was in an airport, she was taken into custody on suspicion of murder. She shivered involuntarily at the memory of being left alone in that sterile room at Heathrow, where that odious security officer Naylor had taken her for questioning.

Gregory must have sensed what she must be thinking because he put his hand under elbow. Philip flanked her on the other side. She permitted her body to relax slightly. No one would be dragging her off this time.

A young man in his thirties with thick jet-black hair and a dusky olive complexion, dressed in a black suit, pristine white shirt, and sporting a somber maroon tie approached them before they had taken five paces into the terminal. "Miss Kirby and Mr. Longdon? Mr. Acheson?"

Emmeline and Gregory had decided on the plane that it would be best if it wasn't known that they were married. She had kept Kirby as her professional name. Therefore, she was in Malta covering a story. Meanwhile, Gregory was there as Symington's chief investigator to follow a lead on the disappearance of the Pink Courtesan and Philip as a representative of Her Majesty's government.

"Yes," Philip responded cautiously.

The man's face broke into a smile, as he extended a hand. "How do you do? I'm Joseph Spiteri," he said solicitously. "Mr. Millbank sent me to meet you." He shook Emmeline and Gregory's hands in turn. "If you'll follow me to the car, I'll take you to your hotel. Mr. Millbank has reserved rooms for you at the Corinthia Palace Hotel in Attard. It's where all the dignitaries stay, when they visit Malta. The queen has stayed there too. It's next to the President's Palace and the San Anton botanical gardens."

Emmeline offered him a smile. "That was very kind of Mr.

Millbank. But I think we'd rather go straight to Valletta to meet with him. I'm afraid time is of the essence." She shot a quizzical glance at both Gregory and Philip to see whether they concurred.

Philip and Gregory nodded in unison. "Yes, that would be best," Philip agreed. "If it's not too much trouble."

Spiteri inclined his head and relieved Emmeline of her bag with a smile. "As you wish. I'll drive you into Valletta and then drop your bags at the hotel. I'll make certain that they are taken to your rooms."

"Splendid," Gregory murmured. "Please lead the way."

Spiteri guided them efficiently through the terminal and out into the car park. They were soon merging with the traffic on Route 1, which was moderate. Fifteen minutes later, they were alighting in front of Whitehall Mansions, the elegant cream-gold home of the British High Commission along the seafront in Ta'Xbiex across the bay from old Valletta.

Spiteri told them that the colonial building also housed the embassies of the Netherlands, Ireland, Spain, Portugal and Austria. "It was formerly the residence of the members of the Fleet Air Arm Wrens," he explained, "who served in Malta during and after the Second World War."

Emmeline shielded her eyes from the sun and tipped her head back to admire the five-story building. "How interesting," she commented.

"Of course, you know that King George VI awarded the George Cross to Malta for 'acts of greatest heroism' fighting the Nazis." He beamed with pride.

"Indeed. It took tremendous courage," Philip agreed. He, like Emmeline and Gregory, had a keen interest in history. "The island was pounded by the Luftwaffe between March and April 1942. It was more intense and sustained than the Battle of Britain." The others nodded in astonishment.

"Yes, my grandparents told me the stories. It was a terrible time." A pensive expression fell across Spiteri's features. Clearly, his mind lingered on the bravery of the islanders of past generations. "Well, I don't want to delay you," he said briskly. He gestured with his hand. "Just walk into the building and Mrs. Denning, Mr. Millbank's secretary, will be waiting to greet you. I'll take your bags to your hotel. Enjoy your stay in Malta."

They thanked him and climbed the stairs. Philip pushed open the glass door and stood aside to allow Emmeline to pass inside. He and Gregory followed on her heels. Once their eyes adjusted from the brightness outside to the darker interior, they saw a tall, slender woman in her mid-fifties with auburn hair that had faded to a mellow red-gold. She was hovering by the royal coat of arms hanging on a ridged, wooden wall, which informed visitors that they had the privilege of being inside the British High Commission.

The woman crossed toward them in three strides. She proffered a bony hand. "Miss Kirby, Mr. Longdon, Mr. Acheson," she said, her slate-green eyes crinkling at the corners. "Welcome to Malta. I'm Valerie Denning, Mr. Millbank's secretary. He's expecting you. I'll take you straight to him."

After pleasantries were exchanged, they followed her down a corridor. She ushered them into a small, airy reception room with gleaming white walls. She gestured toward a grouping of chairs around a low coffee table in front of a fireplace shielded by a black metal fire guard.

"Mr. Millbank will be with you shortly. I'm certain you must be parched from your flight and would like some refreshment. Tea will be sent in. Is there anything else I can do for you?"

"No, you've been very thoughtful," Emmeline replied for all of them. "Tea will be lovely."

Mrs. Denning inclined her head and offered them a smile, before disappearing from the room.

As promised, tea arrived shortly with a plate of biscuits. Emmeline poured a cup for each of them. A companionable silence filled the room as they settled back to wait for the high commissioner.

Half an hour later, Reggie Millbank bustled in. "I do apologize." He put up a hand. "No, please don't get up. Please enjoy your tea." His voice was rather nasally and grated on the nerves. However, he appeared amiable.

He lowered himself into the chair directly opposite Philip. "I'll join you in a cup, if I may. I've been in meetings all morning."

Emmeline studied Millbank over the rim of her cup. She guessed that he was younger than Villiers. She judged that he must be in his late fifties, perhaps sixty. He had perfectly coiffed wavy steel gray hair. A faint trace of stubble shadowed his cheeks. His most arresting feature was his cornflower-blue eyes. They were full of eagerness mingled with affability.

Millbank leaned back in his chair and crossed one lean leg over the other. He took a long swallow of tea and immediately got down to business. "Now, I'm always happy to assist the press. How precisely can I help you, Miss Kirby? Laurence was rather vague when he rang." He flicked a glance at Gregory and Philip. "Please forgive me Mr. Longdon and Mr. Acheson. I'm a bit baffled as to why Laurence sent an investigator from Symington's and a MI5 agent." He gave a nervous chuckle. "I assure you we're not under siege here."

Philip offered him a bland smile. "All will become clear shortly," he murmured.

Millbank accepted this with a nod as he took another sip of tea.

Where to begin? Emmeline took a deep breath as she attempted to organize her thoughts. "Simply put, Mr. Millbank, we're here about murder and corruption."

His mouth curved into a smile, but there was a hint of wariness in his eyes. He set his cup and saucer down on the table. "Indeed. How intriguing. Are you certain you want me and not James Bond?" He laughed again. "I don't want you to be disappointed. I'm merely a humble diplomat."

"Mr. Villiers felt that in the circumstances you would be able to provide the information we need or at least put us in contact with someone who could. I'm afraid we have very little time to find the answers."

Emmeline perched on the edge of her chair and went on to tell him as much as she felt was necessary about Sebastian Jardine's death and his links to Alastair Swanbeck, who they had strong reason to believe had taken up residence on Malta. She left out the bit about Swanbeck's threat to ruin Villiers's career and his personal vendetta against Gregory.

"From what we've been able to piece together, Swanbeck has obtained a so-called Golden Visa and therefore is now a Maltese citizen. Circumstantial though it is, everything points to Swanbeck having Jardine killed," she concluded.

She sat back and watched as Millbank digested the unsavory tale. His complexion had gone an unbecoming shade of gray. He pursed his lips. The silence stretched out for several minutes.

Finally, he found his voice again. "I never expected anything so…so horrid." He wrung his hands. His gaze met and held Emmeline's. "I really wish you hadn't told me any of it."

"We know it's distasteful," Gregory observed. "But we felt that you were owed an explanation."

Millbank nodded. "Yes, yes. Quite right. I appreciate it. However, you place me in an untenable position. I'm terribly sorry, but I can't get involved with the political situation here in any way. I'm Her Majesty's representative. If there's even the slightest perception that I've embroiled myself in this…this scandal, it would be devastating for Britain's relations with Malta. I find it astounding that Laurence even suggested that you come to see me." He slashed the air with his hands in a gesture of finality. "The answer is an unequivocal no. I can't provide any official assistance."

"I rather think Villiers had the unofficial sort in mind," Gregory quipped, a smile playing about his mouth.

"I don't find this conversation remotely amusing, Mr. Longdon," Millbank shot back.

Emmeline sought to smooth his ruffled feathers. "Naturally, we don't expect you to involve yourself directly. We were merely hoping…"

Millbank gave a curt shake of his head. "No, I'm sorry, Miss Kirby. Gentlemen." He rose stiffly. "I can't help you, particularly if as you say, the man has become a Maltese citizen. And if he's not, I don't intend to create an international incident. No, sorry. My hands are tied."

Emmeline leaped to her feet, her hands curling into fists at her side. *Don't lose your temper*, she instructed herself. *It will only make things worse.*

She swallowed down the bitter taste of bile rising to her throat. Drawing in air through her nostrils, she willed her body to relax. Gregory and Philip were standing now too.

"Mr. Millbank," she began slowly, choosing her words carefully. "I quite understand your position. But in this situation, justice must take precedence over diplomatic protocols. Surely you can make a few discreet inquiries. Will your conscience allow you to sleep at night knowing that a ruthless criminal, a man who has had people *murdered*, is roaming free because you were unwilling to do anything to stop him?"

"My sleeping habits are none of your concern," he retorted brusquely. "You will not make me feel guilty." He shook his head to emphasize his point. "Catching this Swanbeck fellow is a policeman's job. I'm a diplomat. I'm bound by certain rules."

Stuff your rules, her brain screamed. She couldn't believe what a fool he was.

An acerbic rejoinder danced on the tip of her tongue, but she was prevented from unleashing it because Philip cut in. "I'm sorry we bothered you, Mr. Millbank. We'll leave." He extended a hand toward the loathsome man.

Ooh, how she hated diplomatic niceties. Her head whirled round to glare at him, but his gaze was focused on Millbank. It was probably just as well. She was certain her withering disappointment was patently evident on her face.

Gregory grasped her firmly by the elbow. One eyebrow arched upward in silent warning.

No matter how much the bureaucratic oaf irked her, she wasn't really going to give Millbank a punch on the nose. Even though he sorely deserved it. Fine. She drew her shoulders back and pasted a smile on her lips. She murmured her goodbyes in the best tradition of diplomatic aplomb and handed him one of her business cards, in the event he felt he could assist them. Gran would have applauded her performance.

⌘

Once out of earshot on the pavement in front Whitehall Mansions, they gave vent to their collective frustration.

"I thought that went extraordinarily well," Gregory commented with more than a modicum of irony, as he slipped his arm around Emmeline's waist, drawing her to his side.

Emmeline sniffed. "Sound, indeed. How could Villiers say that? Millbank is a spineless weasel. He went to great lengths to put us off. Why? What is he hiding?"

A thoughtful expression flitted across Philip's face as he stared out as white-hot embers of sunlight danced upon the cobalt waters of Marsamxetto Harbor. "Oh, no doubt about it. He was nervous. But what I'm curious about is how he knew I'm with MI5. Officially, I work for the Foreign Office. I never mentioned otherwise, neither did the two of you. And Villiers is so closemouthed that he doesn't disclose what he had for breakfast. Therefore, it beggars belief that he would have told Millbank."

⌘

Millbank couldn't get out of the reception room fast enough. He had bolted down the corridor to his office and locked the door. Beads of perspiration had formed on his brow and his breath was coming in ragged gulps. He hurried over to his desk. It unnerved him to see that his hand was trembling as he reached for his phone. When his secretary answered, he issued a terse order saying that Miss Kirby, Mr. Longdon and Mr. Acheson were to be escorted off the premises if they returned to the embassy. When he terminated the conversation, he regretted being so rude to Valerie. But he couldn't risk them sniffing around.

He ran a hand through his hair distractedly. His heart was hammering against his rib cage. How could that bloody reporter have found out?

He was getting out *now*, before Emmeline Kirby had a chance to destroy him.

Millbank grabbed his private mobile and cursed as he punched in a number. He couldn't risk the call appearing on the embassy's phone log.

"Come on, pick up, you bastard," he muttered aloud as the phone rang.

At last, a male voice echoed in his ear. "This is not wise. What do you want?"

"You took your bloody time answering."

"I'm not at your beck and call. You have thirty seconds to tell me what this is about, or I'll ring off."

"Emmeline Kirby, Longdon and Acheson were just here. *At the embassy*. They were asking questions about Jardine and you."

Swanbeck chuckled. "Ah, the games begin. I knew it wouldn't take long for our little Emmeline's curiosity to be aroused."

"Didn't you hear me? They *know*. It's only a matter of time before they fit all the pieces together. I'm finished. I want no part of this anymore."

"You're in no position to issue an ultimatum. You're finished when I say you are and not a minute sooner." Swanbeck's voice held a note of steely menace.

"I have done everything you demanded," Millbank replied querulously. "Surely we're even?"

The sound of Swanbeck's laughter sent a shiver slithering down Millbank's spine. "Oh, Reggie, you are an amusing fellow. Remember, I know what you did, you naughty boy. You're mine until the day you die. If you ever attempt to step out of line again, I will squash you *and* your pretty niece. Now, pull yourself together and get back to work."

"But what about the Kirby woman and the others?"

"It's none of your concern. It's time to set my plans in motion."

The line went dead.

Millbank felt as if his knees would buckle under his weight. He gripped the edge of the desk for a moment to steady himself. He took a deep breath to slow down his racing heart. Then with trembling fingers, he pressed the buttons and made another call.

"Emmeline Kirby is in Valletta," he said in a hoarse whisper. "God help us now."

CHAPTER 31

On a subconscious level, Emmeline had registered Millbank's slip about Philip working for MI5. But it was soon swept away on a tide of annoyance at the high commissioner's obdurate lack of cooperation.

She tossed a glance over her shoulder at Whitehall Mansions. She frowned when she saw Mrs. Denning watching them intently through the glass door. The woman stepped back into the shadows and scurried off the instant their eyes met.

"Hmph," Emmeline grunted. "Millbank's secretary was spying on us just now. Don't bother looking. She's already run off to make a report to her boss, although she'll have precious little to tell him."

Philip kept up a stream of inconsequential banter as his gaze casually surveyed the harbor, the Msida Yacht Marina, the parked cars, and the people out and about in their immediate vicinity. Gregory threw his head back and chuckled, but he appeared to be carrying out the same exercise.

"If anyone's watching, he's a professional," Philip mumbled.

Gregory nodded in agreement.

Even though the weather was milder than in London,

Emmeline's skin prickled with goosebumps. "Could Millbank be in Swanbeck's pocket?" she asked, her voice pitched low.

One of Philip's shoulders twitched in a shrug. "As we are acutely aware, anything's possible when it comes to Swanbeck."

"Perhaps, we should ring Villiers to do a bit of checking on Millbank."

Gregory gave a curt shake of his head. "Not Villiers."

Emmeline looked up into his face. "Darling," she said gently, "I know things are a bit tricky with you and Villiers at the moment but…"

He interrupted her. "Emmy, things are always tricky when it comes to Villiers, but that's not why we shouldn't involve him. We have no idea if Special Branch is keeping track of his movements in the hopes of catching Acheson. I suggest we ring Oliver. He's fully restored to the force, albeit quietly. He and Finch can handle it without making a fuss. They know the situation."

"Yes, good idea," Philip concurred. "In the meantime, let's catch a taxi to take us into old Valletta. We won't stick out as much in the crowds there."

These words had barely spilled from his lips, when Millbank's gleaming black Audi drew to a halt along the curb. A broad smile broke out on Spiteri's face as he opened the door and stepped out of car.

"Hello again. I see you're still here. I hope your meeting with Mr. Millbank was successful. I dropped your bags at the Corinthia Palace. Your rooms were ready. Just ask for the keys at the desk. Would you like me to take you to the hotel?"

"Thank you. That's very kind of you," Emmeline replied, as she made a sweeping gesture with one hand, "but we thought we'd take a taxi to old Valletta and explore for a bit."

"Taxi? No. No. No. I'll drive you. You can take a taxi to your hotel later."

"Won't Mr. Millbank miss you?" she asked.

Spiteri made a dismissive gesture in the air. "No, it's fine. He doesn't know that I've returned. Besides," he lowered his voice conspiratorially, "I know for a fact that he doesn't have any engagements this afternoon, so I'll likely be hanging about on the off chance that something unexpected might come up. I assure you I'll be back before anyone notices that I've been gone."

Emmeline exchanged glances with Gregory and Philip. They nodded in unison.

"We'll take you up on your generous offer," Philip answered for all of them.

"Good." Spiteri held open the door to the back seat and waved his hand with a gallant flourish at Emmeline. "Please Miss Kirby." She inclined her head and clambered into the car with the two men following suit.

In no time at all, Spiteri was pulling up on Strait Street, which was only a short walk from St. George's Square, where the Grandmaster's Palace was located. He apologized because he couldn't take them door to door, explaining that Republic Street, the city's principal thoroughfare, was largely set aside for pedestrians. Only in the early morning were commercial and general maintenance vehicles allowed to use the street.

After the car had disappeared in a dip in the road, the trio made a right onto Old Theatre Street and followed it to end of the block as Spiteri had directed. There they found Caffe Cordina, which was just a few steps from St. George's Square. He had assured them that the café was the ideal spot to enjoy a coffee and a pastry or a light meal. They were grateful for his recommendation because they hadn't eaten anything since leaving London and they suddenly realized that they were famished.

Caffe Cordina was an elegant oasis that sought to entice the palette with its plethora of tempting offerings. Everything gleamed, from the marble floor in alternating patterns of black-and-white checks along either side of the coffee bar, which dominated the center of the café, to the arched ceiling in a soft egg-cream with gilded moldings and delightful frescos of Roman boys frolicking. Suspended from the ceiling was an exquisite Venetian glass chandelier, whose sparkling curlicues and flowers in shades of sky blue, red, and gold merrily captured the light.

The café was crowded, but they were shown to a small table near a curving staircase with a polished wooden banister with insets of swirling leaves that led to an upper floor. The tabletops were made of the same black-veined marble as the floor in this section.

Their mouths watered as they perused the menu. In the end, Emmeline and Gregory decided to try the traditional Maltese *pastizzi*. She opted for one with ricotta, while he selected the mushy peas and minced-beef filling. Philip chose a *bombette*, a deep-fried dough with spinach, mozzarella and ham. They all ordered cappuccino. As they waited for their food, Emmeline tried not to glance at the display cases with pastries that they had passed on the way to the table. However, it was proving quite difficult as she had them in her direct line of sight. There were one or two sinful chocolate confections that kept winking at her.

She attempted to distract herself from these invitations by musing aloud, "Millbank appeared quite willing to help us when he first arrived. Granted, Swanbeck's reputation is enough to make anyone nervous. But I get the sense that there's more going on beneath surface than simply fear of a vicious criminal."

Philip, who was sitting directly opposite her, leaned back in his chair. A slight frown crossed his features. "What's patently obvious is that our Mr. Millbank is a liar. And not a very good one."

"Diplomacy is the ultimate lying game, if you think about it. No one says what they really mean"—Gregory peered over the rim of his cup at Philip—"present company excluded, of course."

Philip pressed a hand to his chest and dipped his head. "I feel honored."

Gregory went on, "Behind the smiles, everyone is cursing the other side for being unreasonable until they get what they want. And if they don't manage to do so, they come up with another lie to save face and justify coming home empty-handed."

Philip sipped his cappuccino, as he mulled this over. "I never took you for a cynic, Longdon."

"I'm not blind," Gregory countered. He raised an eyebrow and his eyes held a mischievous glint. "You must admit I'm right to a certain extent."

Philip gave a casual shrug. "I admit nothing. I'm not a diplomat in the strictest sense of the word. As you both know, I tiptoe between two vastly different worlds."

Gregory grinned and pitched his voice low. "But to be a good spy, isn't one of the prerequisites diplomacy? Think of all the juggling of sensibilities required of a double or triple agent, if he or she is to survive. Or perhaps it's simply a matter of living dangerously."

"I think you mean betrayal, not diplomacy. There's a difference," Philip murmured.

"All right, boys," Emmeline interjected, tapping the table with her spoon to get their attention. "That's quite enough. You've gone completely off the subject. We were talking about Millbank."

At this point, their food arrived. They were silent for an interval as they tucked in, each lost in his or her troubled thoughts.

They were nearly finished eating, when Gregory threw his napkin down and muttered under his breath, "Bloody hell."

The sound of his chair scraping against the marble floor as he jumped to his feet startled not only Emmeline but everyone at the surrounding tables.

She touched his arm. "What is it?"

Gregory shook off her hand. His eyes were glued to the window that overlooked Republic Street. "I'll be back in a minute," he mumbled out of the corner of his mouth. Without another word, he was hurrying out of the café.

Emmeline whirled back to Philip. His gaze was full of bafflement, as she was certain hers must be.

They craned their necks to see where Gregory had gone, but he had shot off somewhere to the right of the window and out of their line of sight. About five minutes had elapsed, when he made a reappearance. But Gregory was not alone. He had one hand on Roger's collar and the other clamped on his upper arm.

Gregory marched his friend to their table. Roger, his lips pressed in a tight line, chafed at being handled in such a rough manner.

Emmeline's eyes widened in surprise, when they came to a halt at Philip's elbow "Roger," she said in stunned greeting.

He gave her a crooked smile. "Emmeline, always a pleasure." He inclined his head toward Philip and then his gaze warily came to rest on Gregory. "Fancy meeting all of you here. It's a small world indeed."

"Hmph," Gregory snorted, as he pressed Roger into the chair beside Philip. "Sit."

"What a gracious invitation," Roger mumbled. "It seems I have no choice." Gregory shook his head in confirmation.

Roger shrugged nonchalantly as if to say so be it. He rubbed his hands together as he his gaze trailed over each of them. It lingered longest on Emmeline's face. What was going on inside his head? Did he believe he could gain the most sympathy from her? She curled her fist into a ball. Was he frantically attempting to come up with a plausible lie that would explain away his suspicious behavior? He had better not be. Too many lies had been bandied about. One thing was certain. Roger knew a great deal more about Jardine and Swanbeck than he had told them thus far.

Gregory folded his hands on the table and flashed one of those dazzling smiles that oozed charm. But had the outside observer bothered to cast a second glance in his direction, he would have seen that Gregory's eyes were ablaze.

He leaned across the table toward Roger. "Why did you run?"

Roger peered into Gregory's half-drunk, now cold cup of cappuccino. "Is that cappuccino? I'd love a cup." He swiveled his neck around. "Where's the waiter?"

Gregory's smile grew wider, but his tone was edged with steel. "No coffee until you answer our questions."

Roger's roaming eye traveled from Emmeline to Philip, before settling once more on Gregory. "You don't seriously plan to interrogate me in this lovely café?" He clucked his tongue. "That would be quite crass. I always thought you were a gentleman."

"I'll throttle you, if you don't start talking," Gregory hissed through clenched teeth.

Philip dropped his arm around Roger's shoulders. "And I'll gladly help him," he whispered in his ear. "Too much is at stake. We don't have time for one of your little con games." He clapped Roger on the shoulder, hard, to reinforce his point.

Roger shook off Philip's arm and leaned back in his chair

with a resigned sigh. "All right. You've painted me as a villain and it's totally unfair. I'm on your side, Greg."

"Prove it," Gregory challenged. "Ever since you popped up in London, you've done nothing but lie. Why didn't you turn over Seb's papers to the police?"

Roger folded his arms over his chest. "How do you know I didn't?"

"Finch told us."

"Perhaps the sergeant was lying. It's been known to happen. Some coppers are dirty."

"Not Finch. And certainly not Oliver," Gregory sneered with disdain. He pounded his fist on the table, making the plates and saucers rattle. "Now, talk." He wagged a finger at him. "No more half-truths or lies by omission."

Roger sniffed. "I can see your hand in this, Emmeline. Greg never used to be so tetchy, when he was a bachelor."

Emmeline smiled at him, but her voice dripped ice. "You know, Roger, your behavior makes you look very, *very* guilty. Anyone would think you had something to do with Jardine's murder."

Roger's jaw clenched and the bemused expression was replaced with something darker. His brow furrowed. "You *know* I didn't kill Seb."

"Do I? How? You were at the airport. By your own account, you were there to meet Jardine. Perhaps the two of you had a row and you killed him. His bag ended up in your possession. Sadly, these are not the actions of an innocent man."

Roger drew in a sharp breath. "I may not be pure as the driven snow, but I draw the line at murder." He then glared at Gregory. "As do you, Greg, I might point out. We're not that much different. Only you have a pretty wife."

Gregory murmured something unintelligible and Emmeline simply ignored the latter comment. Roger was not going to squirm his way out of this with flattery. "How noble that murder offends your sensibilities. But it appears that you're not averse to a bit of blackmail."

A smile played about Roger's mouth as he shrugged. "A man's got to live."

"Your days are numbered at the rate you're going," Philip snapped, his patience reaching its breaking point.

Roger shook his head. "What I've got is pure gold," he said with smug confidence. "It only comes along once in a lifetime. Swanbeck will pay anything to buy my silence. So will others."

"You're delusional," Philip retorted with asperity. "You'd be dead before you had a chance to spend even a penny."

CHAPTER 32

his is about the diamond. You have the Pink Courtesan, don't you?" Emmeline clenched her fists, her nails digging deep into her palms. She propped her elbows on the table and leaned forward to impale Roger with her eyes. Blood was thundering in her ears. "It was *you*. You're the one who coshed Gregory over the head and stole the diamond."

Roger suddenly went still and became tongue-tied.

"Answer me," she demanded in a venomous hiss.

"Emmy—" Whatever soothing platitudes Gregory had been intending to utter, they evaporated the instant her eyes locked on his face.

She channeled her fury at Roger once more. "You could have killed my husband. *Your* supposed friend. Gregory trusted you. *I* trusted you. All along you were playing us. You're only interested in the diamond. You feigned concern about us and wormed your way into our lives because you thought we could lead you to the Pink Courtesan." Her tone was laced with scorn. "You're nothing but a devious opportunist."

Gregory patted her arm and gently pressed her back down into her chair. "It's all right, darling."

He looked her directly in the eye and she melted into the caress of his gaze. But she was still seething with outrage. How could he remain so calm? "Aren't you bothered? Nothing that has come out of his mouth has been the truth."

What she despised above all else was lies and betrayal. She had experienced far too much of both over the last two years. The scars lingered, even if they were no longer painfully raw and exposed.

Gregory took her hand in both of his. "Roger is merely human like the rest of us." He flicked a sideways glance at his disgraced, disloyal friend. "The Pink Courtesan was too tempting a prize to pass up. I can understand that."

Her eyes widened in disbelief. "Too tempting a prize to pass up," she muttered. "You've gone crackers. You must have concussion." If he didn't already, she certainly wanted to give him one to knock some sense into him.

Gregory chuckled, but she saw him wince. Maybe the pain would wake him up.

She held his gaze. "Don't you see that Roger is likely the person who poisoned Swanbeck's mind and fueled his thirst for revenge?"

"For the record, I didn't," Roger countered in his defense. "That was entirely Seb."

"Why should we believe anything that you say?" She hurled these words at him. "Lying is second nature to you."

Roger gave a curt shake of his head. "Only about taking the diamond from Greg. And I only found out about it because of Seb's twisted obsession."

"You went along with his scheme," Philip pointed out. "That means you're no better than Jardine was."

Roger's chest heaved with a sigh. "I just…All I wanted was the Pink Courtesan. What man wouldn't? I could disappear and not have to worry another day in my life. I tried to talk some sense into Seb, but he was beyond reason.

Therefore, I did what I could to find out exactly what he was up to. Everything I told you about his mother, the Cannizzaros and Swanbeck was the truth. Everything." He turned to Gregory. "I swear that when I took Seb's bag my goal was to find something you could use as leverage to get Swanbeck off your back for good. I knew the police would be coming soon to investigate Seb's murder. I ducked into a restaurant for a couple of hours to come up with a plan. I didn't dare risk being seen wandering about the airport with the bag. In the end, I decided to stow it in a locker. I was going to hop in a taxi and leave Heathrow before anyone could connect me to Seb. I had intended to come back in a few days to collect the bag." He sighed again. "Things changed when I saw you and Emmeline, and the coppers, being questioned by that prat of a security officer about Seb's murder. I watched you and Finch slip away and thought I'd better step in to extricate Emmeline. I knew she was your wife. I had seen your wedding announcement in the paper. You know the rest of the story."

Gregory smoothed down the corners of his mustache. The low buzz of conversation from the other tables drifted around them. At last, he cleared his throat. "No one else but you would come up with such a ludicrous story."

Roger's shoulders hunched forward. Some of the tension eased from his face. One corner of his mouth quirked into a smile. "Truce," he mumbled and extended a hand across the table.

Gregory stared at it hovering in the air for a fraction of a second, before clasping it.

Emmeline groaned and slumped back. "Why is it always all boys together?"

"A more important question that you've avoided to this point is what are you doing in Malta?" Philip demanded.

Roger studiously examined his manicure.

"I can hazard a guess," Gregory said, his eyes on Roger. "You're going to sell the diamond to the highest bidder."

Roger lifted his eyes and spread his hands wide. "I thought a silent auction would level the playing field. Highest bid gets the prize." He tapped the breast pocket of his jacket. "I'm accepting bids by mobile."

Emmeline's jaw dropped as she gaped at Roger. "You…you can't," she stammered. "It's stolen for goodness sake." She raked a hand through her curls. "It's *illegal*. You must turn over the Pink Courtesan to the police."

Roger blinked at her. "I don't see why. The police will only ask a series of awkward questions—more than you do—and they'll have to file a stack of tedious reports. On the other hand, the diamond will do me a great deal of good. So you see, in the end, I'm actually saving the police an awful lot of distress."

Emmeline opened her mouth to reply, but no words would come. What Roger was proposing was sheer insanity. Not to mention dangerous as hell.

"As a government official," Philip intoned with gravitas, "I cannot condone, nor can I be a party to, your scheme."

Roger inched his chair closer to Philip and, leaning toward him, whispered out of the corner of his mouth, "I won't tell, if you don't."

The smile on his lips faded when it collided with Philip's stone-faced intractability. Roger cleared his throat. "It's not like it's your diamond." He shot a sideways glance across the table. "Or yours, Emmeline. Why should either of you care? It's a simple business transaction. That's all."

Emmeline drew in a sharp breath. She poked Gregory in the arm. "Are all your friends unhinged? Were you like this in the wicked old days?"

"Ouch, darling," he said as he rubbed his upper arm. "Please don't take your frustrations out on your poor, hapless husband. I have absolutely no idea what you are referring to. I have always been a model of a law-abiding citizen."

She rolled her eyes toward the ceiling. "That line is getting old. Don't play the innocent. Even though we're married, it doesn't mean that I'm blind to your faults. You were born as sly as a fox."

One of Gregory's brows arched upward. "What faults?" He lifted his forearm to shield himself in mock fear. "No, don't hit me again. I don't think my defenseless arm could stand it."

She ignored his piffle and gestured with her chin at Roger. "Talk some sense into your deranged friend."

"My faculties are in perfecting working order. Thank you very much," Roger sniffed.

"Not to the outside observer," Philip tossed back at him. "If you don't go to the authorities *immediately*, it will be my duty to inform them of your illicit plans. You will leave me no choice." His glacial stare was enough to make a normal person think twice about crossing him.

However, Roger was not impressed. "You forget, Acheson, that we're in Malta, not dear old London. I don't think your government credentials will hold much sway here. Besides when I make an anonymous call to Interpol and the local police telling them that Special Branch has a warrant for your arrest, you'll be the one who will have a good deal of explaining to do. It will likely take hours. And by then"—a smug smile curled around his lips—"I will have concluded my business. It's nothing personal, I quite assure you. But you must understand, I've been waiting for precisely such an opportunity my entire life and I'm not going to allow you—" He shot a warning look that encompassed both Emmeline and Gregory. "—Or anyone else to jeopardize it. For the record, I would hate to have any unpleasantness ruin our friendship."

"If you treat your friends this way, I'd much rather be an

enemy," Philip scoffed.

Roger clucked his tongue. "I can see your pride has been wounded, but there's no reason to take that tone." He paused. "Now, if all of you are willing to be reasonable…"

Philip snorted. "By reasonable you mean let you get on with your dodgy diamond auction."

Roger's mouth twisted into a grimace. "Dodgy has such a negative connotation, but I'll let it pass. If you won't interfere with my business affairs, I'm quite disposed to give you something in return."

Emmeline crossed her arms over her chest. "How can we possibly trust you again?"

"It's tragic that one so young is jaded." He sighed. "Trust is a complicated thing," he explained. "It requires a leap of faith. On both sides."

"Hmph," she grunted.

Roger folded his hands in front of him on the table and trained his gaze on Gregory. "The diamond for Seb's papers. I think it's more than generous. What do you say?"

CHAPTER 33

N o," Emmeline responded through clenched teeth before Gregory had a chance to say a word. She struggled to keep her voice barely above a whisper. "You will *not* make us your accomplices. This may be a game to you, but it is not to us. We came to Malta to find Swanbeck. He must pay for his crimes once and for all, including the murder of your friend Jardine. Or have you conveniently forgotten him?"

"That would be rather difficult," Roger replied laconically.

"Despite the fact that Jardine had dubious morals, his killer must answer to the law. If Swanbeck is not brought to justice, it will only embolden him. And God help us all if that happens."

Roger put a hand over his heart and smiled at her. "Your fierce dedication is breathtaking to behold, Emmeline. But sadly, the world is not black and white. There are shades of gray. This falls into one of those gray areas." He put up a hand to preempt the verbal assault she was preparing to fire at him. "In our short acquaintance, I've grown to respect and admire you deeply. It's quite true. And of course, I owe Greg a debt. That's why I've offered you Seb's papers. You must know that I could have gotten quite a lot of money for them, but I'll content myself with the Pink Courtesan. By midnight, the transaction should be concluded."

He shot his cuff and glanced at his watch. "Is that the time?" he exclaimed as he pushed himself to his feet. "I really must go. I have preparations to make. I only have ten hours and there's so much still left to do. Greg, it's now or never. Do we have a deal?"

"If I say no?"

Roger's brows knit together. "I really wish you wouldn't. It would pain me greatly. I am on your side." The hint of irritation in his tone was far from reassuring.

"I agree on two conditions."

Roger sighed. "You're in no position to make demands."

Gregory's mouth curved into a smile. "Humor me."

"Well, get on with it," the other man countered with asperity.

"Give us the papers now and tell us where Swanbeck is."

Roger threw his head back and laughed. "Oh, come on. And lose my leverage, not to mention my life in the process?" Defiance was etched in every line of his face. "No. You get the papers *after* the auction. Once I've safely left Malta, I'll get word to you where you can find Swanbeck."

"Longdon, he'll do a runner," Philip interjected. "He's been stringing us along."

Gregory ignored this comment and rose. "Then we come to the auction. Just to keep you honest."

Emmeline's dark eyes widened, and her head bobbed up down vigorously. "Yes, that's the most sensible thing I've heard in the last hour."

Gregory smiled down and took her small hand in his. "Not you, darling. You're going to the hotel to wait. Acheson and I will accompany Roger." He let go of her hand and clapped Roger on the shoulder. "We're not going to let him out of our sight until the auction is over."

Philip stood now too. "Longdon's right, Emmeline. Best leave it to us."

Her fists curled into balls on the table. "Ooh," she protested. "Why are men always so patronizing?"

"Neanderthal instincts," Roger suggested in an attempt at humor that failed miserably, as evidenced by Emmeline leaping up.

"This is deadly serious."

Roger wiped the smile from his lips. "Sorry. Of course, you're quite right."

"As for you"—her eyes locked on her husband's face—"I'll deal with you later." Her gaze flitted to Philip. "Both of you." She flapped a hand at the trio. "Go now. I'll settle the bill."

Gregory flashed one his brilliant smiles. "That's my girl. I knew you would be reasonable. Go directly to the hotel and stay there until tomorrow morning."

Her smile matched his in intensity as she reached up to give him a peck on the cheek. "And miss the sights in beautiful Valletta." Another kiss. "I have no intention of going to the hotel. Off you go, boys. Have fun."

Gregory and Philip exchanged worried looks.

"Emmy, what are you up to?"

Her eyebrows shot up. "Up to? I have no idea what you mean. I'm simply going to do what any journalist would do when working on a story: ask questions."

"*Emmy*." Gregory's tone was infused with disapproval. However, he was sorely mistaken if he thought it would make her back down.

"Yes, darling?" she asked, her smile growing broader.

"You *know* that is not wise. You have a tendency to step on the wrong toes."

She cast a glance at her feet and then looked up at him

again. "Don't worry. I'll tiptoe."

Roger chuckled. "Game, set, and match, I'd say. It's fascinating to watch the dynamics of a modern marriage."

Gregory cast a pointed glance at him. "Oh, shut up. This doesn't involve you."

Roger made a show of twisting an invisible key to lock his lips.

Philip intervened. "Longdon, perhaps you should stay with Emmeline."

"I don't need a babysitter," she said tartly.

"No, you need a good bang on the head" was Gregory's wry observation.

Her chin jutted mulishly in the air. "It doesn't seem to have done you much good." His brow furrowed, but she pressed her case, "I'm just going to ask a few questions. That's all. I'll be fine. You were going to leave me on my own anyway. What you and Philip intend to do is far more reckless." She wrinkled her nose. "God knows what unsavory characters Roger's auction has drawn out of the woodwork."

"I hate to see the two of you at each other's throats on my account," Roger ventured. "There's really no need for Greg and Acheson to tag along. You can all go to your hotel, relax after your flight and I'll…"

"Think again," Philip advised. "You just threatened to have me arrested."

"It's nothing personal. I quite like you," Roger offered in a conciliatory tone.

"Hmph," Philip grunted.

Roger turned to Gregory. "I'm getting the distinct impression that you still don't trust me."

"Whatever gave you that idea? We simply enjoy your company. Isn't that right, Acheson?"

Philip nodded and took a step closer to Roger. "Indeed, we do. I can't tell you the last time I spent such a delightful afternoon. Threats of being arrested always put me in a jolly mood," he quipped facetiously.

Roger tried a different tack. "Don't you think it's ungentlemanly to leave Emmeline on her own?"

Before either her husband or Philip could utter a word, she said, "I'm quite resourceful. I'll find a way to kill the rest of the afternoon."

"That's what I'm afraid of," Gregory remarked.

She placed her hand on his arm and her tone softened. "How about a compromise? I'll visit the *Times of Malta*'s office to see if I can speak with the editor. Then I'll go the hotel. We can all have dinner in the restaurant and see where things stand." She lifted a brow in askance. "All right?"

Gregory reluctantly acquiesced. "It's useless to argue. I married an obstinate, impetuous woman, who is determined to drive me mad." He gave her a crooked smile and bent to brush her cheek with a kiss. "Be careful, darling."

She fluttered her eyelashes at him. "I'm as careful as you are. What's good for the goose is good for the gander, as the saying goes."

"Touché." Then Gregory clamped his fingers on Roger's upper arm and said, "Let's go."

"Go where precisely?"

"Wherever it was you were so anxious to get off to a few moments ago."

"Oh, yes. Right. I have a…meeting. A *private* meeting. I can't possibly turn up with the two of you in tow."

"If I didn't know better, Roger," Gregory replied. "I'd say you were embarrassed by us. I assure you Acheson and I are quite respectable, aren't we?"

"The epitome of propriety."

Roger huffed a nervous laugh. "No question about it. It's just that…The thing is…It's a rather sensitive matter and this chap jealousy guards his privacy."

"Look, Delahunt," Philip said sharply. "We don't care how many illegal pies you have your thumb in. Our interest is strictly in Swanbeck. We only have twenty-four hours to find him, before he destroys several lives and quite possibly tries to kill Emmeline and Longdon. Again."

Roger thrust his hand in his pockets. "Well, if you put it that way…" His voice trailed off. He pursed his lips. "Look, let me make one call. Then, I'm all yours."

"Fine. Go ahead."

"A private call. I'll step outside, if you don't mind. You wait here."

"We'll join you," Gregory offered, tugging on Roger's sleeve. "Come along. You can make your call in the middle of St. George's Square. Acheson and I can keep you in our sights the whole time. You'll have nowhere to run."

And off they went with Roger keeping up a stream of frivolous chatter.

✁✁

The editor of *Times of Malta*, a seasoned journalist in his mid-fifties, was more than happy to take a half-hour out of his day to talk with Emmeline. He provided insight about the political climate and the pervasive corruption it had spawned. He also discussed how the Mafia had insinuated itself into government and business circles. Naturally, the editor was well aware of Swanbeck. He confirmed several rumors she had heard, including that Swanbeck was operating out of Malta. Unfortunately, the editor had no idea where Swanbeck was hiding nor could he tell her anything about Jardine or his movements over the past few months. There was no doubt in his mind, though, that either Swanbeck or the Cannizzaros were responsible for his death.

Emmeline left the paper a good deal wiser than when she

had arrived, but she still didn't have irrefutable proof that tied Swanbeck and Jardine together. She hadn't dared to tell the editor about the Pink Courtesan. More than likely, the Mafia was closely monitoring what was being reported. She didn't want the Cannizzaros coming after the editor simply because he had been kind enough to share his knowledge with a colleague.

She glanced at her watch. Three-thirty. She debated ringing Gregory to see what was happening with Roger. But he probably wouldn't tell her. She couldn't believe he would actually allow Roger to go through with the auction. She wasn't as confident as Gregory that Roger would keep his word. A niggling voice at the back of her mind was beginning to wonder whether the papers with the evidence on Swanbeck even existed.

A frustrated sigh escaped her lips. She couldn't go back to the hotel to wait for news. She had to do something. She smiled as an idea struck her. She would set the cat among the pigeons and see what she could stir up. Gregory would be livid, if he knew.

So being a thoughtful wife, she wasn't going to tell him. Not until *after* the fact.

CHAPTER 34

Emmeline caught the No. 52 bus from the Central Business District, where the *Times of Malta* was located, into downtown Valletta. The trip took just under half an hour. The bus dropped her off at the Tritons' Fountain at the edge of the city gate. A ten-minute walk straight up Republic Street led her back to St. George's Square. Along the way, her eyes feasted on glimpses of the harbor, as she cast glances down the steep, narrow side streets to her left and right. She would have liked to linger and perhaps pop into some of the shops selling the lovely silver filigree jewelry. Alas, this wasn't a holiday. However, she did allow herself to admire the elegant architecture of the golden Baroque and neoclassical buildings she passed. Some had enclosed balconies painted in a range of bright hues.

Once she arrived at the Grandmaster's Palace, she ducked through the arched, cobblestone passageway. It opened onto a neat courtyard with an arcade running all the way around. A clocktower rose to caress the wisps of clouds in the cerulean sky. Palm trees and bushes, and a few benches, were scattered about the forecourt. A huge circular flowerbed shaded by the contorted branches of a palm tree was the focal point in the center. There were two smaller flowerbeds over which stood sentinel a bronze statue of Neptune. Two stone lion statues, which reminded her of the ones in Trafalgar Square back in London, flanked a forged openwork, metal lace door.

The House of Representatives held its sessions at the palace. She was hoping to waylay Antonio Cannizzaro, who had now risen to the powerful role of finance minister. She had called his office and was told that he would be attending today's session. The prime minister had dispatched him to make the case for a bill the government wanted enacted.

A young guard in a smart navy-blue uniform with a red stripe running across the shoulders and down the sides of his trousers was posted at the entrance. His pristine white colonial helmet had a golden emblem and was perfectly centered on his head. He stood at attention, holding a rifle in front of him.

Emmeline approached him cautiously, her mouth curving into a broad smile. "Hello, I wonder if you could help me."

The guard's expression remained impassive, but not intimidating. "Yes, miss?"

"My name is Emmeline Kirby. I'm the editorial director of investigative features at *The Clarion* in London. I would like to speak to Minister Antonio Cannizzaro. His office told me that he would be at the House of Representatives today."

"If you do not have an appointment with the minister," he replied in a clipped tone, "I'm afraid I cannot allow the press beyond this point." His white-gloved fingers tightened around the barrel of his rifle. "You will have to leave the premises."

Well, there's no need to get tetchy, Emmeline thought. Her smile broadened. "I assure you it will only take a few moments of the minister's time." Her voice was deliberately soft and cajoling. "Five minutes is all I ask. Surely, he can spare that."

The guard's brows knit together and his brown eyes narrowed. "No, miss. If you persist, I will have to arrest you."

"Arrest me?" She laughed, but there was no mirth in it. "For what, I haven't done anything illegal. Don't tell me you arrest journalists in Malta for doing their jobs." With every word, her voice rose an octave.

His brown gaze darted around the courtyard. "Miss, you are making a scene. You will have to leave."

"Not until I speak with Minister Cannizzaro," she asserted stubbornly. "I'm prepared to wait. However long it takes."

"As I've already explained, that is not possible. Please, miss, don't make any difficulties."

"From my vantage point, you're the one who is being quite tiresome. There is something called freedom of the press. You…"

She broke off when a tall, dark-haired man bustled out of a door on the other side of the courtyard and hurried down the arcade. Three men, who were all speaking over one another, trailed close on his heels. It appeared to be a heated argument.

The dark-haired man shook his head and finally spun around. "Enough," he roared. "The answer is no. That is final. There is no deal."

"Be reasonable, Cannizzaro," one of the others urged.

Emmeline's ears perked up when this name floated on the air. She exchanged a glance with the guard, smiled, and hurried across the square. As she had surmised, he couldn't follow her because he couldn't abandon his post.

The guard did call after her, though. "Miss Kirby." It was not quite a shout, but it was definitely more than a hiss.

Naturally, she disregarded him. She was not going to allow Cannizzaro to slip away.

When she was only a few feet away from the group of men, she raised her voice to be heard above the din. "Minister

Cannizzaro, may I have a word?"

The conversation came to an abrupt halt and four pair of male eyes glanced in her direction.

Cannizzaro broke away from his colleagues and took several steps toward her. "What is the meaning of this? Who are you?"

Up close, he was taller than she realized. He had to be well over six feet. His nostrils flared in annoyance as he stared down his aquiline nose at her.

She offered him an ingratiating smile and proffered a hand. He inclined his head and clasped her hand in his own. "How do you do, Minister. I'm Emmeline Kirby. I'm the editorial director of investigative features at *The Clarion* in London. I have a few questions I'd like to ask you about your family's business dealings with Alastair Swanbeck, a known criminal."

Cannizzaro tossed a glance over his shoulder at his colleagues and then turned back to her, a smirk on his face. "Swanbeck? I've never heard of this man. As you know, I'm no longer part of the family business because I decided to dedicate my life to public service. But I can't stress it enough, my family has the highest integrity. Ask anyone. They would never do anything illegal," he bristled with indignation. "You were obviously given incorrect information. I'd check my sources, if I were you. You wouldn't want your paper sued for libel."

"That sounds suspiciously like a threat, Minister. It makes me wonder what you are trying desperately to hide."

Her last words hung upon the breeze. Cannizzaro's jaw clenched into a hard line as his eyes shot daggers at her. He tore his gaze away for an instant to look at his colleagues, who were staring at him open-mouthed. "Please forgive me, gentleman," he murmured. Despite his efforts to remain unfazed, a spasm of annoyance flickered across his features. He waved his hand in the air impatiently. "As you can see, I'm left with no choice. I must deal with this young woman's nonsense, before she makes an even greater nuisance of herself. We will continue our discussions tomorrow."

He gave a curt nod and they dispersed, muttering amongst themselves in frustration.

Once Cannizzaro was certain they were alone, he rounded on Emmeline. "How dare you come here hurling your baseless accusations? In the space of a few minutes, you have single-handedly damaged my reputation. There is no justification for such vile behavior."

Emmeline felt a nervous flutter in the pit of her stomach. His dark eyes blazed, and his voice trembled with fury, but she would not give him the satisfaction of seeing her flinch.

She stood her ground. "I am following a legitimate lead and in the interest of fairness…"

He snorted derisively, "Fairness? You don't know the meaning of the word."

She went on as if he hadn't spoken. "—In the interest of fairness, I came to give you an opportunity to provide your side of the story."

"There is no story," he snarled. "You came to ambush me with a pack of lies in front of my colleagues. I am an honest man. I would never associate with a criminal, neither would my family. Please leave now, before I'm forced to call a guard to escort you out of the palace."

She glared at him in silence for several seconds. The determined expression on his face told her that he wasn't bluffing. She hitched her handbag higher on her shoulder. Without another word, she pivoted on her heel, leaving him standing in the middle of the courtyard.

She had only taken a few steps, when he called to her. "You and Longdon made a grave mistake. Malta is not London. People here know better than to make trouble and those who don't tend to pay a heavy price for their arrogance. I'd keep that in mind as you and your husband wander the streets of this beautiful city. Anything can happen."

Her back stiffened, but she didn't turn around. *If you're as innocent as you profess*, she speculated darkly, *why are you trying to frighten me and Gregory, who for all intents and purposes are tourists?*

She forced herself to place one foot in front of the other, putting as much distance between them as possible. She didn't stop until she was outside in St. George's Square again, where there were lots of people milling about or ambling along Republic Street.

She managed to walk a few yards, but her legs were shaking so hard that she had to stop and lean against the corner of the palace. She drew deep gulps of air into her lungs.

It was not the first time she had been threatened. However, she would never get used to it. After a couple of minutes, she had regained her composure. Judging by Cannizzaro's reaction, she had succeeded in her mission of stirring things up.

But was it enough to bait Swanbeck? And if it was, what would be his next move?

ⱷⱷⱷ

Cannizzaro lingered in the courtyard. He chuckled to himself as Emmeline skittered off like a frightened deer. It served her right for meddling in things that were none of her concern.

And yet, her appearance at the palace worried him. She and Longdon were getting too close for comfort. They would ruin everything. He silently let loose a string of expletives. It was Swanbeck's fault that they were even in Malta. He shook his head. He had warned his father and his brother against getting tangled up with Swanbeck. The man had too much dirty laundry. But, as usual, his advice was ignored and once again it was left up to him to clean up the mess.

He exhaled a long sigh as he pulled out his mobile from the inner pocket of his suit jacket.

He punched in a number. His call was answered almost immediately. "The girl was here asking questions. I've had enough of her and Longdon's interference." He listened for a few seconds. "Don't argue with me. I want them to become a distant memory. It's time to divide and conquer. I will get rid of their friend the MI5 agent. You take care of the Longdons. But not until the Pink Courtesan is safely back in my family's hands. For all my aggravation, I want the Blue Angel too. Then, it's Swanbeck's turn to pay for his treachery."

CHAPTER 35

Emmy?" The sound of Gregory's voice made her jump out of her skin.

She only had a few seconds to arrange her face in what she hoped was a relaxed expression. With her stomach coiled into a knot, she felt anything but serene. Pasting a smile on her lips, she spun around.

She gave a little wave as Gregory sliced his way through a group of tourists to reach her side. "Darling," she murmured and tried to give him a peck on the cheek.

He grasped her by the elbows to prevent her from distracting him. "Why are you still hanging about here? You were supposed to go back to the hotel and wait for us."

Just as he uttered these words, Philip hurried toward them. "Where's Delahunt?" His gaze scanned the tourists taking photos or strolling around aimlessly.

Gregory's head whirled round. "What do you mean? Roger was with you when I went to have a word with a chap I know."

"The scheming bastard." Philip spit out these words in disgust. "Five minutes after you left us, he got a call on his mobile. He said you needed him and off he went like a shot around the corner after you."

"I'll wring his bloody neck," Gregory said through clenched teeth. "In any event, I found out from my acquaintance that there have been whispers for the past several days about a party tonight on the *Sea Predator*. It's docked across the harbor in the Vittoriosa Yacht Marina. The boat belongs to none other than the esteemed Antonio Cannizzaro, minister of finance and spawn of the notorious Mafia clan."

A low whistle escaped from Philip's lips, while Emmeline felt the blood drain from her face at the mention of Cannizzaro.

Gregory, always keenly attuned to what was going on around him especially when it concerned her, noticed her reaction. "Emmy, what's the matter?"

"Nothing," she mumbled. She looked up at him from under her eyelashes. "Absolutely nothing."

Gregory's eyes narrowed with suspicion. "I don't believe you."

"Neither do I," Philip chimed in, his expression just as dubious.

She shrugged and tried to bluster. "It must be something in the air here."

Gregory smiled and tucked her arm through the crook of his elbow. "What have you been doing in our absence?"

She felt the full force of two pairs of male eyes, one cinnamon and the other as blue as the waters in the harbor. "Don't look at me as if I've committed a crime."

"Have you?" Philip queried. "You have a fertile imagination and are capable of getting up to *all* sorts of mischief when left to your own devices."

"Ha. Ha. Very droll," she shot back. "That doesn't even deserve a response."

Gregory's smile grew broader. He lifted her hand to his lips to brush her knuckles with a kiss. His eyes met hers. His face was a hairs breadth away. "But you're going to give us one, my darling."

She snatched her hand away and glared up at him. "Don't treat me as if I'm a child."

He straightened up, all amusement vanishing from his features. "I wouldn't dream of it," he said, his tone clipped. "Just tell us how you kept yourself occupied over the last two hours."

The moment of reckoning had come. She had intended to tell him anyway. However, she had hoped he would be in a better frame of mind when she did. She took a deep breath and related an account of her meeting with the editor of the *Times of Malta*. That went smoothly. When it came to her encounter with Cannizzaro, her tongue rushed to get the words out. And then it was all in the open.

"Have you flipped your lid?" Philip exploded. "What possessed you to approach Cannizzaro?"

"We weren't getting anywhere, so I thought I'd shake things up to see what dropped out," she hurled back defiantly.

"Well, you've certainly succeeded. You got his back up. Now, he's on his guard."

"Then, he'll make a mistake and betray himself or Swanbeck. Either way, we'll get to the truth."

Philip snorted. "Oh, come on, Emmeline. Don't pretend to be naïve. You intentionally goaded Cannizzaro in the name of journalism. You claim it springs from the purest motives, but it was really out of some bizarre desire for excitement. When will you learn that type of adrenaline rush will get you killed?"

She opened her mouth to respond, but then thought better of it. She was loath to admit it, but she had miscalculated.

Out of the corner of her eye, she slid a glance at Gregory. He had remained silent, his lips twisted into a grim line, during her exchange with Philip. Now, he asked, "What did I tell you in the café?"

She chafed at his cool detachment. One shoulder twitched up in a shrug. "You said a lot of things. What precisely are you referring to?"

"I said go to the hotel after your meeting at the paper. I seem to recall my darling wife promising to do so. Did you somehow get lost along the way?"

She threw her hands up in the air. *Damn and blast*, she cursed inwardly.

"You know I need to be doing *something*. I couldn't sit at the hotel twiddling my thumbs waiting for all of you to return. I would have gone mad."

"We've already established that you are," Philip muttered under his breath.

She gave him a quelling look.

Gregory ran a hand through his wavy hair and groaned, "What's done is done. It doesn't help matters being at each other's throats."

She laid a hand on his arm and gave it a squeeze. "Thank you, darling, for understanding."

He gave her a crooked smile. "Until my dying day, I will *never* understand you."

Her mouth curled into a smile. "But think of all of the fun you will have trying."

"Now that domestic bliss has once again been restored," Philip interjected, "we must come up with a plan of action to deal with Cannizzaro, Swanbeck, and the elusive Delahunt."

"It's a virtual certainty that the auction will take place on Cannizzaro's yacht this evening. A party is a perfect cover," Emmeline reasoned. "I wonder how Roger persuaded Cannizzaro to play host. Could Roger have already sold the Pink Courtesan to Cannizzaro? And the party is merely a charade to gather some rivals together to settle some old scores?" This set her pulse racing. "Perhaps he's lured Swanbeck out of his shell."

Philip nodded. "That's a distinct possibility. Delahunt always seems to have something up his sleeve."

"If it is a trap," Gregory observed ominously, "several bodies might be turning up at the bottom of the harbor by morning."

"That would attract too much unwanted attention," Philip remarked. "The Cannizzaros are not that reckless."

"They might limit it to one body," Gregory quipped.

Emmeline had been turning over thoughts in her mind. "The way I see it," she said matter-of-factly, "our only option is to crash the party."

She beamed at the two men, who were staring down at her in exasperation.

"Mad was the wrong term," Philip commented. "You're completely unhinged." He clapped Gregory on the shoulder in a gesture of male camaraderie. "You have my sympathies, you poor chap. I'd be old before my time, if Maggie ran around like your wife does."

Gregory pressed a hand to his chest and gave an exaggerated sigh. "It's the cross I have to bear."

Emmeline rolled her eyes toward the sky. "Playing the martyr doesn't suit you. Do either of you have any better ideas?" she challenged.

Her hard gaze flitted between them. "Huh," she sniffed, when they remained silent. "I thought not. When it's a race against time, one must throw caution to the wind."

"Now, why does that turn of phrase send chills straight to my bones?" Philip pondered.

Emmeline pitched her voice low. "That's rich coming from a MI5 agent."

Philip opened his mouth to respond, but he would never get a chance to say what he had intended.

A hand clamped around his arm. "Philip Acheson?" asked a male voice, infused with the crisp sternness of officialdom.

Philip whirled round, trying to shake off the grasp of whoever it was. "What's the meaning of this?"

The offending hand was attached to the arm of a dour middle-aged man. His blue-gray cap was pulled down low on his forehead, casting a shadow over his face. He was dressed in a navy pullover with the word "Pulizija" embroidered in white over the left breast. *Police.*

A younger man, perhaps in his early forties, in a somber charcoal suit and maroon tie, peered at Philip with contempt. "You are Philip Acheson of Her Majesty's Foreign and Commonwealth Office and a spy for MI5."

Curious onlookers were hovering nearby, their interest piqued by the drama unfolding.

"Keep your bloody voice down," Philip hissed out of the corner of his mouth.

"I give the orders here," the younger man snapped. "I am Inspector Silvio Azzopardi of the Malta Police Force and this is Sergeant Paul Camilleri." He paused to allow this to sink in. "Your furtive behavior leads me to only one conclusion. You *are* Philip Acheson. Since that is the case, I must inform you that you are under arrest."

"This is a mistake," Emmeline asserted. "He hasn't done anything."

Although the policemen ignored her, Gregory took the precaution of drawing her out of the line of fire before they turned their attention on her. "Shh," he ordered. He stepped in front of her, trying to shield her with his body. She was having none of it, though. She elbowed him in the ribs and nudged him aside. He scowled down at her and gave a disapproving shake of his head.

"What's the charge?" Philip demanded of Azzopardi.

"You are a fugitive from justice. Special Branch and Interpol have warrants out for your arrest. I am not prepared to say more for the moment. You will come with us to the station *at once*."

Azzopardi suddenly seemed to notice Gregory and Emmeline's presence. He drew himself up to his full height of over six feet. His chin jutted out and his brown eyes narrowed. Emmeline wondered whether he practiced that air of frosty hauteur or whether it came naturally.

"And who are you?" Azzopardi probed impatiently.

Gregory offered the inspector an ingratiating smile and took Emmeline by the elbow, giving it a warning squeeze. "I'm Percival Smythe-Jones, Inspector." His smile grew wider. "My friends call me Percy. And this lovely lady"—he slipped his arm around Emmeline's waist and drew her to his side—"is my wife, Maud. We're newlyweds. It was our dream to come to Malta on our honeymoon. Isn't that right, love?"

Maud and Percy? Ugh, Emmeline groaned inwardly. *You couldn't have come up with something better? And Smythe-Jones? Isn't that a teeny bit obvious?* However, she nodded mutely and glanced up at him with what she hoped the inspector would consider a besotted wife's adoring gaze.

Azzopardi inclined his head, but a skeptical frown puckered his brow. "Mrs. Smythe-Jones, Mr. Smythe-Jones, my congratulations. May you have a long and happy marriage. But I must ask"—he gestured toward Philip—"how do you know Mr. Acheson?"

"Oh, we don't," Gregory replied matter-of-factly without glancing at Philip. "Never saw him before in our lives. We were just asking him directions to St. John's Cathedral."

Azzopardi's mouth curved into a reptilian smile. "If that's case, why was Mrs. Smythe-Jones so distressed about him a moment ago? To the outside observer, it appeared as if you knew each other quite well. Quite well, indeed." His voice was soft and deceptively sweet, as his hard stare locked on her face.

Emmeline opened her mouth to reply, but Gregory was too quick for her.

He sighed melodramatically. "My wife is too kind-hearted, Inspector. She's always ready to champion the underdog. If I tell you she takes in stray cats, you'll understand. I'm afraid that someone will take advantage of her good nature one of these days." He looked down at her and patted her hand. "And then where will you be, Maud dear?"

Maud will give you a kick in the shins, if this charade goes on much longer, Emmeline thought silently.

She looked up into his eyes and blushed at the absurdity of it all. "Yes, I know, darling." She adopted the meek voice of a witless woman. "But I can't help it."

Gregory shook his head and shrugged at Azzopardi. "You see what I mean."

The inspector cleared his throat. Apparently, his patience had been exhausted and he was eager to get away. "My advice is to be more careful with whom you have contact during your stay in Malta, Mr. and Mrs. Smythe-Jones." Had he placed an extra emphasis on their phony surname?

"Camilleri," Azzopardi barked at the sergeant, "let's go back to the station. Mr. Acheson has a lot of questions to answer."

Camilleri grabbed Philip's arm. "Yes, sir."

Philip struggled against him. "I'm a British subject. I have rights. I insist on speaking to someone from the high commission."

The inspector made a dismissive gesture in the air. "Yes, yes. All in good time. First, Special Branch and Interpol must be informed of your capture," he said with relish, a triumphant gleam in his eyes.

Likely, he was calculating whether this would get him a promotion, Emmeline speculated in disgust.

Azzopardi became brisk. "It's best if you were on your

way, Mr. and Mrs. Smythe-Jones. This is none of your concern. By the way, the cathedral is a three-minute walk back that way." He jerked his thumb over his shoulder. "Retrace your steps along Republic Street and turn left at the pharmacy onto Triq San Gwann." He smirked. "You can't miss it. I'm surprised you did initially."

"Oh, you know how it is when you're in a new place." Gregory extended his hand. "Thank you, Inspector Azzopardi." He took Emmeline's elbow, giving her a pointed look and a nudge. "Come along, Maud. We can't stand in the way of these police officers doing their duty."

Philip gave them an imperceptible nod and allowed himself to be marched off. He was flanked on either side by Azzopardi and Camilleri. There was no way he could make a break for it. With so many things in flux at the moment, it was probably better that he didn't.

Gregory tugged at Emmeline's sleeve. "Let's not linger," he whispered out of the corner of his mouth as he kept his gaze focused straight ahead.

They turned down Triq San Gwann, in the event Azzopardi had sent someone to trail them. They stopped when they reached the cathedral. As Gregory pretended to point out features of the Baroque façade, he surreptitiously surveyed their surroundings. "It's clear, as far as I can tell," he murmured.

"It has to be Cannizzaro," Emmeline muttered, cursing herself bitterly for showing him their hand. "It's all my fault that Philip is in custody."

"Never mind, darling." He grimaced. "I suppose I have no choice but to ring Villiers to let him know about Acheson. After the chilly reception Millbank gave us, I very much doubt he'd be of any use in this situation."

She nodded, pained to see the chagrin reflected in his gaze at the prospect of speaking to his father. "I suppose that's best. Villiers will know how to handle Azzopardi." She clutched at his sleeve. "Gregory, we have to go to that black-tie affair on the *Sea Predator* tonight. I know you disagree, but…"

"Far from it, darling. We can't possibly miss the social event of the season. Everybody who's anybody will be there." He shot his cuff and glanced at his watch. "Time to get cracking. We only have a few hours to find something suitable to wear. I know a chap who can kit me out in a tuxedo and I'm certain procuring a smashing cocktail dress for you will be no problem."

Of course, doesn't everyone 'know a chap' who has eve-rything imaginable at his fingertips? Emmeline mused. Her eyes skimmed over the planes and angles of her husband's faces. *One of these days, my darling, you're going to tell me how you know all these mysterious chaps.*

CHAPTER 36

They had only been in their room at the Corinthia Palace Hotel for ten minutes, when there was a soft tapping at the door. Gregory answered it. There, hovering in the corridor were two bellboys. One was carrying two champagne flutes and a bucket with a bottle of Dom Perignon nestled on ice, while the other held two garment bags aloft.

He waved a hand at the champagne. "What's all this?"

"Compliments of Mr. Alastair," the bellboy replied casually. "He wishes you a pleasant stay in Malta."

Gregory heard Emmeline draw a sharp breath, as he told the chap to place the bucket and glasses on the table by the sliding glass door overlooking the terrace. Her complexion had taken on an ashen hue. She stared at the bottle of champagne as if it were a snake rearing its head out of the bucket.

"Would you like me to hang these in the cupboard for you, sir?" the other chap asked. "Just leave them on the bed," Gregory directed, wishing to get rid of them.

The bellboy nodded and gingerly laid out the garment bags.

Gregory gave both chaps a generous tip and ushered them out.

He bolted the door and crossed to the table. He slid the glass door open and smashed the bottle on the terrace. He put a hand to his lips in mock horror. "Oops, how clumsy of me."

He closed the door and turned to the bed. He kept an eye on Emmeline. She hadn't moved or uttered a word. "Darling," he called gently, as he started unzipping one of the garment bags. "Aren't you curious to see the dress Maurice found for you? I assure you he has extremely good taste."

Her head swiveled slowly, as her dark gaze locked on his face. "Swanbeck knows we're here. He knows we're at this hotel. He's *watching* us."

Gregory sighed and came to stand before her. He folded her into his embrace, his chin resting on top of her head. "Of course, he is." He drew back and searched her face. "Emmy, you said so yourself. He's been leading us by the nose, dropping crumbs here and there, enough to keep us wary and off balance. He's been plotting his revenge from the moment Oliver and Finch arrested him at Melnikov's flat over the summer. Alastair couldn't risk showing his face in the U.K., so he made us come to him. That little game at the airport with the knife in your bag was the opening gambit to put you on the scent. He knew you wouldn't stop until you discovered everything you could about the victim. Alastair just had to sit back and wait for me to identify the dead man as Seb. At that point, he knew we would put the whole sordid story together very quickly. His only miscalculation was not getting his hands on the Pink Courtesan before Seb was murdered."

"So you don't believe Swanbeck had Jardine killed?"

He shook his head. "After watching the CCTV footage, it's clear that Webb and his cohort at the airport were shocked when Seb was murdered right before their eyes. They were ready with the wheelchair to spirit him off to a quiet corner so that they could interrogate him with their fists until he turned over the Pink Courtesan. I have no doubt that Alastair gave them orders to kill Seb, once they had the diamond. But someone else beat them to it. The only ones ruthless enough are the Cannizzaros. Obviously, it came to their ears that the Pink Courtesan was in Seb's possession and they wanted it back. The only thing that makes sense is that they found out that Seb was really Matteo Pappalardo's son and put a contract out on him."

She nodded. "Yes, that must be what happened. And look how far we've come. Roger has the diamond. Philip's in police custody for God knows what crime. Villiers will likely be arrested on a false treason charge any day now. Millbank won't help. Inspector Azzopardi can't be trusted. And Superintendent Burnell and Sergeant Finch are back in London. That leaves only us."

Gregory smiled and rubbed his forehead against hers. "Don't underestimate us, darling. We make a formidable team, when we put our heads together."

She tilted her head back to look up at him. "It doesn't bother you that we're outnumbered?"

"Not at all. Remember Goliath's shock, when David let loose his sling and brought him down with a stone. It's the same principle. Besides, we're British. We have Queen and Country on our side. And we're rather clever."

She couldn't help but laugh at this remark. "So we simply keep calm and carry on, and everything will turn out right in the end?"

"That's my girl. I knew you would understand." He flashed a cheeky grin.

"You're incorrigible."

"When we got married, I did promise that life would never be dull. Now," he said as he glanced at his watch, "we mustn't be late for the party. Would you like to take a shower first or shall I?"

She waved him off. "You go. I'll take a look at the dress."

"You could join me in the shower, if you like." He gave her a suggestive wink. "To save water."

She felt her cheeks flame but pointed at the bathroom. "Go. We don't have time for your nonsense."

He sniffed. "Pity. The hot water might be gone by the time it's your turn."

"I'll take that chance." She gave him a gentle shove. "Now go."

She heard the hiss of water and Gregory moving about in the bathroom, as she unzipped the garment bag and lifted an elegant black lace dress with long tapered sleeves and a plunging V in the back. The dress would fall just below her knees. It was accompanied by a black stain shawl and velvet pumps with a modest heel. She slipped her foot into one shoe. It fit perfectly. She had to admit that Gregory's friend Maurice did indeed have exquisite taste.

She was laying out Gregory's tuxedo, when her mobile began ringing. She fumbled in her handbag. She frowned at the unfamiliar number, when she drew it out.

She hesitated before flipping it open. "Hello," she answered circumspectly.

"Miss Kirby, is that you?" a slightly breathless female voice asked.

"Who's calling?"

"It's Alessia Summergill, one of the associates at Saliba, Mifsud and Zammit Advocates in Valletta. We spoke yesterday. You were seeking information about Sebastian Jardine and Alastair Swanbeck."

Emmeline dropped into a chair. Her pulse started to race. "Yes. You seemed reluctant to help at the time. Have you had a change of heart?"

Please say yes, she implored silently as she scrabbled for her notebook and a pen.

"I must apologize for my reticence yesterday. If you look

it at from my point of view, you have to concede I had a right to be suspicious. Someone I had never heard of before calls out of the blue to ask questions about a dead man and a known international criminal."

"Quite understandable. It's only natural for a lawyer to be on his or her guard, when it comes to a client." She paused and drew a breath. She hoped she hadn't pressed too hard trying to probe whether Jardine had indeed been one of the firm's clients. "But you're willing to talk to me now?"

"Yes. I did some digging into your background to verify you were who you purported to be. Miss Kirby, your reporting and pursuit of the truth has garnered respect in many circles. But I'm embarrassed to admit that I had never heard of you."

"Never mind about that, Mrs. Summergill. I'm just a journalist doing my job like any of my colleagues. Do please call me Emmeline."

"Emmeline." The other woman said the name as if she were testing how it sounded on her tongue. "And I'm Alessia."

Emmeline smiled. The ice was broken and she was gaining the woman's confidence, but she still sensed a hesitation on Alessia's part.

"I'm prepared to tell you all I know about Sebastian Jardine and Alastair Swanbeck, but…" Her voice trailed off.

"If you're concerned about a direct attribution, I could say you were a source close to…"

Alessia cut across her. "No, it's not that…Well, it is in a sense. I can't be seen to do anything that would damage Saliba, Mifsud and Zammit's reputation. The firm would be ruined, if our clients suddenly became worried that they could no longer trust us to safeguard their confidentiality. I can't possibility have that on my conscience."

"I would never ask that of you. All I'm after is the truth.

Surely as a lawyer, you want to see that justice is served. Criminals should not be allowed to flout the law."

"No, certainly not. It's just that…I'm afraid. These are dangerous men we're talking about and…" Alessia broke off in midsentence.

Silence filled the void. "Alessia. Mrs. Summergill," Emmeline barked down the line. "Are you still there?"

"Darling, the bathroom awaits," Gregory said as he padded into the room barefoot, hair still damp, and wrapped in a terry robe the hotel had provided.

Emmeline leaped to her feet and snapped her fingers to silence him. He gave her a quizzical look as she asked again, "Alessia?" Her voice had risen an octave.

Her body relaxed when the other woman whispered in her ear, "I'm here but…Talking to you is too risky." Emmeline's heart sank at these words. "Anyone could overhear." There was a long pause and then she hissed, "I'm sorry. This was a mistake."

"Please don't ring off," Emmeline urged desperately. "We could meet in person. You choose the spot."

"That's impossible since you're in London," Alessia replied, confusion echoing in her tone.

"No, I'm in Malta. We arrived today. I'm staying at the Corinthia Palace Hotel in Attard. I'm getting ready to go to a party tonight in Vittoriosa."

"In Malta? I can't believe it."

"Please meet with me," Emmeline pressed. "You know this story is important. Otherwise, you never would have called me back. If you share the information you have, you would be striking a blow for the truth."

Her eyes widened and she shot an anxious look at Gregory, who came to her side. She crossed her fingers and shifted the mobile so that he could hear. "Alessia, what do you say?"

"Yes." The word came out on a shuddering sigh. "You're

right. Somebody must stand up for what's right. A group of friends and I have been trying to fight the insidious corruption that has gripped Malta. I can't allow fear to stop me now."

Emmeline beamed at Gregory. "That's the spirit. I'm at your disposal. Just tell me where and when to meet."

Alessia lowered her voice, forcing their ears to strain to hear her. "I can't have you come to the office. It's absolutely out of the question. I could be sacked, if anyone discovered I had spoken to you. I'm also fairly certain that I'm being watched."

"I wouldn't want to do anything to jeopardize your position or your safety," Emmeline replied.

"I think it would be best if we met somewhere out in the open. How about the Lower Barrakka Gardens? It's a small park overlooking the harbor. Do you know where it is?"

"I can find it."

"I don't think we'll be disturbed. I'm still at the office. I can't get away before seven o'clock."

"Seven is perfect. I'll be there."

"Good…I…Oh, I must go." Alessia rung off abruptly without saying goodbye.

"*We* will be there at seven," Gregory stressed as Emmeline snapped her mobile shut and stuffed it in her handbag.

"Don't be ridiculous, darling. She's a source. I can't possibly turn up with you."

"Why not?"

"First of all, she has no idea who you are…"

"I'll introduce myself and then we'll all become chums. If you haven't noticed, I'm an extremely charming fellow. Helen and Maggie can provide glowing references should Alessia require them."

Emmeline pressed a hand against his chest. "Gran and Maggie are biased, and you know it. We've had this conversation before about meetings with my sources." She stood on tiptoe and kissed his nose. "You are definitely *persona non grata*. I can't have you frightening off Alessia. She sounds highly strung."

He slipped his arms around her waist and drew her against his body and kissed her throat. "Modesty forbids, but I think I must remind you that a certain type of female finds me utterly irresistible."

She gave a slight moan at the touch of his lips and then she broke free of his embrace. "It's completely unfair to do that."

A roguish grin played about his mouth. "Why?" he asked, as he leaned in for another kiss.

She held up a hand. "No, I will not allow you to seduce me and wear down my resolve. You are *not* tagging along."

Gregory imprisoned her with his unforgiving stare. Any trace of a smile was gone. "I am not letting you out of my sight for the rest of what I hope will be our short stay in Malta. I needn't have to remind you what happened to Acheson this afternoon. We have no official assistance here, if things get a bit sticky. So, love"—he gave her bottom a gentle slap—"you had better hurry and take your shower. We don't want to keep the nervous Alessia waiting."

CHAPTER 37

Gregory made certain that they arrived at the Lower Barrakka Gardens before the appointed meeting to ensure he had time to reconnoiter the area. When he was stealing jewels, he had always been disciplined and meticulous about discovering every detail about the lay of the land and potential pitfalls. It was the only way, if one was to get the prize *and* elude the coppers. This situation was no different. In fact, it required even greater vigilance because of the element of danger posed by Swanbeck and the Cannizzaros.

The garden terrace, perched atop St. Christopher's Bastion, provided breathtaking views of the mouth of the Grand Harbor and the breakwater below. At this hour, the garden was deserted. The monument to Sir Alexander Ball, the British admiral who was the first commissioner of Malta, stood sentinel. The rhythmic *splish splash* from the single jet of water shooting up from the round reflecting pool in front of the neoclassical pavilion cooed softly, serenading them with its watery love song. Gregory tucked Emmeline's arm through his elbow as they strolled along the flagstone path. The muted glow of lamps scattered at intervals cast shadows over the manicured hedges and small trees that lined the borders.

Although he smiled down at her, he remained on his guard.

They still had a few minutes, so they ambled to the golden colonnade. They leaned against a metal railing and gazed out at the Memorial Siege Bell, which was all lit up. The belfry, shaped like a neoclassical temple, contained a huge bronze bell. They had been told that it commemorated the service personnel and civilians who lost their lives during the Siege of Malta during the Second World War. The bells rang every day at noon in their memory. Their eyes gradually were drawn across the harbor to the massive solidity of Fort Ricasoli and Fort St. Angelo, both of which were built by the Order of St. John. Emmeline rested her head against Gregory's shoulder, a companionable silence enveloping them. She was thoroughly enchanted by the twinkling lights reflected upon the water's dusky surface.

She could have remained rooted on that spot forever. But she couldn't. She had a story to write. She sighed regretfully and straightened up, gathering the shawl more tightly around her shoulders against the light breeze. "We'd better go back," she said, gesturing with her thumb in the direction of the garden behind them. "I don't want Alessia to think I've stood her up." Gregory nodded.

They retraced their steps to the pool with its chattering fountain. They could see a woman's silhouette walking down the path toward them, her footsteps echoing awkwardly. She was still too far away to make out her features, but her gait appeared stiff. Her arm pressed her handbag tightly against her body.

"It must be her," Emmeline mumbled out of the corner of mouth. She raised a hand and waved, as she called out, "Alessia."

The woman halted in her tracks several feet away from the pool. "Emmeline?" she asked.

"Yes, it's me."

"You were supposed to come alone," Alessia said, a tremor of trepidation mingled with reproach in her voice. She pointed an accusatory finger at Gregory, who was frowning slightly. "Who are you?"

Emmeline shot a pointed look at Gregory and mouthed, "I told you."

She rushed to the opposite side of the pool, but stopped a few feet from Alessia, not wishing to frighten her further. "I'm sorry. But you have nothing to worry about," she told her in soothing tones, "This is my husband, Gregory Longdon. He's the chief investigator for Symington's, the insurance firm. He can be trusted implicitly."

Gregory had already reached her side by this time. He exuded charm, offering her a smile and extending a hand. "How do you do, Mrs. Summergill." His smile broadened. "Forgive me. I know it may sound silly, but I feel as if we've met somewhere before."

Alessia's dark, straight hair fell past her shoulders, leaving half her face in shadow and making it difficult to gauge her expression. She left Gregory's hand hanging in the air and took a half-step backward, her arm clutching her handbag even more closely against her side. "I don't care who you are. And you know very well that we haven't laid eyes on each other until now."

Before he could offer a reply, she rounded on Emmeline. "You lied to me and lured me out here on false pretenses." She took another step backward.

Emmeline surged forward to close the space between them. "I promise everything I told you was the truth. I need your help, Alessia. If you have information…"

The other woman recoiled and held up a hand. "Stay right there. I took a big risk coming here tonight. My life could be in jeopardy." She cast a furtive glance over her shoulder and then scowled at Gregory.

He cleared his throat. "Then you'll understand precisely why I couldn't allow my wife to meet you alone," he observed reasonably. "This could very well have been a trap."

"How do I know it isn't?" Alessia shot back. "This was a mistake."

She turned and bolted down the path, her heels clicking furiously against the flagstones.

Emmeline started to go after her. "No, wait. Come back. We can go somewhere else and talk alone."

Gregory snatched her arm and pulled her back. "Let her go, Emmy."

She shook off his grasp and glared up at him. "Against my better judgment, I gave in to you. I knew this would happen. How can a source be open with me, if I bring my husband along as a bodyguard?"

Gregory smoothed down the corners of his mustache and reached for her arm again. "I am not going to apologize for wanting to keep my wife safe. I promised to love you till death do us part, but I have no intention of that time coming in the near future. Now if we don't hurry, we'll be late for the party of the year."

ɛ◡ɛ◡ɔ

Philip had been sequestered in a small, windowless room, ever since Inspector Azzopardi and Sergeant Camilleri had brought him to the police station. Azzopardi had made a half-hearted attempt to question him and then seemed to lose interest because he had no idea what the situation was all about. He was not the only one, Philip thought.

Philip drummed his fingers in an angry tattoo on the wooden table. They police couldn't keep him here indefinitely. He leaped to his feet and started to pace back and forth. His mind was awhirl with questions. Why hadn't anyone from the embassy come to his aid? What were these phony charges against him? But what concerned him the most was whether Longdon and Emmeline had been able to get away.

Philip stopped his perambulations, when the door was flung open by Azzopardi.

"Time to face the music, Acheson," he said with evident glee.

"Oh, yes?" He flicked a glance around the room. "Just when I was beginning to think of this charming place as home."

The inspector frowned and waggled his fingers. "All right. That's enough. Come on."

Philip circled around the table to the door. "I hope you're taking me to the high commission. I don't have to remind you that I'm a British subject."

"Fortunately, you are no longer my concern," Azzopardi replied, as he took Philip's arm. "An Interpol officer is here for you. You're his problem."

"I work for the Foreign Office. You can't simply hand me over to Interpol," Philip fumed. He tried to shake off the inspector's grasp.

Azzopardi stopped and turned to face him. "You're wrong, Mr. Acheson. I must transfer you into Interpol's custody. You are a fugitive. I have sworn to uphold the law." He smirked. "I would be breaking it, if I didn't."

"I'll wager that if someone did an audit of your bank account, he'd find that you have a very flexible view of the law," Philip hissed. "You're not fooling anyone. I know Cannizzaro put you up to this charade. These charges against me are pure fantasy. There's not a shred of evidence to back them up."

The inspector's mouth curved into a lupine smile. "I can't tell you how many times I've heard that line. It's what all the criminals say. It is not my place to judge you. You'll have your reckoning in a court and before God." His gaze darted to his right and left. Then he pitched his voice so that only Philip could hear. "I'd watch my tongue, if I were you, Mr. Acheson. You are far from London. Spouting scurrilous accusations against a powerful man like our illustrious Minister of Finance is unwise and could be fatal."

Philip stiffened. He was not surprised by the threat itself, rather the bald temerity and smug arrogance with which it was delivered right in the middle of the police station. "Do you always threaten the prisoners in your charge?"

Azzopardi's brown eyes widened. He pressed a hand to his chest. "What threat?" he asked in mock innocence. "I was offering you a piece of sound advice. If you're too headstrong and conceited to accept it"—he spread his hands wide and shrugged—"then you're more of a fool than I thought."

"Hmph," Philip grunted.

"Azzopardi, what's the delay? I'm not here on holiday, now am I?" a clearly irritated male voice called.

The inspector and Philip turned to see a slender man with thinning steel-gray hair and slate-green eyes, hands thrust deep in his trouser pockets, hovering by the entrance.

Azzopardi's eyes narrowed and he pursed his lips, as the man stalked over to them.

The man raised his wrist and tapped his watch in front of the inspector's face. "I've been kept waiting for twenty minutes. I'm from Interpol, not one of the lackeys that inhabit your station." He cast a disgusted glance around him. Then he jerked his thumb at Philip. "Is this Acheson?"

"Yes, I was just…"

The Interpol man held up a hand to silence him. "You can put a cork in it. I don't have time to waste with the excuses of a provincial policeman," he sneered.

Philip repressed a smile. Azzopardi's cheeks had flushed an unnatural shade of pink beneath his olive complexion and his nostrils flared. His Adam's apple convulsed up and down, but no words rose to his lips. A hush had descended on the station and all eyes were glued to the unfolding drama.

Through clenched teeth, Azzopardi replied acidly, "Take your prisoner and get out of my station." He gave Philip a rough shove toward the other man.

Philip thought it was lucky for the Interpol chap that Azzopardi didn't have a weapon readily at hand. Otherwise, he was certain there would have been a great deal of blood to clean up.

"Hey, wait a moment," Philip said as the Interpol officer clamped his long, bony fingers around his arm. "I demand to see some identification and to be taken to the high commission at once."

"Do you hear this?" the man asked of no one in particular. "He *demands*. That's rich." He wagged a finger at Philip. "Listen, I want none of your lip, do you understand?"

Philip's crossed his arms over his chest. "I refuse to take one step out of here, until you show me some identification."

The Interpol officer muttered something unintelligible and made a great show of taking his identification out of his inside jacket pocket. He flipped it open. "There. Satisfied." He snapped it shut before Philip could get a proper look. All he saw was a photo and some blurred words. "We've wasted enough time. Get a move on, Acheson."

Philip was propelled out the door. The Interpol man had a grip like iron as he dragged Philip along the cobblestone street.

Philip studied the man's profile. Instinct told him that there was something dodgy about what had just taken place at the station. "How about you slow down and show me your identification again?"

The man ignored him.

"Right. At least tell me your name."

Still nothing.

"Your mother must have called you something. Everyone has a name."

At this, the corners of the man's eyes crinkled into a smile. He tossed a glance over his shoulder, before ducking into a street to his right and coming to a sudden stop. His slate-green stare locked on Philip's face. "The name's Dunbar."

Philip nodded, as the truth dawned on him. "You wouldn't happen to be Terence Dunbar, retired Interpol criminal intelligence officer and friend of a certain Scotland Yard detective."

"Yes, Philip," Superintendent Burnell said as he and Sergeant Finch emerged from the doorway of a nearby pub. "There's only one Terry."

Philip grinned at the two policemen and then thrust out a hand to Dunbar. "Thank you. I owe you one."

Dunbar clasped his hand and gave it a hearty shake, his mouth curling into a smile. "My pleasure. Anything to help Oliver. Mind you, I thought the game was up when you asked to see some identification."

"Forgive me. I have a naturally suspicious mind."

"Just like an overly inquisitive journalist we all know, who gets into a good deal of trouble," Burnell muttered. He raised an eyebrow. "Out of curiosity, where are Emmeline and Longdon?"

"I'm afraid that they're walking into the lion's den as we speak."

Burnell rubbed his stomach. "I needn't have bothered asking, my ulcer already knew the answer."

CHAPTER 38

The sleek silhouette of the *Sea Predator* shivered on the inky surface of the water, appearing and melting away with each undulating sigh of the brisk breeze. The yacht was ablaze with light. People mingled inside the main lounge and spilled out onto the deck. Laughter and the low buzz of conversation floated to their ears, as Emmeline and Gregory stepped onto the gangway at eight fifteen.

Halfway up, Emmeline stopped and placed a hand on Gregory's shoulder. He was behind and slightly below her. "Wait a moment, darling," she murmured. "Your tie is crooked. Let me fix it."

Gregory's eyes widened for an instant. He flicked a glance down at his tie and then nodded up at her. "What would I do without you?"

She turned her back to the ship and leaned one hip against the railing to steady herself. She gave a playful laugh. "You'd be utterly lost, of course." Then, she pitched her voice so that only he could hear. "How are we going to get around those two stout fellows stationed at the top of the gangway? They look as if they're made of stone."

As she was pretending to adjust his perfectly straight bow tie, he listed a fraction to the right to peer over her shoulder.

He whispered out of the corner of his mouth, "You mean those two pussycats?" He choked back a laugh at the startled expression on her face. "Don't worry, Emmy. Just follow my lead."

He put a hand on her elbow and gave it a reassuring squeeze. "Thank you for making me presentable," he said aloud. "Now, I hope we can actually enjoy the party. We barely stepped aboard the first time. Then Melita decided to have one of her hysterical episodes and we had to take her home." He sighed wearily and halted as they neared the top, where Cannizzaro's lackeys were hovering.

"Don't get me wrong, darling," he went on. "Tonio is one of my dearest friends. I would do anything in the world for him. But I'm getting rather tired of his tawdry affairs. I wish he would find a more docile mistress."

Emmeline didn't miss a beat. She clucked her tongue in disapproval. "Hmph. You know my opinion on that score. His behavior is quite disgraceful." She craned her neck, as she cast a glance along the deck. "I have a good mind to tell his wife about the way he carries on. The poor woman has a right to know. This can't go on."

Gregory grabbed her arm and raised his voice. "I forbid you to open your mouth."

She snorted. "Forbid? In your dreams. This isn't the Middle Ages. You are not my lord and master. Merely my husband." Out of the corner of her eye, she saw that the two men were smirking. She folded her arms over her chest and tapped her foot against one of the rungs. "You're always so quick to defend him." Her eyes narrowed. "Perhaps a night in the guest bedroom will help you to reflect on the importance of marriage vows."

He smiled like a husband who wanted to get back into his wife's good graces. "Come on, darling. Why are we arguing? Tonio and Pietra's marriage is none of our business. Let's put them out of our mind. It's a lovely night for a party." He dropped an arm around her shoulders and pressed a kiss to her temple. "Hmm. What do you say, my angel?" he cooed sweetly.

She threw up her hands in surrender. "You're right. What wife would like her husband's infidelities brought to her attention?"

"Indeed," Gregory mumbled as he deftly guided her between the two guards.

One of them winked at him, while other gave him a thumbs-up sign.

Emmeline groaned inwardly at the primitive instincts of the male species to stick together.

The heels of her pumps echoed off the polished wooden planks of the deck as they made their way down the starboard side of the boat. Keeping her gaze focused straight ahead, she asked, "How the devil did you know that Cannizzaro has a mistress?"

"It was an educated guess, my dear wife," he replied with an off-hand wave of his wrist, "Cannizzaro is the sort who is always enamored of his own power and influence, and thinks women fall all over themselves to bask in his glow. Some do, of course."

"Hmph. Women are putty in your hands, my darling. Don't get any ideas in your head. Stand warned. I will rip your eyes out *for a start*, if you decide to take a mistress."

Gregory threw his head back and laughed. He stopped and drew her into his embrace. "Emmy, my love, what more could I want, if I have you? You are the earth, the sun, the entire universe."

She smiled up at him and kissed the tip of his nose. "Good. Keep it that way."

His warm breath ruffled her hair and his mustache brushed her cheek as he chuckled again. He placed a hand on the small of her back. "Right. Now, that we've settled that point. Are you ready to face Cannizzaro and whatever else is in store tonight?"

She took a deep breath, squared her shoulders, and nodded. "As ready as I'll ever be. This is our one chance to smoke out Swanbeck. The only thing that I feel guilty about is Philip. It's like we've abandoned him."

"Nonsense, Emmy," Gregory said as he gave her a gentle nudge forward. "Acheson is all right. I very much doubt that Inspector Azzopardi would dare do anything to upset the Foreign Office."

Emmeline bit her lip, still skeptical. "But he's clearly in Cannizzaro's pocket or Swanbeck's, which would be worse."

"Whether the inspector is or isn't, it's out of our hands. Villiers will take care of Acheson."

"Yes, but..."

Gregory cut her off as they reached the bow. "No, we can't allow Acheson to distract us at this stage. We have bigger fish to fry. Ah, smile, darling. Here comes our charming host."

She followed his gaze and saw Cannizzaro threading his way through the throng of guests. He made a halfhearted attempt at a smile. But his clenched jaw rather marred the effect, making it look more like the grimace of rigor mortis. It didn't help that his features were contorted into a fierce scowl.

"Miss Kirby." Cannizzaro kept his voice even. However, there a was brittle edge to it, like a violin string stretched too taut and in danger of snapping at any moment. The tip of his tongue moistened his lips, as his gaze darted to his right and left. Then, he leaned toward her. "You and your husband are trespassing."

Gregory beamed and brashly extended a hand toward the man. "Ah, there you have me at a disadvantage, sir. You apparently know who am I, but we haven't had the pleasure of being properly introduced. You are?" The insolence of the question only served to work up Cannizzaro into a seething lather.

He curled his fists tightly at his sides. "Longdon, you and your nosy wife will regret ever setting foot onto my yacht." He took a step closer. "I'm going to have you both arrested."

Gregory's smile grew wider. "On what charge? Even on Malta, I hardly think crashing a party constitutes a criminal offense."

Cannizzaro leered at him. "You forget that I'm a man of tremendous influence in many circles." His voice dropped to barely a whisper. "I can have you"—he flicked a glance at Emmeline—"and your lovely wife disappear. And your bodies would never be found."

Emmeline gasped at his audacity. She curled a hand around Gregory's arm. He patted it reassuringly. "Don't worry, darling. The distinguished Minister of Finance is merely bluffing."

Cannizzaro's mouth curved into a lupine grin. "I assure you I am not."

Gregory inclined his head. "For argument's sake, let's say you're not. You're a clever fellow. Do you really suppose no one knows we're here tonight? As the proverbial saying goes, if anything happens to us, we've made arrangements for certain documents to fall into the hands of Interpol and a number of other legal authorities. I must tell you, old chap, your shady schemes make for hours of colorful reading. You have been a busy boy in the past few years, haven't you?" He snatched two champagne flutes off the tray of a passing waiter and handed one to Emmeline. After taking an appreciative sip, he continued, "Mmm. Quite refreshing. Now, where was I? Oh, yes." He gestured with the glass at Cannizzaro, whose cheeks flamed beneath his olive complexion. "Of course, your family's business ventures are a whole other kettle of fish that the authorities will find fascinating." He took another sip of champagne. "Naturally, the *coup de grace* is the little matter of Sebastian Jardine's murder."

"Jardine was a nuisance, but I had nothing to do with his murder. My family is well-respected…"

Gregory threw his head back and laughed. "Among the criminal classes indubitably," he retorted. "I know for a fact that the name Cannizzaro carries a certain mystique as does Alastair Swanbeck."

Cannizzaro blanched slightly at the mention of Swanbeck, but he tried to bluster. "Swanbeck? I'm afraid I've never heard of him."

Gregory smoothed the lapels of Cannizzaro's tuxedo jacket. "Shall I give you a few moments to come up with something more plausible? Because I must say that comment lacked any semblance of verisimilitude."

Cannizzaro gave a careless shrug. "Frankly, your thoughts and opinions are of no interest to me. Jardine was a thief and a liar. He was a means to an end, and he got what he deserved."

"I'm sensing some bitterness and hostility, Tonio. It sounds as if you had a strong personal grudge against him. It wouldn't have anything to do with a certain lady of dubious morals who has a penchant for the color pink?"

A primitive growl erupted from the back of Cannizzaro's throat. He lunged at Gregory and grabbed him by the lapels. This drew startled glances and gasps from the guests closest to them. Emmeline held her breath.

Gregory's smile never faltered. He casually pried Cannizzaro's fingers loose and smoothed out the wrinkles from his lapels. "Ah, that's better. Thankfully, no permanent damage. You were lucky. I'm rather fond of this jacket. The cut suits me perfectly. Wouldn't you agree?"

Cannizzaro straightened his spine and shot his cuffs. He

plastered a smile on his lips and waved a hand at the guests gaping at him. "A minor disagreement among friends." He gave phony chortle. "Please ladies and gentlemen, have some more champagne."

He snapped his fingers and the waiters hurried to refill empty glasses with the effervescent golden liquid. He waited until the party settled into a more mellow rhythm once more. Then, his head whirled round and he glared at Gregory. "At last, we come to the matter at hand. The only reason you are still among the living is because of the Pink Courtesan. You *will* give it to me."

Gregory raised a quizzical eyebrow. "My dear, Tonio," he said, as he brushed an imaginary piece of lint from the Cannizzaro's jacket. He had the satisfaction of seeing the other man grit his teeth at the use of his first name. It was nearly as amusing as needling Burnell. Almost, but not quite. "You seem to be under some misapprehension. I'm not acquainted with—What was the lady's name? My memory is not what it used to be."

"I've had enough of your taunts and little jokes." He jerked his chin and the two Neanderthals they had managed to slip past at the gangway suddenly materialized at his elbow.

When he turned back to face Gregory, his onyx eyes gleamed with malevolence. "Longdon, you are going to have to make some hard choices tonight."

"Oh, yes? Do tell. I'm all ears."

The smile that played about Cannizzaro's lips didn't reach his eyes. "You are going to hand over the diamond."

Gregory flashed one of his most engaging grins. "My dear chap, you haven't been listening. I don't…"

Cannizzaro didn't allow him to finish. "It would be a pity if you decided to be greedy about the matter."

Gregory folded his arms over his chest and leaned toward

him. "Why? We live in a world of commerce."

"Indeed, we do, Longdon. Would you like to know what the Pink Courtesan is worth?"

"I'm certain you're going to tell me. Although I'm not interested in making any sort of deal."

"But I believe you'd consider it priceless and well worth your while." He paused for a beat, heightening the tension that had them all gripped in its thrall. "The Pink Courtesan for your lovely wife's life. My other demand is the Blue Angel…as a token of your esteem."

CHAPTER 39

Before Gregory could react, the splayed fingers of a bony hand clamped around his arm as Cannizzaro's lackeys flanked him. Despite the low hum of conversation, they heard the soft *click* of a safety catch being eased off. Gregory felt the bulging solidity of a gun's muzzle digging into his ribs. The brawnier of the two men, whose nose looked as if it had been broken more than once, was attempting to be discreet by holding his hand in his pocket.

"A precaution, you understand, Longdon," Cannizzaro intoned. "One can't be too careful these days, when there are so many thieves about. I'm sure you can appreciate that. Now, back to the matter at hand. The diamonds."

Gregory's brow puckered into a frown. "Diamonds? As in more than one? I didn't know precious jewels multiplied like rabbits. Hmph. Funny that. One learns something new every day."

Cannizzaro gave an exaggerated sigh. "You are beginning to try my patience…"

"Only beginning. I must make a concerted effort," Gregory quipped. "You haven't seen my full potential yet."

Cannizzaro's hand whipped out and grabbed Emmeline by the nape of her neck, tugging on her curls until her scalp screamed silently and her eyes stung with tears. "I could snap your wife's pretty little neck right here and wash my hands of both of you. But it would be so messy. Everything has a time and place. I advise you not to rush me."

Terror clutched at her throat, strangling any words before they could reach her lips. She threw a pleading glance at Gregory.

He strained against his captors but couldn't break free. "Let Emmy go. *Now,*" he ordered acidly, a muscle pulsing along his rigid jaw.

"You are in no position to make demands, Longdon. Remember, you are on my turf. Without an invitation. A serious miscalculation on your part."

They glared at one another in silence for several seconds. Then, Cannizzaro released Emmeline. She staggered back a few steps at the unexpectedness of the gesture. She saw Gregory's shoulders slump forward slightly and read the relief in the depths of his eyes.

Cannizzaro cleared his throat. "That's better. If you've quite finished with your tantrum, we can get down to business." His gaze swept over the deck. "We can't talk here. It's much too public for our delicate negotiations. I say negotiations, but there can be only one outcome." He nodded at his thugs. "Take him to my office."

"What about my wife?" Gregory asked.

"Ah, yes, the fair Emmeline," Cannizzaro sneered at her. "She remains here to enjoy the party. Under supervision, of course." He inclined his head and a lean, muscular fellow with closely cropped salt-and-pepper hair and a gaunt face, pushed himself away from the railing nearby and came to stand beside Emmeline. "This is Nestu. He will be your companion for the evening and see to your every need."

The iciness of Nestu's touch seeped through the gossamer lace sleeves of her dress, as he curled his fingers around her upper arm. She stiffened as a shiver slithered down her spine.

"Keep your bloody paws off my wife," Gregory snarled. He turned to Cannizzaro. "He lays a hand on her again and there's no deal."

The corners of Cannizzaro's eyes crinkled with amusement, but he nodded. "Nestu, as you can see Longdon is rather possessive. We wouldn't want to do anything to make him jealous."

Nestu dropped his hand, as if he had been scalded. "Satisfied, Longdon?" Cannizzaro asked with a smirk.

Gregory grunted in reply.

"Good. Let's go. We've wasted enough time."

Gregory winked at Emmeline and mouthed "Don't worry" as he was shuffled off toward the lounge. She caught a glimpse of his profile reflected in a window, before he was swallowed up by the crowd and lost to view.

She snaked a glance up at Nestu. He was well over six feet. There was a wicked glint in his hooded brown eyes. He leaned down and whispered, "Don't even think about running. You'll be dead before you reach the gangway."

Such a charming sentiment, she thought. *One doesn't have to be a genius to surmise that you're unmarried. What woman would have you?*

His lips curled back to reveal uneven, nicotine-stained teeth. "Just relax. It's a party."

Emmeline pressed her tongue against her cheek. Her gaze dropped to the deck. She was debating which would be more effective. Stomping on his foot and grinding her heel into his toe or a swift kick dead center to his shin.

❧❦❧

Cannizzaro opened the door to his study, which was swathed in shadows. He crossed to his desk and tugged on the chain of the green-shaded banker's lamp. Light spilled across the credenza on the mahogany desk.

He lowered himself into the leather swivel armchair with a sigh, as his men shoved Gregory over the threshold. His footsteps were muted by the plush maroon carpeting.

Gregory cast a brief glance around the study. "Tonio, either you enjoy subdued lighting—though you don't strike me as the romantic type—or you're trying to save on your electric bill. I can't figure out which is it."

An elbow to his ribs winded him. He should have expected the vicious punch to his kidneys, which followed before he could recover his breath. Inflicting pain was the stock in trade of Cannizzaro's men and their ilk. As his knees buckled beneath him and he crumpled into a heap on the floor, he had to admit that they were experts at their *métier*.

Cannizzaro folded his hands on the desk and peered over the edge at Gregory. A nasty smile spread over his face. "That was an aperitif."

Gregory rolled over onto his side. His back throbbed mercilessly. He squeezed his eyes shut to gather his wits and then he met Cannizzaro's smug gaze. "It must...be...an acquired taste," he rasped, his voice hoarse with pain. "I'm...rather partial...to a dry sherry. It's gentler on the palate."

Cannizzaro slammed the desk with his open palm, sending a pen and some papers fluttering to the floor. "Enough. I'm tired of your games, Longdon. I want the diamonds."

Gregory gingerly sat up, making a quick internal assessment. Emmy would not be pleased by the colorful bruises that would sprout upon his body within the next few days, if not already, but he was quite sure there was no permanent damage. He supposed he could chalk that up to one of life's little blessings. The challenge now was to resume an upright and more seemly position.

He drew in air through his nostrils. Groaning with the

effort, he managed to heave himself to his feet once again without having to lean on the desk to do so.

"I've had an opportunity to observe you, Tonio." He folded one arm over his chest and tilted his head to one side to rest his chin on the other hand. "I must say it's not a flattering picture. You're an awfully greedy sort of chap." Cannizzaro's hands curled into fists. "First, you were chuntering on about the Pink Courtesan. Now, it appears you want a treasure trove of diamonds." He punctuated this statement with a smile.

Cannizzaro's lips pressed into a tight line. He wagged an accusatory finger at him. "Your problem, Longdon, is that you are arrogant and glib."

Gregory's smile broadened. "You've only seen one side of me. If you scratch below the surface, you'll be astounded by the hidden depths of my personality. I'm quite an agreeable fellow, Tonio."

"My case in point. I am the Minister of Finance. You will accord me the respect and deference to which I am entitled."

Gregory cocked his head to one side. "Let me guess. You became Minister of Finance because your expertise lies in money laundering. If I were you, that's not a skill I would bandy about. The authorities tend to take a dim view of it."

The minister's nostrils flared. "Respect," he bellowed.

Gregory frowned. "Forgive me," he replied in mock innocence. "I thought this was an intimate gathering of friends. It's a bit heavy-handed to stand on ceremony."

Cannizzaro brought his fist down on the desk with a *thud.* "You have no friends in Malta. No, I stand corrected. There may be one." He settled back in his chair and steepled his fingers over his stomach. Then he sighed and shook his head, dragging out the moment as he chose his next words carefully. "The old days are gone. Such a pity. There's no honor among thieves anymore. Today all anyone is interested in is money, money, money."

Gregory threw him a quizzical glance.

Cannizzaro became brisk. "No use wallowing in nostalgia." He nodded his chin and the chap who had left the imprints of his knuckles in Gregory's back went to open the door.

"Ah, there you are," Cannizzaro boomed in a convivial manner. He waved a hand. "Do come in and join us. Longdon was getting restless. He will welcome a familiar face."

Fury coiled itself into knots in the pit of Gregory's stomach.

He ground his teeth together. "Roger. I can't say this is a pleasure, but neither is it a surprise." The words tumbled off his tongue in a cascade of venom.

Roger offered him a sheepish grin as he pressed the door closed behind him. "Greg, long time no see." His voice was slightly husky. *With fear? Contrition? Or indifference?* Gregory couldn't discern precisely which it was.

"You were working for Cannizzaro the entire time." It was a statement of fact, not a question.

Roger lowered himself into a caramel leather armchair near the door. Half his face was cloaked in shadow, almost as if he was two men at once. The image only served to reinforce his duplicitous, two-faced nature. "No, you're quite wrong. I started out with the purest of motives…"

Gregory snorted. "Come off it. There's nothing pure about you. You're mercenary to the core."

Roger's bottom lip curled down into a pout. "That hurts. It really does. As I was saying when you rudely interrupted, I really did set out to find the evidence Seb had uncovered so that you could take down Swanbeck. But then…"

Gregory cut across him. "You found out about the Pink Courtesan and you wagered that old Tonio here would offer you a better deal."

Roger spread his hands wide and gave a helpless shrug of his shoulders. "I knew you would see my dilemma. Put yourself in my shoes, Greg. If you're honest, you'll admit that you would have jumped at the chance. It simply fell into my lap."

Gregory shook his head in disbelief. "So you gave Tonio the files on Swanbeck and the Pink Courtesan?"

"Stop the pretense," Cannizzaro intervened. "I have the files that show that Swanbeck has been double-crossing my family…"

"If you lie down with dogs, you have to expect to wake up with fleas," Gregory sneered.

Cannizzaro flapped a hand impatiently in the air. "I can do without your inane English proverbs. Let's get to the heart of the issue at hand. While I am grateful to Delahunt for the proof of Swanbeck's perfidy, I want the Pink Courtesan returned to my family. It is ours. Swanbeck tricked my gullible brother into selling it for a fraction of what it's worth. Then the meddlesome Jardine had the nerve to steal it. Can you imagine? Our family's heritage."

"You'll find that Seb had as much right to the diamond." He smiled at the perplexed expression on Cannizzaro's face. "Ah, Roger has failed to tell you the whole story. Which is not surprising. He's a master of omission. I see that I will have to enlighten you. Sebastian Jardine was born Sebastiano Pappalardo." Two vertical lines appeared between the other man's brows. "I see the surname rings a bell. Seb was the son of Matteo Pappalardo. Your mother's brother. The man your father killed in cold blood. Seb was her nephew and your cousin." He waited to allow the salt to permeate the wound. "It appears your family affairs are messier than most."

"You're lying," Cannizzaro growled.

"You give me too much credit. I'm not that imaginative."

"I don't believe you. You have every reason to lie. You're stalling for time."

"My dear, Tonio," Gregory said as if he were speaking to child, "Haven't you heard the old adage that truth is stranger than fiction?"

Cannizzaro blinked twice and then his eyes snaked over to Roger. "Delahunt, is any of this true?"

Roger, in typical fashion, kept his counsel to see how things would play out.

"Come now, Tonio," Gregory taunted. "I grant that you're an excitable fellow. But you're laying it on a bit thick. Whether you knew about the family connection or not, you're the one who had Seb killed. Obviously, whoever you hired bungled the job because Seb died before you could get your hands on the diamond."

Cannizzaro surged to his feet. "I had nothing—I repeat *nothing*—to do with that rat Jardine's murder. His blood is on Swanbeck's hands."

Gregory smoothed down the corners of his mustache and calmly hitched a hip on the desk next to the lamp. His leg swung back and forth like a pendulum. "I suppose if you keep telling a lie long enough, you begin to believe it. But the truth is out there." He swept one hand in an arc that encompassed the room, as his voice dipped lower. "Any day now it will explode in your face. And the family will go down in flames."

Cannizzaro's spine stiffened. The words seemed to hang upon the air between them. Before Gregory could react, the other man opened the middle drawer of his desk. When his hand reappeared, a nine-millimeter Beretta was being leveled at Gregory's head.

"At this range, I can't miss." Cannizzaro eased off the safety catch. "I will shoot you like the dog that you are because you deserve nothing less"—he held out an outstretched hand palm up—"but first you will give me the Pink Courtesan and the Blue Angel. I know you have them on you because I had the boys check your hotel room this afternoon."

Gregory threw his head back, a throaty chuckle erupting from his lips. "You're barking up the wrong tree, mate. You didn't find them because I don't have the diamonds." He jerked a thumb over his shoulder at Roger. "Your newfound friend is in possession of the Pink Courtesan. I have a goose egg on the back of my head to attest to that fact. He's making a fool of you, Tonio. Think about it. Roger has been playing all the angles from the outset. He's admitted as much. He's the one who can't be trusted. How do you know he hasn't made the same offer to Swanbeck?"

"You're lying again," Cannizzaro growled, but Gregory could see a glimmer of doubt in his eye.

"You know I'm right," Gregory cooed, hoping to throw the other man off balance.

If he could just get out of the study, freedom would be within reach. He'd find Emmy and…But he was getting ahead of himself. First, he'd have to get past the sinewy, muscled bulk of Cannizzaro's two thugs, who every second that ticked by looked more and more like boulders of granite that had been nailed to the floor for eternity.

He was still judging the distance to the door, when Cannizzaro broke into his thoughts. "What I *know* is that you're a thief. Rumors of your daring exploits abound across Europe. You're the only one with the skill and brashness to have stolen both the Blue Angel and the Pink Courtesan." He took a deep breath. "This ends now. The diamonds are mine."

The door flung open, catching them all by surprise. A man hovered on the threshold, the light streaming in from behind him. Although they couldn't distinguish his features because of the gloom in the study, it was evident that he was carrying a gun in his right hand.

"Tonio, I'm disappointed." The cold voice was laced with menace. "I expected better of you."

Gregory's heart stopped between beats and his breath

caught in his throat. *Swanbeck.*

In the next second, his nemesis took a step into the room. Shadows and light dappled his features as he stood mere steps from the desk. For a moment, a sense of unreality saturated the air.

"Plotting behind my back to cheat me." Swanbeck shook his head. "*Tsk-tsk.* The lack of remorse is astounding to say the least. And the sense of betrayal leaves a bitter taste in one's mouth."

Cannizzaro squared his shoulders. "You have a nerve waltzing onto my yacht and accusing me of cheating," he bristled. "You hypocrite. You set out to systematically cheat my family. You were always hiding things."

Swanbeck huffed a harsh laugh. "So you thought you'd get your own back by stealing *my* diamonds?"

"You're under some sort of delusion, Alastair," Cannizzaro sneered. "The diamonds were never yours."

Swanbeck's jaw tightened. Through clenched teeth, he hissed, "Oh yes, they were." His sea-green gaze flickered toward Gregory. "Until Longdon decided, not once, but twice, to take something that didn't belong to him. But no matter, the day of judgment has arrived."

There was a soft *click*, as Swanbeck released the safety catch. "I'm going to savor every second, as you watch your nosy little wife die before your eyes. Then I'm going to make sure your father is disgraced before his peers. And for my *pièce de résistance*, I've saved the pleasure of killing you myself. An eye for eye. You never did pay for murdering Dad."

Gregory's body went rigid. He schooled his features into a bland expression. But his pulse was racing, sending blood thundering to his brain. Out of the corner of his eye, he sensed Roger shifting uncomfortably in the armchair.

"But to set all the fun in motion," Swanbeck droned on, "you will have to hand over the Blue Angel and Pink

Courtesan."

He thrust his hand into the pool of light cast by the banker's lamp. Gregory stared down at the lines crisscrossing Swanbeck's upturned palm. Oh, the stories those lines told. Of a life steeped in crime and violence. And now, revenge.

Gregory edged his hip back a fraction on the desk and lifted his eyes to meet the other man's gaze. "I can't understand why everyone keeps insisting that I have the diamonds."

Cannizzaro gave vent to his pent-up frustration by pressing to the Beretta to Gregory's temple. "You shut up," he commanded. To Swanbeck, he said, "The boys are going to escort you off my boat and they're going to make sure you're on the next plane out of Malta. I don't care where you go, as long as you never show your face here again." He gritted his teeth. "Your business with my family is null and void. Consider yourself lucky that I'm allowing you to leave here with your life."

Swanbeck leaned toward him, the skin of his face stretched taut with fury. "Big talk from a weak man," he scoffed. "I'm not going anywhere without the diamonds. And if your goons lay a finger on me, they will never live to see tomorrow."

Cannizzaro opened his mouth, but he never got a chance to hurl back another threat in this battle of wills because Gregory's elbow lashed out, landing a vicious blow against his jaw. Gregory had the satisfaction of hearing bones crunching followed by a strangled groan from Cannizzaro.

As he whirled his body in an arc, the lamp came crashing down beside him as he hit the floor. He felt broken shards of the lampshade sprinkle his hair. The study was plunged in darkness. Male grunts and scuffling sucked the air from the room.

A gun fired off a shot quite close to his ear. He heard a low moan and assumed Cannizzaro must have been hit. The door was flung open and in the next instant it slammed shut. Someone must have dashed out, snuffing out the light once more. Gregory had no idea where Swanbeck was in this pit of hell and he wasn't going to wait around to find out.

His eyes became accustomed to the gloom again. He could make out the outline of the door. He was only about a hundred feet away. He began crawling on his belly. *Oof.* Someone landed heavily onto his back. The air swished past his face as he narrowly avoided a fist to the head. By reflex, his hand whipped out blindly. He was able to parry a second blow, instead landing one of his own. *Good guys one, baddies nil*, he quipped in his head.

Gregory was now in front of the door. He drew himself up onto his haunches, rocked on the balls of his feet, and swiftly stood. He gave the knob a twist and opened the door. Light flooded in from the corridor.

The bullet came hurtling out of the gloom behind him. It burned as it ripped his flesh and lodged itself in his body. The coppery scent of blood filled his nostrils, as its warm, sticky wetness soaked his tuxedo jacket.

CHAPTER 40

Emmeline held her breath, biding her time until the waiter with the hors d'oeuvres was nearly in front of them. She turned into him so quickly that the poor chap didn't have a chance to avoid her. The tray he was carrying flew into the air and its contents landed all over Nestu. Just as Emmeline had intended.

"Oh, how clumsy of me," she tittered, as she bent down and attempted to help the hapless waiter upright. "Are you all right? I'm mortified."

A pink flush spread across the waiter's cheeks. He jumped to his feet. "I'm fine, madam," he replied brusquely, clearly embarrassed by the incident and hoping it wouldn't cost him his job. His eyes alighted on Nestu, who was covered in the detritus of what had been some quite appetizing canapés. Emmeline bit back a smile. The man was quite a sight.

The waiter swallowed hard. "I'm terribly sorry, sir." He drew a white cloth from his pocket. A *crack* echoed on the air as he snapped it open. "Allow me to help you." He began to dab at some of the mess on a lapel.

Nestu's eyes shot daggers at him. He waved him back. "Give me that." He snatched the cloth. "Get out of my sight, you stupid fool."

"But, sir, it was an accident…"

Nestu was preoccupied with his ruined suit and berating the waiter that he didn't notice that Emmeline had edged away from the little drama and into the lounge. She lost herself among the other guests. Her glance darted to all the windows. She didn't see any of Cannizzaros henchmen, but she knew it was only a matter of time before Nestu, at least, came after her. She made a mental note of all the doors, in the event she needed to bolt.

She had to find Gregory. She reckoned that Cannizzaro had taken him to his private quarters to conduct his illicit business away from prying eyes so that he could maintain his virtuous public image. She bit her lip. She didn't know which of the doors led down below and she couldn't afford to attract attention by asking a member of the crew.

Her mind sifted through and discarded potential plans of attack. There had to be a way. She would tear every plank from the deck and yell at the top of her lungs, if necessary. She was not going to leave her husband behind.

Just as this thought took root, some oaf bumped into her and trod on her foot. "Hey, watch it." Her eyes widened, when her gaze locked on Reggie Millbank. "High Commissioner."

Millbank fell back a pace and was jostled by another guest. "Pardon me," he murmured. Then he dropped his voice, hissing at Emmeline, "What the devil are you doing here, Miss Kirby?"

"I could ask you the same question."

Millbank cast a nervous glance around him. "You ask far too many questions than is good for you."

Emmeline's brows knit together. "That sounds suspiciously like a threat, Mr. Millbank."

The high commissioner made a dismissive gesture with his hand. "Take it however you like. From the minute you set foot on Malta, you've done everything in your power to stir up a hornet's nest. Why can't you leave things you understand nothing about in the past? Jardine got what he deserved. It does no good to persecute the innocent."

Innocent? she wondered. As far as she could see, no one was innocent in this matter.

Beads of perspiration sprouted on his brow and he swiped at them with the back of his hand. "Swanbeck and Cannizzaro are the Devil's spawns. They crawled out from under a rock in the same corner of hell. Everything they touch shrivels up and dies. My advice is to pack your bags and go back to London. Otherwise, you might end up in jail like Mr. Acheson. Or worse."

"You *know* Philip has been arrested?" This came out on a ragged breath. "And you haven't lifted a finger to help him?"

He bent his head close to hers. She felt his warm breath tickle her cheek, as he whispered in her ear. "Believe me, he's far safer where he is than you and Longdon are out here in the open. You're as good as dead. Swanbeck is not the only one who is watching you and…"

She didn't hear the rest of the sentence. A tendril of icy dread clutched at her chest. *Swanbeck is here,* her brain screamed.

With a hand that was far from steady, she clutched at his sleeve. "Where is my husband? What have they done to him?"

The muffled sound of a gunshot shattered the festive mood in the lounge. All conversation petered out and guests stared at one another in bewilderment.

Emmeline dug her fingers into Millbank's arm. "Where…"

She choked on her words, when the second shot rang out. Shocked gasps bounced off the polished wood paneling. Seized by panic, the guests stampeded toward the closest doors and out onto the deck.

Against her will, Emmeline was carried outside on a terrified wave of humanity. She lost track of Millbank in the crush.

"Emmeline. Thank God." She heard above the din.

She flattened herself against a wall and craned her neck around. Through a blur of stinging tears, she saw Philip, Burnell and Finch muscling their way toward her. A tall, slim man she had never seen before was close on their heels.

Philip reached her side first. She collapsed against him. She was trembling from head to toe. She held onto him, as if he were a life buoy.

When the others caught up, he asked, "Are you hurt? We heard shots."

She took a great gulp of air. "Cannizzaro and his men took Gregory somewhere below. They think he has the diamonds." She saw Philip exchange a wary look with the two detectives, but she ignored it. "I managed to slip away from the man Cannizzaro had guarding me." Her words were coming out in a stumbling rush. "I ran into Millbank. He said Swanbeck is here." Her watery gaze swept over all of them. "Then we heard the shots. I have to find Gregory."

She disentangled herself from Philip and impatiently wiped the tears clinging to her lashes. "I have to find Gregory," she repeated. "I must know he's safe." Her voice cracked on this last word.

People were still streaming past, all with a single purpose: to get off the yacht before the evening turned even uglier.

Burnell gave her arm a reassuring squeeze. "Don't worry about Longdon. Beneath that flippant exterior, he's as tough as nails. Leave it to us. We'll find him." He turned to the others. "Philip, Finch, come with me. Terry, could you stay with Emmeline?"

The stranger smiled at her. "It would be my pleasure." He

proffered a hand. "By the way, I'm Terence Dunbar. I'm an old friend of Oliver's."

Emmeline inclined her head. "Yes, of course. The criminal intelligence officer from Interpol."

Dunbar winked. "Former. I'm retired now."

"And yet you happened to be in Malta."

A ghost of a smile tugged at his mouth. "There's no such thing as coincidence." He took her gently by the elbow. "Why don't we go wait inside?"

She nodded and allowed him to lead her into the deserted lounge. They settled down on a plush beige sofa. She guessed the crew members were trying to deal with the crisis.

Her shawl had slipped from her shoulders and was draped loosely across her arms. She drew it around herself like a cocoon. She suddenly felt chilled. She didn't know whether it was from being out in the night air or from fear.

Dunbar kept his watchful gaze on her but had tactfully fallen silent. She was grateful because she didn't think she could have made idle conversation at that moment. Instead, she attempted to smile at him. She failed miserably.

Her mind was awhirl. What was taking so bloody long? She glanced at her watch.

Dunbar seemed to sense her troubled thoughts. "They've only been gone about five minutes. It only seems like an eternity."

❦

Gregory staggered down the corridor. His arm throbbed like the Devil, but fortunately it was the only part of his anatomy that had been injured. He would live. The problem was that the wound was bleeding profusely. He ducked into a stateroom and gingerly removed his tuxedo jacket. He grimaced when he saw that the sleeve of what had been a pristine dress shirt was now soaked crimson. He drew out his handkerchief and gritted his teeth, as he tied it around his arm to try to stanch the flow of blood. Then, he eased his jacket back on. It wouldn't pass the scrutiny of prying eyes, but it would do long enough for him to get Emmy out of harm's way and off the boat.

He opened the door a sliver and put his eye to the crack. Not a sole was in the corridor. His heart hammered against his rib cage. His head was swimming slightly, probably from the loss of blood. He forced his ears to concentrate. He thought he heard a creak on the staircase at the other end of the corridor, but he wasn't going to hang about to investigate. It was now or never. He pulled the door open just wide enough to slip out. He didn't look back. In three strides, he was at the staircase closest to him that led up to the main deck.

When he was halfway up the stairs, he froze. Footsteps were hurrying toward him. Any second, the person—no it was more than one—would be upon him. He couldn't retreat back the way he had come because Cannizzaro or Swanbeck would likely be waiting for him, unless they had already scarpered. There was nothing for it. He would simply have to take his chances.

He pressed his shoulder blades into the wall behind him and lowered himself into a semi-crouch. His muscles tingled with anticipation. He kept his eyes locked on the curve of the staircase.

His body sagged with relief, when Philip's blond head appeared. Almost immediately, Burnell and Finch's faces came into view.

"Fancy meeting you here, chaps," he drawled as he climbed the stairs to meet them. "Were you out for an evening constitutional after breaking Acheson out of the Maltese police's clutches?"

"Don't you ever stop with the jokes?" Burnell grumbled.

Gregory favored him with a smile. "I always get a warm glow right here"—he pressed a hand to his chest—"when I see your cheerful face, Oliver. Your sunny disposition always boosts my spirits."

"Hmph," was the superintendent's response. Then his eyes flew to Gregory's face. "Bloody hell. You're turning gray." His gaze traveled down to his injured arm. "You're hurt."

"A mere scratch," Gregory replied with bravado, but he stumbled and missed a step.

If Finch hadn't grasped his arm, he would have fallen on his face. He winced at the pressure.

"Steady on. You're gushing like a sieve, Longdon," the sergeant observed.

Gregory straightened his spine and gave his jacket a tug to smooth it back into a semblance sartorial elegance. "Nonsense. I'm perfectly fine."

"And I'm the fairy godmother," Burnell quipped.

Gregory squinted at him. "I'd never noticed it before. You must have been incognito."

"*Longdon.*" Burnell's tone held a note of warning.

Gregory tossed a quick glance over his shoulder, before addressing the superintendent again. "Look, Oliver, I promise to unburden my soul. But now is not the time. Cannizzaro or Swanbeck could burst upon us at any moment. Where's Emmy? Is she all right?"

"She's unharmed," Philip answered. "Dunbar's with her. Needless to say, she's bloody worried about you."

Some of the tension and pain eased from his body at this news. "Thank God. Not a word to her about this." He lifted his arm in the air.

"You're crackers, if you think she won't notice. Emmeline has the eyes of a hawk," Finch said.

"I'll tell her in my own way. Please, chaps," he implored. They nodded reluctantly. "Good. Now, lead the way to my wife. It's not polite to keep a lady waiting."

Emmeline had been staring down at her hands in her lap, when the air stirred. Her head shot up. Tears stung her eyelids, when she saw Gregory enter the lounge.

"Gregory." His name tumbled from lips on a breathless whisper.

She leaped to her feet and ran over to him, flinging her arms around his waist. "Oh, darling. I was so frightened when I heard the shots."

She drew back and reached up to cup his face between her hands. He took one of her hands and turned it over to press a kiss to her palm. "I'm fine. It was all a storm in a teacup."

Emmeline frowned because she caught the exchange of glances between Philip and the two detectives, who were hovering behind Gregory. Dunbar had joined the group by this time. He inclined his head and introduced himself to Gregory.

Emmeline tilted her head to one side, as her gaze scoured her husband's face. "What are you keeping from me? It's useless to hide anything. Millbank told me Swanbeck was here."

Philip, Burnell and Finch studiously dropped their eyes to their feet. Gregory gave her shoulders a squeeze. "Did he? I wonder what else the High Commissioner knows."

"Quite a lot, judging by how nervous he was. But don't change the subject. I know something's wrong. I can read it in your eyes, so out with it otherwise…"

She broke off, when Philip exploded, "Lord, that's all we need."

They all followed his gaze. She and Gregory were just as displeased to see Inspector Azzopardi and some of his officers boarding the *Sea Predator*. "What the bloody hell is he doing here?" Dunbar exploded.

"You can bet that Cannizzaro rang him," Philip replied, a scowl marring his features.

"Right." Burnell took charge. "Philip, Terry, make your-selves scarce. We can't have the inspector clapping eyes on you two. He doesn't know Finch and me. We'll handle him." He flicked a glance at Gregory. "Are you up to it?"

Gregory winked at him. "There's nothing I'd like more than to have a natter with the charming inspector."

Burnell dropped his voice. "Don't overdo it."

They didn't have time for more because Azzopardi and his entourage burst into the lounge.

"Well, if it isn't Mr. and Mrs. Smythe-Jones. I feel like we're old friends. Would you mind if I called you Percy and Maud?"

Burnell and Finch shot puzzled glances at them, but Emmeline merely rolled her eyes toward the ceiling.

"Not at all," Gregory replied smoothly. "It's an unex-pected pleasure to see you."

Azzopardi fixed his onyx stare on Gregory's face. "I'll bet it is. What are you doing on the Minister's yacht? Don't tell me that you got lost again on the way to the cathedral?"

Gregory chuckled and wagged a finger at the policeman. "Very droll. No, no. Your directions were perfect. The cathe-dral took our breath away, didn't it, Maud?"

Emmeline smiled weakly. "Indeed. It was beautiful," she murmured.

"I see you've found some companions on your wander-ings." Azzopardi pointed at Burnell and Finch.

"Ah, where are my manners?" Gregory said. "Let me in-troduce Detective Superintendent Oliver Burnell and Detec-tive Sergeant Jack Finch of Scotland Yard."

Azzopardi raised an eyebrow. "Scotland Yard? How curi-ous. What brings the two of you to Malta? I hope you're not conducting an investigation without first having the courtesy to inform the local police."

Burnell smiled, as he proffered a hand. "No, no. Nothing

like that. It's just a short stopover. We're on our way to a conference."

Azzopardi nodded, but his tone was skeptical. "Indeed? A conference. How…nice."

"Yes, isn't it," the superintendent responded, mimicking his false tone. No one was fooling anyone here tonight. They were all tiptoeing on hot coals, trying to avoid being scorched.

"And did you arrange to meet in Valletta with Mr. and Mrs. Smythe-Jones?" He wiped a hand across his lips. "Forgive me. Your name is quite a mouthful for a simple policeman."

"Don't be modest," Gregory retorted. "There's nothing simple about you, Inspector. I believe that beneath that unctuous exterior you're quite shrewd." Azzopardi inclined his head. "In fact, you strike me as a ruthless and calculating sort of chap who would do anything to get ahead in this world. Even going so far as to be in the pay of a rich and powerful man…say a member of the government, perhaps?"

Gregory's smile did nothing to take the sting out of this accusation. Azzopardi's back stiffened and his features hardened. "*I* ask the questions here, Mr. Smythe-Jones. What are you and your wife doing on Minister Cannizzaro's yacht tonight?"

Gregory ignored this volley. "It's funny. I was wondering the same thing about you and your men. Why are you here?"

Azzopardi waved a hand vaguely toward the guests still filing off the boat. "My men and I are here on official business. We've been keeping a close watch on Minister Cannizzaro. That's why were able to get here so quickly. The Minister has received threats recently. In fact, there was a call tonight about a bomb threat. We have to take such things seriously."

One of Gregory's eyebrows quirked upward. "A bomb?

Really. Naturally, the call was anonymous."

"That's none of your concern" was the inspector's terse rejoinder. "I had two men under cover at the party tonight. They informed me immediately, when the shots were heard. I was told that a man fitting your description took the minister down below at gunpoint."

"A bomb and a gun? My, my. I didn't realize what a seething den of iniquity Valletta was. The police really ought to do something to keep the good citizens safe in their beds at night."

"How dare you call into question my ability to keep the peace?" Azzopardi bristled with indignation. "One of my men is checking on the minister as we speak. In the interim, I find it odd that the minister would invite a couple of British newlyweds to a party on his yacht. Were you acquainted with him?"

"Never laid eyes on him before tonight," Gregory answered smoothly.

"Fascinating. Then how do you explain your presence here? This was an exclusive party."

"Maud and I are friends of Pietra's cousin Rita. She procured invitations for us."

Azzopardi shot him a quizzical look. "Pietra?"

"Mrs. Cannizzaro," Gregory explained and shook his head in disapproval at his apparent ignorance.

The inspector grunted. They could tell he didn't believe a word of what Gregory had just said, but he couldn't disprove it either. "We'll see what Sergeant Camilleri has to say, when he returns from the minister's study."

Gregory inclined his head. "By all means. That's your prerogative entirely. And for the record, I never carry a gun. They're nasty things that leave holes in bits of one's anatomy."

Azzopardi frowned and his fists curled into balls at his

side.

Emmeline lightly touched Gregory's arm in warning. She was surprised that his sleeve felt wet to her touch. When she glanced down, she was horrified to see that her fingers were smeared with blood and there was a droplet on the edge of his shirt cuff, which was peeping out from his tuxedo jacket.

Her eyes flew to his face. He gave an imperceptible shake of his head. She darted a glance at Azzopardi. The inspector didn't seem to realize that anything was amiss, but he would soon if this interrogation lasted much longer.

"Darling, it's rather warm in here. Would you mind holding my shawl, while I get a glass of water?" She carefully eased the shawl from her shoulders and draped it over Gregory's injured arm. She pressed a hand to her temple and swayed slightly.

"Certainly. You do look a bit flushed. It's all the excitement I suppose. Finch, could you fetch my wife a glass of water?"

Azzopardi appeared flustered by this display of feminine frailty and did not relish the idea of her fainting in his presence. He waved a hand toward a sofa. "Perhaps you should sit down, Mrs. Smythe-Jones."

"I have better idea," Burnell chimed in. "The rest of your questions can wait until tomorrow. Clearly, Mrs. Smythe-Jones is unwell. I think we should get her to her hotel and ring for a doctor."

Azzopardi threw up his hands in surrender and exhaled a frustrated sigh. "Oh, very well. Go. But I want to see you— *all* of you—at the station first thing in the morning."

Gregory sketched a little salute and draped an arm around Emmeline's shoulders. "We'll be counting the minutes with bated breath."

∽∾∽

Emmeline tamped down the urge to turn around and check on Gregory. Aside from the fact that they could only go down the gangway in single file, Azzopardi was leaning his elbows on the railing and watching them from the deck. She could feel the inspector's gaze burning a hole between her shoulder blades and did not want to arouse his suspicions by rushing. Only a few more steps and they would be on *terra firma* again.

She spun around on her heel as soon as her feet hit the pavement. Her fingers gripped her clutch tightly, as she waited for the others to reach her side. It may have been the moon and shadows conspiring, but Gregory's face looked gray. Burnell and Finch brought up the rear. They flanked Gregory as they made their way toward her.

Emmeline didn't utter a word. She slipped her arm around Gregory's waist. He dropped his good arm around her shoulders. A spasm of pain flitted over his handsome features, but he tried to cover it up with a smile.

"There are Terry and Acheson." Burnell was pointing to a dark-colored Peugeot SUV that had just switched on its ignition and was rolling away from the curb about a hundred yards up ahead.

Burnell raised an eyebrow. "All right, Longdon?"

Gregory's smile grew wider. "Lead on, Oliver. I like nothing better than a stroll by moonlight."

He lost his footing and Emmeline had to steady him as they made their way toward the car. "I'm fine," he mumbled and insisted on walking the remainder of the way without any assistance.

Philip got out of the SUV and came around to slide the door open. "Look lively, gentleman and lady."

"Gregory needs a doctor, and you and Mr. Dunbar can't afford to be seen by Azzopardi," Emmeline said hurriedly. "I could stay behind and get a taxi, if you think I'll delay you."

"No," Burnell overruled her before any of the other men could speak. "You go, where we go. From here on out, no more setting off on your own—*anywhere*. We'll manage."

"Of course, we will, Emmy," Gregory said, his lips pressed into a strained smile. He reached out and patted Burnell's bulging mid-section. "I could rest my head on Oliver's shoulder. He won't mind."

The superintendent swatted his hand away and raised a warning finger in the air. "Longdon, count your lucky stars that you're injured. Otherwise…"

Gregory cut across him. "Otherwise what? You'd give me a great, big bear hug. Oh, Oliver, I always knew you cared. You still can if you like, just be gentle with me."

Burnell tilted his head back. "Why Lord? Why me?" he asked of the inky-blue sky. To Emmeline, he said, "Get your husband in the SUV and see that he keeps his mouth shut."

To Burnell's chagrin, Gregory did not keep quiet on the journey to the Corinthia Palace Hotel that evening. He regaled his captive audience with a detailed description of what had occurred on the *Sea Predator* from the instant he was led away by Cannizzaro. He left nothing out about Cannizzaro's threats, Swanbeck's presence, and Roger's not-so-unexpected reappearance. "And, that is the unvarnished truth."

Emmy laced her fingers through his and squeezed hard when he finished his harrowing tale. "When I think about what could have happened…" Her sentence trailed off.

He raised her hand to his lips and brushed her knuckles with a kiss. "Darling, you worry far too much. As you can see, I'm fine."

"You seem to have forgotten the little matter of a bullet hole in your arm."

"A mere graze," he sought to reassure her as his thumb rubbed the soft web of skin between her thumb and forefinger.

Burnell, who was in the front passenger seat, tossed a glance over his shoulder. "Emmeline, your husband is too much of a scoundrel to die."

His gaze met Gregory's and they exchanged a conspiratorial look.

Emmeline rolled her eyes. "Hmph, men," she groused.

The superintendent chuckled, but soon a somber mood settled in the car. "I never trusted Delahunt. Too smarmy. I knew he was up to his neck in this sordid business."

Gregory glanced out the window. "Yes," he murmured.

Emmeline studied his profile. His mouth was pursed as he brooded over his friend's betrayal. The others also retreated into a sullen silence.

After a long interval, Gregory's voice, hoarse from a mixture of pain and disillusionment, echoed from gloom in the rear of the SUV. "Roger didn't have anything to do with Seb's murder."

Finch tossed over his shoulder. "You're in denial, Longdon."

"I'm not. My eyes are wide open," Gregory countered. "Roger is an opportunist, yes. But his only objective in all this was to get his hands on the Pink Courtesan with the Blue Angel tossed in as an unexpected bonus, if he could pull it off. One has to be thoroughly cold and calculating to be a killer. To show absolutely no remorse for his crime. You've met Roger. As a trained policeman, can you really say that he has it in him?"

Finch turned to Burnell. They stared at one another in the flickering shadows. At last, the superintendent answered for both of them, "No, in my opinion he isn't capable of it."

"Then, it must be Cannizzaro," Finch reasoned. "He discovered Jardine's true identity and his efforts to steal the Pink Courtesan. After that, Cannizzaro couldn't let him live."

"When I told Cannizzaro about the family connection," Gregory continued, "he was completely shocked. I don't think it was an act. He didn't bother denying his family's illicit links to Swanbeck, but he swore he had nothing to do with Seb's murder. I believe him."

Burnell's head craned round. "Why?" he asked suspiciously.

"Cannizzaro had no reason to lie at that stage. He was planning to have his boys kill me. A dead man tells no tales."

Burnell exhaled a weary sigh. "Then we've come full circle. Only one man is ruthless and vindictive enough to have orchestrated this elaborate scheme. Swanbeck."

The name hung lugubriously upon air. No one dared to put it into words, but they were all thinking, *Swanbeck won't stop. Not until his thirst for revenge is slaked.*

CHAPTER 41

Emmeline had a fitful night. If she got an hour of sleep, she was lucky. Between her concern for Gregory and their conclusions about Swanbeck, her tired mind chased thoughts round and round.

One bit of good news was that Gregory's wound was not serious. The doctor who Dunbar had rousted out of bed and brought to the hotel had pronounced the injury as a graze. He said it looked worse than it actually was. He cleaned and dressed the wound. However, the doctor warned that they had to watch for infection.

The burden of worrying was left to her, as always. Every hour on the hour, Emmeline would lean over to check whether Gregory was in any distress. To her annoyance, he had fallen asleep the minute his head hit the pillow. The few times he did stir, it was only to change his position. His breathing was even and a serene smile touched his lips. How this was possible she couldn't fathom, considering everything that had occurred the day before. Not for the first time, she mused, that men were strange creatures.

She fumbled on the night table for her watch. It was about five minutes to eight. It was still early. They had made arrangements to meet the two detectives and Dunbar in the dining room for breakfast at nine. She settled back against the pillows and closed her eyes. They still had time. She was loath to wake Gregory. The doctor had ordered him to take it easy today. She didn't want to let him out of her sight. And yet, she couldn't remain cooped up in their hotel room all day long, even if it did have a quiet terrace.

Her eyes popped open and she sat up, drawing her knees to her chest. There were too many loose ends. While they now knew that Swanbeck had been behind everything from the outset, it was all still conjecture. They couldn't even tie him to last night's drama in Cannizzaro's study. Of course, Cannizzaro was the last person who would want to attract attention to the fact that he had been meeting with an international pariah. It would do untold damage to the minister's carefully constructed public image. If only someone had seen Swanbeck.

But someone had. High Commissioner Reggie Millbank, who had gotten lost in the crush of fleeing guests, conveniently evading Azzopardi's interrogation.

Emmeline flipped back the bedclothes and eased her legs over the edge of the bed. She shot a glance at Gregory over her shoulder, as she wriggled her feet into the slippers the hotel had provided. He was still sleeping. She tiptoed across the room to the table, where her handbag sat open. She rummaged around until her fingers found her mobile. With her prize in her hand, she hurried to the bathroom and shut the door.

It was time to rattle Millbank's cage.

She punched in the number of the embassy. It was eight-fifteen. She was taking a chance, but she reckoned that Millbank's secretary had to be there already even if he wasn't yet.

The phone was answered after the first ring. "Good morning. The High Commissioner's office. How may I help you?"

"Good morning, Mrs. Denning. It's Emmeline Kirby. I met with Mr. Millbank yesterday."

There was a silence. "Yes, I remember quite well," Mrs. Denning replied curtly. "As the High Commissioner explained at the time, he is unable to provide you with any assistance. Good day."

"Please don't ring off," Emmeline implored. "I ran into Mr. Millbank at Minister Cannizzaro's party last night. We had a long talk and he told me to call the office today to schedule an appointment to continue our conversation."

"Did he?" the secretary asked, her tone laced with skepticism.

"Yes, he did. As you can imagine, it's a rather delicate and urgent subject. So, I'd appreciate an appointment as early as possible."

"Well." The other woman was wavering. "I suppose if the High Commissioner felt it was important." Emmeline heard paper rustling. "He has an unexpected opening at eleven, but he can only spare about twenty minutes. The rest of his day is rather full."

"I'll be there at eleven on the dot. I don't intend to keep him long. Thank you very much, Mrs. Denning." She ended the call, before the secretary had second thoughts.

She leaped off the edge of the bathtub. Adrenaline was rushing through her veins. The chase was on again. When she slowly opened the door, she nearly jumped out of her skin. Gregory was standing there blocking her way.

"Where do you *think* you'll be at eleven?" The planes and angles of his face were set in stern lines.

She smiled and reached up to press a soft kiss to his lips, as her hands caressed his tousled hair. "Do you know you look especially handsome and dashing in the morning?"

He touched the tip of her nose with his finger. "When you answer a question with a question, I know that you're hiding something. Something rather dangerous."

"Nonsense," she said as she ducked past him.

He trailed her into the room and snatched her wrist, forcing her to turn around and face him. "There's no escape, so you might as well tell me what you're up to."

"Be careful or you'll start bleeding again," she cautioned.

"The doctor said I'm fine." He would not be fobbed off. "I'm waiting for an answer."

Laughter bubbled in her throat. "How does it feel to have the shoe on the other foot?"

"Emmy." There was no hint of amusement in his tone.

She shook off his grasp. "Oh, very well. I've arranged to see Millbank at the embassy."

He dropped his chin to his chest and shook his head.

"It's a public place," she pointed out. "Nothing can happen at the embassy. He wouldn't dare."

He lifted his head and pinned her with his forbidding stare. "Have your forgotten that Azzopardi would like to have another audience with us? What if you run into him on your little jaunt?"

"The inspector can't touch me if I'm in the embassy. It's British soil," she retorted triumphantly.

"He'll be waiting for you when you leave. I'm coming with you."

"You are not. The doctor said you have to rest."

"How can I bloody rest, if my wife is offering herself up as a sacrifice to the Devil?"

She snorted. "Don't be ridiculous."

"Am I? If Millbank is working for Swanbeck—which it's looking increasingly likely—that's exactly what you'll be doing. Emmy, the embassy is Millbank's turf."

She groaned. "I don't see that we have any other choice. It's either Swanbeck or us. He's going to destroy your fath—" She broke off when he stiffened and corrected herself hurriedly, "—to destroy Villiers and he's vowed to kill us. I don't plan to wait around until he does. I'm going to fight for the truth. I'm going to fight him until there's no more breath left in my body."

"A heroic image. But do you always have to do it alone?"

She pressed a hand to his chest. "I'm merely thinking about your health."

"Emmy, my love, trying to pull the wool over my eyes won't work."

She batted her eyelashes at him. "Would I do that?"

He smiled, brushed her lips with a kiss, and rubbed his forehead against hers. "Yes. You have devious tendencies."

"That's the pot calling the kettle black," she muttered under her breath.

∞∞∞

It came as no surprise to Emmeline that when they joined Dunbar, Philip and the two detectives at breakfast, her announcement about her imminent meeting with Millbank cast a pall over the meal and made her the focus of a chorus of male displeasure.

Well, it was too bad. She would not be swayed.

When their arguments had petered out and they were beginning to repeat themselves, she put up a hand to halt the flow of hot air. "Right. While I appreciate your concern, my mind is set. I am going to meet Millbank. You will simply have to lump it."

Philip leaned back in his chair and folded his arms over his chest. "We could always tie you to a chair in your room."

"That's a very good idea, Acheson," Gregory said. "I hadn't thought of that."

Emmeline pulled a face at Philip. "Ha. Ha. If Maggie were here, she would give you a punch on the nose. Speaking of

Maggie, have you called your wife yet?"

Philip made a dismissive gesture in the air with his hand. "Maggie's fine."

"Emmeline, I cannot in good conscience allow you to go alone," Burnell interjected.

She threw up her hands in exasperation. "I will not allow Gregory to set foot outside the hotel."

"That goes without saying. If you insist on doing this, Philip, Terry, Finch and I will go with you."

"That sounds eminently sensible to me," Dunbar chimed in, as he took a bite of toast.

Meanwhile, Gregory murmured, "I would be much more comfortable, if I was the one keeping a watch over my wife."

"Forget it. All of you," she hissed so that the other guests couldn't overhear. "Millbank is the weakest link. He won't talk, if I walk in there with an entourage. He may even bolt." She looked at each of them in turn. "You must realize that."

Burnell slumped back and gave a disapproving shake of his head. "I've had a discussion with my ulcer and we've both come to the conclusion that it's not worth the risk. Too many things could go wrong. You'll be too exposed."

"You know how much I admire and respect you, Superintendent Burnell." She favored him with a bright smile. "But I am keeping my appointment with Millbank," she declared with finality.

Burnell held her gaze. "I see that your mind is made up."

Her chin jutted in the air in defiance. "It is."

He sighed and his shoulders twitched in a resigned shrug. "You're a grown woman. I can't stop you."

For a moment, she was taken aback at his capitulation. "Thank you for understanding. Now, I will leave you all to enjoy your breakfast, while I go upstairs to gather a couple of things." She bent to give Gregory a peck on the cheek. "Don't overdo it today, darling."

"Emmy, I'm not a bloody invalid." He grabbed her wrist and drew her toward him. "Don't go."

She kissed her finger and pressed it to the tip of his nose. "See you this afternoon." And with that, she swanned off.

When she had gone, Gregory rounded on Burnell. "Oliver, I must say I'm disappointed in you. The last thing Emmy needs is encouragement."

The superintendent's lips curled into a Cheshire cat grin. "I agreed no one would go *with* her, but there's no crime in Philip, Terry, Finch and I doing a bit of sightseeing, is there? If our wanderings *happen* to take us near the embassy—at a discreet distance, of course—we could always claim we were lost. We are tourists after all."

Gregory and the others shared a conspiratorial smile. He extended a hand across the table to the superintendent. "You sly old fox," he murmured. "I know it was a slip of the tongue, but you neglected to include me in your clandestine group."

Burnell clasped his hand. "Ah, that's because you're not going to be joining us."

❧❦❧

After gathering her handbag and her notebook from their room, Emmeline went down to the lobby and asked the young woman at the reception desk to call a taxi to take her into Valletta.

"Of course, Mrs. Longdon. By the way, there are number of messages for you. Just a moment, I'll get them."

Emmeline frowned. "Really?"

The woman turned to the small cubbyhole with their room number and drew out a stack of paper slips. "Here you are. Most of them are from last night. My colleague who was on the desk apologizes, but he thought it would be better not to bother you at that time. It was rather late when you returned and your husband appeared unwell. I do hope he's all right now."

Emmeline smiled and took the messages from her. "Yes, my husband's fine. The doctor said it was…a minor stomach upset."

The woman's face flooded with relief. "Oh, good. I mean I'm glad it wasn't anything serious."

Emmeline nodded. "Thanks for the messages."

"You can wait over there." The woman gestured toward a group of chairs and a sofa across the lobby. "Or the garden is rather pleasant. It's a lovely day. A taxi should be here within ten minutes. I can come out to get you."

With its palm trees, bushes and fountains, the garden appealed to Emmeline. She perched herself on a bench in front of a fountain, as she flipped through the messages. They were all from the same person. Alessia Summergill. Each sounded increasingly more desperate than the previous one. She pursed her lips and shook her head. She understood that Alessia was frightened. Who wouldn't be when the stakes involved Swanbeck and an influential politician like Cannizzaro? However, Emmeline didn't like being lured out with the promise of a story, only to have the source get cold feet at the last moment. It was a waste of her time.

Annoyance made her crumple the messages into balls with unnecessary ferocity. She gave them to the receptionist to toss in the rubbish bin, before she walked over to the taxi.

The driver wished her a cheery "Good Morning" as she clambered into the back seat. She went over the questions in her head and made a few notes on the short journey. When she decided to check her mobile, she found that Alessia had left four voicemails, one from last night and three this morning. "Doesn't the woman ever give up?" she muttered under her breath as she deleted them with a punch of her finger.

"Excuse me, madam," the driver asked as he flicked a

glance at her in the rearview mirror.

"It was nothing. Never mind."

He gave a casual shrug. "As you say. We've arrived."

Emmeline thanked him and hurriedly scrambled out of the taxi. She gave him a generous tip and he wished her a pleasant day. She waited until he was gone, before climbing the stairs into the embassy.

She was about ten minutes early. As Millbank's secretary had gone out of her way to stress that the high commissioner had a busy schedule, perhaps he would be willing to see her ahead of her appointment. Emmeline knew this was wishful thinking because Millbank didn't want to see her at all.

She gave her name at the reception desk and said she had a meeting with the high commissioner. She was asked to wait by the middle-aged man at the desk, who rang Millbank's secretary. The man had barely set the receiver back in the cradle, when Mrs. Denning swooped down upon her.

"Miss Kirby, you misled me," she said with more than a dollop of asperity. The deferential and pleasant woman of her last visit was nowhere to be seen.

The secretary's eyes were ablaze with anger as she drew Emmeline aside. "You are here under false pretenses," she hissed. "The High Commissioner was quite upset when I told him about your appointment with him. He said that he had made no such arrangements."

Emmeline forced a smile upon her lips. "I am here, out of courtesy, to give the High Commissioner a chance to tell his side of the story. Some rather serious allegations have come to light." She hitched her handbag higher on her shoulder. "But if he feels so strongly, I'll just go ahead and write the piece and he'll have to explain himself later." She turned on her heel and started to walk away.

"No wait," Mrs. Denning called after her.

Emmeline pivoted to face the secretary again. "Yes?"

"You can have ten minutes. No more." She jerked her head. "Follow me."

Emmeline bit back a smile as she trailed after Mrs. Denning.

The secretary rapped her knuckles lightly on the door to the high commissioner's office. They heard Millbank's muffled voice telling her to enter. A pain expression flitted across the secretary's face, as she opened the door and stood aside to allow her to enter.

"Miss Kirby is here to see you, sir."

Millbank's head snapped up and his eyes shot daggers, when they locked on Emmeline's face. "I gave express instructions that I did not want to see this woman."

Before Mrs. Denning could reply or offer an apology for her insubordination, Emmeline intervened, "I think you had better, Mr. Millbank. You might live to regret it otherwise."

Millbank's jaw clenched with anger. "Go," he ordered the secretary, who was relieved to escape.

Once the door closed behind her, Millbank assailed Emmeline. "You turn up like a bad penny. I warned you last night. You are ruining lives. All in the name of freedom of the press."

"I know you're afraid of Cannizzaro and Swanbeck."

He huffed a bitter laugh. "Minister Cannizzaro is missing. No one has seen him since he went to his study last night with Longdon."

Emmeline's jaw dropped at this unexpected tidbit. "I…I didn't know." She swallowed hard and squared her shoulders. "My husband had absolutely nothing to do with Cannizzaro's disappearance. It had to be Swanbeck."

Millbank's already ashen complexion turned chalk white. He dropped heavily into his chair. "Maybe, maybe not. But your questions are doing untold damage by casting aspersions and spreading innuendos."

"You know it's Swanbeck. That's why you're afraid. What is his hold over you?"

The high commissioner slammed his open palm against the desk and surged to his feet. "Enough," he roared. "I'm not going to risk my career by talking to you. I could be recalled to London."

Emmeline pressed on, determined to get answers. "Isn't the truth more important? You're Swanbeck's captive. It's a prison of your own making. Don't you realize that you'll never be free, unless you tell me what you know."

She held her breath and waited. Something flickered in his eye. He appeared to be wrestling with his conscience. Her pulsed raced. She had gotten through to him.

He opened his mouth and then snapped it shut, as if he had changed his mind. His face was pinched with stubbornness and fear. The wall went up again. "I have nothing to say to you, Miss Kirby." His tone was clipped and formal. "Either now or in the future."

"I can help. This is your chance to set the record straight. Give me something on Swanbeck," she beseeched. "Anything that will put him behind bars. He has to pay for his litany of crimes."

Millbank held her gaze as he reached for his phone. Then, he calmly asked his secretary to call a guard to have Emmeline escorted out of the embassy.

CHAPTER 42

For one moment, Emmeline had been confident Millbank would crack. What was the awful secret that he was willing to remain under Swanbeck's thumb for the rest of life, rather than tell the world what he knows about the man? Millbank was frightened of his own shadow.

As she stood on the steps of the embassy, something niggled at the back of her mind and she couldn't put her finger on what it was that was bothering her. It was something the high commissioner had said last night on the *Sea Predator*.

She bit her lip and stared out at the harbor without appreciating its beauty. The peal of her mobile jarred her from her brooding.

She drew it out of her handbag and answered the call, expecting it to be Gregory. "Right. Are you going to be ringing me up on the hour to check on my whereabouts?"

Silence followed for a moment. "I'm sorry, Miss Kirby."

It wasn't Gregory.

Emmeline pursed her lips. "Alessia," she replied crisply.

The woman rushed on, "I don't blame you for being upset with me. I apologize for running off like that. But I expected you to come alone. You *promised* to come alone. I am taking a tremendous risk."

"Look, Alessia, either you're willing to talk to me or this conversation ends now."

She heard the woman exhale a long breath at the other end of the line. "Yes." It was a hoarse whisper. "I…I will trust you to do what's right with the information I have."

Emmeline relented at these words. "You made a wise decision. As it happens, I'm across the harbor in Valletta. I could meet…"

Alessia cut her off. "No, no. I'm at work. I can't get away now."

Emmeline frowned. "I don't have time to play these games. I'm leaving Malta tomorrow."

"Please, please, Miss Kirby, be reasonable. You don't live here. You're not the one who will have to suffer the repercussions, if it ever was revealed that I went to the press. I could lose my job. Or worse."

Emmeline silently conceded this point, but she was fast losing her patience. Not that she had a high threshold when it came to patience. She curled her fist into a tight ball, while Alessia Summergill dithered with her conscience.

"Let's meet in a neutral place. You said that you're staying at the Corinthia Palace Hotel in Attard. It's not far from Mdina. Do you know it? It's a fortified city that sits on a hill. Mdina is known as the Silent City. I'll tell you all the evil secrets you want to know there. You could easily get a cab from your hotel. It will drop you off at the city gate. You'll walk across the bridge. I'll be waiting for you just inside the city walls at five o'clock. But only you."

Emmeline hesitated for only a fraction of a second. She had promised the others that she wouldn't go off on her own. But her instincts whispered that this was a lead she couldn't afford to pass up. "Agreed. Don't let me down again."

"I won't. Please don't make me regret my decision. I'm putting my faith in your oath as a journalist not to betray me."

"You have nothing to fear. My sources are sacred. No one will pry their names from my lips."

"I'm relieved to hear it. I'm counting on your discretion and integrity."

There was a soft *click* and then the line went dead.

∽∾∽∾

Gregory checked his watch. He had waited a decent interval. Burnell and the others were probably in Valletta by now. It put his mind at ease knowing that they would be watching over Emmy. Therefore, he was free to pursue Swanbeck without placing her in harm's way. His first visit would be to the *Sea Predator*. He had reckoned that was the only logical place where Cannizzaro would hide the files with the dirt on Swanbeck. Cannizzaro wouldn't risk keeping them in his office or at home, where anyone could find them. After all, the files revealed all the juicy details about how the family and Swanbeck were doing a brisk trade in the smuggling of guns, drugs, people, and other naughty goods that warmed the cockles of a criminal's heart. He couldn't risk having their business dealings exposed. Suspicion was one thing. One could always dismiss rumors as the envy of a political or business rival. But dates, names, bank records, wire transfers, and contracts in glaring black and white for the world to see, that was quite another story.

Once he had sorted out Swanbeck and Cannizzaro, he would go after good, old duplicitous Roger. The best way to punish him would be to liberate the Pink Courtesan from his undeserving clutches. Gregory reasoned that it was a fair exchange. He had some old friends keeping an eye out for Delahunt. He was certain that Roger was still in Malta. His greed would be his downfall. The man wouldn't leave if there was even a remote chance that he could get his hands on the Blue

Angel too. Gregory's lips twitched into a smile. Roger was deluding himself, if he thought that was ever going to happen.

A knock at the door interrupted these musings. He didn't know why, but the line from *Macbeth* flew to mind.

"By the pricking of my thumbs, Something wicked this way comes."

❦❦❦

The hairs on the back of Emmeline's neck prickled. Someone was watching her. She whirled around, expecting to catch Mrs. Denning's disapproving stare reflected in the glass door of the embassy. But Millbank's secretary was nowhere in sight. Emmeline darted a glance up and down the road. The pavement was virtually deserted.

She shook her head in disgust and put it down to nerves. Gregory being shot last night had rattled her more than she had been willing to admit. He could have been killed. As lovely as Malta was, she would be glad when they were back safe in their townhouse in Holland Park.

Her smile faded quickly. But they would never be safe, unless Swanbeck was locked away in prison or *dead*. She sent up a silent prayer hoping that Alessia wouldn't get cold feet again.

She pressed her handbag against her body, as she tossed a look over her shoulder. Someone *was* watching. She could feel it in the marrow of her bones. It had to be Swanbeck. Or, Cannizzaro could very well have sent lackeys to conclude last night's unfinished business. Both men were looking to feast on a cold dish of revenge. It was a good thing that Alessia couldn't get away at the moment.

She had to get away, though. She was too isolated on this side of the harbor. For an instant, she contemplated running back into the embassy and begging for assistance. However, she dismissed the idea. No doubt Millbank had instructed all embassy staff, especially the guards, that she was not permitted on the premises again. But would he really go that far? It would be going against his sworn duty to help British citizens in trouble on Maltese soil. On the other hand, fear was a powerful motivator and Millbank had proven himself to be a weak man. If it came down to her life or betraying Swanbeck, she was certain that the diplomat would offer her up as the sacrificial lamb.

As this thought crossed her mind, a dark blue Ford Fiesta seemed to materialize out of nowhere. It was hurtling toward her, but then it continued on its merry way. She squeezed her eyes shut in relief.

The tooting of a horn made her eyes pop open again.

"Hello, Miss Kirby," Joseph Spitieri, Millbank's driver, shouted from across the road. He gave her a little wave. "May I offer you a ride again?"

She stared at him. Was this a trap? Had Millbank sent him to report on her whereabouts?

She gave a violent shake of her head and hitched her handbag higher on her shoulder. "No, thank you. You're not going in my direction. I must dash." And she did just that before he could utter another word.

She hurried down the block. She needed to be near people. She would find a taxi and ask to be dropped off at the *Times of Malta*'s office, rather than returning to the hotel. It was bad enough that Gregory had been shot. She wasn't going to give Swanbeck or Cannizzaro a second chance to finish the job. No one would dare try anything at the paper. She could speak to the editor again. They had struck up a rapport when she had been there yesterday. She didn't think he would mind her hanging about until it was time to go meet Alessia in Mdina. Once she got to the paper, she would ring Gregory to see how he was faring and to tell him about her intention to see

Alessia. She needed to hear his voice.

"Who the devil is that?" Burnell demanded, as he scrambled to free himself from the seat belt.

He, Philip and Dunbar were keeping a close eye on Emmeline's exchange with Spitieri from the hired Peugeot SUV, which was parked a few hundred yards from the embassy.

Burnell flung open the door and was halfway out of the car, when Emmeline started running up the block.

Philip reached across and put a restraining hand on his arm. "That's Millbank's driver. Don't rush in. Something Spitieri said spooked her, but Emmeline's all right. Wherever she's rushing off to, he's not following."

Reluctantly, the superintendent settled back into the passenger seat and closed the door. He kept his gaze glued on Spitieri. "I don't like it. Where is she going now?"

"Back to the hotel?" Dunbar suggested.

Philip and Burnell gave him a pitying look and shook their heads.

"That would be the safe thing to do in this situation," Burnell remarked. "However, Emmeline always does the opposite of what is safe."

Dunbar nodded. "Mmm. In my extremely short acquaintance with her, I have to say that she struck me as a tad…overenthusiastic when she gets an idea in her head."

Philip and Burnell both laughed. "That's a diplomatic way of putting it," the superintendent quipped. "If retirement ever gets too dull, you can always ask Philip to find you a job at the Foreign Office."

"Mind you," Philip offered, "Emmeline is not the only one who throws caution to the wind. Longdon is just as bad."

Burnell groaned. "Let's not start on the topic of Longdon. I don't have the energy to deal with it today too. All this running around is for the young."

Dunbar chuckled. "Is that why you tasked poor Finch with surveilling him today?"

"Yes. He's young. He has the stamina to keep up with Longdon's devious schemes."

"Come off it, Oliver. You're not old. You could run rings around all of them. It's the truth and you know it."

Burnell inclined his head at the compliment and gave a casual shrug. Then he sat up straight, suddenly becoming alert. "Oi. There's Millbank."

They saw him walk out to the car and bend down to speak to Spitieri. The driver listened intently. He gave a brisk nod of his head as he started the ignition. Millbank watched as the car pulled away from the curb. He lingered on the pavement for another moment or two to take a call on his mobile. They watched the diplomat grow more agitated. The conversation must have ended abruptly because Millbank stared at his mobile for several seconds in disbelief. He began pacing along the pavement, rubbing the back of his neck and shaking his head.

"Could it be that Millbank's house of cards is tumbling before his eyes?" Burnell asked facetiously.

Dunbar slumped against the back seat. "Millbank," he murmured more to himself than anyone in particular. "I suppose it is possible. But it was all such a long time ago. And yet, hatred festers over time. So it *could* be true. It's too much of a coincidence."

He lapsed into silence, a pensive expression settling on his face.

Burnell and Philip both swiveled around to look at him. "Don't keep us in suspense, Terry," the superintendent prompted.

Dunbar tore himself from his ruminations and met Burnell's gaze. "Remember I told you about Jardine's sordid family history?"

"Yes," Burnell replied cautiously.

"You'll recall that his mother took up with a chap on Malta, her so-called husband, the one who committed suicide six months after she left him…his name was Clive Millbank. I was just wondering whether he could be related"—he gestured with his chin—"to our friend over there the high commissioner."

"Bloody hell," Burnell exploded. To Philip, he said, "After your unsatisfactory meeting yesterday with Millbank, Longdon rang and asked me to check up on the high commissioner. The information hadn't come in yet by the time Finch, Terry and I had to leave for the airport."

Philip nodded. "Millbank did his utmost to dissuade us—Emmeline in particular—from pursuing the story about Jardine and Swanbeck any further. We left with the strong impression that he was hiding something. Then he happens to make an appearance on the *Sea Predator* last night and conveniently vanishes when the fireworks start. As Dunbar pointed out, the coincidences are piling up and it's getting a bit uncomfortable."

"Ye-es," Burnell muttered as he drew out his mobile. "I'm ringing the Yard to see what Sergeant Roberts was able to pull up on Millbank." He waited a few seconds. "Roberts, good I've caught you. I need to know everything you found out about the high commissioner in Malta, Reginald Millbank."

His frown deepened as he listened. He grunted a couple of times and shook his head. Then, he thanked the sergeant and severed the connection.

"Our dodgy diplomat has a lot of explaining to do. He is indeed the brother of the late Clive Millbank. The gloves are off, gentlemen. We need to find out what his connection is to Swanbeck." He paused to sort out his plan. "Philip, you're the one with the Foreign Office credentials. You can get us into the embassy to see Millbank. He's going to have cancel whatever he has scheduled for this afternoon. Terry, someone has to keep an eye on Emmeline. You take the SUV and try to catch up with her. She hasn't been gone long and Spitieri didn't follow her, so we know she's all right for the moment."

"Right, Oliver." Dunbar was already slipping out of his seat. "How will the two of you get back?" he asked as Burnell and Philip exited the car.

"Don't worry about us. We'll get a taxi back to the hotel. Keep in touch by mobile. If you can't get through to one of us, ring Finch. I'll fill him on Millbank in the meantime."

Dunbar sketched a little salute as he got behind the wheel. "Already moving. See you later, chaps."

Philip and Burnell crossed the road and slowly climbed the embassy steps.

"Criminals never learn," Burnell muttered under his breath as they entered the building. "The truth always comes out, *always*. No matter the lengths one goes to hide it. It's the lies that trip them up in the end. They have to tell so many that they lose track." He fixed his eye on Philip. "Moral of the story: never tell a lie. It will only lead you to perdition."

"I'll keep it mind. But what do you do with someone like Longdon?"

Burnell groaned. "Personally, I'd rather have nothing to do with him. A psychiatrist, on the other hand, would find that he was a case sent from heaven."

Philip chuckled. But the moment for levity was short-lived. His manner became serious, crisp and unbending in its determination, when he presented his Foreign Office identification and demanded to see Millbank on an urgent matter. He vouched for Burnell, who also flashed his warrant card. The man at the reception desk gave Burnell a long, appraising look. He appeared about to protest, when he caught Philip's severe gaze. He shrugged and reached for the phone to ring

Mrs. Denning.

He spoke softly for a few seconds. "Yes, Mrs. Denning, I do realize that it is an imposition, but the gentlemen are quite insistent. They said that they have to see Mr. Millbank at once. The matter cannot wait." He flicked a glance at Philip.

Philip smiled and leaned over to whisper. "Tell her that either Millbank sees us now or I will call his boss in London and order him to see us."

The man cleared his throat. "I will relay your message." Which he promptly did and was dressed down, judging by the way he held the receiver from his ear. The conversation concluded a few seconds later. "Mrs. Denning will be out in a moment."

"That wasn't difficult, now was it?" Burnell asked. "Things go so much more smoothly, when everyone cooperates."

The man sniffed. "The old cow has her back up. All I can wish you is good luck."

They heard the angry *click-clack* of Mrs. Denning's heels, before the rest of her came into view.

"Ah, Mrs. Denning," Philip hailed her diplomatically as he extended a hand. "How nice to see you again."

Her eyes narrowed and she refused to shake his hand. "Unfortunately, I cannot say the same, Mr. Acheson," she replied tersely. "This is highly irregular. Mr. Millbank had a number of important meetings today. You, of all people, should understand the delicacy involved."

"Let's put it this way," Burnell intervened. "Millbank can talk to us here at the embassy or we can put him on a plane and he can answer the questions in Whitehall. It's his choice."

The secretary shot him a venomous look, but it merely bounced off Burnell. Without another word, she pivoted on her heel. They took that as a signal and followed her down the corridor.

"Thank for your cooperation," Philip murmured to her rigid back.

She tapped on Millbank's door and then opened it. She stood aside to allow Philip and Burnell to enter, but she refused to look them in the eye again.

Millbank halted his nervous pacing and looked up, when the two men walked into the room. Burnell noticed that the hand that pushed his glasses higher up the bridge of his nose was trembling.

Always best to take the upper hand from the outset was the superintendent's motto.

"We know about your brother."

Millbank's face crumpled in anguish and his shoulders slumped forward. He dropped heavily onto his chair. "Oh, God." His Adam's apple worked up and down. "She was poison. She killed him." The words were laced with pain, disgust and rage. "Death was too good for her. She deserved to rot in hell for eternity."

Philip shot Burnell a questioning look, but the superintendent ignored him. In his experience, once a criminal started talking, he wouldn't stop. He craved validation for his crime.

"You wanted Rosalie Jardine to pay," Burnell nudged him toward a confession. *Come on*, he silently prompted. *You know you want to tell me how clever you were.*

Millbank tossed up his head defiantly. "She was guilty and she was roaming around free, while poor Clive was six feet under. He had been a brilliant lawyer with an even brighter future. She robbed him of everything. That was not fair. The books had to be balanced.

"I hired a private detective. He was a conscientious fellow. Found out everything there was to know about Rosalie's routine. She was a creature of habit." He huffed a bitter laugh. "She made it terribly easy. You could say that she was an unwitting accomplice to her own demise. All I had to do was wait for the next time she went up to London and then *bang*"—his hands came together like a thunderclap reverberating upon the air—"I knew what time her train arrived at Waterloo Station and I waited. The minute she stepped off the curb…I hit her. No more Rosalie."

"It must have been a disappointment that young Sebastian wasn't with her," the superintendent probed.

"Yes, it was a pity," Millbank conceded matter-of-factly.

"I must say you were very patient. It must have cost a fortune to track Jardine's whereabouts for years." Burnell was conjecturing now, but he trusted his instinct. "I bet you couldn't believe your luck that shortly after you were appointed as high commissioner, Jardine came to Valletta. Like the proverbial fly inadvertently straying into the spider's web."

Millbank gripped his armrests so hard, the skin stretched taut across his knuckles. "He was a living, breathing reminder of *her*. Jardine looked like her. It turned my stomach seeing him."

"Of course, he had to die too. So you hired someone to have him killed?"

Millbank blinked and said nothing for several seconds. "I wish I had. But someone took the problem out of my hands."

"You really expect us to believe that?" Philip asked incredulously.

"I had nothing to do with Jardine's murder." He bit his lip. "It must have been—" He broke off abruptly.

"It must have been Swanbeck. Is that what you were going to say?" Burnell pressed.

"I don't have to answer any more of your questions. I have diplomatic immunity. You can't charge me with anything," he shot back smugly.

"You're correct to a certain point, Mr. Millbank," Burnell explained. "If Rosalie Jardine and her son Sebastian had been murdered in Malta, then yes you can claim diplomatic immunity. However, they were both killed in England. You are a British subject and bound by the laws of the land. Just like everybody else. And there's no statute of limitations on murder."

A blue vein stood out along the high commissioner's jaw, pulsing with blood and dread at the realization that his past had caught up with him at last.

"I didn't kill the son," he insisted.

Burnell ignored this. "Is Swanbeck blackmailing you? Did he find out about Rosalie and threaten to wash your dirty laundry in the court of public opinion, unless you did his bidding?"

Millbank swallowed the lump that rose in his throat. "He left me with no choice. He's like a cancer that eats away at your body. I was trapped. I was only trying to protect..."

"What did he ask you to do? It's time for the truth," Philip demanded.

"That's not important now. Swanbeck is going to kill Longdon this afternoon, but he's going to make sure he gets the diamonds first."

"What?" Burnell exploded. "And you were blithely going to sit by and allow that to happen?"

Philip braced his hands on the desk and loomed over Millbank. "Talk fast and don't leave out any details."

"Don't forget about Emmeline," Burnell interrupted.

All the blood drained from Millbank's face. "Emmeline Kirby. Oh my God. I'd nearly forgotten about her. This is all my fault."

CHAPTER 43

Gregory knew he should never have answered the door. But then, one can see things with crystalline clarity with the benefit of hindsight. His unexpected visitor turned out to be Azzopardi. He wasn't alone. He had brought along a Beretta nine-millimeter gun as a companion, which he pointed directly at Gregory's heart. The inspector made certain that Gregory knew that he had absolutely no qualms about pulling the trigger. In fact, he would relish the chance to do so.

"Well, at least we know where we stand," Gregory had remarked wryly.

The smile on Azzopardi's lips had not touched his eyes. "I know you like adventure…"

"That rather depends on the company."

A spark of annoyance flared in the inspector's dark eyes. "We're going for a drive and then we're going to return to the scene of the crime, where you're going to confess your sins and return Swanbeck's property."

And here they were in the study on the *Sea Predator*. Gregory surveyed the room. The detritus of last night's fracas had been tidied up.

"I suppose corruption has its perks. For a time," he observed. "I don't know many coppers who can come and go as he pleases on the Minister of Finance's yacht."

Azzopardi gave him shove. "Shut up, Longdon."

"I'm curious about something. How did you cotton on that Percy Smythe-Jones was an alias?"

Azzopardi chuckled. "Really, Longdon. I knew who you were the first time we met, but I must admit I enjoyed your little charade. How's Miss Kirby today?"

Gregory didn't like Emmy's name on the man's tongue, but he willed himself not to react.

"I suppose she's doing what she does best: making a nuisance of herself." He sighed and gave a sad shake of his head. "No matter. We have more important things to discuss. The diamonds."

Gregory cocked his head to one side. "Diamonds? What diamonds?" he asked in mock innocence.

Azzopardi eased off the safety catch on the gun. "Don't be tiresome. Make it easy on yourself and just hand over the Blue Angel and Pink Courtesan."

"I would have never taken you for a Judas. Betraying poor, old Tonio for the thirty pieces of silver Swanbeck dangled in front of your nose. For shame."

"Minister Cannizzaro I fear was past his prime. Mr. Swanbeck is a man of bold vision and strength."

One of Gregory's brows quirked upward. "Was?"

The lupine smile touched Azzopardi's lips again. "Didn't you hear? No one has seen the minister since last night?"

Gregory's stomach tightened with apprehension. "What happened to Cannizzaro?"

Azzopardi casually lowered himself into the armchair Roger had occupied last night and crossed one leg over the other. "No one knows precisely, but I suspect that his body will be found floating in the harbor in a few days." He clucked his tongue and shook his head. "Pity. But then, a man like that must have had enemies. It has come to my ears that several guests saw *you* having a heated argument with the minister at the party. You both disappeared down below. Now, I find you have come back to the boat. A known jewel thief. I caught you in the act of trying to steal. You resisted arrest." He spread his hands wide. "It goes without saying that I had to shoot you."

"Now, why doesn't that surprise me in the least?" One of Azzopardi's shoulders twitched up in a shrug. "Let me guess. You're going to find evidence—manufactured, of course— that I was the one who helped Cannizzaro meet his maker."

The inspector wagged a finger at him. "I knew you were an astute fellow, Longdon." He smoothed a crease from his trouser leg. "To business. The diamonds, if you please."

The engine shuddered to life all of a sudden.

The look of surprise on Azzopardi's face must have matched his own. They heard the crew shouting up on the deck and then the boat was gliding,

Gregory burst out of the study first. He ran to the end of the corridor and took the stairs two at a time.

"You took your time to join us, Longdon," Swanbeck drawled from the comfort of a sofa in the lounge. "I thought perhaps you had suddenly become shy."

Swanbeck bounced a gun with a silencer in the palm of his hand. He saw where Gregory's gaze was trained. "You like it." He brandished the gun in the air. "It's new. I bought it especially for you. I've waited a long time for this moment. Cannizzaro cheated me out of the pleasure last night. Greedy sod. Speaking of greed." His sea-green eyes alighted on Az- zopardi, who appeared at the top of the staircase a pace or two behind Gregory. "Ah, Silvio. Better late than never."

"Swanbeck," the inspector whispered. "What…what are you doing here?"

"Seeing to my interests as usual." He chuckled, clearly amused by the look of terror that had settled on the policeman's face. "I didn't want to believe it, when a little bird told me that you were going behind my back to steal my diamonds. 'Not Silvio,' I said. 'He's as loyal as they come.' Sadly, my trust seems to have been misplaced."

"I…I can explain," Azzopardi stammered. He forced a laugh. "It's just a misunderstanding."

"Is it?" Swanbeck stared at him stone-faced.

"It appears you and Cannizzaro had more things in common than you realized, Alastair," Gregory commented. "You have to be wary of a chap, who is willing to betray the hand that feeds him at the drop of a hat."

"No one asked for your opinion, Longdon. If I were you, I'd be looking at the grand scheme of things and trying to come to a decision about which you hold more dear: your wife's life or the diamonds?"

Icy dread pressed down on his chest. "Where's Emmy? What have done to her?"

Swanbeck threw his head back chuckled. "I'm glad to see that I've got your full attention at last. Forgive me for a moment. Silvio and I have some unfinished business. I'm sure you understand."

He didn't wait for a response and turned on Azzopardi. His lips drew back from his teeth in a macabre resemblance of a smile. "Silvio, Silvio." He exhaled regretful sigh. "I will have to terminate our arrangement and, consequently, your life. You do see that, don't you? I find your willingness to deceive me extremely hurtful. I can't have word spreading to my rivals that I had been duped."

"Wait, Swanbeck. You're making a mistake." Azzopardi's voice thrummed with fear. "Whoever it was that told you I betrayed you is playing you for a fool."

"Silvio, I would have been willing to give you the benefit

of the doubt, but your presence here on the boat rather belies your protestations of innocence."

"Who is the liar? I demand to know who my accuser is."

Swanbeck raised his hands in the air and clapped. "Bravo. That was a rather good demonstration of outrage."

"Tell me who he is. I'll prove to you that he's a liar."

"Oh, why not. This should be rather fun. Let's step out on the deck for a bit of fresh air."

The boat rounded the point and passed through the mouth of the Grand Harbor. They were on open water. The late afternoon sun's lashes caressed Valletta's golden buildings setting them ablaze with rose and tangerine fire.

"You can come out now," Swanbeck called into the wind.

A door opened somewhere, and Roger slunk out onto the deck. He studiously avoided meeting Gregory's gaze.

"Delahunt," Azzopardi hissed. To Swanbeck, he said, "This is your informant? Can't you see that he's the one who has been playing both ends against the middle from the start. First, it was Jardine. Then he moved onto Cannizzaro and now you. I can't believe you're willing to listen to his lies. He's Longdon's friend. They probably cooked up this whole scheme together. Longdon has always hated you."

"Enough. Silvio, you've had your chance to plead your case. As I'm the judge, it's time to issue my decision. I find you guilty as charged. Your punishment is death."

A shot rang out seemingly from nowhere. Azzopardi collapsed to the deck like a stone. No one had to check his pulse. His sightless stare made it clear he was no longer among the living.

Two crew members came out and, without emotion or signs of disgust, hefted Azzopardi's body over the railing. One minute the man was standing there talking and the next he was gone.

Gregory knew that would be his fate, if he didn't think

fast.

"Now, then, Longdon, if you don't want to fish dear Emmeline out of the harbor, I suggest you turn over the diamonds to Delahunt." Swanbeck waved the gun in the air. "Nice and easy. No tricks, unless you want your wife to be a mere memory."

Delahunt shuffled toward him. His eyes were on Gregory, but the words were directed at Swanbeck. "I know he has the diamonds on him. He wouldn't risk leaving them in his room at the hotel."

"Don't dawdle. Search him and give me the diamonds. And remember, this gun is aimed squarely at your back. There's nowhere to run."

When Roger was standing directly in front of Gregory, he ordered, "Unzip your jacket and put your arms out to the sides."

Gregory did as he was commanded. Through gritted teeth, he hissed, "You won't get away with this. If anything happens to Emmy…"

"Shut up and listen," Roger murmured as he went through the motions of patting down Gregory's trouser legs.

When he rose again, he pitched his voice lower, "There's a bomb on the boat. Once Swanbeck gets the diamonds, he's going to have you tied up and leave you to your fate. The crew are already lowering the launch, so that he can get away." He pressed something hard into Gregory's palm. "Here take the Pink Courtesan."

Gregory's eyes flickered a fraction. "I never betrayed you, Greg. Now, hit me hard and jump over the side. It's your only chance. Emmeline would never forgive me, if something happened to you."

"I can't leave you here with Swanbeck," Gregory whispered out of the corner of his mouth.

"Just hit me and run like hell."

"*Sea Predator* this is the Armed Forces of Malta. Stop your engines. AFM officers are going to board you," a male voice boomed over a loudspeaker. "I repeat, stop your engines *Sea Predator.*"

Swanbeck let loose a string of curses. He ran and leaned over the starboard railing. The launch was suspended halfway in the air. It swung back and forth on the brisk wind. "Keep lowering it. Don't stop," he screamed.

Gregory and Roger took advantage of Swanbeck's and the crew's momentary distraction to run toward the stern of the yacht, where the AFM boat was anchored. Gregory was in the lead with Roger close on his heels.

Gregory waved his arms wildly in the air and screamed a warning about the bomb to the AFM boat, but his words were carried away by a gust of wind.

Bloody hell, he swore. Despite the chill air, his brow was moist with beads of perspiration. His heart was hammering against his ribs. His chest felt as if it was going to explode. His brain was no longer in control. He was being driven by the adrenaline surging through his veins.

Today is not my day to die. He repeated these words over and over, trying to convince himself that they were the truth.

When he reached the stern, he drew a big gulp of air into his lungs. He flapped his arms as if he were a human semaphore flag. "Don't shoot," he yelled.

Finch and several AFM officers raced to the bow of the boat. Finch cupped his hands around his mouth and shouted, "Are you all right?"

Gregory took another deep breath. "Swanbeck. BOMB. Push off. There's a bomb."

Finch and AFM officers exchanged sharp glances. They bent their heads together in hurried conversation. They had gotten the message about the danger.

One of the officers, he appeared to be the commander,

bellowed at the top of his lungs, "Jump and swim as hard as you can away from the boat. We'll pick you up."

Through sign language, Gregory telegraphed that there would be two of them in need of rescue. The commander gave a thumbs-up sign in recognition. "Jump. NOW."

The AFM boat already was maneuvering away from the *Sea Predator*.

Gregory nodded. "Did you hear all that Roger?" He turned around only to find Roger slumped against the wall of the lounge semi-conscious. His trouser leg was soaked in blood.

Damn and blast, Gregory cursed silently as he bent down close to Delahunt. He put his arm around his friend's shoulders and tried to prop him up better. "Get up, Roger. Stay awake. Listen to me. We have to jump. The bomb." He slapped Roger's face. The other man moaned. "Come on, Roger. We've come this far. You can't give up now."

Delahunt's eyes flickered open for an instant. "You…go." He was struggling to get out the words. "Emmeline."

He didn't have the strength to say more. His eyes closed again.

Gregory pressed two fingers to his throat. Roger's pulse was faint and irregular, but it was still beating.

He cast a desperate glance to his right and left. His gaze locked on a life buoy attached to the railing a few feet from them. He freed his arm and scrambled to his feet. He snatched the buoy. He skidded on the deck, twisting his ankle in his haste to get back to Roger, but he ignored the throbbing.

He slapped Roger's face a couple of times. "Wake up." There was no reaction this time.

As gently as possible, he eased the buoy over his friend's head. Gregory draped one of Roger's arms over his shoulders and slipped his arm around his waist. He braced his back against the wall. With a primitive grunt, he lifted Roger to his feet and dragged him to the railing.

"Time for a dip, old chap," he observed through clenched teeth, as every muscle in his body strained with the effort of trying to heave Roger over the side. His injured arm, in particular, protested in excruciating terms.

Suddenly, his burden lightened and the Mediterranean welcomed Roger into her embrace with a big splash.

Gregory had one leg over the railing, when the hot rush of the explosion propelled him high into the air.

He was rising in an arc. Higher and higher. Just as he reached out to touch the clouds, he was cruelly sucked back down. He clawed at the air, as the ringing in his ears rose to a crescendo.

And then silence filled the void and all pain ceased. With a serene smile upon his lips, he surrendered to the tender ministrations of oblivion.

CHAPTER 44

At four-thirty, Emmeline tried Gregory's mobile again. It rang three times and went straight to voicemail. Damn. He still had it turned off. She had been hoping to speak to him. He left her with no choice but to leave a message. Briefly, she explained about her meeting with Alessia in Mdina. She promised that she wouldn't linger and then she'd come straight back to the hotel. She also rang the hotel and left a message at the reception desk, in case he had gone out with the others.

She felt a flutter in the pit of her stomach. Why wasn't Gregory answering? What the devil had he been doing all afternoon? Perhaps, his arm was bothering him and he had gone to the doctor. She was tempted to call Alessia to cancel. She would return to the hotel to see for herself how Gregory was faring. But then the thought struck her that he didn't like her fussing.

She was torn.

She glanced at her watch. *Gregory's probably fine*, she tried to reassure herself. Perhaps he had fallen asleep out on the terrace and had left his mobile in the room. Yes, that must it be it. It was a warm afternoon. He was taking advantage of the weather.

The knots of tension eased in her body and the last twinge of guilt melted away. She hailed a taxi in front of the *Times of Malta*'s offices and went off to Mdina with a clear conscience.

ᘒᘒᘒ

He wished the chap with the nasally voice would stop chuntering on. His words only served to amplify the ringing in his ears. Bloody hell, he cursed. Now, the irksome chap had taken to shaking him rather violently. Didn't he realize that every part of his body ached? On and on it went. *Shake. Shake. Shake.* Right, that was enough of that. But to unleash his ire, he would have to see this individual who possessed offensive manners. Alas, that was easier said than done. At the moment, everything was plunged in a blinding onyx fog. Where was he? In a corner of Hades?

Shake. Shake. Not again. A chap could only take so much.

Using every ounce of willpower, he forced his eyelids to flutter open.

"Longdon, at last," a male voice boomed in close proximity.

He blinked a couple of times and then his eyes roamed until his gaze locked on the owner of the voice. A faint smile played about his mouth. "Oliver," he croaked. "It's nice to see a familiar face in the Devil's lair. We can atone for our sins together."

A grin spread across Burnell's features. A flush of relief could be seen beneath his beard. "You're not dead, Longdon. You just made an awfully good attempt at it. You're on the AFM boat."

The faces of Philip, Finch and Dunbar suddenly filled his line of vision. They seemed to be talking at once.

He squeezed his eyes shut for a moment and everything

came flooding back. The *Sea Predator*, Swanbeck, Roger…the bomb.

His eyes flew open again and he tried to sit up. He groaned as every single sinew tingled with pain.

"The man is a maniac," an unfamiliar voice, the nasally one, said. "Listen, Mr. Longdon, you can't go rushing around. You have a concussion. Lie back." Two strong hands pressed him down on the pillows. "That's it. You're lucky to be alive. I'm amazed you escaped with only a handful of bruises and abrasions. But the concussion can be quite serious. You need rest."

Doctor, Gregory decided. He must be a doctor. Only doctors spoke as if they were addressing a child. Doctors and Emmy.

Emmy.

He sat bolt upright this time, ignoring the chorus of protest echoing around him.

"Emmy," he rasped. "Swanbeck said that he was going after Emmy."

"Relax, Longdon," Burnell sought to reassure him. "Before we dashed over here to see what happened to you, Terry tracked her down to the *Times of Malta*'s offices. She was still there when he left. It appeared she would be there for the rest of the afternoon."

Gregory was not mollified. "How long ago was that?"

"About an hour ago."

Gregory violently shrugged off the light blanket that had been covering him and planted his feet on the floor. He frowned at the unfamiliar clothes he was wearing. They must have removed his own clothes because they had gotten wet from his "dip" in the ocean.

"A lot can happen in an hour," he asserted. "Swanbeck could have…"

Burnell cut him off. "Swanbeck couldn't have survived

the explosion."

"Hmph. I'll believe it when I see his roasted body," Gregory shot back. "It sounded like he already put his plan in motion. His thugs might not know that he's dead…if he's dead."

The others fell silent as this very real prospect sank in.

"I'll ring the paper," Finch said as he pulled out his mobile. "I'll ask to speak to the editor Emmeline met with yesterday."

Gregory nodded his thanks. He had almost forgotten about Roger. "Is Roger all right?"

Philip and Burnell exchanged a wary look. "He was gravely injured. He needs surgery immediately. He's been taken to hospital, but the doctor thinks he will make a full recovery. You saved his life. If you hadn't thrown him overboard, he never would have made it off the yacht. He was pretty far gone."

Gregory waved off these compliments. He was relieved that Roger would eventually be all right, but at this moment he focused on Emmy. He kept remembering the malevolent smirk on Swanbeck's face.

"Mdina? Why?" Finch's sharp tone broke through his troubled thoughts and aroused his concern.

Finch covered the mobile with one hand and mouthed, "Emmeline left about half an hour ago to go to Mdina." He turned his attention back to the call. "She said she was going to meet someone. Did she say who? I see. She didn't say anything else. A lead, of course. What else is new? Thank you, sir."

"What did he say?" Gregory pressed.

"The editor said that Emmeline had been at the paper all afternoon. As you heard, she left a short while ago to meet Alessia Summergill in Mdina. It's a nearby town. Emmeline mentioned something about following up on a lead. She's all right, Longdon. Swanbeck was merely bluffing to force your hand."

"I suppose you're right," Gregory murmured.

"Of course, he is," Burnell asserted. "Following leads is Emmeline's bread and butter."

Gregory lifted his gaze to meet the superintendent's. "Yes, I just hope that Emmy's not wasting her time again. Alessia couldn't seem to make up her mind whether she wanted to share her knowledge or not."

"Fear can do that to a person," Philip offered. "Look at it this way, if Alessia gets cold feet again, Emmeline will go back to the hotel to wait for you. Ahem." He cleared his throat. "She's not going to be best pleased with your afternoon's adventures. After all, you were meant to be resting."

Gregory made a dismissive gesture with his hand. "I can deal with Emmy." He slowly rose to his feet. His head swam and swayed for an instant, before regaining his equilibrium. "Let's go. I want to be at the hotel when Emmy returns."

Philip flicked a glance at the doctor. "Dr. Cassar, what is your assessment? Can Mr. Longdon leave or should he go to hospital as well?"

"No hospital," Gregory insisted.

Dr. Cassar threw his hands up in the air. "My diagnosis is that your friend suffers stubbornness. I can't force him to go to hospital, although I would prefer to have him observed overnight." He raised an eyebrow in askance. The forbidding scowl on Gregory's face told him that this suggestion was a nonstarter. "No. I already knew what the answer would be. Therefore, Mr. Acheson, take your friend with you. His bruises and cuts will heal. Just keep a watch over him. If he passes out again or begins to feel nauseous, take him directly to hospital."

Philip proffered his hand. "Thank you for everything, Doctor."

Cassar nodded.

Gregory also extended a hand. "Thank you for your care."

Cassar wagged a finger at him. "I don't ever want to see you again as a patient. You've made a lasting first impression."

Gregory chuckled and then regretted it because it rattled around his skull.

The two detectives and Dunbar also shook hands with the doctor, before they disembarked from the AFM boat. The hired Peugeot SUV was parked a few steps away. None of them appreciated how the sun's slanting last rays glinted off the water in the Vittoriosa Yacht Marina. A farewell kiss to the day. A day that had been too long in each man's opinion.

Each of them was glad to clamber into the car and allowed their minds to rest on the drive back. After a bit, Gregory asked how the AFM boat had come to chase down the *Sea Predator*. Finch explained that he had been trailing Gregory since he had left the hotel with Azzopardi. It didn't sit well with the sergeant, when he saw that Azzopardi had brought him back to the yacht. When the engines started, Finch immediately called the AFM and identified himself as a police officer. He said that he had reason to suspect that a man had been taken hostage. The rest of the story Gregory knew up until the explosion.

Philip and Burnell related how they had kept watch over Emmeline as she went to the embassy, her subsequent departure and Dunbar's suggestion that Millbank might be related to Rosalie Jardine's hapless paramour, who had committed suicide. They also told him that Scotland Yard had confirmed that Clive Millbank was the high commissioner's brother. As Burnell recounted their confrontation with Millbank and his confession that he had killed Rosalie, something stirred at the back of Gregory's brain but he couldn't quite grasp it.

"I find it revolting," the superintendent went on. "Millbank showed absolutely no remorse for his crime. He kept going on about how Rosalie deserved to die. How she was responsible for his brother taking his own life. He hated your friend Jardine because he was her son. He said he was the spitting image of his mother. He swore, though, that he hadn't killed Jardine. He said that Swanbeck was responsible."

That's when all the pieces fell into place in Gregory's mind. "Of course, he looked like her. They were related. That's the source of the problem. It was about revenge all along."

Burnell stopped talking and tossed a glance over his shoulder. "That's what I've been saying. Longdon, is your head all right? Have you been listening at all?"

"Yes, Oliver, to every word. The concussion was precisely what I needed. It was right in front of my nose, but I was too blind to see it."

"Too blind to see what?" Philip asked.

So Gregory told them.

❦❦❦

Vilhena Gate, the entrance to Mdina, sparkled against the evening's cobalt mantle. A few clouds scudded across the sky, carried on a soft breeze. Emmeline crossed over the cobblestone bridge and ducked through the gate's arch. She had done some research on Mdina before she came. Just inside, she knew the elegant building on her right was the National Museum of Natural History. It was formerly the Grand Masters Vilhena's palace. Across from it was the Torre Dello Standardo, which had been built in 1725 by the Knights of Malta and formed part of the city's fortifications. Today, it housed a tourist information office.

Alessia said to meet her at the gate, so she hovered by the wrought-iron fence in front of the museum.

"Miss Kirby, here I am," Alessia said in a breathy whisper

as she stepped out of the shadow of the gate. She extended a hand. "Thank you so much for coming, especially after my behavior yesterday. It was unforgivable."

Emmeline took the woman's hand. "It's all right. I understand that you're frightened. I actually think it's very brave of you to come and talk with me."

Alessia's gaze slid away, embarrassed. "I don't think I'm very brave. However, let's sit down and have a coffee. I promise to tell you everything."

Emmeline smiled. "Lead the way. I'm the tourist."

"I thought we could go to Fontanella. It's a tearoom. It's only a short walk. That way, you can enjoy these old streets as we go along. Mdina is nice during the day, but now at night it's quieter. The tourists and horse carts are gone."

They fell in step and made small talk, as Emmeline glanced up and down the narrow streets and at the ancient buildings. They soon came upon the main square where the Baroque-style Metropolitan Cathedral of Saint Paul loomed. Its façade was lit up, making it even more impressive.

They tarried in the square for a few minutes. "When I was a little girl, my parents used to take me here on weekends. It was such a treat. I loved to wander down these old streets," Alessia remarked, a fond smile upon her lips at the memories.

"It's lovely from what I've seen thus far. You were fortunate to have been born here on Malta. You mentioned that you married recently. You said your husband was British and that he works at the embassy. Do you and he live near your parents?"

Alessia's brow puckered in a frown. "Both my parents are dead. They died a long time ago, when I was small. They were both were British. That's why I was sent to England to live with my uncle and aunt. But my heart was always in Malta. I came back here to university and never left again."

"Except when you went to England to meet your

husband's parents," Emmeline pointed out.

"Yes, of course. But that was a short visit. Thank God." She rolled her eyes and laughed. "Derek's parents are dreadful."

Emmeline laughed with her. "I'm sorry to hear that. You know our backgrounds are similar. My parents died when I was five. My grandmother, my mother's mother, raised me. Gran made me the woman I am today. She happens to adore Gregory, my husband. They're as thick as thieves."

Alessia nodded politely. "How nice for your husband," she murmured as they strolled on. They passed a shop that sold blown glass figurines and bowls, and all sorts of other decorative objects.

"Ooh, come this way. You must see this." Alessia slipped her arm through Emmeline's and tugged her down a winding street that was cloaked in the shadow of tall buildings on either side.

Emmeline felt goosebumps prickle her skin and halted. "Where are you taking me? There doesn't appear to be much of interest to see down this way."

"Oh, but you're wrong," Alessia corrected her. "It's a place of revelations. You can't miss it. You'll regret it for the rest of your life."

It didn't feel right. Emmeline shook off the other woman's arm. "I think I can live without seeing whatever it is. I'm going back to the square."

Alessia's movement had been so subtle that Emmeline hadn't realized what she was doing, until she was staring down the barrel of a gun. "I can't allow that, Emmeline. You know far too much."

The other woman's face was half in shadow. The eye that was toward the light was full of hatred. It was like staring at a two-sided mask of Janus.

That's when she knew the truth.

"You killed Sebastian Jardine. Not Swanbeck. It was you. Why?"

"Why? You have the nerve to ask me why." The words were whispered, but they were laced with menace. "Because he was my mother's son. The one she loved more than anything. She left Papa and me because of him." Her voice softened. "Papa was a wonderful man. I loved him very much. I became a lawyer just like him. But he killed himself because he couldn't live without *her* and she only had eyes for Sebastian."

"Oh, my God. You're the child Rosalie Jardine left behind when she fled to England."

"To save my brother," Alessia spat the words. "She chose *him*. What kind of mother abandons one child in favor of another? A mother shouldn't play favorites. I was three and she left me.

"Can you imagine my shock when he walked into the office one day three months ago? He was the spitting image of her. He was referred to me for legal advice because my friends knew of my anti-corruption work. He didn't even recognize me. I wanted to stab him in the heart right at that moment. But I knew I couldn't. I would have wait and come up with a plan for his punishment. And I did. It was perfect. Until you got in the way."

Her voice was choked with tears and venom. If she hadn't been holding a pistol, Emmeline would have pitied her.

Alessia waved the gun in front her face. "Don't you dare look at me like that."

"I'm not looking at you in any particular way." She put her hands up in the air in a silent plea for the other woman to calm down. "Please put the gun away, Alessia. You don't need it. We can go somewhere quiet and talk. I'm not going to hurt you."

"Ha," Alessia sneered, as she swiped away the tears with

the back of her hand. "You're just trying to trick me. We've had enough talk. I can't let you live anymore, now that you know everything."

She paused and then, like a scorpion, lashed out with her stinger. "And your husband knows." Emmeline stiffened at the mention of Gregory. "I saw the way he looked at me last night. He knows about Sebastian. But it doesn't matter anymore. Swanbeck will have finished him off by now. One less thief in the world."

Emmeline's heart leaped to her throat and the sour taste of bile coated her tongue. "Swanbeck? What's happened to Gregory?" She heard the panic rising in her voice and tried to stop her body from trembling.

"What have you done, you vindictive little witch?" she hissed.

Alessia threw her head back and laughed. The sound sent an icy tendril slithering down Emmeline's spine.

"I'm certain Swanbeck planned something spectacular. You know, he despised your husband." She gave a casual shrug. "But that was his business. All I did was tell him where to find your precious husband. But don't worry. It won't be long now before you will join him in hell."

"Enough, Alessia," a male voice commanded.

Alessia froze, her gaze locked on Emmeline.

They both turned around slowly. A man materialized out of the gloom.

"Uncle Reggie," Alessia whispered. "Please go away. This doesn't concern you."

Uncle Reggie? Emmeline gaped at Millbank. Of course, now it all made sense.

"Stop. This ends now." As he spoke, he kept walking toward them. "Rosalie and her son were different. That was justice." He pointed at Emmeline. "This is not right. We don't have a quarrel with Miss Kirby."

"She *knows*," his niece whispered. "She has to die too."

"No, Alessia." He was standing before her, barely a hairsbreadth of space between them. He took her hands between his own. "Give me the gun."

She stared up at him through a curtain of tears. She didn't move a muscle for an excruciating moment. Then, she uncurled her fingers and the gun was in his palm.

He put an arm around her shoulders. "Good girl." She pressed her face into his chest and all the hurt she had kept inside since childhood came cascading out in a flood of tears.

"Emmy."

Still stunned by the evening's turn of events, she spun around to see Gregory at the opening to the narrow street. She ran toward him and flung herself into his arms.

"*Oof.* Steady on, darling," he murmured, his lips against her curls.

She pulled away and squinted at him. "You're hurt. These are not your clothes. What happened?"

His mouth curved into an impish smile. "Why is it that I'm always subjected to an interrogation by you? Questions, always questions." He sighed. "I'll be fine. But it's a long story that will have to wait for another time."

Emmeline's eyes narrowed. She prepared to press him further, but she was prevented from doing so by the appearance of Philip, Burnell, Finch and Dunbar.

Once they had satisfied themselves that she had come to no harm, Philip, Burnell and Finch moved toward Millbank and his niece.

"You do realize that your career, and life as you know it, is over," Philip said.

Millbank looked down at Alessia, who was still pressed against his side. He gave a sad nod. "Yes," he muttered. "To tell you the truth, I'm glad. I'm tired. I want a bit of peace. I"—he glanced down at his niece again—"the family hasn't had peace in a long time."

EPILOGUE

Their little band was taking one last putter around the garden in front of the Corinthia Palace Hotel, while they waited for the car to take them to the airport. Emmeline was looking forward to going home. She felt guilty about leaving Roger behind, but he couldn't travel yet. Philip had spoken to some chaps at the embassy. They would keep an eye on Roger and make certain that he got back to the U.K. safely.

They were sitting on a bench, the fountain pleasantly chattering in the background. The men took turns filling her in on their discoveries about the Millbanks and their connection to the Jardines. Two families tied by blood and murder. It was terribly sad.

When it came to Gregory's harrowing escape from the *Sea Predator*, she shuddered and squeezed his hand. There by the grace of God…

Would they ever have a normal life? she wondered. Then again, they weren't a conventional couple.

"What about Swanbeck?" she asked. Everything else had fallen neatly into place. Swanbeck was the only missing piece of the puzzle.

Burnell must have seen the worry etched on her face. "He

couldn't have survived the explosion."

"But they haven't found his body," she insisted.

"No and they likely never will," Burnell pointed out.

"That means we will never know for sure." Which is what worried her.

She slid a sideways glance at Gregory. She caught him when his guard was down and saw that this troubling thought plagued him too.

LEAD ME INTO DANGER

Here is a quick look at how the series began. Please enjoy this peek into *Lead Me Into Danger* by Daniella Bernett

LEAD ME INTO DANGER

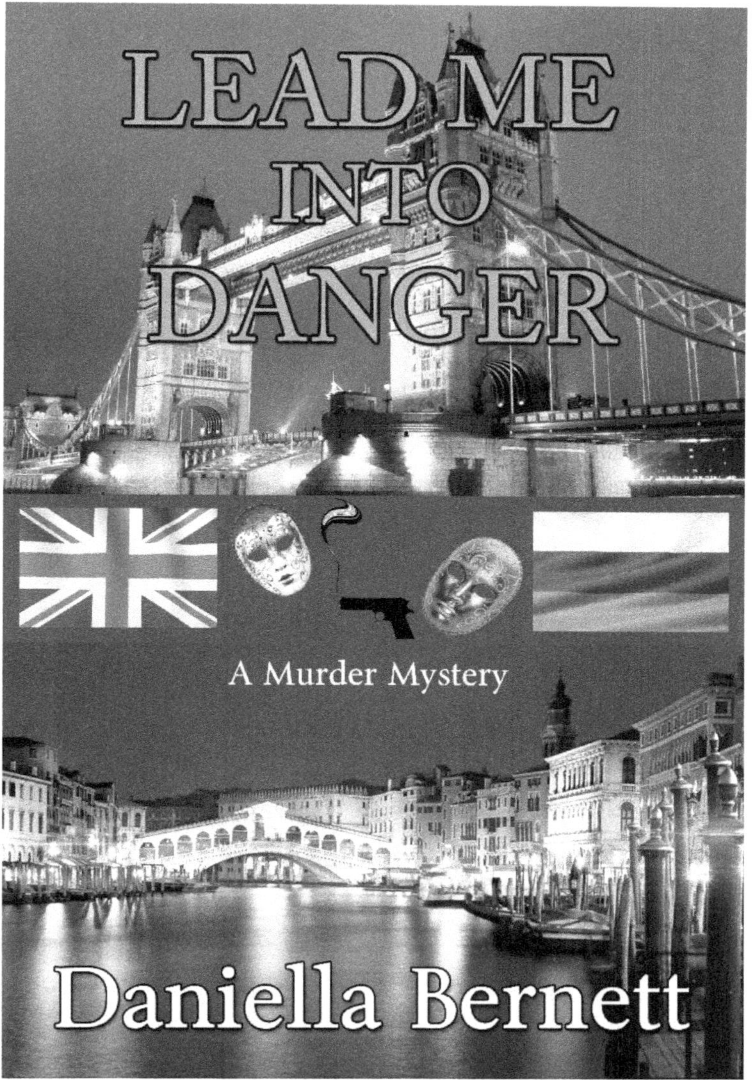

LEAD ME
INTO
DANGER
A Murder Mystery
Daniella Bernett

LEAD ME INTO DANGER

CHAPTER 1

London

February 2010:

He turned up the collar of his overcoat against the thickening fog. The damp chill seemed to permeate his leather gloves, so he dug his hands deeper into his pockets. His footsteps echoed hollowly as he walked along Kennington Road in Lambeth. He turned into Fitzalan Street, where the bare tree branches cast eerie shadows upon the square, like the ghouls and goblins in a children's story. He stopped in the middle of the block in front of Number Thirty-Two, one of those nineteenth-century mansions that had long ago been converted into flats. The steps were still slick from the rain earlier in the evening. He searched the names of the tenants listed on the intercom panel beside the door.

He pressed several buttons, hoping that someone would buzz him in.

The intercom crackled as a disembodied female voice broke the silence. "It's about time you showed up, Derek. I'd nearly given up on you. I've been waiting for over an hour." There was a loud buzz and a click as the door was unlocked.

He smiled to himself as he walked into the hall and silently thanked Derek—whoever he was—for being late. He took the lift up to the fourth floor. Number Five was down the corridor to his right. As luck would have it, there was no one about. His pick slipped easily into the lock, a couple of twists and, within seconds, the door was open. The thin beam from his torch bounced quickly over the living room.

From the layout of the flat he had memorized, he knew that the study was down the short hallway next to the bedroom. Once he found it, he crossed the room and turned on the desk lamp. He sat in the swivel chair and began methodically going through all the drawers. After half an hour without any success, he began riffling through the paperbacks and leather-bound volumes in the two bookcases along the opposite wall. He was beginning to lose his patience. *Nothing.* Where would he have hidden it? But his thoughts were interrupted, when he heard someone unlocking the front door.

He quickly turned off the desk lamp and waited. "Mr. Latimer, is that you? You're back early. I thought you'd be in Italy until Monday," a woman's voice called out. "Are you hungry, Mr. Latimer? Would you like me to fix you a light supper?"

Damn, he thought. Mrs. Saunders, the old busybody who came in twice a week to cook and clean for Latimer. Maybe she'd go away.

"*Mr. Latimer?*"

He heard her coming down the hall toward the study. She hesitated. "Mr. Latimer, are you in there?"

She slowly opened the door and flicked on the switch. She saw a heap of books on the floor and papers strewn all over the desk. "Dear, oh dear. What's been happening here?"

Mrs. Saunders took a step into the room. The last thing she would ever hear before her neck was snapped was the door closing behind her. She crumpled to the ground. One minute alive, the next dead. It had happened so quickly she didn't have time to struggle or cry out.

His search had yielded nothing, so there was no point for the assassin to hang about any longer. He didn't have to worry about fingerprints because he was wearing gloves.

He opened the door into the corridor a crack. It was empty. Quietly, he hurried toward the stairs. He didn't want to wait for the lift and risk being seen. In five minutes, he was outside and was immediately swallowed up by the fog. He retraced his steps up Kennington Road, walking at a steady pace so as not to attract any undue attention. He crossed Lambeth Road and continued along Kennington until it turned into Westminster Bridge Road.

The assassin crossed Westminster Bridge. Once on the other side of the Thames, he pulled out his mobile and called a certain number in the Russian embassy.

He heard the phone ring twice. He hung up and dialed again, allowing it to ring two more times. The signal. This time a male voice with a heavy Russian accent answered. "Yes?"

"It was not in the flat. Latimer must have it with him."

"I see," the voice at the other end of the line said.

"The housekeeper came while I was there."

"And?"

"I dealt with her."

"I see. Is there any way to connect it to you?"

"No."

"Good. Your job is done. Your money is waiting for you in a locker at Heathrow."

The assassin heard a click and then silence. He tossed the mobile over the parapet and it disappeared into the murky depths of the Thames with a soft splash. He had stolen it that afternoon from an unsuspecting businessman exiting a taxi on Regent Street. There was no way to trace him to the call to the embassy.

He whistled as he descended the few steps into the Westminster tube station. Within seconds, he was lost amid the crush of commuters hurrying home.

Soon afterward, a call was made on a secure line from the embassy in Kensington Palace Gardens to an apartment on Via Veneto in Rome. "It was not in the flat. Latimer has it."

"We'll take over from here." The line went dead.

ABOUT THE AUTHOR

Daniella Bernett is a member of the Mystery Writers of America New York Chapter and the International Thriller Writers. She graduated summa cum laude with a B.S. in Journalism from St. John's University. *Lead Me Into Danger*, *Deadly Legacy*, *From Beyond The Grave*, *A Checkered Past*, *When Blood Runs Cold* and *Old Sins Never Die* are the other books in the Emmeline Kirby-Gregory Longdon mystery series. She also is the author of two poetry collections, *Timeless Allure* and *Silken Reflections*. In her professional life, she is the research manager for a nationally prominent engineering, architectural and construction management firm. Daniella is currently working on Emmeline and Gregory's next adventure. Visit www.daniellabernett.com or follow her on Facebook and Goodreads.